The Sorrows of Satan

The Sorrows of Satan

Marie Corelli

MINT EDITIONS

The Sorrows of Satan was first published in 1895.

This edition published by Mint Editions 2021.

ISBN 9781513277776 | E-ISBN 9781513278186

Published by Mint Editions®

 MINT
EDITIONS
minteditionbooks.com

Publishing Director: Jennifer Newens
Design & Production: Rachel Lopez Metzger
Project Manager: Micaela Clark
Typesetting: Westchester Publishing Services

Contents

I

D o you know what it is to be poor? Not poor with the arrogant poverty complained of by certain people who have five or six thousand a year to live upon, and who yet swear they can hardly manage to make both ends meet, but really poor,—downright, cruelly, hideously poor, with a poverty that is graceless, sordid and miserable? Poverty that compels you to dress in your one suit of clothes till it is worn threadbare,—that denies you clean linen on account of the ruinous charges of washerwomen,—that robs you of your own self-respect, and causes you to slink along the streets vaguely abashed, instead of walking erect among your fellow-men in independent ease,—this is the sort of poverty I mean. This is the grinding curse that keeps down noble aspiration under a load of ignoble care; this is the moral cancer that eats into the heart of an otherwise well-intentioned human creature and makes him envious and malignant, and inclined to the use of dynamite. When he sees the fat idle woman of society passing by in her luxurious carriage, lolling back lazily, her face mottled with the purple and red signs of superfluous eating,—when he observes the brainless and sensual man of fashion smoking and dawdling away the hours in the Park, as if all the world and its millions of honest hard workers were created solely for the casual diversion of the so-called 'upper' classes,— then the good blood in him turns to gall, and his suffering spirit rises in fierce rebellion, crying out—"Why in God's name, should this injustice be? Why should a worthless lounger have his pockets full of gold by mere chance and heritage, while I, toiling wearily from morn till midnight, can scarce afford myself a satisfying meal?"

Why indeed! Why should the wicked flourish like a green bay-tree? I have often thought about it. Now however I believe I could help to solve the problem out of my own personal experience. But. . . such an experience! Who will credit it? Who will believe that anything so strange and terrific ever chanced to the lot of a mortal man? No one. Yet it is true;—truer than much so-called truth. Moreover I know that many men are living through many such incidents as have occurred to me, under precisely the same influence, conscious perhaps at times, that they are in the tangles of sin, but too weak of will to break the net in which they have become voluntarily imprisoned. Will they be taught, I wonder, the lesson I have learned? In the same bitter school, under the same formidable taskmaster? Will they realize as I have been forced to do,—aye, to the very fibres of my intellectual perception,—the vast, individual, active Mind, which behind all matter, works unceasingly, though silently, a very eternal and positive God? If so, then dark problems will become clear to them, and what seems injustice in the world will prove pure equity! But I do not write with any hope of either persuading or enlightening my fellow-men. I know their obstinacy too well;—I can gauge it by my own. My proud belief in myself was, at one time, not to be outdone by any human unit on the face of the globe. And I am aware that others are in similar case. I merely intend to relate the various incidents of my career in due order exactly as they happened,— leaving to more confident heads the business of propounding and answering the riddles of human existence as best they may.

During a certain bitter winter, long remembered for its arctic severity, when a great wave of intense cold spread freezing influences not alone over the happy isles of Britain, but throughout all Europe, I, Geoffrey Tempest, was alone in London and well-nigh starving. Now a starving man seldom gets the sympathy he merits,—so few can be persuaded to believe in him. Worthy folks who have just fed to repletion are the most incredulous, some of them being even moved to smile when told of existing hungry people, much as if these were occasional jests invented for after-dinner amusement. Or, with that irritating vagueness of attention which characterizes fashionable folk to such an extent that when asking a question they neither wait for the answer nor understand it when given, the well-dined groups, hearing of some one starved to death, will idly murmur 'How dreadful!' and at once turn to the discussion of the latest 'fad' for killing time, ere it takes to killing them with sheer *ennui*. The pronounced fact of being hungry sounds coarse and common, and is not a topic for polite society, which always eats more than sufficient for its needs. At the period I am speaking of however, I, who have since been one of the most envied of men, knew the cruel meaning of the word hunger, too well,— the gnawing pain, the sick faintness, the deadly stupor, the insatiable animal craving for mere food, all of which sensations are frightful enough to those who are, unhappily, daily inured to them, but which when they afflict one who has been tenderly reared and brought up to consider himself a 'gentleman,'—God save the mark! are perhaps still more painful to bear. And I felt that I had not deserved to suffer the wretchedness in which I found myself. I had worked hard. From the time my father died, leaving me to discover that every penny of the fortune I imagined he possessed was due to swarming creditors, and that nothing of all our house and estate was left to me except a jewelled miniature of my mother who had lost her own life in giving me birth,—from that time I say, I had put my shoulder to the wheel and toiled late and early. I had turned my University education to the only use for which it or I seemed fitted,—literature. I had sought for employment on almost every journal in London,—refused by many, taken on trial by some, but getting steady pay from none. Whoever seeks to live by brain and pen alone is, at the beginning of such a career, treated as a sort of social pariah. Nobody wants him,—everybody despises him. His efforts are derided, his manuscripts are flung back to him unread, and he is less cared for than the condemned murderer in gaol. The murderer is at least fed and clothed,—a worthy clergyman visits him, and his gaoler will occasionally condescend to play cards with him. But a man gifted with original thoughts and the power of expressing them, appears to be regarded by everyone in authority as much worse than the worst criminal, and all the 'jacks-in-office' unite to kick him to death if they can. I took both kicks and blows in sullen silence and lived on,—not for the love of life, but simply because I scorned the cowardice of self-destruction. I was young enough not to part with hope too easily;—the vague idea I had that my turn would come,—that the ever-circling wheel of Fortune would perchance lift me up some day as it now crushed me down, kept me just wearily capable of continuing existence,—though it was merely a continuance and no more. For about six months I got some reviewing work on a well-known literary journal. Thirty novels a week were sent to me to 'criticise,'—I made a habit of glancing hastily at about eight or ten of them, and writing one column of rattling abuse concerning these thus casually selected,—the remainder were never noticed at all. I found that this mode of action was considered 'smart,' and I managed for a time to please my editor who paid me the munificent sum of fifteen shillings for my weekly labour. But on one fatal occasion I happened to change my tactics and warmly praised a work which my own conscience told me was both original and excellent. The author of it happened to be an old enemy of the proprietor of the journal on which I was employed;— my eulogistic review of the hated individual, unfortunately for me, appeared, with the result that private spite outweighed public justice, and I was immediately dismissed.

After this I dragged on in a sufficiently miserable way, doing 'hack work' for the dailies, and living on promises that never became realities, till, as I have said, in the early January of the bitter winter alluded to, I found myself literally penniless and face to face with starvation, owing a month's rent besides for the poor lodging I occupied in a back street not far from the British Museum. I had been out all day trudging from one newspaper office to another, seeking for work and finding none. Every available post was filled. I had also tried, unsuccessfully, to dispose of a manuscript of my own,—a work of fiction which I knew had some merit, but which all the 'readers' in the publishing offices appeared to find exceptionally worthless. These 'readers' I learned, were most of them novelists themselves, who read other people's productions in their spare moments and passed judgment on them. I have always failed to see the justice of this arrangement; to me it seems merely the way to foster mediocrities and suppress originality. Common sense points out the fact that the novelist 'reader' who has a place to maintain for himself in literature would naturally rather encourage work that is likely to prove ephemeral, than that which might possibly take a higher footing than his own. Be this as it may, and however good or bad the system, it was entirely prejudicial to me and my literary offspring. The last publisher I tried was a kindly man who looked at my shabby clothes and gaunt face with some commiseration.

"I'm sorry," said he, "very sorry, but my readers are quite unanimous. From what I can learn, it seems to me you have been too earnest. And also, rather sarcastic in certain strictures against society. My dear fellow, that won't do. Never blame society,—it buys books! Now if you could write a smart love-story, slightly *risqué*,—even a little more than *risqué* for that matter; that is the sort of thing that suits the present age."

"Pardon me," I interposed somewhat wearily—"but are you sure you judge the public taste correctly?"

He smiled a bland smile of indulgent amusement at what he no doubt considered my ignorance in putting such a query.

"Of course I am sure,"—he replied—"It is my business to know the public taste as thoroughly as I know my own pocket. Understand me,—I don't suggest that you should write a book on any positively indecent subject,—that can be safely left to the 'New' woman,"—and he laughed,—"but I assure you high-class fiction doesn't sell. The critics don't like it, to begin with. What goes down with them and with the public is a bit of sensational realism told in terse newspaper English. Literary English,—Addisonian English,—is a mistake."

"And I am also a mistake I think," I said with a forced smile—"At any rate if what you say be true, I must lay down the pen and try another trade. I am old-fashioned enough to consider Literature as the highest of all professions, and I would rather not join in with those who voluntarily degrade it."

He gave me a quick side-glance of mingled incredulity and depreciation.

"Well, well!" he finally observed—"you are a little quixotic. That will wear off. Will you come on to my club and dine with me?"

I refused this invitation promptly. I knew the man saw and recognised my wretched plight,—and pride—false pride if you will—rose up to my rescue. I bade him a hurried good-day, and started back to my lodging, carrying my rejected manuscript with me. Arrived there, my landlady met me as I was about to ascend the stairs, and asked me whether I would 'kindly settle accounts' the next day. She spoke civilly enough, poor soul, and not without a certain compassionate hesitation in her manner. Her evident pity for me galled my spirit as much as the publisher's offer of a dinner had wounded my pride,— and with a perfectly audacious air of certainty I at once promised her the money at the time she herself appointed, though I had not the least idea where or how I should get the required sum. Once past her, and shut in my own room, I flung my useless manuscript on the floor and myself into a chair, and—swore. It refreshed me to swear, and it seemed natural,—for though temporarily weakened by lack of food, I was not yet so weak as to shed tears,—and a fierce formidable oath was to me the same sort of physical relief which I imagine a fit of weeping may be to an excitable woman. Just as I could not shed tears, so was I incapable of apostrophizing God in my despair. To speak frankly, I did not believe in any God—*then*. I was to myself an all-sufficing mortal, scorning the time-worn superstitions of so-called religion. Of course I had been brought up in the Christian faith; but that creed had become worse than useless to me since I had intellectually realized the utter inefficiency of Christian ministers to deal with difficult life-problems. Spiritually I was adrift in chaos,—mentally I was hindered both in thought and achievement,—bodily, I was reduced to want. My case was desperate,—I myself was desperate. It was a moment when if ever good and evil angels play a game of chance for a man's soul, they were surely throwing the dice on the last wager for mine. And yet, with it all, I felt I had done my best. I was driven into a corner by my fellow-men who grudged me space to live in, but I had fought against it. I had worked honestly and patiently;—all to no purpose. I knew of rogues who gained plenty of money; and of knaves who were amassing large fortunes. Their prosperity appeared to prove that honesty after all was *not* the best policy. What should I do then? How should I begin the jesuitical business of committing evil that good, personal good, might come of it? So I thought, dully, if such stray half-stupefied fancies as I was capable of, deserved the name of thought.

The night was bitter cold. My hands were numbed, and I tried to warm them at the oil-lamp my landlady was good enough to still allow me the use of, in spite of delayed cash-payments. As I did so, I noticed three letters on the table,—one in a long blue envelope suggestive of either a summons or a returned manuscript,—one bearing the Melbourne postmark, and the third a thick square missive coroneted in red and gold at the back. I turned over all three indifferently, and selecting the one from Australia, balanced it in my hand a moment before opening it. I knew from whom it came, and idly wondered what news it brought me. Some months previously I had written a detailed account of my increasing debts and difficulties to an old college chum, who finding England too narrow for his ambition had gone out to the wider New world on a speculative quest of gold mining. He was getting on well, so I understood, and had secured a fairly substantial position; and I had therefore ventured to ask him point-blank for the loan of fifty pounds. Here, no doubt, was his reply, and I hesitated before breaking the seal.

"Of course it will be a refusal," I said half-aloud,—"However kindly a friend may otherwise be, he soon turns crusty if asked to lend money. He will express many regrets, accuse trade and the general bad times and hope I will soon 'tide over.' I know the sort of thing. Well,—after all, why should I expect him to be different to other men? I've no claim on him beyond the memory of a few sentimental arm-in-arm days at Oxford."

A sigh escaped me in spite of myself, and a mist blurred my sight for the moment. Again I saw the grey towers of peaceful Magdalen, and the fair green trees shading the walks in and around the dear old University town where we,—I and the man whose letter I now held in my hand,—strolled about together as happy youths, fancying that we were young geniuses born to regenerate the world. We were both fond of classics,—we were brimful of Homer and the thoughts and maxims of all the immortal Greeks and Latins,—and I verily believe, in those imaginative days, we thought we had in us such stuff as heroes are made of. But our entrance into the social arena soon robbed us of our sublime conceit,—we were common working units, no more,—the grind and prose of daily life put Homer into the background, and we soon discovered that society was more interested in the latest unsavoury scandal than in the tragedies of Sophocles or the wisdom of Plato. Well! it was no doubt extremely foolish of us to dream that we might help to regenerate a world in which both Plato and Christ appear to have failed,—yet the most hardened cynic will scarcely deny that it is pleasant to look back to the days of his youth if he can think that at least then, if only once in his life, he had noble impulses.

The lamp burned badly, and I had to re-trim it before I could settle down to read my friend's letter. Next door some-one was playing a violin, and playing it well. Tenderly and yet with a certain amount of *brio* the notes came dancing from the bow, and I listened, vaguely pleased. Being faint with hunger I was somewhat in a listless state bordering on stupor,—and the penetrating sweetness of the music appealing to the sensuous and æsthetic part of me, drowned for the moment mere animal craving.

"There you go!" I murmured, apostrophizing the unseen musician,—"practising away on that friendly fiddle of yours,—no doubt for a mere pittance which barely keeps you alive. Possibly you are some poor wretch in a cheap orchestra,—or you might even be a street-player and be able to live in this neighbourhood of the *élite* starving,—you can have no hope whatever of being the 'fashion' and making your bow before Royalty,—or if you have that hope, it is wildly misplaced. Play on, my friend, play on!—the sounds you make are very agreeable, and seem to imply that you are happy. I wonder if you are?—or if, like me, you are going rapidly to the devil!"

The music grew softer and more plaintive, and was now accompanied by the rattle of hailstones against the window-panes. A gusty wind whistled under the door and roared down the chimney,—a wind cold as the grasp of death and searching as a probing knife. I shivered,—and bending close over the smoky lamp, prepared to read my Australian news. As I opened the envelope, a bill for fifty pounds, payable to me at a well-known London banker's, fell out upon the table. My heart gave a quick bound of mingled relief and gratitude.

"Why Jack, old fellow, I wronged you!" I exclaimed,—"Your heart is in the right place after all."

And profoundly touched by my friend's ready generosity, I eagerly perused his letter. It was not very long, and had evidently been written off in haste.

Dear Geoff,

I'm sorry to hear you are down on your luck; it shows what a crop of fools are still flourishing in London, when a man of your capability cannot gain his proper place in the world of letters, and be fittingly acknowledged. I believe it's all a question of wire-pulling, and money is the only thing that will pull the wires. Here's the fifty you ask for and welcome,—don't hurry about paying it back. I am doing you a good turn this year by sending you a friend,—a real friend, mind you!—no sham. He brings you a letter of introduction from me, and between ourselves, old man, you cannot do better than put yourself and your literary affairs entirely in his hands. He knows everybody, and is up to all the dodges of editorial management and newspaper cliques. He is a great philanthropist besides,—and seems particularly fond of the society of the clergy. Rather a queer taste you will say, but his reason for such preference is, as he has explained to me quite frankly, that he is so enormously wealthy that he does not quite know what to do with his money, and the reverend gentlemen of the church are generally ready to show him how to spend some of it. He is always glad to know of some quarter where his money and influence (he is very influential) may be useful to others. He has helped me out of a very serious hobble, and I owe him a big debt of gratitude. I've told him all about you,—what a smart fellow you are, and what a lot dear old Alma Mater thought of you, and he has promised to give you a lift up. He can do anything he likes; very naturally, seeing that the whole world of morals, civilization and the rest is subservient to the power of money,—and *his* stock of cash appears to be limitless. *Use him*; he is willing and ready to be used,—and write and let me know how you get on. Don't bother about the fifty till you feel you have tided over the storm.

Ever yours
Boffles

I laughed as I read the absurd signature, though my eyes were dim with something like tears. 'Boffles' was the nickname given to my friend by several of our college companions, and neither he nor I knew how it first arose. But no one except the dons ever addressed him by his proper name, which was John Carrington,—he was simply 'Boffles,' and Boffles he remained even now for all those who had been his intimates. I refolded and put by his letter and the draft for the fifty pounds, and with a passing vague wonder as to what manner of man the 'philanthropist' might be who had more money than he knew what to do with, I turned to the consideration of my other two correspondents, relieved to feel that now, whatever happened, I could settle up arrears with my landlady the next day as I had promised. Moreover I could order some supper, and have a fire lit to cheer my chilly room. Before attending to these creature comforts however, I opened the long blue envelope that looked so like a threat of legal proceedings, and unfolding the paper within, stared at it amazedly. What was it all about? The written characters danced before my eyes,—puzzled and bewildered, I found myself reading the thing over and over again without any clear comprehension of it. Presently a glimmer of meaning flashed upon me, startling my senses like an electric shock, . . . no—no—!—impossible! Fortune never could be so mad as this!—never so wildly capricious and grotesque of humour! It was some senseless hoax that was being practised upon me, . . . and yet, . . . if it were a joke, it was a very elaborate and remarkable one! Weighted with the majesty of the law too! . . . Upon my word and by all the fantastical freakish destinies that govern human affairs, the news seemed actually positive and genuine!

II

S teadying my thoughts with an effort, I read every word of the document over again deliberately, and the stupefaction of my wonder increased. Was I going mad, or sickening for a fever? Or could this startling, this stupendous piece of information be really true? Because,—if indeed it were true, . . . good heavens!—I turned giddy to think of it,—and it was only by sheer force of will that I kept myself from swooning with the agitation of such sudden surprise and ecstasy. If it were true—why then the world was mine!—I was king instead of beggar;—I was everything I chose to be! The letter,—the amazing letter, bore the printed name of a noted firm of London solicitors, and stated in measured and precise terms that a distant relative of my father's, of whom I had scarcely heard, except remotely now and then during my boyhood, had died suddenly in South America, leaving me his sole heir.

"*The real and personal estate now amounting to something over Five Millions of Pounds Sterling, we should esteem it a favour if you could make it convenient to call upon us any day this week in order that we may go through the necessary formalities together. The larger bulk of the cash is lodged in the Bank of England, and a considerable amount is placed in French government securities. We should prefer going into further details with you personally rather than by letter. Trusting you will call on us without delay, we are, Sir, yours obediently. . . *"

Five Millions! I, the starving literary hack,—the friendless, hopeless, almost reckless haunter of low newspaper dens,—I, the possessor of "over Five Millions of Pounds Sterling"! I tried to grasp the astounding fact,—for fact it evidently was,—but could not. It seemed to me a wild delusion, born of the dizzy vagueness which lack of food engendered in my brain. I stared round the room;—the mean miserable furniture,— the fireless grate,—the dirty lamp,—the low truckle bedstead,—the evidences of penury and want on every side;—and then,—then the overwhelming contrast between the poverty that environed me and the news I had just received, struck me as the wildest, most ridiculous incongruity I had ever heard of or imagined,—and I gave vent to a shout of laughter.

"Was there ever such a caprice of mad Fortune!" I cried aloud— "Who would have imagined it! Good God! I! I, of all men in the world to be suddenly chosen out for this luck! By Heaven!—If it is all true,

MARIE CORELLI

I'll make society spin round like a top on my hand before I am many months older!"

And I laughed loudly again; laughed just as I had previously sworn, simply by way of relief to my feelings. Some one laughed in answer,—a laugh that seemed to echo mine. I checked myself abruptly, somewhat startled, and listened. Rain poured outside, and the wind shrieked like a petulant shrew,—the violinist next door was practising a brilliant roulade up and down his instrument,—but there were no other sounds than these. Yet I could have sworn I heard a man's deep-chested laughter close behind me where I stood.

"It must have been my fancy;" I murmured, turning the flame of the lamp up higher in order to obtain more light in the room—"I am nervous I suppose,—no wonder! Poor Boffles!—good old chap!" I continued, remembering my friend's draft for fifty pounds, which had seemed such a godsend a few minutes since—"What a surprise is in store for you! You shall have your loan back as promptly as you sent it, with an extra fifty added by way of interest for your generosity. And as for the new Mæcenas you are sending to help me over my difficulties,— well, he may be a very excellent old gentleman, but he will find himself quite out of his element this time. I want neither assistance nor advice nor patronage,—I can buy them all! Titles, honours, possessions,—they are all purchaseable,—love, friendship, position,—they are all for sale in this admirably commercial age and go to the highest bidder! By my soul!—The wealthy 'philanthropist' will find it difficult to match me in power! He will scarcely have more than five millions to waste, I warrant! And now for supper,—I shall have to live on credit till I get some ready cash,—and there is no reason why I should not leave this wretched hole at once, and go to one of the best hotels and swagger it!"

I was about to leave the room on the swift impulse of excitement and joy, when a fresh and violent gust of wind roared down the chimney, bringing with it a shower of soot which fell in a black heap on my rejected manuscript where it lay forgotten on the floor, as I had despairingly thrown it. I hastily picked it up and shook it free from the noisome dirt, wondering as I did so, what would be its fate now?—now, when I could afford to publish it myself, and not only publish it but advertise it, and not only advertise it, but 'push' it, in all the crafty and cautious ways known to the inner circles of 'booming'! I smiled as I thought of the vengeance I would take on all those who had scorned and slighted me and my labour,—how they should cower before me!—

how they should fawn at my feet like whipt curs, and whine their fulsome adulation! Every stiff and stubborn neck should bend before me;—this I resolved upon; for though money does not always conquer everything, it only fails when it is money apart from brains. Brains and money together can move the world,—brains can very frequently do this alone without money, of which serious and proved fact those who have no brains should beware!

Full of ambitious thought, I now and then caught wild sounds from the violin that was being played next door,—notes like sobbing cries of pain, and anon rippling runs like a careless woman's laughter,—and all at once I remembered I had not yet opened the third letter addressed to me,—the one coroneted in scarlet and gold, which had remained where it was on the table almost unnoticed till now. I took it up and turned it over with an odd sense of reluctance in my fingers, which were slow at the work of tearing the thick envelope asunder. Drawing out an equally thick small sheet of notepaper also coroneted, I read the following lines written in an admirably legible, small and picturesque hand.

Dear Sir

I am the bearer of a letter of introduction to you from your former college companion Mr. John Carrington, now of Melbourne, who has been good enough to thus give me the means of making the acquaintance of one, who, I understand, is more than exceptionally endowed with the gift of literary genius. I shall call upon you this evening between eight and nine o'clock, trusting to find you at home and disengaged. I enclose my card, and present address, and beg to remain,

Very faithfully yours
Lucio Rimânez

The card mentioned dropped on the table as I finished reading the note. It bore a small, exquisitely engraved coronet and the words

PRINCE LUCIO RIMÁNEZ.

while, scribbled lightly in pencil underneath was the address 'Grand Hotel.'

I read the brief letter through again,—it was simple enough,—expressed with clearness and civility. There was nothing remarkable about it,—nothing whatever; yet it seemed to me surcharged with meaning. Why, I could not imagine. A curious fascination kept my eyes fastened on the characteristic bold handwriting, and made me fancy I should like the man who penned it. How the wind roared!—and how that violin next door wailed like the restless spirit of some forgotten musician in torment! My brain swam and my heart ached heavily,— the drip drip of the rain outside sounded like the stealthy footfall of some secret spy upon my movements. I grew irritable and nervous,—a foreboding of evil somehow darkened the bright consciousness of my sudden good fortune. Then an impulse of shame possessed me,—shame that this foreign prince, if such he were, with limitless wealth at his back, should be coming to visit me,—*me*, now a millionaire,—in my present wretched lodging. Already, before I had touched my riches, I was tainted by the miserable vulgarity of seeking to pretend I had never been really poor, but only embarrassed by a little temporary difficulty! If I had had a sixpence about me, (which I had not) I should have sent a telegram to my approaching visitor to put him off.

"But in any case," I said aloud, addressing myself to the empty room and the storm-echoes—"I will not meet him to-night. I'll go out and leave no message,—and if he comes he will think I have not yet had his letter. I can make an appointment to see him when I am better lodged, and dressed more in keeping with my present position,—in the meantime, nothing is easier than to keep out of this would-be benefactor's way."

As I spoke, the flickering lamp gave a dismal crackle and went out, leaving me in pitch darkness. With an exclamation more strong than reverent, I groped about the room for matches, or failing them, for my hat and coat,—and I was still engaged in a fruitless and annoying search, when I caught a sound of galloping horses' hoofs coming to an abrupt stop in the street below. Surrounded by black gloom, I paused and listened. There was a slight commotion in the basement,—I heard my landlady's accents attuned to nervous civility, mingling with the mellow tones of a deep masculine voice,—then steps, firm and even, ascended the stairs to my landing.

"The devil is in it!" I muttered vexedly—"Just like my wayward luck!—here comes the very man I meant to avoid!"

III

The door opened,—and from the dense obscurity enshrouding me I could just perceive a tall shadowy figure standing on the threshold. I remember well the curious impression the mere outline of this scarcely discerned Form made upon me even then,—suggesting at the first glance such a stately majesty of height and bearing as at once riveted my attention,—so much so indeed that I scarcely heard my landlady's introductory words "A gentleman to see you sir,"—words that were quickly interrupted by a murmur of dismay at finding the room in total darkness. "Well to be sure! The lamp must have gone out!" she exclaimed,—then addressing the personage she had ushered thus far, she added—"I'm afraid Mr. Tempest isn't in after all, sir, though I certainly saw him about half-an-hour ago. If you don't mind waiting here a minute I'll fetch a light and see if he has left any message on his table."

She hurried away, and though I knew that of course I ought to speak, a singular and quite inexplicable perversity of humour kept me silent and unwilling to declare my presence. Meanwhile the tall stranger advanced a pace or two, and a rich voice with a ring of ironical amusement in it called me by my name—

"Geoffrey Tempest, are you there?"

Why could I not answer? The strangest and most unnatural obstinacy stiffened my tongue,—and, concealed in the gloom of my forlorn literary den I still held my peace. The majestic figure drew nearer, till in height and breadth it seemed to suddenly overshadow me; and once again the voice called—

"Geoffrey Tempest, are you there?"

For very shame's sake I could hold out no longer,—and with a determined effort I broke the extraordinary dumb spell that had held me like a coward in silent hiding, and came forward boldly to confront my visitor.

"Yes I *am* here," I said—"And being here I am ashamed to give you such a welcome as this. You are Prince Rimânez of course;—I have just read your note which prepared me for your visit, but I was hoping that my landlady, finding the room in darkness, would conclude I was out, and show you downstairs again. You see I am perfectly frank!"

"You are indeed!" returned the stranger, his deep tones still vibrating with the silvery clang of veiled satire—"So frank that I cannot fail to understand you. Briefly, and without courtesy, you resent my visit this evening and wish I had not come!"

This open declaration of my mood sounded so brusque that I made haste to deny it, though I knew it to be true. Truth, even in trifles, always seems unpleasant!

"Pray do not think me so churlish,"—I said—"The fact is, I only opened your letter a few minutes ago, and before I could make any arrangements to receive you, the lamp went out, with the awkward result that I am forced to greet you in this unsociable darkness, which is almost too dense to shake hands in."

"Shall we try?" my visitor enquired, with a sudden softening of accent that gave his words a singular charm; "Here is my hand,—if yours has any friendly instinct in it the twain will meet,—quite blindly and without guidance!"

I at once extended my hand, and it was instantly clasped in a warm and somewhat masterful manner. At that moment a light flashed on the scene,—my landlady entered, bearing what she called 'her best lamp' alit, and set it on the table. I believe she uttered some exclamation of surprise at seeing me,—she may have said anything or nothing,—I did not hear or heed, so entirely was I amazed and fascinated by the appearance of the man whose long slender hand still held mine. I am myself an average good height, but he was fully half a head taller than I, if not more than that,—and as I looked straightly at him, I thought I had never seen so much beauty and intellectuality combined in the outward personality of any human being. The finely shaped head denoted both power and wisdom, and was nobly poised on such shoulders as might have befitted a Hercules,—the countenance was a pure oval, and singularly pale, this complexion intensifying the almost fiery brilliancy of the full dark eyes, which had in them a curious and wonderfully attractive look of mingled mirth and misery. The mouth was perhaps the most telling feature in this remarkable face,—set in the perfect curve of beauty, it was yet firm, determined, and not too small, thus escaping effeminacy,—and I noted that in repose it expressed bitterness, disdain and even cruelty. But with the light of a smile upon it, it signified, or seemed to signify, something more subtle than any passion to which we can give a name, and already with the rapidity of a lightning flash, I caught myself wondering what that mystic undeclared something might be. At a glance I comprehended these primary details of my new acquaintance's eminently prepossessing appearance, and when my hand dropped from his close grasp I felt as if I had known him all my life! And now face to face with him in the bright lamp-light, I remembered my actual surroundings,—the bare cold room, the lack of fire, the black soot that sprinkled the nearly carpetless floor,—my own shabby clothes and deplorable aspect, as compared with this regal-looking individual, who carried the visible evidence of wealth upon him in the superb Russian sables that lined and bordered his long overcoat which he now partially unfastened and threw open with a carelessly imperial air, the while he regarded me, smiling.

"I know I have come at an awkward moment," he said—"I always do! It is my peculiar misfortune. Well-bred people never intrude where they are not wanted,—and in this particular I'm afraid my manners leave much to be desired. Try to forgive me if you can, for the sake of this,"—and he held out a letter addressed to me in my friend Carrington's familiar handwriting. "And permit me to sit down while you read my credentials."

He took a chair and seated himself. I observed his handsome face and easy attitude with renewed admiration.

"No credentials are necessary," I said with all the cordiality I now really felt—"I have already had a letter from Carrington in which he speaks of you in the highest and most grateful terms. But the fact is—well!—really, prince, you must excuse me if I seem confused or astonished. . . I had expected to see quite an old man. . ."

And I broke off, somewhat embarrassed by the keen glance of the brilliant eyes that met mine so fixedly.

"No one is old, my dear sir, nowadays!" he declared lightly—"even the grandmothers and grandfathers are friskier at fifty than they were at fifteen. One does not talk of age at all now in polite society,—it is ill-bred, even coarse. Indecent things are unmentionable—age has become an indecent thing. It is therefore avoided in conversation. You expected to see an old man you say? Well, you are not disappointed—I *am* old. In fact you have no idea how very old I am!"

I laughed at this piece of absurdity.

"Why, you are younger than I,"—I said—"or if not, you look it."

"Ah, my looks belie me!" he returned gaily—"I am like several of the most noted fashionable beauties,—much riper than I seem. But come, read the introductory missive I have brought you,—I shall not be satisfied till you do."

Thus requested, and wishing to prove myself as courteous as I had hitherto been brusque, I at once opened my friend's note and read as follows,—

Dear Geoffrey

The bearer of this, Prince Rimânez, is a very distinguished scholar and gentleman, allied by descent to one of the oldest families in Europe, or for that matter, in the world. You, as a student and lover of ancient history, will be interested to know that his ancestors were originally princes of Chaldea, who afterwards settled in Tyre,—from thence they went to Etruria and there continued through many centuries, the last scion of the house being the very gifted and genial personage who, as my good friend, I have the pleasure of commending to your kindest regard. Certain troublous and overpowering circumstances have forced him into exile from his native province, and deprived him of a great part of his possessions, so that he is, to a considerable extent a wanderer on the face of the earth, and has travelled far and seen much, and has a wide experience of men and things. He is a poet and musician of great skill, and though he occupies himself with the arts solely for his own amusement, I think you will find his practical knowledge of literary matters eminently useful to you in your difficult career. I must not forget to add that in all matters scientific he is an absolute master. Wishing you both a cordial friendship, I am, dear Geoffrey,

Yours sincerely
John Carrington

The signature of 'Boffles' had evidently been deemed out of place this time and somehow I was foolishly vexed at its omission. There seemed to be something formal and stiff in the letter, almost as if it had been written to dictation, and under pressure. What gave me this idea I know not. I glanced furtively at my silent companion,—he caught my stray look and returned it with a curiously grave fixity. Fearing lest my momentary vague distrust of him had been reflected in my eyes I made haste to speak—

"This letter, prince, adds to my shame and regret that I should have greeted you in so churlish a manner this evening. No apology can condone my rudeness,—but you cannot imagine how mortified I felt and still feel, to be compelled to receive you in this miserable den,—it is not at all the sort of place in which I should have liked to welcome you. . ." And I broke off with a renewed sense of irritation, remembering how actually rich I now was, and that in spite of this, I was obliged to seem poor. Meanwhile the prince waived aside my remarks with a light gesture of his hand.

"Why be mortified?" he demanded. "Rather be proud that you can dispense with the vulgar appurtenances of luxury. Genius thrives in a garret and dies in a palace,—is not that the generally accepted theory?"

"Rather a worn-out and mistaken one I consider,"—I replied; "Genius might like to try the effect of a palace for once,—it usually dies of starvation."

"True!—but in thus dying, think how many fools it afterwards fattens! There is an all-wise Providence in this, my dear sir! Schubert perished of want,—but see what large profits all the music-publishers have made since out of his compositions! It is a most beautiful dispensation of nature,—that honest folk should be sacrificed in order to provide for the sustenance of knaves!"

He laughed, and I looked at him in a little surprise. His remark touched so near my own opinions that I wondered whether he were in jest or earnest.

"You speak sarcastically of course?" I said—"You do not really believe what you say?"

"Oh, do I not!" he returned, with a flash of his fine eyes that was almost lightning-like in its intensity—"If I could not believe the teaching of my own experience, what would be left to me? I always realize the '*needs must*' of things—how does the old maxim go—'needs must when the devil drives.' There is really no possible contradiction to offer to the accuracy of that statement. The devil drives the world, whip in hand,—and oddly enough, (considering that some belated folk still fancy there is a God somewhere) succeeds in managing his team with extraordinary ease!" His brow clouded and the bitter lines about his mouth deepened and hardened,—anon he laughed again lightly and continued—"But let us not moralize,—morals sicken the soul both in church and out of it,—every sensible man hates to be told what he *could* be and what he *won't* be. I am here to make friends with you if you permit,—and to put an end to ceremony, will you accompany me back to my hotel where I have ordered supper?"

MARIE CORELLI

By this time I had become indescribably fascinated by his easy manner, handsome presence and mellifluous voice,—the satirical turn of his humour suited mine,—I felt we should get on well together,—and my first annoyance at being discovered by him in such poverty-stricken circumstances somewhat abated.

"With pleasure!" I replied—"But first of all, you must allow me to explain matters a little. You have heard a good deal about my affairs from my friend John Carrington, and I know from his private letter to me that you have come here out of pure kindness and goodwill. For that generous intention I thank you! I know you expected to find a poor wretch of a literary man struggling with the direst circumstances of disappointment and poverty,—and a couple of hours ago you would have amply fulfilled that expectation. But now, things have changed,—I have received news which completely alters my position,—in fact I have had a very great and remarkable surprise this evening. . ."

"An agreeable one I trust?" interposed my companion suavely.

I smiled.

"Judge for yourself!" And I handed him the lawyer's letter which informed me of my suddenly acquired fortune.

He glanced it through rapidly,—then folded and returned it to me with a courteous bow.

"I suppose I should congratulate you,"—he said—"And I do. Though of course this wealth which seems to content you, to me appears a mere trifle. It can be quite conveniently run through and exhausted in about eight years or less, therefore it does not provide absolute immunity from care. To be rich, really rich, in my sense of the word, one should have about a million a year. Then one might reasonably hope to escape the workhouse!"

He laughed,—and I stared at him stupidly, not knowing how to take his words, whether as truth or idle boasting. Five millions of money a mere trifle! He went on without apparently noticing my amazement—

"The inexhaustible greed of a man, my dear sir, can never be satisfied. If he is not consumed by desire for one thing, he is for another, and his tastes are generally expensive. A few pretty and unscrupulous women for example, would soon relieve you of your five millions in the purchase of jewels alone. Horse-racing would do it still more quickly. No, no,—you are not rich,—you are still poor,—only your needs are no longer so pressing as they were. And in this I confess myself somewhat disappointed,—for I came to you hoping to do a good turn to some one for once in my life, and to play the foster-father to a rising genius—and here I am—forestalled,—as usual! It is a singular thing, do you know, but nevertheless a fact, that whenever I have had any particular intentions towards a man I am always forestalled! It is really rather hard upon me!" He broke off and raised his head in a listening attitude.

"What is that?" he asked.

It was the violinist next door playing a well-known "Ave Maria." I told him so.

"Dismal,—very dismal!" he said with a contemptuous shrug. "I hate all that kind of mawkish devotional stuff. Well!—millionaire as you are, and acknowledged lion of society as you shortly will be, there is no objection I hope, to the proposed supper? And perhaps a music-hall afterwards if you feel inclined,—what do you say?"

He clapped me on the shoulder cordially and looked straight into my face,—those wonderful eyes of his, suggestive of both tears and fire, fixed me with a clear masterful gaze that completely dominated me. I made no attempt to resist the singular attraction which now possessed me for this man whom I had but just met,—the sensation was too strong and too pleasant to be combated. Only for one moment more I hesitated, looking down at my shabby attire.

"I am not fit to accompany you, prince," I said—"I look more like a tramp than a millionaire."

He glanced at me and smiled.

"Upon my life, so you do!" he averred.—"But be satisfied!—you are in this respect very like many another Croesus. It is only the poor and proud who take the trouble to dress well,—they and the dear 'naughty' ladies, generally monopolize tasteful and becoming attire. An ill-fitting coat often adorns the back of a Prime Minister,—and if you see a woman clad in clothes vilely cut and coloured, you may be sure she is eminently virtuous, renowned for good works, and probably a duchess!" He rose, drawing his sables about him.

"What matter the coat if the purse be full!" he continued gaily.—"Let it once be properly paragraphed in the papers that you are a millionaire, and doubtless some enterprising tailor will invent a 'Tempest' ulster coloured softly like your present garb, an artistic mildewy green! And now come along,—your solicitor's communication should have given you a good appetite, or it is not so valuable as it seems,—and I want you to do justice to my supper. I have my own *chef* with me, and he is not without skill. I hope, by the way, you will at least do me this much service,—that pending legal discussion and settlement of your affairs, you will let me be your banker?"

This offer was made with such an air of courteous delicacy and friendship, that I could do no more than accept it gratefully, as it relieved me from all temporary embarrassment. I hastily wrote a few lines to my landlady, telling her she would receive the money owing to her by post next day,—then, thrusting my rejected manuscript, my only worldly possession, into my coat-pocket, I extinguished the lamp, and with the new friend I had so suddenly gained, I left my dismal lodgings and all its miserable associations for ever. I little thought the time would come when I should look back to the time spent in that small mean room as the best period of my life,—when I should regard the bitter poverty I then endured, as the stern but holy angel meant to guide me to the highest and noblest attainment,—when I should pray desperately with wild tears to be as I was then, rather than as I am now! Is it well or ill for us I wonder, that the future is hidden from our knowledge? Should we steer our ways clearer from evil if we knew its result? It is a doubtful question,—at anyrate my ignorance for the moment was indeed bliss. I went joyfully out of the dreary house where I had lived so long among disappointments and difficulties, turning my back upon it with such a sense of relief as could never be expressed in words,—and the last thing I heard as I passed into the street with my companion, was a plaintive long-drawn wail of minor melody, which seemed to be sent after me like a parting cry, by the unknown and invisible player of the violin.

IV

O utside, the prince's carriage waited, drawn by two spirited black horses caparisoned in silver; magnificent thoroughbreds, which pawed the ground and champed their bits impatient of delay,—at sight of his master the smart footman in attendance threw the door open, touching his hat respectfully. We stepped in, I preceding my companion at his expressed desire; and as I sank back among the easy cushions, I felt the complacent consciousness of luxury and power to such an extent that it seemed as if I had left my days of adversity already a long way behind me. Hunger and happiness disputed my sensations between them, and I was in that vague light-headed condition common to long fasting, in which nothing seems absolutely tangible or real. I knew I should not properly grasp the solid truth of my wonderful good luck till my physical needs were satisfied and I was, so to speak, once more in a naturally balanced bodily condition. At present my brain was in a whirl,—my thoughts were all dim and disconnected,—and I appeared to myself to be in some whimsical dream from which I should wake up directly. The carriage rolled on rubber-tyred wheels and made no noise as it went,—one could only hear the even rapid trot of the horses. By-and-by I saw in the semi-darkness my new friend's brilliant dark eyes fixed upon me with a curiously intent expression.

"Do you not feel the world already at your feet?" he queried half playfully, half ironically—"Like a football, waiting to be kicked? It is such an absurd world, you know—so easily moved. Wise men in all ages have done their best to make it less ridiculous,—with no result, inasmuch as it continues to prefer folly to wisdom. A football, or let us say a shuttlecock among worlds, ready to be tossed up anyhow and anywhere, provided the battledore be of gold!"

"You speak a trifle bitterly, prince"—I said—"But no doubt you have had a wide experience among men?"

"I have," he returned with emphasis—"My kingdom is a vast one."

"You are a ruling power then?" I exclaimed with some astonishment— "Yours is not a title of honour only?"

"Oh, as your rules of aristocracy go, it *is* a mere title of honour"—he replied quickly—"When I say that my kingdom is a vast one, I mean that I rule wherever men obey the influence of wealth. From this point of view, am I wrong in calling my kingdom vast?—is it not almost boundless?"

"I perceive you are a cynic,"—I said—"Yet surely you believe that there are some things wealth cannot buy,—honour and virtue for example?"

He surveyed me with a whimsical smile.

"I suppose honour and virtue *do* exist—" he answered—"And when they are existent of course they cannot be bought. But my experience has taught me that I can always buy everything. The sentiments called honour and virtue by the majority of men are the most shifty things imaginable,—set sufficient cash down, and they become bribery and corruption in the twinkling of an eye! Curious—very curious. I confess I found a case of unpurchaseable integrity once, but only once. I may find it again, though I consider the chance a very doubtful one. Now to revert to myself, pray do not imagine I am playing the humbug with you or passing myself off under a *bogus* title. I am a *bona-fide* prince, believe me, and of such descent as none of your oldest families can boast,—but my dominions are long since broken up and my former subjects dispersed among all nations,—anarchy, nihilism, disruption and political troubles generally, compel me to be rather reticent concerning my affairs. Money I fortunately have in plenty,—and with that I pave my way. Some day when we are better acquainted, you shall know more of my private history. I have various other names and titles besides that on my card—but I keep to the simplest of them, because most people are such bunglers at the pronunciation of foreign names. My intimate friends generally drop my title, and call me Lucio simply."

"That is your christian name—?" I began.

"Not at all—I have no 'christian' name,"—he interrupted swiftly and with anger—"There is no such thing as 'christian' in my composition!"

He spoke with such impatience that for a moment I was at a loss for a reply. At last—

"Indeed!" I murmured vaguely.

He burst out laughing.

"'Indeed!' That is all you can find to say! Indeed and again indeed the word 'christian' vexes me. There is no such creature alive. *You* are not a Christian,—no one is really,—people pretend to be,—and in so damnable an act of feigning are more blasphemous than any fallen fiend! Now I make no pretences of the kind,—I have only one faith—"

"And that is?"—

"A profound and awful one!" he said in thrilling tones—"And the worst of it is that it is true,—as true as the workings of the Universe.

But of that hereafter,—it will do to talk of when we feel low-spirited and wish to converse of things grim and ghastly,—at present here we are at our destination, and the chief consideration of our lives, (it is the chief consideration of most men's lives) must be the excellence or non-excellence of our food."

The carriage stopped and we descended. At first sight of the black horses and silver trappings, the porter of the hotel and two or three other servants rushed out to attend upon us; but the prince passed into the hall without noticing any of them and addressed himself to a sober-looking individual in black, his own private valet, who came forward to meet him with a profound salutation. I murmured something about wishing to engage a room for myself in the hotel.

"Oh, my man will see to that for you"—he said lightly—"The house is not full,—at anyrate all the best rooms are not taken; and of course you want one of the best."

A staring waiter, who up to that moment, had been noting my shabby clothes with that peculiar air of contempt commonly displayed by insolent menials to those whom they imagine are poor, overheard these words, and suddenly changing the derisive expression of his foxy face, bowed obsequiously as I passed. A thrill of disgust ran through me, mingled with a certain angry triumph,—the hypocritical reflex of this low fellow's countenance, was, I knew, a true epitome of what I should find similarly reflected in the manner and attitude of all 'polite' society. For there the estimate of worth is no higher than a common servant's estimate, and is taken solely from the money standard;—if you are poor and dress shabbily you are thrust aside and ignored,—but if you are rich, you may wear shabby clothes as much as you like, you are still courted and flattered, and invited everywhere, though you may be the greatest fool alive or the worst blackguard unhung. With vague thoughts such as these flitting over my mind, I followed my host to his rooms. He occupied nearly a whole wing of the hotel, having a large drawing-room, dining-room and study *en suite*, fitted up in the most luxurious manner, besides bedroom, bathroom, and dressing-room, with other rooms adjoining, for his valet and two extra personal attendants. The table was laid for supper, and glittered with the costliest glass, silver and china, being furthermore adorned by baskets of the most exquisite fruit and flowers, and in a few moments we were seated. The prince's valet acted as head-waiter, and I noticed that now this man's face, seen in the full light of the electric lamps, seemed very dark and unpleasant,

MARIE CORELLI

even sinister in expression,—but in the performance of his duties he was unexceptionable, being quick, attentive, and deferential, so much so that I inwardly reproached myself for taking an instinctive dislike to him. His name was Amiel, and I found myself involuntarily watching his movements, they were so noiseless,—his very step suggesting the stealthy gliding of a cat or a tiger. He was assisted in his work by the two other attendants who served as his subordinates, and who were equally active and well-trained,—and presently I found myself enjoying the choicest meal I had tasted for many and many a long day, flavoured with such wine as connoisseurs might be apt to dream of, but never succeed in finding. I began to feel perfectly at my ease, and talked with freedom and confidence, the strong attraction I had for my new friend deepening with every moment I passed in his company.

"Will you continue your literary career now you have this little fortune left you?" he inquired, when at the close of supper Amiel set the choicest cognac and cigars before us, and respectfully withdrew—"Do you think you will care to go on with it?"

"Certainly I shall"—I replied—"if only for the fun of the thing. You see, with money I can force my name into notice whether the public like it or not. No newspaper refuses paying advertisements."

"True!—but may not inspiration refuse to flow from a full purse and an empty head?"

This remark provoked me not a little.

"Do you consider me empty-headed?" I asked with some vexation.

"Not at present. My dear Tempest, do not let either the Tokay we have been drinking, or the cognac we are going to drink, speak for you in such haste! I assure you I do not think you empty-headed,—on the contrary, your head, I believe from what I have heard, has been and is full of ideas,—excellent ideas, original ideas, which the world of conventional criticism does not want. But whether these ideas will continue to germinate in your brain, or whether, with the full purse, they will cease, is now the question. Great originality and inspiration, strange to say, seldom endow the millionaire. Inspiration is supposed to come from above,—money from below! In your case however both originality and inspiration may continue to flourish and bring forth fruit,—I trust they may. It often happens, nevertheless that when bags of money fall to the lot of aspiring genius, God departs and the devil walks in. Have you never heard that?"

"Never!" I answered smiling.

"Well, of course the saying is foolish, and sounds doubly ridiculous in this age when people believe in neither God nor devil. It implies however that one must choose an up or a down,—genius is the Up, money is the Down. You cannot fly and grovel at the same instant."

"The possession of money is not likely to cause a man to grovel"—I said—"It is the one thing necessary to strengthen his soaring powers and lift him to the greatest heights."

"You think so?" and my host lit his cigar with a grave and pre-occupied air—"Then I'm afraid, you don't know much about what I shall call natural psychics. What belongs to the earth tends earthwards,—surely you realize that? Gold most strictly belongs to the earth,—you dig it out of the ground,—you handle it and dispose of it in solid wedges or bars—it is a substantial metal enough. Genius belongs to nobody knows where,—you cannot dig it up or pass it on, or do anything with it except stand and marvel—it is a rare visitant and capricious as the wind, and generally makes sad havoc among the conventionalities of men. It is as I said an 'upper' thing, beyond earthly smells and savours,—and those who have it always live in unknown high latitudes. But money is a perfectly level commodity,—level with the ground;—when you have much of it, you come down solidly on your flat soles and down you stay!"

I laughed.

"Upon my word you preach very eloquently against wealth!" I said— "You yourself are unusually rich,—are you sorry for it?"

"No, I am not sorry, because being sorry would be no use"—he returned—"And I never waste my time. But I am telling you the truth— Genius and great riches hardly ever pull together. Now I, for example,— you cannot imagine what great capabilities I had once!—a long time ago—before I became my own master!"

"And you have them still I am sure"—I averred, looking expressively at his noble head and fine eyes.

The strange subtle smile I had noticed once or twice before lightened his face. "Ah, you mean to compliment me!" he said—"You like my looks,—many people do. Yet after all there is nothing so deceptive as one's outward appearance. The reason of this is that as soon as childhood is past, we are always pretending to be what we are not,—and thus, with constant practice from our youth up, we manage to make our physical frames complete disguises for our actual selves. It is really wise and clever of us,—for hence each individual is so much flesh-wall through which neither friend nor enemy can spy. Every man is a solitary soul imprisoned in a self-made den,—when he is quite alone he knows and frequently hates himself,—sometimes he even gets afraid of the gaunt and murderous monster he keeps hidden behind his outwardly pleasant body-mask, and hastens to forget its frightful existence in drink and debauchery. That is what I do occasionally,—you would not think it of me, would you?"

"Never!" I replied quickly, for something in his voice and aspect moved me strangely—"You belie yourself, and wrong your own nature."

He laughed softly.

"Perhaps I do!" he said carelessly—"This much you may believe of me—that I am no worse than most men! Now to return to the subject of your literary career,—you have written a book, you say,—well, publish it and see the result—if you only make one 'hit' that is something. And there are ways of arranging that the 'hit' shall be made. What is your story about? I hope it is improper?"

"It certainly is not;"—I replied warmly—"It is a romance dealing with the noblest forms of life and highest ambitions;—I wrote it with the intention of elevating and purifying the thoughts of my readers, and wished if I could, to comfort those who had suffered loss or sorrow—"

Rimânez smiled compassionately.

"Ah, it won't do!" he interrupted—"I assure you it won't;—it doesn't fit the age. It might go down, possibly, if you could give a 'first-night' of it as it were to the critics, like one of my most intimate friends, Henry Irving,—a 'first-night' combined with an excellent supper and any amount of good drinks going. Otherwise it's no use. If it is to succeed by itself, it must not attempt to be literature,—it must simply be indecent. As indecent as you can make it without offending advanced women,— that is giving you a good wide margin. Put in as much as you can about sexual matters and the bearing of children,—in brief, discourse of men and women simply as cattle who exist merely for breeding purposes, and your success will be enormous. There's not a critic living who won't applaud you,—there's not a school-girl of fifteen who will not gloat over your pages in the silence of her virginal bedroom!"

Such a flash of withering derision darted from his eyes as startled me,—I could find no words to answer him for the moment, and he went on—

"What put it into your head, my dear Tempest, to write a book dealing with, as you say, 'the noblest forms of life'? There are no noble forms of life left on this planet,—it is all low and commercial,—man is a pigmy, and his aims are pigmy like himself. For noble forms of life seek other worlds!—there *are* others. Then again, people don't want their thoughts raised or purified in the novels they read for amusement—they go to church for that, and get very bored during the process. And why should you wish to comfort folks who, out of their own sheer stupidity generally, get into trouble? They wouldn't comfort *you*,—they would not give you sixpence to save you from starvation. My good fellow, leave your quixotism behind you with your poverty. Live your life to yourself,—if you do anything for others they will only treat you with the blackest ingratitude,—so take my advice, and don't sacrifice your own personal interests for any consideration whatever."

He rose from the table as he spoke and stood with his back to the bright fire, smoking his cigar tranquilly,—and I gazed at his handsome figure and face with just the faintest thrill of pained doubt darkening my admiration.

"If you were not so good-looking I should call you heartless"—I said at last—"But your features are a direct contradiction to your words. You have not really that indifference to human nature which you strive to assume,—your whole aspect betokens a generosity of spirit which you cannot conquer if you would. Besides, are you not always trying to do good?"

He smiled.

"Always! That is, I am always at work endeavouring to gratify every man's desire. Whether that is good of me, or bad, remains to be proved. Men's wants are almost illimitable,—the only thing none of them ever seem to wish, so far as I am concerned, is to cut my acquaintance!"

"Why, of course not! After once meeting you, how could they!" I said, laughing at the absurdity of the suggestion.

He gave me a whimsical side-look.

"Their desires are not always virtuous," he remarked, turning to flick off the ash of his cigar into the grate.

"But of course you do not gratify them in their vices!" I rejoined, still laughing—"That would be playing the part of a benefactor somewhat too thoroughly!"

"Ah now I see we shall flounder in the quicksands of theory if we go any further"—he said—"You forget, my dear fellow, that nobody can decide as to what *is* vice, or what *is* virtue. These things are chameleon-like, and take different colours in different countries. Abraham had two or three wives and several concubines, and he was the very soul of virtue according to sacred lore,—whereas my Lord Tom-Noddy in London to-day has one wife and several concubines, and is really very much like Abraham in other particulars, yet he is considered a very dreadful person. 'Who shall decide when doctors disagree!' Let's drop the subject, as we shall never settle it. What shall we do with the rest of the evening? There is a stout-limbed, shrewd wench at the Tivoli, dancing her way into the affections of a ricketty little Duke,—shall we go and watch the admirable contortions with which she is wriggling into a fixed position among the English aristocracy? Or are you tired, and would you prefer a long night's rest?"

To tell the truth I was thoroughly fatigued, and mentally as well as physically worn out with the excitements of the day,—my head too was heavy with the wine to which I had so long been unaccustomed.

"Upon my word I think I would rather go to bed than anything—" I confessed—"But what about my room?"

"Oh, Amiel will have attended to that for you,—we'll ask him." And he touched the bell. His valet instantly appeared.

"Have you got a room for Mr. Tempest?"

"Yes, your Excellency. An apartment in this corridor almost facing your Excellency's suite. It is not as well furnished as it might be, but I have made it as comfortable as I can for the night."

"Thanks very much!" I said—"I am greatly obliged to you."

Amiel bowed deferentially.

"Thank *you*, sir."

He retired, and I moved to bid my host good-night. He took my proffered hand, and held it in his, looking at me curiously the while.

"I like you, Geoffrey Tempest;" he said—"And because I like you, and because I think there are the makings of something higher than mere earthy brute in you, I am going to make you what you may perhaps consider rather a singular proposition. It is this,—that if you don't like *me*, say so at once, and we will part now, before we have time to know anything more of each other, and I will endeavour not to cross your path again unless you seek me out. But if on the contrary, you do like me,—if you find something in my humour or turn of mind congenial to your own disposition, give me your promise that you will be my friend and comrade for a while, say for a few months at any rate. I can take you into the best society, and introduce you to the prettiest women in Europe as well as the most brilliant men. I know them all, and I believe I can be useful to you. But if there is the smallest aversion to me lurking in the depths of your nature"—here he paused,—then resumed with extraordinary solemnity—"in God's name give it full way and let me go,—because I swear to you in all sober earnest that I am not what I seem!"

Strongly impressed by his strange look and stranger manner, I hesitated one moment,—and on that moment, had I but known it, hung my future. It was true,—I had felt a passing shadow of distrust and repulsion for this fascinating yet cynical man, and he seemed to have guessed it. But now every suspicion of him vanished from my mind, and I clasped his hand with renewed heartiness.

"My dear fellow, your warning comes too late!" I said mirthfully—"Whatever you are, or whatever you choose to think you are, I find you most sympathetic to my disposition, and I consider myself most fortunate in knowing you. My old friend Carrington has indeed done me a good turn in bringing us together, and I assure you I shall be proud of your companionship. You seem to take a perverse delight in running yourself down!—but you know the old adage, 'the devil is not so black as he is painted'?"

"And that is true!" he murmured dreamily—"Poor devil! His faults are no doubt much exaggerated by the clergy! And so we are to be friends?"

"I hope so! I shall not be the first to break the compact!"

His dark eyes rested upon me thoughtfully, yet there seemed to be a lurking smile in them as well.

"Compact is a good word"—he said—"So,—a compact we will consider it. I meant to improve your material fortunes,—you can dispense with that aid now; but I think I can still be of service in pushing you on in society. And love—of course you will fall in love if you have not already done so,—have you?"

"Not I!" I answered quickly, and with truth—"I have seen no woman yet who perfectly fulfils my notions of beauty."

He burst out laughing violently.

"Upon my word you are not wanting in audacity!" he said—"Nothing but perfect beauty will suit you, eh? But consider, my friend, you, though a good-looking well-built man, are not yourself quite a Phoebus Apollo!"

"That has nothing to do with the matter"—I rejoined—"A man should choose a wife with a careful eye to his own personal gratification, in the same way that he chooses horses or wine,—perfection or nothing."

"And the woman?"—Rimânez demanded, his eyes twinkling.

"The woman has really no right of choice"—I responded,—for this was my pet argument and I took pleasure in setting it forth—"She must mate wherever she has the chance of being properly maintained. A man is always a man,—a woman is only a man's appendage, and without beauty she cannot put forth any just claim to his admiration or his support."

"Right!—very right, and logically argued!"—he exclaimed, becoming preternaturally serious in a moment—"I myself have no sympathy with the new ideas that are in vogue concerning the intellectuality of woman. She is simply the female of man,—she has no real soul save that which is a reflex of his, and being destitute of logic, she is incapable of forming a correct opinion on any subject. All the imposture of religion is kept up by this unmathematical hysterical creature,—and it is curious, considering how inferior a being she is, what mischief she has contrived to make in the world, upsetting the plans of the wisest kings and counsellors, who as mere men, should undoubtedly have mastered her! And in the present age she is becoming more than ever unmanageable."

"It is only a passing phase"—I returned carelessly—"A fad got up by a few unloved and unlovable types of the feminine sex. I care very little for women—I doubt whether I shall ever marry."

"Well you have plenty of time to consider, and amuse yourself with the fair ones, *en passant*"—he said watching me narrowly—"And in the meantime I can take you round the different marriage-markets of the world if you choose, though the largest one of them all is of course this very metropolis. Splendid bargains to be had, my dear friend!—wonderful blonde and brunette specimens going really very cheap. We'll examine them at our leisure. I'm glad you have yourself decided that we are to be comrades,—for I am proud;—I may say damnably proud;—and never stay in any man's company when he expresses the slightest wish to be rid of me. Good-night!"

"Good-night!" I responded. We clasped hands again and they were still interlocked, when a sudden flash of lightning blazed vividly across the room, followed instantaneously by a terrific clap of thunder. The electric lights went out, and only the glow of the fire illumined our faces. I was a little startled and confused,—the prince stood still, quite unconcerned, his eyes shining like those of a cat in the darkness.

"What a storm!" he remarked lightly—"Such thunder in winter is rather unusual. Amiel!"

The valet entered, his sinister countenance resembling a white mask made visible in the gloom.

"These lamps have gone out,"—said his master—"It's very odd that civilized humanity has not yet learned the complete management of the electric light. Can you put them in order, Amiel?"

"Yes, your excellency." And in a few moments, by some dexterous manipulation which I did not understand and could not see, the crystal-cased jets shone forth again with renewed brilliancy. Another peal of thunder crashed overhead, followed by a downpour of rain.

"Really remarkable weather for January,"—said Rimânez, again giving me his hand—"Good-night my friend! Sleep well."

"If the anger of the elements will permit!" I returned, smiling.

"Oh, never mind the elements. Man has nearly mastered them or soon will do so, now that he is getting gradually convinced there is no Deity to interfere in his business. Amiel, show Mr. Tempest to his room."

Amiel obeyed, and crossing the corridor, ushered me into a large, luxurious apartment, richly furnished, and lit up by the blaze of a bright fire. The comforting warmth shone welcome upon me as I entered, and I who had not experienced such personal luxury since my boyhood's days, felt more than ever overpowered by the jubilant sense of my sudden extraordinary good fortune. Amiel waited respectfully, now and then furtively glancing at me with an expression which to my fancy had something derisive in it.

"Is there anything I can do for you sir?" he inquired.

"No thank you,"—I answered, endeavouring to throw an accent of careless condescension into my voice—for somehow I felt this man must be kept strictly in his place—"you have been very attentive,—I shall not forget it."

A slight smile flickered over his features.

"Much obliged to you, sir. Good-night."

And he retired, leaving me alone. I paced the room up and down more dreamily than consciously, trying to think,—trying to set in order the amazing events of the day, but my brain was still dazed and confused, and the only image of actual prominence in my mind was the striking and remarkable personality of my new friend Rimânez. His extraordinary good looks, his attractive manner, his curious cynicism which was so oddly mixed with some deeper sentiment to which I could not give a name, all the trifling yet uncommon peculiarities of his

MARIE CORELLI

bearing and humour haunted me and became indissolubly mingled as it were with myself and all the circumstances concerning me. I undressed before the fire, listening drowsily to the rain, and the thunder which was now dying off into sullen echoes.

"Geoffrey Tempest, the world is before you—" I said, apostrophizing myself indolently—"you are a young man,—you have health, a good appearance, and brains,—added to these you now have five millions of money, and a wealthy prince for your friend. What more do you want of Fate or Fortune? Nothing,—except fame! And that you will get easily, for now-a-days even fame is purchaseable—like love. Your star is in the ascendant,—no more literary drudgery for you my boy!—pleasure and profit and ease are yours to enjoy for the rest of your life. You are a lucky dog!—at last you have your day!"

I flung myself upon the soft bed, and settled myself to sleep,—and as I dozed off, I still heard the rumble of heavy thunder in the distance. Once I fancied I heard the prince's voice calling "Amiel! Amiel!" with a wildness resembling the shriek of an angry wind,—and at another moment I started violently from a profound slumber under the impression that someone had approached and was looking fixedly at me. I sat up in bed, peering into the darkness, for the fire had gone out;—then I turned on a small electric night-lamp at my side which fully illumined the room,—there was no one there. Yet my imagination played me such tricks before I could rest again that I thought I heard a hissing whisper near me that said—

"Peace! Trouble him not. Let the fool in his folly sleep!"

V

The next morning on rising I learned that 'his excellency' as Prince Rimânez was called by his own servants and the employés of the 'Grand,' had gone out riding in the Park, leaving me to breakfast alone. I therefore took that meal in the public room of the hotel, where I was waited upon with the utmost obsequiousness, in spite of my shabby clothes, which I was of course still compelled to wear, having no change. When would I be pleased to lunch? At what hour would I dine? Should my present apartment be retained?—or was it not satisfactory? Would I prefer a 'suite' similar to that occupied by his excellency? All these deferential questions first astonished and then amused me,—some mysterious agency had evidently conveyed the rumour of my wealth among those best fitted to receive it, and here was the first result. In reply I said my movements were uncertain,—I should be able to give definite instructions in the course of a few hours, and that in the meantime I retained my room. The breakfast over I sallied forth to go to my lawyers, and was just about to order a hansom when I saw my new friend coming back from his ride. He bestrode a magnificent chestnut mare, whose wild eyes and strained quivering limbs showed she was fresh from a hard gallop and was scarcely yet satisfied to be under close control. She curveted and danced among the carts and cabs in a somewhat risky fashion, but she had her master in Rimânez, who if he had looked handsome by night looked still more so by day, with a slight colour warming the natural pallor of his complexion and his eyes sparkling with all the zest of exercise and enjoyment. I waited for his approach, as did also Amiel, who as usual timed his appearance in the hotel corridor in exact accordance with the moment of his master's arrival. Rimânez smiled as he caught sight of me, touching his hat with the handle of his whip by way of salutation.

"You slept late, Tempest"—he said, as he dismounted and threw the reins to a groom who had cantered up after him,—"To-morrow you must come with me and join what they call in fashionable slang parlance the Liver Brigade. Once upon a time it was considered the height of indelicacy and low breeding to mention the 'liver' or any other portion of one's internal machinery,—but we have done with all that now, and we find a peculiar satisfaction in discoursing of disease and unsavoury medical matters generally. And in the Liver Brigade you see at a glance all those interesting fellows who have sold themselves to the devil for the sake of the flesh-pots of Egypt,—men who eat till they are well-nigh bursting, and then prance up and down on good horses,—much too respectable beasts by the way to bear such bestial burdens—in the hope of getting out of their poisoned blood the evil they have themselves put in. They think me one of them, but I am not."

He patted his mare and the groom led her away, the foam of her hard ride still flecking her glossy chest and forelegs.

"Why do you join the procession then?" I asked him, laughing and glancing at him with undisguised approval as I spoke, for he seemed more admirably built than ever in his well-fitting riding gear—"You are a fraud!"

"I am!" he responded lightly—"And do you know I am not the only one in London! Where are you off to?"

"To those lawyers who wrote to me last night;—Bentham and Ellis is the name of the firm. The sooner I interview them the better,—don't you think so?"

"Yes—but see here,"—and he drew me aside—"You must have some ready cash. It doesn't look well to apply at once for advances,—and there is really no necessity to explain to these legal men that you were on the verge of starvation when their letter arrived. Take this pocket-book,—remember you promised to let me be your banker,—and on your way you might go to some well-reputed tailor and get properly rigged out. Ta-ta!"

He moved off at a rapid pace,—I hurried after him, touched to the quick by his kindness.

"But wait—I say—Lucio!" And I called him thus by his familiar name for the first time. He stopped at once and stood quite still.

"Well?" he said, regarding me with an attentive smile.

"You don't give me time to speak"—I answered in a low voice, for we were standing in one of the public corridors of the hotel—"The fact is I have some money, or rather I can get it directly,—Carrington sent me a draft for fifty pounds in his letter—I forgot to tell you about it. It was very good of him to lend it to me,—you had better have it as security for this pocket-book,—by-the-bye how much is there inside it?"

"Five hundred, in bank notes of tens and twenties,"—he responded with business-like brevity.

"Five hundred! My dear fellow, I don't want all that. It's too much!"

"Better have too much than too little nowadays,"—he retorted with a laugh—"My dear Tempest, don't make such a business of it. Five hundred pounds is really nothing. You can spend it all on a dressing-case for example. Better send back John Carrington's draft,—I don't think much of his generosity considering that he came into a mine worth a hundred thousand pounds sterling, a few days before I left Australia."

I heard this with great surprise, and, I must admit with a slight feeling of resentment too. The frank and generous character of my old chum 'Boffles' seemed to darken suddenly in my eyes,—why could he not have told me of his good fortune in his letter? Was he afraid I might trouble him for further loans? I suppose my looks expressed my thoughts, for Rimânez, who had observed me intently, presently added—

"Did he not tell you of his luck? That was not very friendly of him—but as I remarked last night, money often spoils a man."

"Oh I daresay he meant no slight by the omission," I said hurriedly, forcing a smile—"No doubt he will make it the subject of his next letter. Now as to this five hundred"—

"Keep it, man, keep it"—he interposed impatiently—"What do you talk about security for? Haven't I got *you* as security?"

I laughed. "Well, I am fairly reliable now"—I said—"And I'm not going to run away."

"From *me*?" he queried, with a half cold half kind glance; "No,—I fancy not!"

He waved his hand lightly and left me, and I, putting the leather case of notes in my inner breast-pocket, hailed a hansom and was driven off rapidly to Basinghall Street where my solicitors awaited me.

Arrived at my destination, I sent up my name, and was received at once with the utmost respect by two small chips of men in rusty black who represented 'the firm.' At my request they sent down their clerk to pay and dismiss my cab, while I, opening Lucio's pocket book, asked them to change me a ten-pound note into gold and silver which they did with ready good-will. Then we went into business together. My deceased relative, whom I had never seen as far as I myself remembered, but who had seen me as a motherless baby in my nurse's arms, had left me everything he possessed unconditionally, including several rare collections of pictures, jewels and curios. His will was so concisely and clearly worded that there were no possibilities of any legal hair-splitting over it,—and I was informed that in a week or ten days at the utmost everything would be in order and at my sole disposition.

"You are a very fortunate man Mr. Tempest;"—said the senior partner Mr. Bentham, as he folded up the last of the papers we had been looking through and put it by—"At your age this princely inheritance may be either a great boon to you or a great curse,—one never knows. The possession of such enormous wealth involves great responsibilities."

I was amused at what I considered the impertinence of this mere servant of the law in presuming to moralize on my luck.

"Many people would be glad to accept such responsibilities and change places with me"—I said with a flippant air—"You yourself, for example?"

I knew this remark was not in good taste, but I made it wilfully, feeling that he had no business to preach to me as it were on the responsibilities of wealth. He took no offence however,—he merely gave me an observant side-glance like that of some meditative crow.

"No Mr. Tempest, no"—he said drily—"I do not think I should at all be disposed to change places with you. I feel very well satisfied as I am. My brain is my bank, and brings me in quite sufficient interest to live upon, which is all that I desire. To be comfortable, and pay one's way honestly is enough for me. I have never envied the wealthy."

"Mr. Bentham is a philosopher,"—interposed his partner, Mr. Ellis smiling—"In our profession Mr. Tempest, we see so many ups and downs of life, that in watching the variable fortunes of our clients, we ourselves learn the lesson of content."

"Ah, it is a lesson that I have never mastered till now!" I responded merrily—"But at the present moment I confess myself satisfied."

They each gave me a formal little bow, and Mr. Bentham shook hands.

"Business being concluded, allow me to congratulate you," he said politely—"Of course, if you should wish at any time to entrust your legal affairs to other hands, my partner and myself are perfectly willing to withdraw. Your deceased relative had the highest confidence in us. . ."

"As I have also, I assure you,"—I interrupted quickly—"Pray do me the favour to continue managing things for me as you did for my relative, and be assured of my gratitude in advance."

Both little men bowed again, and this time Mr. Ellis shook hands.

"We shall do our best for you, Mr. Tempest, shall we not Bentham?" Bentham nodded gravely. "And now what do you say—shall we mention it Bentham?—or shall we not mention it?"

"Perhaps," responded Bentham sententiously—"it would be as well to mention it."

I glanced from one to the other, not understanding what they meant. Mr. Ellis rubbed his hands and smiled deprecatingly.

"The fact is Mr. Tempest, your deceased relative had one very curious idea—he was a shrewd man and a clever one, but he certainly had one very curious idea—and perhaps if he had followed it up to any extent, it might—yes, it might have landed him in a lunatic asylum and prevented his disposing of his extensive fortune in the—er—the very just and reasonable manner he has done. Happily for himself and—er—for you, he did not follow it up, and to the last he retained his admirable business qualities and high sense of rectitude. But I do not think he ever quite dispossessed himself of the idea itself, did he Bentham?"

Bentham gazed meditatively at the round black mark of the gas-burner where it darkened the ceiling.

"I think not,—no, I think not," he answered—"I believe he was perfectly convinced of it."

"And what was it?" I asked, getting impatient—"Did he want to bring out some patent?—a new notion for a flying-machine, and get rid of his money in that way?"

"No, no, no!" and Mr. Ellis laughed a soft pleasant little laugh over my suggestion—"No, my dear sir—nothing of a purely mechanical or commercial turn captivated his imagination. He was too,—er—yes, I think I may say too profoundly opposed to what is called 'progress' in the world to aid it by any new invention or other means whatever. You see it is a little awkward for me to explain to you what really seems to be the most absurd and fantastic notion,—but—to begin with, we never really knew how he made his money, did we Bentham?"

Bentham shook his head and pursed his lips closely together.

"We had to take charge of large sums, and advise as to investments and other matters,—but it was not our business to inquire where the cash came from in the first place, was it, Bentham?"

Again Bentham shook his head solemnly.

"We were entrusted with it;"—went on his partner, pressing the tips of his fingers together caressingly as he spoke—"and we did our best to fulfil that trust—with—er—with discretion and fidelity. And it was only after we had been for many years connected in business that our client mentioned—er—his idea;—a most erratic and extraordinary one, which was briefly this,—that he had sold himself to the devil, and that his large fortune was one result of the bargain!"

I burst out laughing heartily.

"What a ridiculous notion!" I exclaimed—"Poor man!—a weak spot in his brain somewhere evidently,—or perhaps he used the expression as a mere figure of speech?"

"I think not;"—responded Mr. Ellis half interrogatively, still caressing his fingers—"I think our client did not use the phrase 'sold to the devil' as a figure of speech merely, Mr. Bentham?"

"I am positive he did not,"—said Bentham seriously—"He spoke of the 'bargain' as an actual and accomplished fact."

I laughed again with a trifle less boisterousness.

"Well, people have all sorts of fancies now-a-days"—I said; "What with Blavatskyism, Besantism and hypnotism, it is no wonder if some folks still have a faint credence in the silly old superstition of a devil's existence. But for a thoroughly sensible man. . ."

"Yes—er, yes;"—interrupted Mr. Ellis—"Your relative, Mr. Tempest, *was* a thoroughly sensible man, and this—er—this idea was the only fancy that ever appeared to have taken root in his eminently practical mind. Being only an idea, it seemed hardly worth mentioning—but perhaps it is well—Mr. Bentham agreeing with me—that we *have* mentioned it."

"It is a satisfaction and relief to ourselves,"—said Mr. Bentham, "to have had it mentioned."

I smiled, and thanking them, rose to go. They bowed to me once more, simultaneously, looking almost like twin brothers, so identically had their united practice of the law impressed itself upon their features.

"Good-day Mr. Tempest,"—said Mr. Bentham—"I need scarcely say that we shall serve you as we served our late client, to the best of our ability. And in matters where advice may be pleasant or profitable, we may possibly be of use to you. May we ask whether you require any cash advances immediately?"

"No, thank you,"—I answered, feeling grateful to my friend Rimânez for having placed me in a perfectly independent position to confront these solicitors—"I am amply provided."

They seemed, I fancied, a trifle surprised at this, but were too discreet to offer any remark. They wrote down my address at the Grand Hotel, and sent their clerk to show me to the door. I gave this man half-a-sovereign to drink my health which he very cheerfully promised to do,—then I walked round by the Law Courts, trying to realize that I was not in a dizzy dream, but that I was actually and solidly, five times a millionaire. As luck would have it, in turning a corner I jostled up against a man coming the other way, the very publisher who had returned me my rejected manuscript the day before.

"Hullo!" he exclaimed stopping short.

"Hullo!" I rejoined.

"Where are you off to?" he went on—"Going to try and place that unlucky novel? My dear boy, believe me it will never do as it is. . ."

"It will do, it shall do;"—I said calmly—"I am going to publish it myself."

He started. "Publish it yourself! Good heavens!—it will cost you—ah!—sixty or seventy, perhaps a hundred pounds."

"I don't care if it costs me a thousand!"

A red flush came into his face, and his eyes opened in astonishment.

"I thought. . . excuse me. . ." he stammered awkwardly; "I thought money was scarce with you—"

"It was," I answered drily—"It isn't now."

Then, his utterly bewildered look, together with the whole topsy-turviness of things in my altered position, struck me so forcibly that I burst out laughing, wildly, and with a prolonged noise and violence that apparently alarmed him, for he began looking nervously about him in all directions as if meditating flight. I caught him by the arm.

"Look here man," I said, trying to conquer my almost hysterical mirth—"I'm not mad—don't you think it,—I'm only a—millionaire!" And I began laughing again; the situation seemed to me so sublimely ridiculous. But the worthy publisher did not see it at all—and his features expressed so much genuine alarm that I made a further effort to control myself and succeeded. "I assure you on my word of honour I'm not joking—it's a fact. Last night I wanted a dinner, and you, like a good fellow, offered to give me one,—to-day I possess five millions of money! Don't stare so! don't have a fit of apoplexy! And as I have told you, I shall publish my book myself at my own expense, and it *shall* succeed! Oh I'm in earnest, grim earnest, grim as death!—I've more than enough in my pocketbook to pay for its publication *now*!"

I loosed my hold of him, and he fell back stupefied and confused.

"God bless my soul!" he muttered feebly—"It's like a dream!—I was never more astonished in my life!"

"Nor I!" I said, another temptation to laughter threatening my composure,—"But strange things happen in life, as in fiction. And that book which the builders—I mean the readers—rejected, shall be the headstone of the corner—or—the success of the season! What will you take to bring it out?"

"Take? I? I bring it out!"

"Yes, you—why not? If I offer you a chance to turn an honest penny shall your paid pack of 'readers' prevent your accepting it? Fie! you are not a slave,—this is a free country. I know the kind of people who 'read' for you,—the gaunt unlovable spinster of fifty,—the dyspeptic book-worm who is a 'literary failure' and can find nothing else to do but scrawl growling comments on the manuscript of promising work,— why in heaven's name should you rely on such incompetent opinion? I'll pay you for the publication of my book at as stiff a price as you choose and something over for good-will. And I guarantee you another thing— it shall not only make my name as an author, but yours as a publisher. I'll advertise royally, and I'll work the press. Everything in this world can be done for money. . ."

"Stop, stop,"—he interrupted.—"This is so sudden! You must let me think of it—you must give me time to consider—"

"Take a day for your meditations then," I said—"But no longer. For if you don't say yes, I'll get another man, and he'll have the big pickings instead of you! Be wise in time, my friend!—good-day!"

He ran after me.

"Stay,—look here! You're so strange, so wild—so erratic you know! Your head seems quite turned!"

"It is! The right way round this time!"

"Dear dear me," and he smiled benevolently—"Why, you don't give me a chance to congratulate you. I really do, you know—I congratulate you sincerely!" And he shook me by the hand quite fervently. "And as regards the book I believe there was really no fault found with it in the matter of literary style or quality,—it was simply too—too transcendental, and unlikely therefore to suit the public taste. The Domestic-Iniquity line is what we find pays best at present. But I will think about it—where will a letter find you?"

"Grand Hotel," I responded, inwardly amused at his puzzled and anxious expression—I knew he was already mentally calculating how much he could make out of me in the pursuit of my literary whim— "Come there, and lunch or dine with me to-morrow if you like—only send me a word beforehand. Remember, I give you just a day's grace to decide,—it must be yes or no, in twenty-four hours!"

And with this I left him, staring vaguely after me like a man who has seen some nameless wonder drop out of the sky at his feet. I went on, laughing to myself inaudibly, till I saw one or two passers-by looking at me so surprisedly that I came to the conclusion that I must put a disguise on my thoughts if I would not be taken for a madman. I walked briskly, and presently my excitement cooled down. I resumed the normal condition of the phlegmatic Englishman who considers it the height of bad form to display any personal emotion whatever, and I occupied the rest of the morning in purchasing some ready-made apparel which by unusual good luck happened to fit me, and also in giving an extensive, not to say extravagant order to a fashionable tailor in Sackville Street who promised me everything with punctuality and despatch. I next sent off the rent I owed to the landlady of my former lodgings, adding five pounds extra by way of recognition of the poor woman's long patience in giving me credit, and general kindness towards me during my stay in her dismal house,—and this done I returned to the Grand in high spirits, looking and feeling very much the better for my ready-made outfit. A waiter met me in the corridor and with the most obsequious deference, informed me that 'his excellency the prince' was waiting luncheon for me in his own apartments. Thither I repaired at once, and found my new friend alone in his sumptuous drawing-room, standing near the full light of the largest window and holding in his hand an oblong crystal case through which he was looking with an almost affectionate solicitude.

"Ah, Geoffrey! Here you are!" he exclaimed—"I imagined you would get through your business by lunch time, so I waited."

"Very good of you!" I said, pleased at the friendly familiarity he displayed in thus calling me by my Christian name—"What have you got there?"

"A pet of mine,"—he answered, smiling slightly—"Did you ever see anything like it before?"

VI

I approached and examined the box he held. It was perforated with finely drilled holes for the admission of air, and within it lay a brilliant winged insect coloured with all the tints and half-tints of the rainbow.

"Is it alive?" I asked.

"It is alive, and has a sufficient share of intelligence,"—replied Rimânez. "I feed it and it knows me,—that is the utmost you can say of the most civilized human beings; they know what feeds them. It is quite tame and friendly as you perceive,"—and opening the case he gently advanced his forefinger. The glittering beetle's body palpitated with the hues of an opal; its radiant wings expanded, and it rose at once to its protector's hand and clung there. He lifted it out and held it aloft, then shaking it to and fro lightly, he exclaimed—

"Off, Sprite! Fly, and return to me!"

The creature soared away through the room and round and round the ceiling, looking like a beautiful iridescent jewel, the whirr of its wings making a faint buzzing sound as it flew. I watched it fascinated, till after a few graceful movements hither and thither, it returned to its owner's still outstretched hand, and again settled there making no further attempt to fly.

"There is a well-worn platitude which declares that 'in the midst of life we are in death'"—said the prince then softly, bending his dark deep eyes on the insect's quivering wings—"But as a matter of fact that maxim is wrong as so many trite human maxims are. It should be 'in the midst of death we are in life.' This creature is a rare and curious production of death, but not I believe the only one of its kind. Others have been found under precisely similar circumstances. I took possession of this one myself in rather a weird fashion,—will the story bore you?"

"On the contrary"—I rejoined eagerly, my eyes fixed on the radiant bat-shaped thing that glittered in the light as though its veins were phosphorescent.

He paused a moment, watching me.

"Well,—it happened simply thus,—I was present at the uncasing of an Egyptian female mummy;—her talismans described her as a princess of a famous royal house. Several curious jewels were tied round her neck, and on her chest was a piece of beaten gold quarter of an inch thick. Underneath this gold plate, her body was swathed round and round in an unusual number of scented wrappings; and when these were removed it was discovered that the mummified flesh between her breasts had decayed away, and in the hollow or nest thus formed by the process of decomposition, this insect I hold was found alive, as brilliant in colour as it is now!"

I could not repress a slight nervous shudder.

"Horrible!" I said—"I confess, if I were you, I should not care to make a pet of such an uncanny object. I should kill it, I think."

He kept his bright intent gaze upon me.

"Why?" he asked. "I'm afraid, my dear Geoffrey, you are not disposed to study science. To kill the poor thing who managed to find life in the very bosom of death, is a cruel suggestion, is it not? To me, this unclassified insect is a valuable proof (if I needed one) of the indestructibility of the germs of conscious existence; it has eyes, and the senses of taste, smell, touch and hearing,—and it gained these together with its intelligence, out of the dead flesh of a woman who lived, and no doubt loved and sinned and suffered more than four thousand years ago!" He broke off,—then suddenly added—"All the same I frankly admit to you that I believe it to be an evil creature. I do indeed! But I like it none the less for that. In fact I have rather a fantastic notion about it myself. I am much inclined to accept the idea of the transmigration of souls, and so I please my humour sometimes by thinking that perhaps the princess of that Royal Egyptian house had a wicked, brilliant, vampire soul,—and that. . . *here it is!*"

A cold thrill ran through me from head to foot at these words, and as I looked at the speaker standing opposite me in the wintry light, dark and tall, with the 'wicked, brilliant, vampire soul' clinging to his hand, there seemed to me to be a sudden hideousness declared in his excessive personal beauty. I was conscious of a vague terror, but I attributed it to the gruesome nature of the story, and, determining to combat my sensations, I examined the weird insect more closely. As I did so, its bright beady eyes sparkled, I thought, vindictively, and I stepped back, vexed with myself at the foolish fear of the thing which overpowered me.

"It is certainly remarkable,"—I murmured—"No wonder you value it,—as a curiosity. Its eyes are quite distinct, almost intelligent in fact."

"No doubt she had beautiful eyes,"—said Rimânez smiling.

"She? Whom do you mean?"

"The princess, of course!" he answered, evidently amused; "The dear dead lady,—some of whose personality must be in this creature, seeing that it had nothing but her body to nourish itself upon."

And here he replaced the creature in its crystal habitation with the utmost care.

"I suppose"—I said slowly, "you, in your pursuit of science, would infer from this that nothing actually perishes completely?"

"Exactly!" returned Rimânez emphatically. "There, my dear Tempest, is the mischief,—or the deity,—of things. Nothing can be entirely annihilated;—not even a thought."

I was silent, watching him while he put the glass case with its uncanny occupant away out of sight.

"And now for luncheon," he said gaily, passing his arm through mine—"You look twenty per cent. better than when you went out this morning, Geoffrey, so I conclude your legal matters are disposed of satisfactorily. And what else have you done with yourself?"

Seated at table with the dark-faced Amiel in attendance, I related my morning's adventures, dwelling at length on my chance meeting with the publisher who had on the previous day refused my manuscript, and who now, I felt sure, would be only too glad to close with the offer I had made him. Rimânez listened attentively, smiling now and then.

"Of course!" he said, when I had concluded. "There is nothing in the least surprising in the conduct of the worthy man. In fact I think he showed remarkable discretion and decency in not at once jumping at your proposition,—his pleasant hypocrisy in retiring to think it over, shows him to be a person of tact and foresight. Did you ever imagine that a human being or a human conscience existed that could not be bought? My good fellow, you can buy a king if you only give a long price enough; and the Pope will sell you a specially reserved seat in his heaven if you will only hand him the cash down while he is on earth! Nothing is given free in this world save the air and the sunshine,—everything else must be bought,—with blood, tears and groans occasionally,—but oftenest with money."

I fancied that Amiel, behind his master's chair, smiled darkly at this,—and my instinctive dislike of the fellow kept me more or less reticent concerning my affairs till the luncheon was over. I could not formulate to myself any substantial reason for my aversion to this confidential servant of the prince's,—but do what I would the aversion remained, and increased each time I saw his sullen, and as I thought, sneering features. Yet he was perfectly respectful and deferential; I could find no actual fault with him,—nevertheless when at last he placed the coffee, cognac, and cigars on the table and noiselessly withdrew, I was conscious of a great relief, and breathed more freely. As soon as we were alone, Rimânez lit a cigar and settled himself for a smoke, looking over at me with a personal interest and kindness which made his handsome face more than ever attractive.

"Now let us talk,"—he said—"I believe I am at present the best friend you have, and I certainly know the world better than you do. What do you propose to make of your life? Or in other words how do you mean to begin spending your money?"

I laughed. "Well, I shan't provide funds for the building of a church, or the endowment of a hospital,"—I said—"I shall not even start a Free Library, for these institutions, besides becoming centres for infectious diseases, generally get presided over by a committee of local grocers who presume to consider themselves judges of literature. My dear Prince Rimânez, I mean to spend my money on my own pleasure, and I daresay I shall find plenty of ways to do it."

Rimânez fanned away the smoke of his cigar with one hand, and his dark eyes shone with a peculiarly vivid light through the pale grey floating haze.

"With your fortune, you could make hundreds of miserable people happy;"—he suggested.

"Thanks, I would rather be happy myself first"—I answered gaily—"I daresay I seem to you selfish,—you are philanthropic I know; I am not."

He still regarded me steadily.

"You might help your fellow-workers in literature. . ."

I interrupted him with a decided gesture.

"That I will never do, my friend, though the heavens should crack! My fellow-workers in literature have kicked me down at every opportunity, and done their best to keep me from earning a bare livelihood,—it is my turn at kicking now, and I will show them as little mercy, as little help, as little sympathy as they have shown me!"

"Revenge is sweet!" he quoted sententiously—"I should recommend your starting a high-class half-crown magazine."

"Why?"

"Can you ask? Just think of the ferocious satisfaction it would give you to receive the manuscripts of your literary enemies, and reject them! To throw their letters into the waste-paper basket, and send back their poems, stories, political articles and what not, with '*Returned with thanks*' or '*Not up to our mark*' type-written on the backs thereof! To dig knives into your rivals through the medium of anonymous criticism! The howling joy of a savage with twenty scalps at his belt would be tame in comparison to it! I was an editor once myself, and I know!"

I laughed at his whimsical earnestness.

"I daresay you are right,"—I said—"I can grasp the vengeful position thoroughly! But the management of a magazine would be too much trouble to me,—too much of a tie."

"*Don't* manage it! Follow the example of all the big editors, and live out of the business altogether,—but take the profits! You never see the real editor of a leading daily newspaper you know,—you can only interview the sub. The real man is, according to the seasons of the year, at Ascot, in Scotland, at Newmarket, or wintering in Egypt,—he is supposed to be responsible for everything in his journal, but he is generally the last person who knows anything about it. He relies on his 'staff'—a very bad crutch at times,—and when his 'staff' are in a difficulty, they get out of it by saying they are unable to decide without the editor. Meanwhile the editor is miles away, comfortably free from worry. You could bamboozle the public in that way if you liked."

"I could, but I shouldn't care to do so," I answered—"If I had a business I would not neglect it. I believe in doing things thoroughly."

"So do I!" responded Rimânez promptly. "I am a very thorough-going fellow myself, and whatever my hand findeth to do, I do it with my might!—excuse me for quoting Scripture!" He smiled, a little ironically I thought, then resumed—"Well, in what, at present does your idea of enjoying your heritage consist?"

"In publishing my book," I answered. "That very book I could get no one to accept,—I tell you, I will make it the talk of London!"

"Possibly you will"—he said, looking at me through half-closed eyes and a cloud of smoke,—"London easily talks. Particularly on unsavoury and questionable subjects. Therefore,—as I have already hinted,—if your book were a judicious mixture of Zola, Huysmans and Baudelaire, or had for its heroine a 'modest' maid who considered honourable marriage a 'degradation,' it would be quite sure of success in these days of new Sodom and Gomorrah." Here he suddenly sprang up, and flinging away his cigar, confronted me. "Why do not the heavens rain fire on this accursed city! It is ripe for punishment,—full of abhorrent creatures not worth the torturing in hell to which it is said liars and hypocrites are condemned! Tempest, if there is one human being more than another that I utterly abhor, it is the type of man so common to the present time, the man who huddles his own loathly vices under a cloak of assumed broad-mindedness and virtue. Such an one will even deify the loss of chastity in woman by the name of 'purity,'—because he knows that it is by her moral and physical ruin alone that he can gratify his brutal lusts. Rather than be such a sanctimonious coward I would openly proclaim myself vile!"

"That is because yours is a noble nature"—I said—"You are an exception to the rule."

"An exception? I?"—and he laughed bitterly—"Yes, you are right; I am an exception among men perhaps,—but I am one with the beasts in honesty! The lion does not assume the manners of the dove,—he loudly announces his own ferocity. The very cobra, stealthy though its movements be, evinces its meaning by a warning hiss or rattle. The hungry wolf's bay is heard far down the wind, intimidating the hurrying traveller among the wastes of snow. But man gives no clue to his intent—more malignant than the lion, more treacherous than the snake, more greedy than the wolf, he takes his fellow-man's hand in pretended friendship, and an hour later defames his character behind his back,—with a smiling face he hides a false and selfish heart,—flinging his pigmy mockery at the riddle of the Universe, he stands gibing at God, feebly a-straddle on his own earth-grave—Heavens!"—here he stopped short with a passionate gesture—"What should the Eternities do with such a thankless, blind worm as he!"

His voice rang out with singular emphasis,—his eyes glowed with a fiery ardour; startled by his impressive manner I let my cigar die out and stared at him in mute amazement. What an inspired countenance!—what an imposing figure!—how sovereignly supreme and almost god-like in his looks he seemed at the moment;—and yet there was something terrifying in his attitude of protest and defiance. He caught my wondering glance,—the glow of passion faded from his face,—he laughed and shrugged his shoulders.

"I think I was born to be an actor"—he said carelessly—"Now and then the love of declamation masters me. Then I speak—as Prime Ministers and men in Parliament speak—to suit the humour of the hour, and without meaning a single word I say!"

"I cannot accept that statement"—I answered him, smiling a little—"You do mean what you say,—though I fancy you are rather a creature of impulse."

"Do you really!" he exclaimed—"How wise of you!—good Geoffrey Tempest, how very wise of you! But you are wrong. There never was a being created who was less impulsive, or more charged with set purpose than I. Believe me or not as you like,—belief is a sentiment that cannot be forced. If I told you that I am a dangerous companion,—that I like evil things better than good,—that I am not a safe guide for any man, what would you think?"

"I should think you were whimsically fond of under-estimating your own qualities"—I said, re-lighting my cigar, and feeling somewhat amused by his earnestness—"And I should like you just as well as I do now,—perhaps better,—though that would be difficult."

At these words, he seated himself, bending his steadfast dark eyes full upon me.

"Tempest, you follow the fashion of the prettiest women about town,—they always like the greatest scoundrels!"

"But you are not a scoundrel;"—I rejoined, smoking peacefully.

"No,—I'm not a scoundrel, but there's a good deal of the devil in me."

"All the better!" I said, stretching myself out in my chair with lazy comfort—"I hope there's something of him in me too."

"Do you believe in him?" asked Rimânez smiling.

"The devil? of course not!"

"He is a very fascinating legendary personage;"—continued the prince, lighting another cigar and beginning to puff at it slowly—"And he is the subject of many a fine story. Picture his fall from heaven!—'Lucifer Son of the Morning'—what a title, and what a birthright! To be born of the morning implies to be a creature formed of translucent light undefiled, with all the warm rose of a million orbs of day colouring his bright essence, and all the lustre of fiery planets flaming in his eyes. Splendid and supreme, at the right hand of Deity itself he stood, this majestic Arch-angel, and before his unwearied vision rolled the grandest creative splendours of God's thoughts and dreams. All at once he perceived in the vista of embryonic things a new small world, and on it a being forming itself slowly as it were into the Angelic likeness,—a being weak yet strong, sublime yet foolish,—a strange paradox, destined to work its way through all the phases of life, till imbibing the very breath and soul of the Creator it should touch Conscious Immortality,—Eternal Joy. Then Lucifer, full of wrath, turned on the Master of the Spheres, and flung forth his reckless defiance, crying aloud—'Wilt thou make of this slight poor creature an Angel even as I? I do protest against thee and condemn! Lo, if thou makest Man in Our image I will destroy him utterly, as unfit to share with me the splendours of Thy Wisdom,—the glory of Thy love!' And the Voice Supreme in accents terrible and beautiful replied; 'Lucifer, Son of the Morning, full well dost thou know that never can an idle or wasted word be spoken before Me. For Free-will is the gift of the Immortals; therefore what thou sayest, thou must needs do! Fall, proud Spirit from thy high estate!—thou and thy companions with thee!—and return no more till Man himself redeem thee! Each human soul that yields unto thy tempting shall be a new barrier set between thee and heaven; each one that of its own choice doth repel and overcome thee, shall lift thee nearer thy lost home! When the world rejects thee, I will pardon and again receive thee,—but *not till then.*'"

"I never heard exactly that version of the legend before,"—I said,—"The idea that Man should redeem the devil is quite new to me."

"Is it?" and he looked at me fixedly—"Well—it is one form of the story, and by no means the most unpoetical. Poor Lucifer! His punishment is of course eternal, and the distance between himself and Heaven must be rapidly increasing every day,—for Man will never assist him to retrieve his error. Man will reject God fast enough and gladly enough—but never the devil. Judge then, how, under the peculiar circumstances of his doom, this 'Lucifer, Son of the Morning,' Satan, or whatever else he is called, must hate Humanity!"

I smiled. "Well he has one remedy left to him"—I observed—"He need not tempt anybody."

"You forget!—he is bound to keep his word, according to the legend"—said Rimânez—"He swore before God that he would destroy Man utterly,—he must therefore fulfil that oath, if he can. Angels, it would seem, may not swear before the Eternal without endeavouring at least to fulfil their vows,—men swear in the name of God every day without the slightest intention of carrying out their promises."

"But it's all the veriest nonsense,"—I said somewhat impatiently—"All these old legends are rubbish. You tell the story well, and almost as if you believed in it,—that is because you have the gift of speaking with eloquence. Nowadays no one believes in either devils or angels;—I, for example, do not even believe in the soul."

"I know you do not"—he answered suavely—"And your scepticism is very comfortable because it relieves you of all personal responsibility. I envy you! For—I regret to say, I am compelled to believe in the soul."

"Compelled!" I echoed—"That is absurd—no one can compel you to accept a mere theory."

He looked at me with a flitting smile that darkened rather than lightened his face.

"True! very true! There is no compelling force in the whole Universe,—Man is the supreme and independent creature,—master of all he surveys and owning no other dominion save his personal desire. True—I forgot! Let us avoid theology, please, and psychology also,—let us talk about the only subject that has any sense or interest in it—namely, Money. I perceive your present plans are definite,—you wish to publish a book that shall create a stir and make you famous. It seems a modest enough campaign! Have you no wider ambitions? There are several ways, you know, of getting talked about. Shall I enumerate them for your consideration?"

I laughed. "If you like!"

"Well, in the first place I should suggest your getting yourself properly paragraphed. It must be known to the press that you are an exceedingly rich man. There is an Agency for the circulation of paragraphs,—I daresay they'll do it sufficiently well for about ten or twenty guineas."

I opened my eyes a little at this.

"Oh, is that the way these things are done?"

"My dear fellow, how else should they be done?" he demanded somewhat impatiently—"Do you think *anything* in the world is done without money? Are the poor, hard-working journalists your brothers or your bosom friends that they should lift you into public notice without getting something for their trouble? If you do not manage them properly in this way, they'll abuse you quite heartily and free of cost,—that I can promise you! I know a 'literary agent,' a very worthy man too, who for a hundred guineas down, will so ply the paragraph wheel that in a few weeks it shall seem to the outside public that Geoffrey Tempest, the millionaire, is the only person worth talking about, and the one desirable creature whom to shake hands with is next in honour to meeting Royalty itself."

"Secure him!" I said indolently—"And pay him *two* hundred guineas! So shall all the world hear of me!"

"When you have been paragraphed thoroughly," went on Rimânez—"the next move will be a dash into what is called 'swagger' society. This must be done cautiously and by degrees. You must be presented at the first Levée of the season, and later on, I will get you an invitation to some great lady's house, where you will meet the Prince of Wales privately at dinner. If you can oblige or please His Royal Highness in any way so much the better for you,—he is at least the most popular royalty in Europe, so it should not be difficult to you to make yourself agreeable. Following upon this event, you must purchase a fine country seat, and have *that* fact 'paragraphed'—then you can rest and look round,—Society will have taken you up, and you will find yourself in the swim!"

I laughed heartily,—well entertained by his fluent discourse.

"I should not," he resumed—"propose your putting yourself to the trouble of getting into Parliament. That is no longer necessary to the career of a gentleman. But I should strongly recommend your winning the Derby."

"I daresay you would!" I answered mirthfully—"It's an admirable suggestion,—but not very easy to follow!"

"If you wish to win the Derby," he rejoined quietly—"you *shall* win it. I'll guarantee both horse and jockey!"

Something in his decisive tone impressed me, and I leaned forward to study his features more closely.

"Are you a worker of miracles?" I asked him jestingly—"Do you mean it?"

"Try me!" he responded—"Shall I enter a horse for you?"

"You can't; it's too late," I said. "You would need to be the devil himself to do it. Besides I don't care about racing."

"You will have to amend your taste then,"—he replied—"That is, if you want to make yourself agreeable to the English aristocracy, for they are interested in little else. No really great lady is without her betting book, though she may be deficient in her knowledge of spelling. You may make the biggest literary *furore* of the season, and that will count as nothing among 'swagger' people, but if you win the Derby you will be a really famous man. Personally speaking I have a great deal to do with racing,—in fact I am devoted to it. I am always present at every great race,—I never miss one; I always bet, and I never lose! And now let me proceed with your social plan of action. After winning the Derby you will enter for a yacht race at Cowes, and allow the Prince of Wales to beat you just narrowly. Then you will give a grand dinner, arranged by a perfect *chef*,—and you will entertain His Royal Highness to the strains of 'Britannia rules the waves,' which will serve as a pretty compliment. You will allude to the same well-worn song in a graceful speech,—and the probable result of all this will be one, or perhaps two Royal invitations. So far, so good. With the heats of summer you will go to Homburg to drink the waters there whether you require them or not,—and in the autumn you will assemble a shooting-party at the country seat before-mentioned which you will have purchased, and invite Royalty to join you in killing the poor little partridges. Then your name in society may be considered as made, and you can marry whatever fair lady happens to be in the market!"

"Thanks!—much obliged!" and I gave way to hearty laughter— "Upon my word Lucio, your programme is perfect! It lacks nothing!"

"It is the orthodox round of social success," said Lucio with admirable gravity—"Intellect and originality have nothing whatever to do with it,—only money is needed to perform it all."

"You forget my book"—I interposed—"I know there is some intellect in that, and some originality too. Surely that will give me an extra lift up the heights of fashionable light and leading."

"I doubt it!" he answered—"I very much doubt it. It will be received with a certain amount of favour of course, as a production of a rich man amusing himself with literature as a sort of whim. But, as I told you before, genius seldom develops itself under the influence of wealth. Then again 'swagger' folks can never get it out of their fuddled heads that Literature belongs to Grub Street. Great poets, great philosophers, great romancists are always vaguely alluded to by 'swagger' society as 'those sort of people.' Those sort of people are so 'interesting' say the blue-blooded noodles deprecatingly, excusing themselves as it were for knowing any members of the class literary. You can fancy a 'swagger' lady of Elizabeth's time asking a friend—'O do you mind, my dear, if I bring one Master William Shakespeare to see you? He writes plays, and does something or other at the *Globe* theatre,—in fact I'm afraid he acts a little—he's not very well off poor man,—but *these sort of people* are always so amusing!' Now you, my dear Tempest, are not a Shakespeare, but your millions will give you a better chance than he ever had in his life-time, as you will not have to sue for patronage, or practise a reverence for 'my lord' or 'my lady,'—these exalted personages will be only too delighted to borrow money of you if you will lend it."

"I shall not lend,"—I said.

"Nor give?"

"Nor give."

His keen eyes flashed approval.

"I am very glad," he observed, "that you are determined not to 'go about doing good' as the canting humbugs say, with your money. You are wise. Spend on yourself,—because your very act of spending cannot but benefit others through various channels. Now I pursue a different course. I always help charities, and put my name on subscription-lists,—and I never fail to assist a certain portion of clergy."

"I rather wonder at that—" I remarked—"Especially as you tell me you are not a Christian."

"Yes,—it does seem strange,—doesn't it?"—he said with an extraordinary accent of what might be termed apologetic derision—"But perhaps you don't look at it in the proper light. Many of the clergy are doing their utmost best to *destroy* religion,—by cant, by hypocrisy, by sensuality, by shams of every description,—and when they seek my help in this noble work, I give it,—freely!"

I laughed "You must have your joke evidently"—I said, throwing the end of my finished cigar into the fire—"And I see you are fond of satirizing your own good actions. Hullo, what's this?"

For at that moment Amiel entered, bearing a telegram for me on a silver salver. I opened it,—it was from my friend the publisher, and ran as follows—

"Accept book with pleasure. Send manuscript immediately."

I showed this to Rimânez with a kind of triumph. He smiled.

"Of course! what else did you expect? Only the man should have worded his telegram differently, for I do not suppose he would accept the book with pleasure if he had to lay out his own cash upon it. 'Accept money for publishing book with pleasure' should have been the true message of the wire. Well, what are you going to do?"

"I shall see about this at once"—I answered, feeling a thrill of satisfaction that at last the time of vengeance on certain of my enemies was approaching—"The book must be hurried through the press as quickly as possible,—and I shall take a particular pleasure in personally attending to all the details concerning it. For the rest of my plans,—"

"Leave them to me!" said Rimânez laying his finely shaped white hand with a masterful pressure on my shoulder; "Leave them to me!—and be sure that before very long I shall have set you aloft like the bear who has successfully reached the bun on the top of a greased pole,—a spectacle for the envy of men, and the wonder of angels!"

VII

The next three or four weeks flew by in a whirl of excitement, and by the time they were ended I found it hard to recognize myself in the indolent, listless, extravagant man of fashion I had so suddenly become. Sometimes at stray and solitary moments the past turned back upon me like a revolving picture in a glass with a flash of unwelcome recollection, and I saw myself worn and hungry, and shabbily clothed, bending over my writing in my dreary lodging, wretched, yet amid all my wretchedness receiving curious comfort from my own thoughts which created beauty out of penury, and love out of loneliness. This creative faculty was now dormant in me,—I did very little, and thought less. But I felt certain that this intellectual apathy was but a passing phase,—a mental holiday and desirable cessation from brain-work to which I was deservedly entitled after all my sufferings at the hands of poverty and disappointment. My book was nearly through the press,—and perhaps the chiefest pleasure of any I now enjoyed was the correction of the proofs as they passed under my supervision. Yet even this, the satisfaction of authorship, had its drawback,—and my particular grievance was somewhat singular. I read my own work with gratification of course, for I was not behind my contemporaries in thinking well of myself in all I did,—but my complacent literary egoism was mixed with a good deal of disagreeable astonishment and incredulity, because my work, written with enthusiasm and feeling, propounded sentiments and inculcated theories which I personally did not believe in. Now, how had this happened, I asked myself? Why had I thus invited the public to accept me at a false valuation? I paused to consider,— and I found the suggestion puzzling. How came I to write the book at all, seeing that it was utterly unlike me as I now knew myself? My pen, consciously or unconsciously, had written down things which my reasoning faculties entirely repudiated,—such as belief in a God,—trust in the eternal possibilities of man's diviner progress,—I credited neither of these doctrines. When I imagined such transcendental and foolish dreams I was poor,—starving,—and without a friend in the world;— remembering all this, I promptly set down my so-called 'inspiration' to the action of an ill-nourished brain. Yet there was something subtle in the teaching of the story, and one afternoon when I was revising some of the last proof sheets I caught myself thinking that the book was nobler than its writer. This idea smote me with a sudden pang,—I pushed my papers aside, and walking to the window, looked out. It was raining hard, and the streets were black with mud and slush,—the foot-passengers were drenched and miserable,—the whole prospect was dreary, and the fact that I was a rich man did not in the least lift from my mind the depression that had stolen on me unawares. I was quite alone, for I had my own suite of rooms now in the hotel, not far from those occupied by Prince Rimânez; I also had my own servant, a respectable, good sort of fellow whom I rather liked because he shared to the full the instinctive aversion I felt for the prince's man, Amiel. Then I had my own carriage and horses with attendant coachman and groom,—so that the prince and I, though the most intimate friends in the world, were able to avoid that 'familiarity which breeds contempt' by keeping up our own separate establishments. On this particular afternoon I was in a more miserable humour than ever my poverty had brought upon me, yet from a strictly reasonable point of view I had nothing to be miserable about. I was in full possession of my fortune,—I enjoyed excellent health, and I had everything I wanted, with the added consciousness that if my wants increased I could gratify them easily. The 'paragraph wheel' under Lucio's management had been worked with such good effect that I had seen myself mentioned in almost every paper in London and the provinces as the 'famous millionaire,'—and for the benefit of the public, who are sadly uninstructed on these matters, I may here state as a very plain unvarnished truth, that for forty pounds,[1] a well-known 'agency' will guarantee the insertion of *any* paragraph, provided it is not libellous, in no less than four hundred newspapers. The art of 'booming' is thus easily explained, and level-headed people will be able to comprehend why it is that a few names of authors are constantly mentioned in the press, while others, perhaps more deserving, remain ignored. Merit counts as nothing in such circumstances,—money wins the day. And the persistent paragraphing of my name, together with a description of my personal appearance and my 'marvellous literary gifts,' combined with a deferential and almost awe-struck allusion to the 'millions' which made me so interesting— (the paragraph was written out by Lucio and handed for circulation to the 'agency' aforesaid with 'money down')—all this I say brought upon me two inflictions,—first, any amount of invitations to social

---

1. A fact.

and artistic functions,—and secondly, a continuous stream of begging-letters. I was compelled to employ a secretary, who occupied a room near my suite, and who was kept hard at work all day. Needless to say I refused all appeals for money;—no one had helped *me* in my distress, with the exception of my old chum 'Boffles,'—no one save he had given me even so much as a word of sympathy,—I was resolved now to be as hard and as merciless as I had found my contemporaries. I had a certain grim pleasure in reading letters from two or three literary men, asking for work 'as secretary or companion,' or failing that, for the loan of a little cash to 'tide over present difficulties.' One of these applicants was a journalist on the staff of a well-known paper who had promised to find *me* work, and who instead of doing so, had, as I afterwards learned, strongly dissuaded his editor from giving me any employment. He never imagined that Tempest the millionaire, and Tempest the literary hack, were one and the same person,—so little do the majority think that wealth can ever fall to the lot of authors! I wrote to him myself however and told him what I deemed it well he should know, adding my sarcastic thanks for his friendly assistance to me in time of need,— and herein I tasted something of the sharp delight of vengeance. I never heard from him again, and I am pretty sure my letter gave him material not only for astonishment but meditation.

Yet with all the advantages over both friends and enemies which I now possessed I could not honestly say I was happy. I knew I could have every possible enjoyment and amusement the world had to offer,—I knew I was one of the most envied among men, and yet,—as I stood looking out of the window at the persistently falling rain, I was conscious of a bitterness rather than a sweetness in the full cup of fortune. Many things that I had imagined would give me intense satisfaction had fallen curiously flat. For example, I had flooded the press with the most carefully worded and prominent advertisements of my forthcoming book, and when I was poor I had pictured to myself how I should revel in doing this,—now that it was done I cared nothing at all about it. I was simply weary of the sight of my own advertised name. I certainly did look forward with very genuine feeling and expectation to the publication of my work when that should be an accomplished fact,— but to-day even that idea had lost some of its attractiveness owing to this new and unpleasant impression on my mind that the contents of that book were as utterly the reverse of my own true thoughts as they could well be. A fog began to darken down over the streets in company with the rain,—and disgusted with the weather and with myself, I turned away from the window and settled into an arm-chair by the fire, poking the coal till it blazed, and wondering what I should do to rid my mind of the gloom that threatened to envelop it in as thick a canopy as that of the London fog. A tap came at the door, and in answer to my somewhat irritable "Come in!" Rimânez entered.

"What, all in the dark Tempest!" he exclaimed cheerfully—"Why don't you light up?"

"The fire's enough,"—I answered crossly—"Enough at any rate to think by."

"And have you been thinking?" he inquired laughing—"Don't do it. It's a bad habit. No one thinks now-a-days,—people can't stand it—their heads are too frail. Once begin to think and down go the foundations of society,—besides thinking is always dull work."

"I have found it so," I said gloomily—"Lucio, there is something wrong about me somewhere."

His eyes flashed keen, half-amused inquiry into mine.

"Wrong? Oh no, surely not! What *can* there be wrong about you, Tempest? Are you not one of the richest men living?"

I let the satire pass.

"Listen, my friend," I said earnestly—"You know I have been busy for the last fortnight correcting the proofs of my book for the press,—do you not?"

He nodded with a smiling air.

"Well I have arrived almost at the end of my work and I have come to the conclusion that the book is not Me,—it is not a reflex of my feelings at all,—and I cannot understand how I came to write it."

"You find it stupid perhaps?" said Lucio sympathetically.

"No," I answered with a touch of indignation—"I do not find it stupid."

"Dull then?"

"No,—it is not dull."

"Melodramatic?"

"No,—not melodramatic."

"Well, my good fellow, if it is not dull or stupid or melodramatic, what is it!" he exclaimed merrily—"It must be something!"

"Yes,—it is this,—it is beyond me altogether." And I spoke with some bitterness. "Quite beyond me. I could not write it now,—I wonder I could write it then. Lucio, I daresay I am talking foolishly,—but it seems to me I must have been on some higher altitude of thought when I wrote the book,—a height from which I have since fallen."

"I'm sorry to hear this," he answered, with twinkling eyes—"From what you say it appears to me you have been guilty of literary sublimity. Oh bad, very bad! Nothing can be worse. To write sublimely is a grievous sin, and one which critics never forgive. I'm really grieved for you, my friend—I never thought your case was quite so desperate."

I laughed in spite of my depression.

"You are incorrigible, Lucio!" I said—"But your cheerfulness is very inspiriting. All I wanted to explain to you is this,—that my book expresses a certain tone of thought which purporting to be *mine*, is not *me*,—in short, I, in my present self have no sympathy with it. I must have changed very much since I wrote it."

"Changed? Why yes, I should think so!" and Lucio laughed heartily— "The possession of five millions is bound to change a man considerably for the better—or worse! But you seem to be worrying yourself most absurdly about nothing. Not one author in many centuries writes from his own heart or as he truly feels—when he does, he becomes well-nigh immortal. This planet is too limited to hold more than one Homer, one Plato, one Shakespeare. Don't distress yourself—you are neither of these three! You belong to the age, Tempest,—it is a decadent ephemeral age, and most things connected with it are decadent and ephemeral. Any era that is dominated by the love of money only, has a rotten core within it and must perish. All history tells us so, but no one accepts the lesson of history. Observe the signs of the time,—Art is made subservient to the love of money—literature, politics and religion the same,—*you* cannot escape from the general disease. The only thing to do is to make the best of it,—no one can reform it—least of all you, who have so much of the lucre given to your share."

He paused,—I was silent, watching the bright fire-glow and the dropping red cinders.

"What I am going to say now," he proceeded in soft, almost melancholy accents—"will sound ridiculously trite,—still it has the perverse prosiness of truth about it. It is this—in order to write with intense feeling, you must first *feel*. Very likely when you wrote this book of yours, you were almost a human hedge-hog in the way of feeling. Every prickly point of you was erect and responsive to the touch of all influences, pleasant or the reverse, imaginative or realistic. This is a condition which some people envy and others would rather dispense with. Now that you, as a hedge-hog, have no further need for either alarm, indignation or self-defence, your prickles are soothed into an agreeable passiveness, and you partially cease to feel. That is all. The 'change' you complain of is thus accounted for;—you have nothing to feel about,—hence you cannot comprehend how it was that you ever felt."

I was conscious of irritation at the calm conviction of his tone.

"Do you take me for such a callous creature as all that?" I exclaimed— "You are mistaken in me, Lucio. I feel most keenly—"

"What do you feel?" he inquired, fixing his eyes steadily upon me— "There are hundreds of starving wretches in this metropolis,—men and women on the brink of suicide because they have no hope of anything in this world or the next, and no sympathy from their kind—do you feel for them? Do *their* griefs affect *you*? You know they do not,—you know you never think of them,—why should you? One of the chief advantages of wealth is the ability it gives us to shut out other people's miseries from our personal consideration."

I said nothing,—for the first time my spirit chafed at the truth of his words, principally because they *were* true. Alas, Lucio!—if I had only known then what I know now!

"Yesterday," he went on in the same quiet voice—"a child was run over here, just opposite this hotel. It was *only* a poor child,—mark that 'only.' Its mother ran shrieking out of some back-street hard by, in time to see the little bleeding body carted up in a mangled heap. She struck wildly with both hands at the men who were trying to lead her away, and with a cry like that of some hurt savage animal fell face forward in the mud—dead. She was only a poor woman,—another 'only.' There were three lines in the paper about it headed 'Sad Incident.' The hotel-porter here witnessed the scene from the door with as composed a demeanor as that of a fop at the play, never relaxing the serene majesty of his attitude,—but about ten minutes after the dead body of the woman had been carried out of sight, he, the imperial, gold-buttoned being, became almost crook-backed in his servile haste to run and open the door of your brougham, my dear Geoffrey, as you drove up to the entrance. This is a little epitome of life as it is lived now-a-days,—and yet the canting clerics swear we are all equal in the sight of heaven! We may be, though it does not look much like it,—and if we are, it does not matter, as we have ceased to care how heaven regards us. I don't want to point a moral,—I simply tell you the 'sad incident' as it occurred,—and

MARIE CORELLI

I am sure you are not the least sorry for the fate of either the child who was run over, or its mother who died in the sharp agony of a suddenly broken heart. Now don't say you are, because I know you're not!"

"How can one feel sorry for people one does not know or has never seen,—" I began.

"Exactly!—How is it possible? And there we have it—how can one feel, when one's self is so thoroughly comfortable as to be without any other feeling save that of material ease? Thus, my dear Geoffrey, you must be content to let your book appear as the reflex and record of your past when you were in the prickly or sensitive stage,—now you are encased in a pachydermatous covering of gold, which adequately protects you from such influences as might have made you start and writhe, perhaps even roar with indignation, and in the access of fierce torture, stretch out your hands and grasp—quite unconsciously—the winged thing called Fame!"

"You should have been an orator,"—I said, rising and pacing the room to and fro in vexation,—"But to me your words are not consoling, and I do not think they are true. Fame is easily enough secured."

"Pardon me if I am obstinate;"—said Lucio with a deprecatory gesture—"Notoriety is easily secured—very easily. A few critics who have dined with you and had their fill of wine, will give you notoriety. But fame is the voice of the whole civilized public of the world."

"The public!" I echoed contemptuously—"The public only care for trash."

"It is a pity you should appeal to it then;"—he responded with a smile—"If you think so little of the public why give it anything of your brain? It is not worthy of so rare a boon! Come, come Tempest,—do not join in the snarl of unsuccessful authors who take refuge, when marked unsaleable, in pouring out abuse on the public. The public is the author's best friend and truest critic. But if you prefer to despise it, in company with all the very little literature-mongers who form a mutual admiration society, I tell you what to do,—print just twenty copies of your book and present these to the leading reviewers, and when they have written you up (as they will do—I'll take care of that) let your publisher advertise to the effect that the 'First and Second Large Editions' of the new novel by Geoffrey Tempest, are exhausted, one hundred thousand copies having been sold in a week! If that does not waken up the world in general, I shall be much surprised!"

I laughed,—I was gradually getting into a better humour.

"It would be quite as fair a plan of action as is adopted by many modern publishers," I said—"The loud hawking of literary wares now-a-days reminds me of the rival shouting of costermongers in a low neighbourhood. But I will not go quite so far,—I'll win my fame legitimately if I can."

"You can't!" declared Lucio with a serene smile—"It's impossible. You are too rich. That of itself is not legitimate in Literature, which great art generally elects to wear poverty in its button-hole as a flower of grace. The fight cannot be equal in such circumstances. The fact that you are a millionaire must weigh the balance apparently in your favour for a time. The world cannot resist money. If I, for example, became an author, I should probably with my wealth and influence, burn up every one else's laurels. Suppose that a desperately poor man comes out with a book at the same time as you do, he will have scarcely the ghost of a chance against you. He will not be able to advertise in your lavish style,—nor will he see his way to dine the critics as you can. And if he should happen to have more genius than you, and you succeed, your success will *not* be legitimate. But after all, that does not matter much— in Art, if in nothing else, things always right themselves."

I made no immediate reply, but went over to my table, rolled up my corrected proofs and directed them to the printers,—then ringing the bell I gave the packet to my man, Morris, bidding him post it at once. This done, I turned again towards Lucio and saw that he still sat by the fire, but that his attitude was now one of brooding melancholy, and that he had covered his eyes with one hand on which the glow from the flames shone red. I regretted the momentary irritation I had felt against him for telling me unwelcome truths,—and I touched him lightly on the shoulder.

"Are *you* in the dumps now Lucio?" I said—"I'm afraid my depression has proved infectious."

He moved his hand and looked up,—his eyes were large and lustrous as the eyes of a beautiful woman.

"I was thinking," he said, with a slight sigh—"of the last words I uttered just now,—*things always right themselves*. Curiously enough in art they always do,—no charlatanism or sham lasts with the gods of Parnassus. But in other matters it is different. For instance *I* shall never right myself! Life is hateful to me at times, as it is to everybody."

"Perhaps you are in love?" I said with a smile.

He started up.

"In love! By all the heavens and all the earths too, that suggestion wakes me with a vengeance! In love! What woman alive do you think could impress *me* with the notion that she was anything more than a frivolous doll of pink and white, with long hair frequently not her own? And as for the tom-boy tennis-players and giantesses of the era, I do not consider them women at all,—they are merely the unnatural and strutting embryos of a new sex which will be neither male nor female. My dear Tempest, I hate women. So would you if you knew as much about them as I do. They have made me what I am, and they keep me so."

"They are to be much complimented then,"—I observed—"You do them credit!"

"I do!" he answered slowly—"In more ways than one!" A faint smile was on his face, and his eyes brightened with that curious jewel-like gleam I had noticed several times before. "Believe me, I shall never contest with you such a slight gift as woman's love, Geoffrey. It is not worth fighting for. And *apropos* of women, that reminds me,—I have promised to take you to the Earl of Elton's box at the Haymarket to-night,—he is a poor peer, very gouty and somewhat heavily flavoured with port-wine, but his daughter, Lady Sibyl, is one of the belles of England. She was presented last season and created quite a *furore*. Will you come?"

"I am quite at your disposition"—I said, glad of any excuse to escape the dullness of my own company and to be in that of Lucio, whose talk, even if its satire galled me occasionally, always fascinated my mind and remained in my memory—"What time shall we meet?"

"Go and dress now, and join me at dinner,"—he answered; "And we'll drive together to the theatre afterwards. The play is on the usual theme which has lately become popular with stage-managers,—the glorification of a 'fallen' lady, and the exhibition of her as an example of something superlatively pure and good, to the astonished eyes of the innocent. As a play it is not worth seeing,—but perhaps Lady Sibyl is."

He smiled again as he stood facing me,—the light flames of the fire had died down to a dull uniform coppery red,—we were almost in darkness, and I pressed the small button near the mantelpiece that flooded the room with electric light. His extraordinary beauty then struck me afresh as something altogether singular and half unearthly.

"Don't you find that people look at you very often as you pass, Lucio?" I asked him suddenly and impulsively.

He laughed. "Not at all. Why should they? Every man is so intent on his own aims, and thinks so much of his own personality that he would scarcely forget his *ego* if the very devil himself were behind him. Women look at me sometimes, with the affected coy and kitten-like interest usually exhibited by the frail sex for a personable man."

"I cannot blame them!" I answered, my gaze still resting on his stately figure and fine head with as much admiration as I might have felt for a noble picture or statue—"What of this Lady Sibyl we are to meet to-night,—how does she regard you?"

"Lady Sibyl has never seen me,"—he replied—"And I have only seen her at a distance. It is chiefly for the purpose of an introduction to her that the Earl has asked us to his box this evening."

"Ha ha! Matrimony in view!" I exclaimed jestingly.

"Yes—I believe Lady Sibyl is for sale,"—he answered with the callous coldness that occasionally distinguished him and made his handsome features look like an impenetrable mask of scorn—"But up to the present the bids have not been sufficiently high. And I shall not purchase. I have told you already, Tempest, I hate women."

"Seriously?"

"Most seriously. Women have always done me harm,—they have wantonly hindered me in my progress. And why I specially abominate them is, that they have been gifted with an enormous power for doing good, and that they let this power run to waste and will not use it. Their deliberate enjoyment and choice of the repulsive, vulgar and common-place side of life disgusts me. They are much less sensitive than men, and infinitely more heartless. They are the mothers of the human race, and the faults of the race are chiefly due to them. That is another reason for my hatred."

"Do you want the human race to be perfect?" I asked astonished— "Because, if you do, you will find that impossible."

He stood for a moment apparently lost in thought.

"Everything in the Universe is perfect,"—he said, "except that curious piece of work—Man. Have you never thought out any reason why he should be the one flaw,—the one incomplete creature in a matchless Creation?"

"No, I have not,"—I replied—"I take things as I find them."

"So do I,"—and he turned away, "And as I find *them*, so they find *me*! Au revoir! Dinner in an hour's time remember!"

The door opened and closed—he was gone. I remained alone for

MARIE CORELLI

a little, thinking what a strange disposition was his,—what a curious mixture of philosophy, worldliness, sentiment and satire seemed to run like the veins of a leaf through the variable temperament of this brilliant, semi-mysterious personage who had by mere chance become my greatest friend. We had now been more or less together for nearly a month, and I was no closer to the secret of his actual nature than I had been at first. Yet I admired him more than ever,—without his society I felt life would be deprived of half its charm. For though, attracted as human moths will be by the glare of my glittering millions, numbers of so-called 'friends' now surrounded me, there was not one among them who so dominated my every mood and with whom I had so much close sympathy as this man,—this masterful, half cruel, half kind companion of my days, who at times seemed to accept all life as the veriest bagatelle, and myself as a part of the trivial game.

VIII

No man, I think, ever forgets the first time he is brought face to face with perfect beauty in woman. He may have caught fleeting glimpses of loveliness on many fair faces often,—bright eyes may have flashed on him like star-beams,—the hues of a dazzling complexion may now and then have charmed him, or the seductive outlines of a graceful figure;—all these are as mere peeps into the infinite. But when such vague and passing impressions are suddenly drawn together in one focus,—when all his dreamy fancies of form and colour take visible and complete manifestation in one living creature who looks down upon him as it were from an empyrean of untouched maiden pride and purity, it is more to his honour than his shame, if his senses swoon at the ravishing vision, and he, despite his rough masculinity and brute strength, becomes nothing but the merest slave to passion. In this way was I overwhelmed and conquered without any chance of deliverance when Sibyl Elton's violet eyes, lifted slowly from the shadow of their dark lashes, rested upon me with that indefinable expression of mingled interest and indifference which is supposed to indicate high breeding, but which more frequently intimidates and repulses the frank and sensitive soul. The Lady Sibyl's glance repelled, but I was none the less attracted. Rimânez and I had entered the Earl of Elton's box at the Haymarket between the first and second acts of the play, and the Earl himself, an unimpressive, bald-headed, red-faced old gentleman, with fuzzy white whiskers, had risen to welcome us, seizing the prince's hand and shaking it with particular effusiveness. (I learned afterwards that Lucio had lent him a thousand pounds on easy terms, a fact which partly accounted for the friendly fervour of his greeting.) His daughter had not moved; but a minute or two later when he addressed her somewhat sharply, saying "Sibyl! Prince Rimânez and his friend, Mr. Geoffrey Tempest," she turned her head and honoured us both with the chill glance I have endeavoured to describe, and the very faintest possible bow as an acknowledgment of our presence. Her exquisite beauty smote me dumb and foolish,—I could find nothing to say, and stood silent and confused, with a strange sensation of bewilderment upon me. The old Earl made some remark about the play, which I scarcely heard though I answered vaguely and at hap-hazard,—the orchestra was playing abominably as is usual in theatres, and its brazen din sounded like the noise of the sea in my ears,—I had not much real consciousness of anything save the wondrous loveliness of the girl who faced me, clad in pure white, with a few diamonds shining about her like stray dewdrops on a rose. Lucio spoke to her, and I listened.

"At last, Lady Sibyl," he said, bending towards her deferentially. "At last I have the honour of meeting you. I have seen you often, as one sees a star,—at a distance."

She smiled,—a smile so slight and cold that it scarcely lifted the corners of her lovely lips.

"I do not think I have ever seen *you*," she replied. "And yet there is something oddly familiar in your face. I have heard my father speak of you constantly,—I need scarcely say his friends are always mine."

He bowed.

"To merely speak to Lady Sibyl Elton is counted sufficient to make the man so privileged happy," he said. "To be her friend is to discover the lost paradise."

She flushed,—then grew suddenly very pale, and shivering, she drew her cloak towards her. Rimânez wrapped its perfumed silken folds carefully round her beautiful shoulders,—how I grudged him the dainty task! He then turned to me, and placed a chair just behind hers.

"Will you sit here Geoffrey?" he suggested—"I want to have a moment's business chat with Lord Elton."

Recovering my self-possession a little, I hastened to take the chance he thus generously gave me to ingratiate myself in the young lady's favour, and my heart gave a foolish bound of joy because she smiled encouragingly as I approached her.

"You are a great friend of Prince Rimânez?" she asked softly, as I sat down.

"Yes, we are very intimate," I replied—"He is a delightful companion."

"So I should imagine!" and she looked over at him where he sat next to her father talking earnestly in low tones—"He is singularly handsome."

I made no reply. Of course Lucio's extraordinary personal attractiveness was undeniable,—but I rather grudged her praise bestowed on him just then. Her remarks seemed to me as tactless as when a man with one pretty woman beside him loudly admires another in her hearing. I did not myself assume to be actually handsome, but I knew I was better looking than the ordinary run of men. So out of sudden pique I remained silent, and presently the curtain rose and the play was resumed. A very questionable scene was enacted, the 'woman with the past' being well to the front of it. I felt disgusted at the performance and looked at my companions to see if they too were similarly moved. There was no sign of disapproval on Lady Sibyl's fair countenance,—her father was bending forward eagerly, apparently gloating over every detail,—Rimânez wore that inscrutable expression of his in which no feeling whatever could be discerned. The 'woman with the past' went on with her hysterical sham-heroics, and the mealy-mouthed fool of a hero declared her to be a 'pure angel wronged,' and the curtain fell amid loud applause. One energetic hiss came from the gallery, affecting the occupants of the stalls to scandalized amazement.

"England has progressed!" said Rimânez in soft half-bantering tones—"Once upon a time this play would have been hooted off the stage as likely to corrupt the social community. But now the only voice of protest comes from the 'lower' classes."

"Are you a democrat, prince?" inquired Lady Sibyl, waving her fan indolently to and fro.

"Not I! I always insist on the pride and supremacy of worth,—I do not mean money value, but intellect. And in this way I foresee a new aristocracy. When the High grows corrupt, it falls and becomes the Low;—when the Low educates itself and aspires, it becomes the High. This is simply the course of nature."

"But, God bless my soul!" exclaimed Lord Elton—"you don't call this play low or immoral do you? It's a realistic study of modern social life—that's what it is. These women you know,—these poor souls with a past—are very interesting!"

"Very!" murmured his daughter.—"In fact it would seem that for women with no such 'past' there can be no future! Virtue and modesty are quite out of date, and have no chance whatever."

I leaned towards her, half whispering,

"Lady Sibyl, I am glad to see this wretched play offends you."

She turned her deep eyes on me in mingled surprise and amusement.

"Oh no, it doesn't," she declared—"I have seen so many like it. And I have read so many novels on just the same theme! I assure you, I am quite convinced that the so-called 'bad' woman is the only popular type of our sex with men,—she gets all the enjoyment possible out of life,—she frequently makes an excellent marriage, and has, as the Americans say 'a good time all round.' It's the same thing with our convicted criminals,—in prison they are much better fed than the

MARIE CORELLI

honest working-man. I believe it is quite a mistake for women to be respectable,—they are only considered dull."

"Ah, now you are only joking!" I said with an indulgent smile. "You know that in your heart you think very differently!"

She made no answer, as just then the curtain went up again, disclosing the unclean 'lady' of the piece, "having a good time all round" on board a luxurious yacht. During the unnatural and stilted dialogue which followed, I withdrew a little back into the shadow of the box, and all that self-esteem and assurance of which I had been suddenly deprived by a glance at Lady Sibyl's beauty, came back to me, and a perfectly stolid coolness and composure succeeded to the first feverish excitement of my mind. I recalled Lucio's words—*I believe Lady Sibyl is for sale*—and I thought triumphantly of my millions. I glanced at the old earl, abjectly pulling at his white whiskers while he listened anxiously to what were evidently money schemes propounded by Lucio. Then my gaze came back appraisingly to the lovely curves of Lady Sibyl's milk-white throat, her beautiful arms and bosom, her rich brown hair of the shade of a ripe chestnut, her delicate haughty face, languid eyes and brilliant complexion,—and I murmured inwardly—"All this loveliness is purchaseable, and I will purchase it!" At that very instant she turned to me and said—

"You are the famous Mr. Tempest, are you not?"

"Famous?" I echoed with a deep sense of gratification—"Well,—I am scarcely that,—yet! My book is not published. . ."

Her eyebrows arched themselves surprisedly.

"Your book? I did not know you had written one?"

My flattered vanity sank to zero.

"It has been extensively advertised," I began impressively,—but she interrupted me with a laugh.

"Oh I never read advertisements,—it's too much trouble. When I asked if you were the famous Mr. Tempest, I meant to say were you the great millionaire who has been so much talked of lately?"

I bowed a somewhat chill assent. She looked at me inquisitively over the lace edge of her fan.

"How delightful it must be for you to have so much money!" she said—"And you are young too, and good-looking."

Pleasure took the place of vexed *amour-propre* and I smiled.

"You are very kind, Lady Sibyl!"

"Why?" she asked laughing,—such a delicious little low laugh—"Because I tell you the truth? You *are* young and you *are* good-looking!

Millionaires are generally such appalling creatures. Fortune, while giving them money, frequently deprives them of both brains and personal attractiveness. And now do tell me about your book!"

She seemed to have suddenly dispensed with her former reserve, and during the last act of the play, we conversed freely, in whispers which assisted us to become almost confidential. Her manner to me now was full of grace and charm, and the fascination she exerted over my senses became complete. The performance over, we all left the box together, and as Lucio was still apparently engrossed with Lord Elton I had the satisfaction of escorting Lady Sibyl to her carriage. When her father joined her, Lucio and I both stood together looking in at the window of the brougham, and the Earl, getting hold of my hand shook it up and down with boisterous friendliness.

"Come and dine,—come and dine!" he spluttered excitedly; "Come—let me see,—this is Tuesday—come on Thursday. Short notice and no ceremony! My wife is paralysed I'm sorry to say,—she can't receive,—she can only see a few people now and then when she is in the humour,—her sister keeps house and does the honours,—Aunt Charlotte, eh Sibyl?—ha-ha-ha! The Deceased Wife's Sister's Bill would never be any use to me, for if my wife were to die I shouldn't be anxious to marry Miss Charlotte Fitzroy! Ha ha ha! A perfectly unapproachable woman sir!—a model,—ha ha! Come and dine with us, Mr. Tempest,—Lucio, you bring him along with you, eh? We've got a young lady staying with us,—an American, dollars, accent and all,— and by Jove I believe she wants to marry me ha ha ha! and is waiting for Lady Elton to go to a better world first, ha ha! Come along—come and see the little American, eh? Thursday shall it be?"

Over the fair features of Lady Sibyl there passed a faint shadow of annoyance at her father's allusion to the "little American," but she said nothing. Only her looks appeared to question our intentions as well as to persuade our wills, and she seemed satisfied when we both accepted the invitation given. Another apoplectic chuckle from the Earl and a couple of handshakes,—a slight graceful bow from her lovely ladyship, as we raised our hats in farewell, and the Elton equipage rolled away, leaving us to enter our own vehicle, which amid the officious roarings of street-boys and policemen had just managed to draw up in front of the theatre. As we drove off, Lucio peered inquisitively at me—I could see the steely glitter of his fine eyes in the semi-darkness of the brougham,—and said—

"Well?"

I was silent.

"Don't you admire her?" he went on—"I must confess she is cold,—a very chilly vestal indeed,—but snow often covers volcanoes! She has good features, and a naturally clear complexion."

Despite my intention to be reticent, I could not endure this tame description.

"She is perfectly beautiful,"—I said emphatically. "The dullest eyes must see that. There is not a fault to be found with her. And she is wise to be reserved and cold—were she too lavish of her smiles and too seductive in manner, she might drive many men not only into folly, but madness."

I felt rather than saw the cat-like glance he flashed upon me.

"Positively, Geoffrey, I believe that notwithstanding the fact that we are only in February, the wind blows upon you due south, bringing with it odours of rose and orange-blossom! I fancy Lady Sibyl has powerfully impressed you?"

"Did you wish me to be impressed?" I asked.

"I? My dear fellow, I wish nothing that you yourself do not wish. I accommodate my ways to my friends' humours. If asked for my opinion I should say it is rather a pity if you are really smitten with the young lady, as there are no obstacles to be encountered. A love-affair, to be conducted with spirit and enterprise should always bristle with opposition and difficulty, real or invented. A little secrecy and a good deal of wrong-doing, such as sly assignations and the telling of any amount of lies—such things add to the agreeableness of love-making on this planet—"

I interrupted him.

"See here, Lucio, you are very fond of alluding to 'this' planet as if you knew anything about other planets"—I said impatiently. "*This* planet, as you somewhat contemptuously call it, is the only one *we* have any business with."

He bent his piercing looks so ardently upon me that for the moment I was startled.

"If that is so," he answered, "why in Heaven's name do you not let the other planets alone? Why do you strive to fathom their mysteries and movements? If men, as you say, have no business with any planet save this one why are they ever on the alert to discover the secret of mightier worlds,—a secret which haply it may some day terrify them to know!"

The solemnity of his voice and the inspired expression of his face awed me. I had no reply ready, and he went on—

"Do not let us talk, my friend, of planets, not even of this particular pin's point among them known as Earth. Let us return to a better subject—the Lady Sibyl. As I have already said, there are no obstacles in the way of your wooing and winning her, if such is your desire. Geoffrey Tempest, as mere author of books would indeed be insolent to aspire to the hand of an earl's daughter, but Geoffrey Tempest, millionaire, will be a welcome suitor. Poor Lord Elton's affairs are in a bad way—he is almost out-at-elbows;—the American woman who is boarding with him—"

"Boarding with him!" I exclaimed—"Surely he does not keep a boarding-house?"

Lucio laughed heartily.

"No, no!—you must not put it so coarsely, Geoffrey. It is simply this, that the Earl and Countess of Elton give the prestige of their home and protection to Miss Diana Chesney (the American aforesaid) for the trifling sum of two thousand guineas per annum. The Countess being paralyzed, is obliged to hand over her duties of chaperonage to her sister Miss Charlotte Fitzroy,—but the halo of the coronet still hovers over Miss Chesney's brow. She has her own suite of rooms in the house, and goes wherever it is proper for her to go, under Miss Fitzroy's care. Lady Sibyl does not like the arrangement, and is therefore never seen anywhere except with her father. She will not join in companionship with Miss Chesney, and has said so pretty plainly."

"I admire her for it!" I said warmly—"I really am surprised that Lord Elton should condescend—"

"Condescend to what?" inquired Lucio—"Condescend to take two thousand guineas a year? Good heavens man, there are no end of lords and ladies who will readily agree to perform such an act of condescension. 'Blue' blood is getting thin and poor, and only money can thicken it. Diana Chesney is worth over a million dollars and if Lady Elton were to die conveniently soon, I should not be surprised to see that 'little American' step triumphantly into her vacant place."

"What a state of topsy-turveydom!" I said, half angrily.

"Geoffrey, my friend, you are really amazingly inconsistent! Is there a more flagrant example of topsy-turveydom than yourself for instance? Six weeks ago, what were you? A mere scribbler, with flutterings of the wings of genius in your soul, but many uncertainties as to whether those wings would ever be strong enough to lift you out of the rut of obscurity in which you floundered, struggling and grumbling at adverse fate. Now, as millionaire, you think contemptuously of an Earl, because he ventures quite legitimately to add a little to his income by boarding an American heiress and launching her into society where she would never get without him. And you aspire, or probably mean to aspire to the hand of the Earl's daughter, as if you yourself were a descendant of kings. Nothing can be more topsy-turvy than *your* condition!"

"My father was a gentleman," I said, with a touch of hauteur, "and a descendant of gentlemen. We were never common folk,—our family was one of the most highly esteemed in the counties."

Lucio smiled.

"I do not doubt it, my dear fellow,—I do not in the least doubt it. But a simple 'gentleman' is a long way below—or above—an Earl. Have it which side you choose!—because it really doesn't matter nowadays. We have come to a period of history when rank and lineage count as nothing at all, owing to the profoundly obtuse stupidity of those who happen to possess it. So it chances, that as no resistance is made, brewers are created peers of the realm, and ordinary tradesmen are knighted, and the very old families are so poor that they have to sell their estates and jewels to the highest bidder, who is frequently a vulgar 'railway-king' or the introducer of some new manure. You occupy a better position than such, since you inherit your money with the farther satisfaction that you do not know how it was made."

"True!" I answered meditatively,—then, with a sudden flash of recollection I added—"By the way I never told you that my deceased relative imagined that he had sold his soul to the devil, and that this vast fortune of his was the material result!"

Lucio burst into a violent fit of laughter.

"No! Not possible!" he exclaimed derisively—"What an idea! I suppose he had a screw loose somewhere! Imagine any sane man believing in a devil! Ha, ha, ha! And in these advanced days too! Well, well! The folly of human imaginations will never end! Here we are!"—and he sprang lightly out as the brougham stopped at the Grand Hotel—"I will say good-night to you, Tempest. I've promised to go and have a gamble."

"A gamble? Where?"

"At one of the select private clubs. There are any amount of them in this eminently moral metropolis—no occasion to go to Monte Carlo! Will you come?"

I hesitated. The fair face of Lady Sibyl haunted my mind,—and I felt, with a no doubt foolish sentimentality, that I would rather keep my thoughts of her sacred, and unpolluted by contact with things of lower tone.

"Not to-night;"—I said,—then half smiling, I added—"It must be rather a one-sided affair for other men to gamble with you, Lucio! You can afford to lose,—and perhaps they can't."

"If they can't, they shouldn't play,"—he answered—"A man should at least know his own mind and his own capacity; if he doesn't, he is no man at all. As far as I have learned by long experience, those who gamble like it, and when *they* like it, *I* like it. I'll take you with me to-morrow if you care to see the fun,—one or two very eminent men are members of the club, though of course they wouldn't have it known for worlds. You shan't lose much—I'll see to that."

"All right,—to-morrow it shall be!"—I responded, for I did not wish to appear as though I grudged losing a few pounds at play—"But to-night I think I'll write some letters before going to bed."

"Yes—and dream of Lady Sibyl!" said Lucio laughing—"If she fascinates you as much when you see her again on Thursday you had better begin the siege!"

He waved his hand gaily, and re-entering his carriage, was driven off at a furious pace through the drifting fog and rain.

IX

M y publisher, John Morgeson,—the estimable individual who had first refused my book, and who now, moved by self-interest, was devoting his energies assiduously to the business of launching it in the most modern and approved style, was not like Shakespeare's *Cassio*, strictly 'an honourable man.' Neither was he the respectable chief of a long-established firm whose system of the cheating of authors, mellowed by time, had become almost sacred;—he was a 'new' man, with new ways, and a good stock of new push and impudence. All the same, he was clever, shrewd and diplomatic, and for some reason or other, had secured the favour of a certain portion of the press, many of the dailies and weeklies always giving special prominence to his publications over the heads of other far more legitimately dealing firms. He entered into a partial explanation of his methods, when, on the morning after my first meeting with the Earl of Elton and his daughter, I called upon him to inquire how things were going with regard to my book.

"We shall publish next week,"—he said, rubbing his hands complacently, and addressing me with all the deference due to my banking account—"And as you don't mind what you spend, I'll tell you just what I propose to do. I intend to write out a mystifying paragraph of about some seventy lines or so, describing the book in a vague sort of way as '*likely to create a new era of thought*'—or, '*ere long everybody who is anybody will be compelled to read this remarkable work,*'—or '*as something that must be welcome to all who would understand the drift of one of the most delicate and burning questions of the time.*' These are all stock phrases, used over and over again by the reviewers,—there's no copyright in them. And the last one always 'tells' wonderfully, considering how old it is, and how often it has been made to do duty, because any allusion to a '*delicate and burning question*' makes a number of people think the novel must be improper, and they send for it at once!"

He chuckled at his own perspicuity, and I sat silent, studying him with much inward amusement. This man on whose decision I had humbly and anxiously waited not so many weeks ago was now my paid tool,—ready to obey me to any possible extent for so much cash,—and I listened to him indulgently while he went on unravelling his schemes for the gratification of *my* vanity, and the pocketing of *his* extras.

"The book has been splendidly advertised"—he went on; "It could not have been more lavishly done. Orders do not come in very fast yet—but they will,—they will. This paragraph of mine, which will take the shape of a 'leaderette,' I can get inserted in about eight hundred to a thousand newspapers here and in America. It will cost you,—say a hundred guineas—perhaps a trifle more. Do you mind that?"

"Not in the least!" I replied, still vastly amused.

He meditated a moment,—then drew his chair closer to mine and lowered his voice a little.

"You understand I suppose, that I shall only issue two hundred and fifty copies at first?"

This limited number seemed to me absurd, and I protested vehemently.

"Such an idea is ridiculous!" I said—"you cannot supply the trade with such a scanty edition."

"Wait, my dear sir, wait,—you are too impatient. You do not give me time to explain. All these two hundred and fifty will be *given away* by me in the proper quarters on the day of publication,—never mind how,—they *must* be given away—"

"Why?"

"Why?" and the worthy Morgeson laughed sweetly—"I see, my dear Mr. Tempest, you are like most men of genius—you do not understand business. The reason why we give the first two hundred and fifty copies away is in order to be able to announce at once in all the papers that '*The First Large Edition of the New Novel by Geoffrey Tempest being exhausted on the day of publication, a Second is in Rapid Preparation.*' You see we thus hoodwink the public, who of course are not in our secrets, and are not to know whether an edition is two hundred or two thousand. The Second Edition will of course be ready behind the scenes, and will consist of another two hundred and fifty."

"Do you call that course of procedure honest?" I asked quietly.

"Honest? My dear sir! Honest?" And his countenance wore a virtuously injured expression—"Of course it is honest! Look at the daily papers! Such announcements appear every day—in fact they are getting rather too common. I freely admit that there are a few publishers here and there who stick up for exactitude and go to the trouble of not only giving the number of copies in an Edition, but also publishing the date of each one as it was issued,—this may be principle if they like to call it so, but it involves a great deal of precise calculation and worry! If the public like to be deceived, what is the use of being exact! Now, to resume,—your second edition will be sent off 'on sale or return' to provincial booksellers, and then we shall announce—"In consequence of the Enormous Demand for the new novel by Geoffrey Tempest, the Large Second Edition is out of print. A Third will be issued in the course of next week." And so on, and so on, till we get to the sixth or seventh edition (always numbering two hundred and fifty each) in three volumes; perhaps we can by skilful management work it to a tenth. It is only a question of diplomacy and a little dexterous humbugging of the trade. Then we shall arrive at the one-volume issue, which will require different handling. But there's time enough for that. The frequent advertisements will add to the expense a bit, but if you don't mind—"

"I don't mind anything," I said—"so long as I have my fun."

"Your fun?" he queried surprisedly—"I thought it was fame you wanted, more than fun!"

I laughed aloud.

"I'm not such a fool as to suppose that fame is secured by advertisement," I said—"For instance I am one of those who think the fame of Millais as an artist was marred when he degraded himself to the level of painting the little green boy blowing bubbles of Pears's Soap. That was an advertisement. And that very incident in his career, trifling though it seems, will prevent his ever standing on the same dignified height of distinction with such masters in art as Romney, Sir Peter Lely, Gainsborough or Reynolds."

"I believe there is a great deal of justice in what you say;" and Morgeson shook his head wisely—"Viewed from a purely artistic and sentimental standpoint you are right." And he became suddenly downcast and dubious. "Yes,—it is a most extraordinary thing how fame does escape people sometimes just when they seem on the point of grasping it. They are 'boomed' in every imaginable way, and yet after a time nothing will keep them up. And there are others again who get kicked and buffeted and mocked and derided—"

"Like Christ?" I interposed with a half smile. He looked shocked,— he was a Non-conformist,—but remembering in time how rich I was, he bowed with a meek patience.

"Yes"—and he sighed—"as you suggest, Mr. Tempest, like Christ. Mocked and derided and opposed at every turn,—and yet by the queerest caprice of destiny, they succeed in winning a world-wide fame and power—"

"Like Christ again!" I said mischievously, for I loved to jar his non-conformist conscience.

"Exactly!" He paused, looking piously down. Then with a return of secular animation he added—"But I was not thinking of the Great Example just then, Mr. Tempest—I was thinking of a woman."

"Indeed!" I said indifferently.

"Yes—a woman, who despite continued abuse and opposition is rapidly becoming celebrated. You are sure to hear of her in literary and social circles"—and he gave me a furtive glance of doubtful inquiry—"but she is not rich, you know,—only famous. However,—we have nothing to do with her just now—so let us return to business. The one uncertain point in the matter of your book's success is the attitude of the critics. There are only six leading men who do the reviews, and between them they cover all the English magazines and some of the American too, as well as the London papers. Here are their names"—and he handed me a pencilled memorandum,—"and their addresses, as far as I can ascertain them, or the addresses of the papers for which they most frequently write. The man at the head of the list, David McWhing, is the most formidable of the lot. He writes everywhere about everything,—being a Scotchman he's bound to have his finger in every pie. If you can secure McWhing, you need not trouble so much about the others, as he generally gives the 'lead,' and has his own way with the editors. He is one of the 'personal friends' of the editor of the *Nineteenth Century* for example, and you would be sure to get a notice there, which would otherwise be impossible. No reviewer *can* review anything for that magazine unless he *is* one of the editor's friends.[2] You must manage McWhing, or he might, just for the sake of 'showing off,' cut you up rather roughly."

"That would not matter," I said, diverted at the idea of 'managing McWhing,'—"A little slating always helps a book to sell."

"In some cases it does,"—and Morgeson stroked his thin beard perplexedly—"But in others it most emphatically does *not*. Where there is any very decided or daring originality, adverse criticism is always the most effective. But a work like yours requires fostering with favour,—wants 'booming' in short—"

"I see!" and I felt distinctly annoyed—"You don't think my book original enough to stand alone?"

---

2. The author has Mr. Knowles's own written authority for this fact.

"My dear sir!—you are really—really—! what shall I say?" and he smiled apologetically—"a little brusque? I think your book shows admirable scholarship and delicacy of thought,—if I find fault with it at all, it is perhaps because I am dense. The only thing it lacks in my opinion is what I should call *tenaciousness*, for want of a better expression,—the quality of holding the reader's fancy fixed like a nail. But after all this is a common failing of modern literature; few authors feel sufficiently themselves to make others feel."

I made no reply for a moment. I was thinking of Lucio's remarks on this very same subject.

"Well!" I said at last—"If I had no feeling when I wrote the book, I certainly have none now. Why man, I felt every line of it!—painfully and intensely!"

"Ay, ay indeed!" said Morgeson soothingly—"Or perhaps you *thought* you felt, which is another very curious phase of the literary temperament. You see, to convince people at all, you must first yourself be convinced. The result of this is generally a singular magnetic attraction between author and public. However I am a bad hand at argument,—and it is possible that in hasty reading I may have gathered a wrong impression of your intentions. Anyhow the book shall be a success if we can make it so. All I venture to ask of you is that you should personally endeavour to manage McWhing!"

I promised to do my best, and on this understanding we parted. I realised that Morgeson was capable of greater discernment than I had imagined, and his observations had given me material for thought which was not altogether agreeable. For if my book, as he said, lacked tenacity, why then it would not take root in the public mind,—it would be merely the ephemeral success of a season,—one of those brief 'booms' in literary wares for which I had such unmitigated contempt,—and Fame would be as far off as ever, except that spurious imitation of it which the fact of my millions had secured. I was in no good humour that afternoon, and Lucio saw it. He soon elicited the sum and substance of my interview with Morgeson, and laughed long and somewhat uproariously over the proposed 'managing' of the redoubtable McWhing. He glanced at the five names of the other leading critics and shrugged his shoulders.

"Morgeson is quite right,"—he said—"McWhing is intimate with the rest of these fellows—they meet at the same clubs, dine at the same cheap restaurants and make love to the same painted ballet-girls. All in a comfortable little fraternal union together, and one obliges the other on their several journals when occasion offers. Oh yes! I should make up to McWhing if I were you."

"But how?" I demanded, for though I knew McWhing's name well enough having seen it signed *ad nauseam* to literary articles in almost every paper extant, I had never met the man; "I cannot ask any favour of a press critic."

"Of course not!" and Lucio laughed heartily again—"If you were to do such an idiotic thing what a slating you'd get for your pains! There's no sport a critic loves so much as the flaying of an author who has made the mistake of lowering himself to the level of asking favours of his intellectual inferiors! No, no, my dear fellow!—we shall manage McWhing quite differently,—*I* know him, though you do not."

"Come, that's good news!" I exclaimed—"Upon my word Lucio, you seem to know everybody."

"I think I know most people worth knowing—" responded Lucio quietly—"Though I by no means include Mr. McWhing in the category of worthiness. I happened to make his personal acquaintance in a somewhat singular and exciting manner. It was in Switzerland, on that awkward ledge of rock known as the Mauvais Pas. I had been some weeks in the neighbourhood on business of my own, and being surefooted and fearless, was frequently allowed by the guides to volunteer my services with theirs. In this capacity of amateur guide, capricious destiny gave me the pleasure of escorting the timid and bilious McWhing across the chasms of the Mer de Glace, and I conversed with him in the choicest French all the while, a language of which, despite his boasted erudition, he was deplorably ignorant. I knew who he was I must tell you, as I know most of his craft, and had long been aware of him as one of the authorised murderers of aspiring genius. When I got him on the Mauvais Pas, I saw that he was seized with vertigo; I held him firmly by the arm and addressed him in sound strong English thus—'Mr. McWhing, you wrote a damnable and scurrilous article against the work of a certain poet' and I named the man—'an article that was a tissue of lies from beginning to end, and which by its cruelty and venom embittered a life of brilliant promise, and crushed a noble spirit. Now, unless you promise to write and publish in a leading magazine a total recantation of this your crime when you get back to England,—*if* you get back!—giving that wronged man the 'honourable mention' he rightly deserves,—down you go! I have but to loosen my hold!' Geoffrey, you should have seen McWhing then! He whined, he wriggled, he clung! Never was an oracle of the press in such an unoracular condition. 'Murder!—murder!' he gasped, but his voice failed him. Above him towered the snow peaks like the summits of that Fame he could not reach and therefore grudged to others,—below him the glittering ice-waves yawned in deep transparent hollows of opaline blue and green,—and afar off the tinkling cowbells echoed through the still air, suggestive of safe green pastures and happy homes. 'Murder!' he whispered gurglingly. 'Nay!' said I, ''tis I should cry Murder!—for if ever an arresting hand held a murderer, mine holds one now! Your system of slaying is worse than that of the midnight assassin, for the assassin can but kill the body,—*you* strive to kill the soul. You cannot succeed, 'tis true, but the mere attempt is devilish. No shouts, no struggles will serve you here,—we are alone with Eternal Nature,—give the man you have slandered his tardy recognition, or else, as I said before—down you go!' Well, to make my story short, he yielded, and swore to do as I bade him,—whereupon placing my arm round him as though he were my tender twin-brother, I led him safely off the Mauvais Pas and down the kindlier hill, where, what with the fright and the remains of vertigo, he fell a'weeping grievously. Would you believe it, that before we reached Chamounix we had become the best friends in the world? He explained himself and his rascally modes of action, and I nobly exonerated him,—we exchanged cards,—and when we parted, this same author's bug-bear McWhing, overcome with sentiment and whisky toddy (he is a Scotchman you know) swore that I was the grandest fellow in the world, and that if ever he could serve me he would. He knew my princely title by this time, but he would have given me a still higher name. 'You are not—*hic*—a poet yourself?' he murmured, leaning on me fondly as he rolled to bed. I told him no. 'I am sorry—very!' he declared, the tears of whisky rising to his eyes, 'If you had been I would have done a great thing for you,—I would have boomed you,—*for nothing*!' I left him snoring nobly, and saw him no more. But I think he'll recognize me, Geoffrey;—I'll go and look him up personally. By all the gods!—if he had only known Who held him between life and death upon the Mauvais Pas!"

I stared, puzzled.

"But he did know"—I said—"Did you not say you exchanged cards?"

"True, but that was afterwards!" and Lucio laughed; "I assure you, my dear fellow, we can 'manage' McWhing!"

I was intensely interested in the story as he told it,—he had such a dramatic way of speaking and looking, while his very gestures brought the whole scene vividly before me like a picture. I spoke out my thought impulsively.

"You would certainly have made a superb actor, Lucio!"

"How do you know I am not one?" he asked with a flashing glance, then he added quickly—"No,—there is no occasion to paint the face and prance over the boards before a row of tawdry footlights like the paid mimes, in order to be histrionically great. The finest actor is he who can play the comedy of life perfectly, as I aspire to do. To walk well, talk well, smile well, weep well, groan well, laugh well—and die well!—it is all pure acting,—because in every man there is the dumb dreadful immortal Spirit who is real,—who cannot act,—who Is,—and who steadily maintains an infinite though speechless protest against the body's Lie!"

I said nothing in answer to this outburst,—I was beginning to be used to his shifting humours and strange utterances,—they increased the mysterious attraction I had for him, and made his character a perpetual riddle to me which was not without its subtle charm. Every now and then I realized, with a faintly startled sense of self-abasement, that I was completely under his dominance,—that my life was being entirely guided by his control and suggestion,—but I argued with myself that surely it was well it should be so, seeing he had so much more experience and influence than I. We dined together that night as we often did, and our conversation was entirely taken up with monetary and business concerns. Under Lucio's advice I was making several important investments, and these matters gave us ample subject for discussion. At about eleven o'clock, it being a fine frosty evening and fit for brisk walking, we went out, our destination being the private gambling club to which my companion had volunteered to introduce me as a guest. It was situated at the end of a mysterious little back street, not far from the respectable precincts of Pall-Mall, and was an unpretentious looking house enough outside, but within, it was sumptuously though tastelessly furnished. Apparently, the premises were presided over by a woman,—a woman with painted eyes and dyed hair who received us first of all within the lamp-lighted splendours of an Anglo-Japanese drawing-room. Her looks and manner undisguisedly proclaimed her as a *demi-mondaine* of the most pronounced type,—one of those 'pure' ladies with a 'past' who are represented as such martyrs to the vices of men. Lucio said something to her apart,—whereupon she glanced at me deferentially and smiled,—then rang the bell. A discreet looking man-servant in sober black made his appearance, and at a slight sign from his mistress who bowed to me as I passed her, proceeded to show us upstairs. We trod on a carpet of the softest felt,— in fact I noticed that everything was rendered as noiseless as possible in this establishment, the very doors being covered with thick baize and swinging on silent hinges. On the upper landing, the servant knocked very cautiously at a side-door,—a key turned in the lock, and we were admitted into a long double room, very brilliantly lit with electric lamps, which at a first glance seemed crowded with men playing at *rouge et noir* and *baccarat*. Some looked up as Lucio entered and nodded smilingly,— others glanced inquisitively at me, but our entrance was otherwise scarcely noticed. Lucio drawing me along by the arm, sat down to watch the play,—I followed his example and presently found myself infected by the intense excitement which permeated the room like the silent tension of the air before a thunderstorm. I recognised the faces of many well known public men,—men eminent in politics and society whom one would never have imagined capable of supporting a gambling club by their presence and authority. But I took care to betray no sign of surprise, and quietly observed the games and the gamesters with almost as impassive a demeanour as that of my companion. I was prepared to play and to lose,—I was not prepared however for the strange scene which was soon to occur and in which I, by force of circumstances was compelled to take a leading part.

X

As soon as the immediate game we were watching was finished, the players rose, and greeted Lucio with a good deal of eagerness and effusion. I instinctively guessed from their manner that they looked upon him as an influential member of the club, a person likely to lend them money to gamble with, and otherwise to oblige them in various ways, financially speaking. He introduced me to them all, and I was not slow to perceive the effect my name had upon most of them. I was asked if I would join in a game of baccarat, and I readily consented. The stakes were ruinously high, but I had no need to falter for that. One of the players near me was a fair-haired young man, handsome in face and of aristocratic bearing,—he had been introduced to me as Viscount Lynton. I noticed him particularly on account of the reckless way he had of doubling his stakes suddenly and apparently out of mere bravado, and when he lost, as he mostly did, he laughed uproariously as though he were drunk or delirious. On first beginning to play I was entirely indifferent as to the results of the game, caring nothing at all as to whether I had losses or gains. Lucio did not join us, but sat apart, quietly observant, and watching me, so I fancied, more than anyone. And as chance would have it, all the luck came my way, and I won steadily. The more I won the more excited I became, till presently my humour changed and I was seized by a whimsical desire to lose. I suppose it was the touch of some better impulse in my nature that made me wish this for young Lynton's sake. For he seemed literally maddened by my constant winnings, and continued his foolhardy and desperate play,—his young face grew drawn and sharply thin, and his eyes glittered with a hungry feverishness. The other gamesters, though sharing in his run of ill-luck, seemed better able to stand it, or perhaps they concealed their feelings more cleverly,—anyhow I know I caught myself very earnestly wishing that this devil's luck of mine would desert me and set in the young Viscount's direction. But my wishes were no use,— again and again I gathered up the stakes, till at last the players rose, Viscount Lynton among them.

"Well, I'm cleaned out!" he said, with a loud forced laugh. "You must give me my chance of a *revanche* to-morrow, Mr. Tempest!"

I bowed.

"With pleasure!"

He called a waiter at the end of the room to bring him a brandy and soda, and meanwhile I was surrounded by the rest of the men, all of them repeating the Viscount's suggestion of a 'revanche,' and strenuously urging upon me the necessity of returning to the club the next night in order to give them an opportunity of winning back what they had lost. I readily agreed, and while we were in the midst of talk, Lucio suddenly addressed young Lynton.

"Will you make up another game with me?" he inquired. "I'll start the bank with this,"—and he placed two crisp notes of five hundred pounds each on the table.

There was a moment's silence. The Viscount was thirstily drinking his brandy-and-soda, and glanced over the rim of his tall tumbler at the notes with covetous bloodshot eyes,—then he shrugged his shoulders indifferently. "I can't stake anything," he said; "I've already told you I'm cleaned out,—'stony-broke,' as the slang goes. It's no use my joining."

"Sit down, sit down, Lynton!" urged one man near him. "I'll lend you enough to go on with."

"Thanks, I'd rather not!" he returned, flushing a little. "I'm too much in your debt already. Awfully good of you all the same. You go on, you fellows, and I'll watch the play."

"Let me persuade you Viscount Lynton," said Lucio, looking at him with his dazzling inscrutable smile—"just for the fun of the thing! If you do not feel justified in staking money, stake something trifling and merely nominal, for the sake of seeing whether the luck will turn"—and here he took up a counter—"This frequently represents fifty pounds,—let it represent for once something that is not valuable like money,—your soul, for example!" A burst of laughter broke from all the men. Lucio laughed softly with them.

"We all have, I hope, enough instruction in modern science to be aware that there is no such thing as a soul in existence"—he continued. "Therefore, in proposing it as a stake for this game at baccarat, I really propose less than one hair of your head, because the hair is a something, and the soul is a nothing! Come! Will you risk that non-existent quantity for the chance of winning a thousand pounds?"

The Viscount drained off the last drop of brandy, and turned upon us, his eyes flushing mingled derision and defiance.

"Done!" he exclaimed; whereupon the party sat down.

The game was brief,—and in its rapid excitement, almost breathless. Six or seven minutes sufficed, and Lucio rose, the winner. He smiled as he pointed to the counter which had represented Viscount Lynton's last stake.

"I have won!" he said quietly. "But you owe me nothing, my dear Viscount, inasmuch as you risked—Nothing! We played this game simply for fun. If souls had any existence of course I should claim yours;—I wonder what I should do with it by the way!" He laughed good-humouredly. "What nonsense, isn't it!—and how thankful we ought to be that we live in advanced days like the present, when such silly superstitions are being swept aside by the march of progress and pure Reason! Good-night! Tempest and I will give you, your full revenge to-morrow,—the luck is sure to change by then, and you will probably have the victory. Again—good-night!"

He held out his hand,—there was a peculiar melting tenderness in his brilliant dark eyes,—an impressive kindness in his manner. Something—I could not tell what—held us all for the moment spellbound as if by enchantment, and several of the players at other tables, hearing of the eccentric stake that had been wagered and lost, looked over at us curiously from a distance. Viscount Lynton, however, professed himself immensely diverted, and shook Lucio's proffered hand heartily.

"You are an awfully good fellow!" he said, speaking a little thickly and hurriedly—"And I assure you seriously if I had a soul I should be very glad to part with it for a thousand pounds at the present moment. The soul wouldn't be an atom of use to me and the thousand pounds would. But I feel convinced I shall win to-morrow!"

"I am equally sure you will!" returned Lucio affably, "In the meantime, you will not find my friend here, Geoffrey Tempest, a hard creditor,—he can afford to wait. But in the case of the lost soul,"—here he paused, looking straight into the young man's eyes,—"of course *I* cannot afford to wait!"

The Viscount smiled vaguely at this pleasantry, and almost immediately afterwards left the club. As soon as the door had closed behind him, several of the gamesters exchanged sententious nods and glances.

"Ruined!" said one of them in a *sotto-voce*.

"His gambling debts are more than he can ever pay"—added another—"And I hear he has lost a clear fifty thousand on the turf."

MARIE CORELLI

These remarks were made indifferently, as though one should talk of the weather,—no sympathy was expressed,—no pity wasted. Every gambler there was selfish to the core, and as I studied their hardened faces, a thrill of honest indignation moved me,—indignation mingled with shame. I was not yet altogether callous or cruel-hearted, though as I look back upon those days which now resemble a wild vision rather than a reality, I know that I was becoming more and more of a brutal egoist with every hour I lived. Still I was so far then from being utterly vile, that I inwardly resolved to write to Viscount Lynton that very evening, and tell him to consider his debt to me cancelled, as I should refuse to claim it. While this thought was passing through my mind, I met Lucio's gaze fixed steadily upon me. He smiled,—and presently signed to me to accompany him. In a few minutes we had left the club, and were out in the cold night air under a heaven of frostily sparkling stars. Standing still for a moment, my companion laid his hand on my shoulder.

"Tempest, if you are going to be kind-hearted or sympathetic to undeserving rascals, I shall have to part company with you!" he said, with a curious mixture of satire and seriousness in his voice—"I see by the expression of your face that you are meditating some silly disinterested action of pure generosity. Now you might just as well flop down on these paving stones and begin saying prayers in public. You want to let Lynton off his debt,—you are a fool for your pains. He is a born scoundrel,—and has never seen his way to being anything else,—why should you compassionate him? From the time he first went to college till now, he has been doing nothing but live a life of degraded sensuality,—he is a worthless rake, less to be respected than an honest dog!"

"Yet some one loves him I daresay!" I said.

"Some one loves him!" echoed Lucio with inimitable disdain—"Bah! Three ballet girls live on him if that is what you mean. His mother loved him,—but she is dead,—he broke her heart. He is no good I tell you,—let him pay his debt in full, even to the soul he staked so lightly. If I were the devil now, and had just won the strange game we played to-night, I suppose according to priestly tradition, I should be piling up the fire for Lynton in high glee,—but being what I am, I say let the man alone to make his own destiny,—let things take their course,—and as he chose to risk everything, so let him pay everything."

We were by this time walking slowly into Pall Mall,—I was on the point of making some reply, when catching sight of a man's figure on the opposite side of the way, not far from the Marlborough Club, I uttered an involuntary exclamation.

"Why there he is!" I said—"there is Viscount Lynton!"

Lucio's hand closed tightly on my arm.

"You don't want to speak to him now, surely!"

"No. But I wonder where he's going? He walks rather unsteadily."

"Drunk, most probably!"

And Lucio's face presented the same relentless expression of scorn I had so often seen and marvelled at.

We paused a moment, watching the Viscount strolling aimlessly up and down in front of the clubs,—till all at once he seemed to come to a sudden resolution, and stopping short, he shouted,

"Hansom!"

A silent-wheeled smart vehicle came bowling up immediately. Giving some order to the driver, he jumped in. The cab approached swiftly in our direction,—just as it passed us the loud report of a pistol crashed on the silence.

"Good God!" I cried reeling back a step or two—"He has shot himself!"

The hansom stopped,—the driver sprang down,—club-porters, waiters, policemen and no end of people starting up from Heaven knows where, were on the scene on an instant,—I rushed forward to join the rapidly gathering throng, but before I could do so, Lucio's strong arm was thrown round me, and he dragged me by main force away.

"Keep cool, Geoffrey!" he said—"Do you want to be called up to identify? And betray the club and all its members? Not while I am here to prevent you! Check your mad impulses, my good fellow,—they will lead you into no end of difficulties. If the man's dead he's dead, and there's an end of it."

"Lucio! You have no heart!" I exclaimed, struggling violently to escape from his hold—"How can you stop to reason in such a case! Think of it! *I* am the cause of all the mischief!—it is my cursed luck at baccarat this evening that has been the final blow to the wretched young fellow's fortunes,—I am convinced of it!—I shall never forgive myself—"

"Upon my word, Geoffrey, your conscience is very tender!" he answered, holding my arm still more closely and hurrying me away despite myself—"You must try and toughen it a little if you want to be successful in life. Your 'cursed luck' you think, has caused Lynton's

MARIE CORELLI

death? Surely it is a contradiction in terms to call luck 'cursed,'—and as for the Viscount, he did not need that last game at baccarat to emphasise his ruin. You are not to blame. And for the sake of the club, if for nothing else, I do not intend either you or myself to be mixed up in a case of suicide. The coroner's verdict always disposes of these incidents comfortably in two words—'Temporary insanity.'"

I shuddered. My soul sickened as I thought that within a few yards of us was the bleeding corpse of the man I had so lately seen alive and spoken with,—and notwithstanding Lucio's words I felt as if I had murdered him.

"'Temporary insanity'"—repeated Lucio again, as if speaking to himself—"all remorse, despair, outraged honour, wasted love, together with the scientific modern theory of Reasonable Nothingness—Life a Nothing, God a Nothing,—when these drive the distracted human unit to make of himself also a nothing, 'temporary insanity' covers up his plunge into the infinite with an untruthful pleasantness. However, after all, it is as Shakespeare says, a mad world!"

I made no answer. I was too overcome by my own miserable sensations. I walked along almost unconscious of movement, and as I stared bewilderedly up at the stars they danced before my sight like fireflies whirling in a mist of miasma. Presently a faint hope occurred to me.

"Perhaps," I said, "he has not really killed himself? It may be only an attempt?"

"He was a capital shot"—returned Lucio composedly,—"That was his one quality. He has no principles,—but he was a good marksman. I cannot imagine his missing aim."

"It is horrible! An hour ago alive, . . . and now. . . I tell you, Lucio, it is horrible!"

"What is? Death? It is not half so horrible as Life lived wrongly,"—he responded, with a gravity that impressed me in spite of my emotion and excitement—"Believe me, the mental sickness and confusion of a wilfully degraded existence are worse tortures than are contained in the priestly notions of Hell. Come come, Geoffrey, you take this matter too much to heart,—you are not to blame. If Lynton has given himself the 'happy dispatch' it is really the best thing he could do,—he was of no use to anybody, and he is well out of it. It is positively weak of you to attach importance to such a trifle. You are only at the beginning of your career—"

"Well, I hope that career will not lead me into any more such tragedies as the one enacted to-night,"—I said passionately—"If it does, it will be entirely against my will!"

Lucio looked at me curiously.

"Nothing can happen to you against your will"—he replied; "I suppose you wish to imply that I am to blame for introducing you to the club? My good fellow, you need not have gone there unless you had chosen to do so! I did not bind and drag you there! You are upset and unnerved,—come into my room and take a glass of wine,—you will feel more of a man afterwards."

We had by this time reached the hotel, and I went with him passively. With equal passiveness I drank what he gave me, and stood, glass in hand, watching him with a kind of morbid fascination as he threw off his fur-lined overcoat and confronted me, his pale handsome face strangely set and stern, and his dark eyes glittering like cold steel.

"That last stake of Lynton's, . . . to you—" I said falteringly—"His soul—"

"Which *he* did not believe in, and which *you* do not believe in!" returned Lucio, regarding me fixedly. "Why do you now seem to tremble at a mere sentimental idea? If fantastic notions such as God, the Soul, and the Devil were real facts, there would perhaps be cause for trembling, but being only the brainsick imaginations of superstitious mankind, there is nothing in them to awaken the slightest anxiety or fear."

"But you"—I began—"you say you believe in the soul?"

"I? I am brainsick!" and he laughed bitterly—"Have you not found that out yet? Much learning hath driven me mad, my friend! Science has led me into such deep wells of dark discovery, that it is no wonder if my senses sometimes reel,—and I believe—at such insane moments—in the Soul!"

I sighed heavily.

"I think I will go to bed," I answered. "I am tired out,—and absolutely miserable!"

"Alas, poor millionaire!" said Lucio gently,—"I am sorry, I assure you, that the evening has ended so disastrously."

"So am I!" I returned despondently.

"Imagine it!" he went on, dreamily regarding me—"If my beliefs,—my crack-brained theories,—were worth anything,—which they are not—I could claim the only positive existing part of our late acquaintance

MARIE CORELLI

Viscount Lynton! But,—where and how to send in my account with him? If I were Satan now. . ."

I forced a faint smile.

"You would have cause to rejoice!" I said.

He moved two paces towards me, and laid his hands gently on my shoulders.

"No, Geoffrey"—and his rich voice had a strange soft music in it— "No, my friend! If I were Satan I should probably lament!—for every lost soul would of necessity remind me of my own fall, my own despair,— and set another bar between myself and heaven! Remember,—the very Devil was an Angel once!"

His eyes smiled, and yet I could have sworn there were tears in them. I wrung his hand hard,—I felt that notwithstanding his assumed coldness and cynicism, the fate of young Lynton had affected him profoundly. My liking for him gained new fervour from this impression, and I went to bed more at ease with myself and things in general. During the few minutes I spent in undressing I became even able to contemplate the tragedy of the evening with less regret and greater calmness,—for it was certainly no use worrying over the irrevocable,—and, after all, what interest had the Viscount's life for me? None. I began to ridicule myself for my own weakness and disinterested emotion,—and presently, being thoroughly fatigued, fell sound asleep. Towards morning however, perhaps about four or five o'clock, I woke suddenly as though touched by an invisible hand. I was shivering violently, and my body was bathed in a cold perspiration. In the otherwise dark room there was something strangely luminous, like a cloud of white smoke or fire. I started up, rubbing my eyes,—and stared before me for a moment, doubting the evidence of my own senses. For, plainly visible and substantially distinct, at a distance of perhaps five paces from my bed, stood three Figures, muffled in dark garments and closely hooded. So solemnly inert they were,—so heavily did their sable draperies fall about them that it was impossible to tell whether they were men or women,—but what paralysed me with amazement and terror was the strange light that played around and above them,—the spectral, wandering, chill radiance that illumined them like the rays of a faint wintry moon. I strove to cry out,—but my tongue refused to obey me—and my voice was strangled in my throat. The Three remained absolutely motionless,—and again I rubbed my eyes, wondering if this were a dream or some hideous optical delusion. Trembling in every limb, I stretched my hand towards the bell intending to ring violently for assistance,—when—a Voice, low and thrilling with intense anguish, caused me to shrink back appalled, and my arm fell nerveless at my side. "*Misery!*"

The word struck the air with a harsh reproachful clang, and I nearly swooned with the horror of it. For now one of the Figures moved, and a face gleamed out from beneath its hooded wrappings—a face white as whitest marble and fixed into such an expression of dreadful despair as froze my blood. Then came a deep sigh that was more like a death-groan, and again the word, "*Misery!*" shuddered upon the silence.

Mad with fear, and scarcely knowing what I did, I sprang from the bed, and began desperately to advance upon these fantastic masqueraders, determined to seize them and demand the meaning of this practical and untimely jest,—when suddenly all Three lifted their heads and turned their faces on me,—such faces!—indescribably awful in their pallid agony,—and a whisper more ghastly than a shriek, penetrated the very fibres of my consciousness—"*Misery!*"

With a furious bound I flung myself upon them,—my hands struck *empty space*. Yet there—distinct as ever—they stood, glowering down upon me, while my clenched fists beat impotently *through* and *beyond* their seemingly corporeal shapes! And then—all at once—I became aware of their eyes,—eyes that watched me pitilessly, stedfastly, and disdainfully,—eyes that like witch-fires, seemed to slowly burn terrific meanings into my very flesh and spirit. Convulsed and almost frantic with the strain on my nerves, I abandoned myself to despair,—this awful sight meant death I thought,—my last hour had surely come! Then—I saw the lips of one of those dreadful faces move. . . some superhuman instinct in me leaped to life, . . . in some strange way I thought I knew, or guessed the horror of what that next utterance would be, . . . and with all my remaining force I cried out—

"No! No! Not that eternal Doom! . . . Not yet!"

Fighting the vacant air, I strove to beat back those intangible weird Shapes that loomed above me, withering up my soul with the fixed stare of their angry eyes, and with a choking call for help, I fell, as it were, into a pit of darkness, where I lay mercifully unconscious.

MARIE CORELLI

XI

How the ensuing hours between this horrible episode and full morning elapsed I do not know. I was dead to all impressions. I woke at last, or rather recovered my senses to see the sunlight pouring pleasantly through the half-drawn curtains at my window, and to find myself in bed in as restful a position as though I had never left it. Was it then merely a vision I had seen?—a ghastly sort of nightmare? If so, it was surely the most abhorrent illusion ever evolved from dreamland! It could not be a question of health, for I had never felt better in my life. I lay for some time quiescent, thinking over the matter, with my eyes fixed on that part of the room where those Three Shapes had seemingly stood; but I had lately got into such a habit of cool self-analysis, that by the time my valet brought my early cup of coffee, I had decided that the whole thing was a dreadful fantasy, born of my own imagination, which had no doubt been unduly excited by the affair of Viscount Lynton's suicide. I soon learned that there was no room left for doubt as to that unhappy young nobleman's actual death. A brief account of it was in the morning papers, though as the tragedy had occurred so late at night there were no details. A vague hint of 'money difficulties' was thrown out in one journal,—but beyond that, and the statement that the body had been conveyed to the mortuary there to await an inquest, there was nothing said, either personal or particular. I found Lucio in the smoking-room, and it was he who first silently pointed out to me the short paragraph headed 'Suicide of a Viscount.'

"I told you he was a good shot!" he commented.

I nodded. Somehow I had ceased to feel much interest in the subject. My emotion of the previous evening had apparently exhausted all my stock of sympathy and left me coldly indifferent. Absorbed in myself and my own concerns, I sat down to talk and was not long before I had given a full and circumstantial account of the spectral illusion which had so unpleasantly troubled me during the night. Lucio listened, smiling oddly.

"That old Tokay was evidently too strong for you!" he said, when I had concluded my story.

"Did you give me old Tokay?" I responded laughing—"Then the mystery is explained! I was already overwrought, and needed no stimulant. But what tricks the imagination plays us to be sure! You have no idea of the distinct manner in which those three phantoms asserted themselves! The impression was extraordinarily vivid."

"No doubt!" And his dark eyes studied me curiously. "Impressions often *are* very vivid. See what a marvellously real impression this world makes upon us, for example!"

"Ah! But then the world *is* real!" I answered.

"Is it? You accept it as such, I daresay, and things are as they appear to each separate individual. No two human beings think alike; hence there may be conflicting opinions as to the reality or non-reality of this present world. But we will not take unnecessary plunges into the infinite question of what *is*, as contrasted with what appears to be. I have some letters here for your consideration. You have lately spoken of buying a country estate—what say you to Willowsmere Court in Warwickshire? I have had my eye on that place for you,—it seems to me just the very thing. It is a magnificent old pile; part of it dates from Elizabeth's time. It is in excellent repair; the grounds are most picturesque, the classic river Avon winds with rather a broad sweep through the park,—and the whole thing, with a great part of the furniture included, is to be sold for a mere song;—fifty thousand pounds cash. I think you had better go in for it; it would just suit your literary and poetic tastes."

Was it my fancy, or had his musical voice the faintest touch of a sneer as he uttered the last words? I would not allow myself to think this possible, and answered quickly,—

"Anything *you* recommend must be worth looking at, and I'll certainly go and see it. The description sounds well, and Shakespeare's country always appeals to me. But wouldn't you like to secure it for yourself?"

He laughed.

"Not I! I live nowhere for long. I am of a roving disposition, and am never happy tied down to one corner of the earth. But I suggest Willowsmere to you for two reasons,—first that it is charming and perfectly appointed; secondly, that it will impress Lord Elton considerably if he knows you are going to buy it."

"How so?"

"Why, because it used to be his property"—returned Lucio quietly—"till he got into the hands of the Jews. He gave them Willowsmere as security for loans, and latterly they have stepped in as owners. They've sold most of the pictures, china, bric-a-brac and other valuables. By the way, have you noticed how the legended God still appears to protect the house of Israel? Particularly the 'base usurer' who is allowed to get the unhappy Christian into his clutches nine times out of ten? And no remedy drops from heaven! The Jew always triumphs. Rather inconsistent isn't it, on the part of an equitable Deity!" His eyes flashed strange scorn. Anon he resumed—"As a result of Lord Elton's unfortunate speculations, and the Jews' admirable shrewdness, Willowsmere, as I tell you is in the market, and fifty thousand pounds will make you the envied owner of a place worth a hundred thousand."

"We dine at the Eltons' to-night, do we not?" I asked musingly.

"We do. You cannot have forgotten that engagement and Lady Sibyl so soon surely!" he answered laughing.

"No, I have not forgotten"—I said at last, after a little silence. "And I will buy this Willowsmere. I will telegraph instructions to my lawyers at once. Will you give me the name and address of the agents?"

"With pleasure, my dear boy!" And Lucio handed me a letter containing the particulars concerning the sale of the estate and other items. "But are you not making up your mind rather suddenly? Hadn't you better inspect the property first? There may be things you object to—"

"If it were a rat-infested barrack," I said resolutely—"I would still buy it! I shall settle the matter at once. I wish to let Lord Elton know this very night that I am the future owner of Willowsmere!"

"Good!"—and my companion thrust his arm through mine as we left the smoking-room together—"I like your swiftness of action Geoffrey. It is admirable! I always respect determination. Even if a man makes up his mind to go to hell, I honour him for keeping to his word, and going there straight as a die!"

I laughed, and we parted in high good-humour,—he to fulfil a club engagement, I to telegraph precise instructions to my legal friends Messrs Bentham and Ellis, for the immediate purchase in my name at all costs, risks or inconveniences, of the estate known as Willowsmere Court in the county of Warwick.

That evening I dressed with more than common care, giving my man Morris almost as much trouble as if I had been a fidgetty woman. He waited upon me however with exemplary patience, and only when I was quite ready did he venture to utter what had evidently been on his mind for some time.

"Excuse me sir,"—he then observed—"but I daresay you've noticed that there's something unpleasant-like about the prince's valet, Amiel?"

"Well, he's rather a down-looking fellow if that's what you mean,"—I replied—"But I suppose there's no harm in him."

"I don't know about that sir,"—answered Morris severely; "He does a great many strange things I do assure you. Downstairs with the servants he goes on something surprising. Sings and acts and dances too, as if he were a whole music-hall."

"Really!" I exclaimed in surprise—"I should never have thought it."

"Nor should I sir, but it's a fact."

"He must be rather an amusing fellow then,"—I continued, wondering that my man should take the accomplishments of Amiel in such an injured manner.

"Oh, I don't say anything against his amusingness,"—and Morris rubbed his nose with a doubtful air—"It's all very well for him to cut capers and make himself agreeable if he likes,—but it's the deceit of him that surprises me sir. You'd think to look at him that he was a decent sort of dull chap with no ideas beyond his duty, but really sir, it's quite the contrary, if you'll believe me. The language he uses when he's up to his games downstairs is something frightful! And he actually swears he learnt it from the gentlemen of the turf, sir! Last night he was play acting, and taking off all the fashionable folks,—then he took to hypnotising—and upon my word it made my blood run cold."

"Why, what did he do?" I asked with some curiosity.

"Well, sir, he took one of the scullery-maids and sat her in a chair and just pointed at her. Pointed at her and grinned, for all the world like a devil out of a pantomime. And though she is generally a respectable sober young woman, if she didn't get up with a screech and commence dancing round and round like a lunatic, while he kept on pointing. And presently she got to jumping and lifting her skirts that high that it was positively scandalous! Some of us tried to stop her and couldn't; she was like mad, till all at once number twenty-two bell rang—that's the prince's room,—and he just caught hold of her, set her down in her chair again and clapped his hands. She came to directly, and didn't know a bit what she'd been doing. Then twenty-two bell rang again, and the fellow rolled up his eyes like a clergyman and said, 'Let us pray!' and off he went."

I laughed.

"He seems to have a share of humour at anyrate,"—I said; "I should not have thought it of him. But do you think these antics of his are mischievous?"

"Well that scullery girl is very ill to-day,"—replied Morris; "I expect she'll have to leave. She has what she calls the 'jumps' and none of us dare tell her how she got them. No sir, believe me or not as you like, there's something very queer about that Amiel. And another thing I want to know is this—what does he do with the other servants?"

"What does he do with the other servants?" I repeated bewilderedly—"What on earth do you mean?"

"Well sir, the prince has a *chef* of his own hasn't he?" said Morris enumerating on his fingers—"And two personal attendants besides Amiel,—quiet fellows enough who help in the waiting. Then he has a coachman and groom. That makes six servants altogether. Now none of these except Amiel are ever seen in the hotel kitchens. The *chef* sends all the meals in from somewhere, in a heated receptacle—and the two other fellows are never seen except when waiting at table, and they don't live in their own rooms all day, though they *may* sleep there,—and nobody knows where the carriage and horses are put up, or where the coachman and groom lodge. Certain it is that both they and the *chef* board out. It seems to me very mysterious."

I began to feel quite unreasonably irritated.

"Look here, Morris," I said—"There's nothing more useless or more harmful than the habit of inquiring into other people's affairs. The prince has a right to live as he likes, and do as he pleases with his servants—I am sure he pays royally for his privileges. And whether his cook lives in or out, up in the skies or down in a cellar is no matter of mine. He has been a great traveller and no doubt has his peculiarities; and probably his notions concerning food are very particular and fastidious. But I don't want to know anything about his ménage. If you dislike Amiel, it's easy to avoid him, but for goodness sake don't go making mysteries where none exist."

Morris looked up, then down, and folded one of my coats with special care. I saw I had effectually checked his flow of confidence.

"Very well, sir,"—he observed, and said no more.

I was rather diverted than otherwise at my servant's solemn account of Amiel's peculiarities as exhibited among his own class,—and when we were driving to Lord Elton's that evening I told something of the story to Lucio. He laughed.

"Amiel's spirits are often too much for him,"—he said—"He is a perfect imp of mischief and cannot always control himself."

"Why, what a wrong estimate I have formed of him!" I said—"I thought he had a peculiarly grave and somewhat sullen disposition."

"You know the trite saying—appearances are deceptive?" went on my companion lightly—"It's extremely true. The professed humourist is nearly always a disagreeable and heavy man personally. As for Amiel, he is like me in the respect of not being at all what he seems. His only fault is a tendency to break the bounds of discipline, but otherwise he serves me well, and I do not inquire further. Is Morris disgusted or alarmed?"

"Neither I think," I responded laughing—"He merely presents himself to me as an example of outraged respectability."

"Ah then, you may be sure that when the scullery-maid was dancing, he observed her steps with the closest nicety;" said Lucio—"Very respectable men are always particular of inspection into these matters! Soothe his ruffled feelings, my dear Geoffrey, and tell him that Amiel is the very soul of virtue! I have had him in my service for a long time, and can urge nothing against his character as a man. He does not pretend to be an angel. His tricks of speech and behaviour are the result of a too constant repression of his natural hilarity, but he is really an excellent fellow. He dabbled in hypnotic science when he was with me in India; I have often warned him of the danger there is in practising this force on the uninitiated. But—a scullery-maid!—heavens!—there are so many scullery-maids! One more or less with the 'jumps' will not matter. This is Lord Elton's."

The carriage stopped before a handsome house situated a little back from Park Lane. We were admitted by a man-servant gorgeous in red plush, white silk hose and powdered wig, who passed us on majestically to his twin-brother in height and appearance, though perhaps a trifle more disdainful in bearing, and he in his turn ushered us upstairs with the air of one who should say "See to what ignominious degradation a cruel fate reduces so great a man!" In the drawing-room we found Lord Elton, standing on the hearth-rug with his back to the fire, and directly opposite him in a low arm chair, reclined an elegantly attired young lady with very small feet. I mention the feet, because as I entered they were the most prominent part of her person, being well stretched out from beneath the would-be concealment of sundry flounced petticoats towards the warmth of the fire which the Earl rather inconsiderately screened from view. There was another lady in the room sitting bolt upright with hands neatly folded on her lap, and to her we were first of all introduced when Lord Elton's own effusive greetings were over.

"Charlotte, allow me,—my friends, Prince Lucio Rimânez—Mr. Geoffrey Tempest; gentlemen, my sister-in-law, Miss Charlotte Fitzroy."

We bowed; the lady gave us a dignified bend of the head. She was an imposing looking spinster, with a curious expression on her features which was difficult to construe. It was pious and prim, but it also suggested the idea that she must have seen something excessively improper once in her life and had never been able to forget it. The pursed-up mouth, the round pale-coloured eyes and the chronic air of insulted virtue which seemed to pervade her from head to foot all helped to deepen this impression. One could not look at Miss Charlotte long without beginning to wonder irreverently what it was that had in her long past youth so outraged the cleanly proprieties of her nature as to leave such indelible traces on her countenance. But I have since seen many English women look so, especially among the particularly 'high bred,' old and plain-featured of the "upper ten." Very different was the saucy and bright physiognomy of the younger lady to whom we were next presented, and who, raising herself languidly from her reclining position, smiled at us with encouraging familiarity as we made our salutations.

"Miss Diana Chesney,"—said the Earl glibly—"You perhaps know her father, prince,—you must have heard of him at any rate—the famous Nicodemus Chesney, one of the great railway-kings."

"Of course I know him"—responded Lucio warmly—"Who does not! I have met him often. A charming man, gifted with most remarkable humour and vitality—I remember him perfectly. We saw a good deal of each other in Washington."

"Did you though?" said Miss Chesney with a somewhat indifferent interest,—"He's a queer sort of man to my thinking; rather a cross between the ticket-collector and custom-house officer combined, you know! I never see him but what I feel I must start on a journey directly—railways seem to be written all over him. I tell him so. I say 'Pa, if you didn't carry railway-tracks in your face you'd be better looking.' And you found him humorous, did you?"

Laughing at the novel and free way in which this young person criticised her parent, Lucio protested that he did.

"Well I don't,"—confessed Miss Chesney—"But that may be because I've heard all his stories over and over again, and I've read most of them in books besides,—so they're not much account to me. He tells some of them to the Prince of Wales whenever he can get a chance,—but he don't try them off on me any more. He's a real clever man too; he's made his pile quicker than most. And you're quite right about his vitality,—my!—his laugh takes you into the middle of next week!"

Her bright eyes flashed merrily as she took a comprehensive survey of our amused faces.

"Think I'm irreverent, don't you?" she went on—"But you know Pa's not a 'stage parent' all dressed out in lovely white hair and benedictions,—he's just an accommodating railway-track, and he wouldn't like to be reverenced. Do sit down, won't you?"—then turning her pretty head coquettishly towards her host—"Make them sit down, Lord Elton,—I hate to see men standing. The superior sex, you know! Besides you're so tall," she added, glancing with unconcealed admiration at Lucio's handsome face and figure, "that it's like peering up an apple-tree at the moon to look at you!"

Lucio laughed heartily, and seated himself near her—I followed his example; the old Earl still kept his position, legs a-straddle, on the hearth-rug, and beamed benevolence upon us all. Certainly Diana Chesney was a captivating creature; one of those surface-clever American women who distinctly divert men's minds without in the least rousing their passions.

"So you're the famous Mr. Tempest?" she said, surveying me critically—"Why, it's simply splendid for you isn't it? I always say it's no use having a heap of money unless you're young,—if you're old, you only want it to fill your doctor's pockets while he tries to mend your poor tuckered-out constitution. I once knew an old lady who was left a legacy of a hundred thousand pounds when she was ninety-five. Poor old dear, she cried over it. She just had sense enough to understand what a good time she couldn't have. She lived in bed, and her only luxury was a halfpenny bun dipped in milk for her tea. It was all she cared for."

"A hundred thousand pounds would go a long way in buns!" I said smiling.

"Wouldn't it just!" and the fair Diana laughed—"But I guess *you'll* want something a little more substantial for your cash Mr. Tempest! A fortune in the prime of life is worth having. I suppose you're one of the richest men about just now, aren't you?"

She put the question in a perfectly naïve frank manner and seemed to be unconscious of any undue inquisitiveness in it.

"I may be one of the richest,"—I replied, and as I spoke the thought flashed suddenly across me how recently I had been one of the poorest!—"But my friend here, the prince, is far richer than I."

"Is that so!" and she stared straight at Lucio, who met her gaze with an indulgent, half satirical smile—"Well now! I guess Pa's no better than a sort of pauper after all! Why, you must have the world at your feet!"

"Pretty much so,"—replied Lucio composedly—"But then, my dear Miss Chesney, the world is so very easily brought to one's feet. Surely *you* know that?"

And he emphasized the words by an expressive look of his fine eyes.

"I guess you mean compliments,"—she replied unconcernedly—"I don't like them as a rule, but I'll forgive you this once!"

"Do!" said Lucio, with one of his dazzling smiles that caused her to stop for a moment in her voluble chatter and observe him with mingled fascination and wonderment.

"And you too are young, like Mr. Tempest,"—she resumed presently.

"Pardon me!" interrupted Lucio—"I am many years older."

"Really!" exclaimed Lord Elton at this juncture—"You don't look it, does he Charlotte?"

Miss Fitzroy thus appealed to, raised her elegant tortoise-shell-framed glasses to her eyes and peered critically at us both.

"I should imagine the prince to be slightly the senior of Mr. Tempest"—she remarked in precise high-bred accents—"But only very slightly."

"Anyhow," resumed Miss Chesney "you're young enough, to enjoy your wealth aren't you?"

"Young enough, or old enough;—just as you please;"—said Lucio with a careless shrug—"But as it happens—I do *not* enjoy it!"

Miss Chesney's whole aspect now expressed the most lively astonishment.

"What does money do for you?" went on Lucio, his eyes dilating with that strange and wistful expression which had often excited my curiosity—"The world is at your feet, perhaps; yes—but *what* a world! What a trumpery clod of kickable matter! Wealth acts merely as a kind of mirror to show you human nature at its worst. Men skulk and fawn about you, and lie twenty times in as many hours in the hope to propitiate you and serve their own interests; princes of the blood willingly degrade themselves and their position to borrow cash of you,—your intrinsic merit (if you have any) is thought nothing of,—your full pockets are your credentials with kings, prime ministers and councillors!

You may talk like a fool, laugh like a hyena and look like a baboon, but if the chink-chink of your gold be only sufficiently loud, you may soon find yourself dining with the Queen if such be your ambition. If, on the contrary you happen to be truly great, brave, patient, and enduring, with a spark in you of that genius which strengthens life and makes it better worth living,—if you have thoughts which take shape in work that shall endure when kingdoms are swept away like dust before the wind, and if, with all this you are yet poor in current coin, why then,— you shall be spurned by all the crowned dummies of the world,—you shall be snubbed by the affluent starch-maker and the Croesus who lives on a patent pill,—the tradesman from whom you buy bedsteads and kitchen ware, can look down upon you with lordly scorn, for does he not by virtue of his wealth alone, drive a four-in-hand, and chat on easy and almost patronizing terms with the Prince of Wales? The wealthy denizens of Snob-land delight in ignoring Nature's elected noblemen."

"But supposing" said Miss Chesney quickly, "you happen to be a Nature's nobleman yourself, and have the advantage of wealth besides, surely you must fairly allow that to be rather a good thing, mustn't you?"

Lucio laughed a little—

"I will retort upon you in your own words fair lady, and say 'I guess you mean compliments.' What I venture to imply however, is that even when wealth does fall to the lot of one of these 'Nature's noblemen,' it is not *because* of his innate nobility that he wins social distinction. It is simply because he is rich. That is what vexes me. I for example, have endless friends who are not my friends so much as the friends of my income. They do not trouble to inquire as to my antecedents,—what I am or where I came from is of no importance. Neither are they concerned in how I live or what I do; whether I am sick or well, happy or unhappy, is equally with them a matter of indifference. If they knew more about me, it would perhaps be better in the long run. But they do not want to know,—their aims are simple and unconcealed,—they wish to make as much out of me, and secure as much advantage to themselves by their acquaintance with me as possible. And I give them their full way,—they get all they want,—and more!"

His musical voice lingered with a curiously melancholy impressiveness on the last word,—and this time, not only Miss Chesney, but we all, looked at him as though drawn by some irresistible magnetic spell, and for a moment there was silence.

MARIE CORELLI

"Very few people have any real friends,"—said Lord Elton presently. "And in that respect I suppose we're none of us worse off than Socrates, who used to keep two chairs only in his house 'one for myself, and another for a friend—when I find him!' But you are a universal favourite Lucio,—a most popular fellow—and I think you're rather hard on your set. People must look after themselves you know—eh?"

Lucio bowed his head gravely.

"They must indeed," he replied—"Especially as the latest news of science is that God has given up the business."

Miss Fitzroy looked displeased,—but the Earl laughed uproariously. At that moment a step was heard outside, approaching the open doorway of the drawing-room, and Miss Chesney's quick ears caught the sound. She shook herself out of her reclining attitude instantly and sat erect.

"It's Sibyl!" she said with a half-laughing half-apologetic flash of her brown eyes at us all—"I never can loll before Sibyl!"

My heart beat fast as the woman whom poets might have called the goddess of their dreams, but whom I was now disposed to consider as an object of beauty lawfully open to my purchase, entered, clad in simple white, unrelieved by any ornaments save a golden waistbelt of antique workmanship, and a knot of violets nestled among the lace at her bosom. She looked far lovelier than when I had first seen her at the theatre; there was a deeper light in her eyes and a more roseate flush on her cheeks, while her smile as she greeted us was positively dazzling. Something in her presence, her movements, her manner, sent such a tide of passion through me that for a moment my brain whirled in a dizzy maze, and despite the cold calculations I had made in my own mind as to the certainty I had of winning her for my wife, there was a wondrous charm of delicate dignity and unapproachableness about her that caused me for the moment to feel ashamed, and inclined to doubt even the power of wealth to move this exquisite lily of maidenhood from her sequestered peace. Ah, what fools men are! How little do we dream of the canker at the hearts of these women 'lilies' that look so pure and full of grace!

"You are late, Sibyl," said her aunt severely.

"Am I?" she responded with languid indifference—"So sorry! Papa, are you an extemporized fire-screen?"

Lord Elton hastily moved to one side, rendered suddenly conscious of his selfish monopoly of the blaze.

"Are you not cold, Miss Chesney?" continued Lady Sibyl, in accents of studied courtesy—"Would you not like to come nearer the fire?"

Diana Chesney had become quite subdued, almost timid in fact.

"Thank-you!"—she murmured, and her eyes drooped with what might have been called retiring maiden modesty, had not Miss Chesney's qualities soared far beyond that trite description.

"We heard some shocking news this morning, Mr. Tempest," said Lady Sibyl, looking at Lucio rather than at me—"No doubt you read it in the papers,—an acquaintance of ours, Viscount Lynton, shot himself last night."

I could not repress a slight start. Lucio gave me a warning glance, and took it upon himself to reply.

"Yes, I read a brief account of the affair—terrible indeed! I also knew him slightly."

"Did you? Well, he was engaged to a friend of mine," went on Lady Sibyl—"I myself think she has had a lucky escape, because though he was an agreeable man enough in society, he was a great gambler, and very extravagant, and he would have run through her fortune very quickly. But she cannot be brought to see it in that light,—she is dreadfully upset. She had set her heart on being a Viscountess."

"I guess," said Miss Chesney demurely, with a sly sparkle of her eyes—"it's not only Americans who run after titles. Since I've been over here I've known several real nice girls marry downright mean dough-heads just for the sake of being called 'my lady' or 'your grace.' I like a title very well myself—but I also like a man attached to it."

The Earl smothered a chuckling laugh,—Lady Sibyl gazed meditatively into the fire and went on as though she had not heard.

"Of course my friend will have other chances,—she is young and handsome—but I really think, apart from the social point of view, that she was a little in love with the Viscount—"

"Nonsense! nonsense!" said her father somewhat testily. "You always have some romantic notion or other in your head Sibyl,—one 'season' ought to have cured you of sentiment—ha-ha-ha! She always knew he was a dissolute rascal, and she was going to marry him with her eyes wide open to the fact. When I read in the papers that he had blown his brains out in a hansom, I said 'Bad taste—bad taste! spoiling a poor cabby's stock-in-trade to satisfy a selfish whim!' ha-ha!—but I thought it was a good riddance of bad rubbish. He would have made any woman's life utterly miserable."

MARIE CORELLI

"No doubt he would!" responded Lady Sibyl, listlessly; "But, all the same, there is such a thing as love sometimes."

She raised her beautiful liquid eyes to Lucio's face, but he was not looking her way, and her steadfast gaze met mine instead. What my looks expressed I know not; but I saw the rich blood mantle warmly in her cheeks, and a tremor seemed to pass through her frame,—then she grew very pale. At that moment one of the gorgeous footmen appeared at the doorway.

"Dinner is served, my lud."

"Good!" and the Earl proceeded to 'pair' us all. "Prince, will you take Miss Fitzroy,—Mr. Tempest, my daughter falls to your escort,—I will follow with Miss Chesney."

We set off in this order down the stairs, and as I walked behind Lucio with Lady Sibyl on my arm, I could not help smiling at the extreme gravity and earnestness with which he was discussing church matters with Miss Charlotte, and the sudden enthusiasm that apparently seized that dignified spinster at some of his remarks on the clergy, which took the form of the most affectionate and respectful eulogies, and were totally the reverse of the ideas he had exchanged with me on the same subject. Some spirit of mischief was evidently moving him to have a solemn joke with the high-bred lady he escorted, and I noted his behaviour with a good deal of inward amusement.

"Then you know the dear Canon?" I heard Miss Charlotte say.

"Most intimately!" replied Lucio with fervour—"and I assure you I am thankful to have the privilege of knowing him. A truly perfect man!—almost a saint—if not quite!"

"So pure-minded!" sighed the spinster.

"So free from every taint of hypocrisy!" murmured Lucio with intense gravity.

"Ah yes! Yes indeed! And so—"

Here they passed into the dining-room and I could hear no more. I followed with my beautiful partner, and in another minute we were all seated at table.

XII

The dinner went on in the fashion of most dinners at great houses,—commencing with arctic stiffness and formality, thawing slightly towards the middle course, and attaining to just a pleasant warmth of mutual understanding when ices and dessert gave warning of its approaching close. Conversation at first flagged unaccountably, but afterwards brightened under Lucio's influence to a certain gaiety. I did my best to entertain Lady Sibyl, but found her like most 'society' beauties, somewhat of a vague listener. She was certainly cold, and in a manner irresponsive,—moreover I soon decided that she was not particularly clever. She had not the art of sustaining or appearing to sustain interest in any one subject; on the contrary, she had, like many of her class, an irritating habit of mentally drifting away from you into an absorbed reverie of her own in which you had no part, and which plainly showed you how little she cared for anything you or anyone else happened to be saying. Many little random remarks of hers however implied that in her apparently sweet nature there lurked a vein of cynicism and a certain contempt for men, and more than once her light words stung my sense of self-love almost to resentment, while they strengthened the force of my resolve to win her and bend that proud spirit of hers to the meekness befitting the wife of a millionaire and—a genius. A genius? Yes,—God help me!—that is what I judged myself to be. My arrogance was two-fold,—it arose not only from what I imagined to be my quality of brain, but also from the knowledge of what my wealth could do. I was perfectly positive that I could buy Fame,—buy it as easily as one buys a flower in the market,—and I was more than positive that I could buy love. In order to commence proving the truth of this, I threw out a 'feeler' towards my object.

"I believe," I said suddenly, addressing the Earl—"you used to live in Warwickshire at Willowsmere Court did you not?"

Lord Elton flushed an apoplectic red, and swallowed a gulp of champagne hastily.

"Yes-er-yes. I—er had the place for some time,—rather a bore to keep up,—wants quite an army of servants."

"Just so;" I replied with a nod of appreciative comprehension—"I presume it will require a considerable domestic retinue. I have arranged to purchase it."

Lady Sibyl's frigid composure was at last disturbed—she looked strangely agitated,—and the Earl stared till his eyes seemed likely to fall out of his head.

"You? *You* are going to buy Willowsmere?" he exclaimed.

"Yes. I have wired to my lawyers to settle the matter as quickly as possible"—and I glanced at Lucio whose steel-bright eyes were fixed on the Earl with curious intentness,—"I like Warwickshire,—and as I shall entertain a great deal I think the place will suit me perfectly."

There was a moment's silence. Miss Charlotte Fitzroy sighed deeply, and the lace bow on her severely parted hair trembled visibly. Diana Chesney looked up with inquisitive eyes and a little wondering smile.

"Sibyl was born at Willowsmere,"—said the Earl presently in rather a husky voice.

"A new charm is added to its possession by that knowledge,"—I said gently, bowing to Lady Sibyl as I spoke—"Have you many recollections of the place?"

"Indeed, indeed I have!" she answered with a touch of something like passion vibrating in her accents—"There is no corner of the world I love so well! I used to play on the lawns under the old oak-trees, and I always gathered the first violets and primroses that came out on the banks of the Avon. And when the hawthorn was in full flower I used to make believe that the park was fairyland and I the fairy queen—"

"As you were and are!" interposed Lucio suddenly.

She smiled and her eyes flashed,—then she went on more quietly—

"It was all very foolish, but I loved Willowsmere, and love it still. And I often saw in the fields on the other side of the river which did not belong to the estate, a little girl about my own age, playing all by herself and making long daisy-chains and buttercup balls,—a little girl with long fair curls and a sweet baby face. I wanted to know her and speak to her, but my nurse would never let me because she was supposed to be 'beneath' me." Lady Sibyl's lip curled scornfully at this recollection. "Yet she was well-born; she was the orphan child of a very distinguished scholar and gentleman, and had been adopted by the physician who attended her mother's deathbed, she having no living relatives left to take care of her. And she—that little fair-haired girl,—was Mavis Clare."

As this name was uttered, a sort of hush fell on our party as though an 'Angelus' had rung; and Lucio looking across at me with peculiar intentness asked,

"Have you never heard of Mavis Clare, Tempest?"

I thought a moment before replying. Yes,—I had heard the name,—connected with literature in some dim and distant way, but I could not remember when or how. For I never paid any attention to the names of women who chose to associate themselves with the Arts, as I had the usual masculine notion that all they did, whether in painting, music or writing, must of necessity be trash and unworthy of comment. Women, I loftily considered, were created to amuse men,—not to instruct them.

"Mavis Clare is a genius,"—Lady Sibyl said presently—"If Mr. Tempest has not heard of her, there is no doubt he *will* hear. I often regret that I never made her acquaintance in those old days at Willowsmere,—the stupidity of my nurse often rankles in my mind. 'Beneath me'—indeed!—and how very much she is above me now! She still lives down there,—her adopted parents are dead and she rents the lovely little house they inhabited. She has bought some extra land about it and improved the place wonderfully. Indeed I have never seen a more ideal poet's corner than Lily Cottage."

I was silent, feeling somewhat in the background on account of my ignorance as to the gifts and the position of the individual they all seemed to recognize as a celebrity of importance.

"Rather an odd name, Mavis, isn't it?"—I at last ventured to observe.

"Yes,—but it suits her wonderfully. She sings quite as sweetly as any thrush, so she merits her designation."

"What has she done in literature?" I continued.

"Oh,—only a novel!" replied Lucio with a smile—"But it has a quality unusual to novels; it lives! I hope, Tempest, that your forthcoming work will enjoy the same vitality."

Here Lord Elton who had been more or less brooding darkly over his glass of wine ever since I had mentioned my purchase of Willowsmere, roused himself from his reverie.

"Why, God bless my soul!" he exclaimed—"You don't mean to tell me you have written a novel Mr. Tempest?" (Was it possible he had never noticed all the prominent advertisements of my book in every paper, I thought indignantly!) "What do you want to do that for, with your immense position?"

"He hankers after fame!" said Lucio half kindly, half satirically.

"But you've got fame!" declared the Earl emphatically—"Everybody knows who you are by this time."

"Ah, my dear lord, that is not enough for the aspirations of my gifted friend"—responded Lucio, speaking for me, his eyes darkening with that mystic shadow of mingled sorrow and scorn which so frequently clouded their lustrous brilliancy; "He does not particularly care for the 'immense position' that is due to wealth alone, because that does not lift him a jot higher than Maple of Tottenham Court Road. He seeks to soar beyond the furniture man,—and who shall blame him? He would be known for that indescribable quality called Genius,—for high thoughts, poetry, divine instincts, and prophetic probings into the heart of humanity,—in short, for the power of the Pen, which topples down great kingdoms like card-houses and sticks foolscaps on the heads of kings. Generally it is the moneyless man or woman who is endowed with this unpurchaseable power,—this independence of action and indifference to opinion,—the wealthy seldom do anything but spend or hoard. But Tempest means to unite for once in his own person the two most strenuously opposed forces in nature,—genius and cash,—or in other words, God and Mammon."

Lady Sibyl turned her head towards me;—there was a look of doubt and wonder on her beautiful face.

"I am afraid,"—she said half smiling, "that the claims of society will take up too much of your time, Mr. Tempest, to allow you to continue the writing of books. I remember you told me the other evening that you were about to publish a novel. I suppose you were— originally I mean—an author by profession?"

A curious sense of anger burned dully within me. 'Originally' an author? Was I not one still? Was I to be given credit for nothing but my banking-book? 'Originally'? Why, I had never been an actual 'author' till now,—I had simply been a wandering literary hack,—a stray 'super' of Grub Street, occasionally engaged to write articles 'to order' on any subject that came uppermost, at a starvation rate of pay, without any visible prospect of rising from that lowest and dirtiest rung of the literary ladder. I felt myself growing red, then pale,—and I saw that Lucio was looking at me fixedly.

"I *am* an author, Lady Sibyl"—I said at last—"and I hope I may soon prove my right to be acknowledged as one. 'Author' is in my opinion, a prouder title than king, and I do not think any social claims will deter me from following the profession of literature, which I look upon as the highest in the world."

Lord Elton fidgetted uneasily in his chair.

"But your people"—he said—"Your family—are they literary?"

"No members of my family are now living,"—I answered somewhat stiffly—"My father was John Tempest of Rexmoor."

"Indeed!" and the Earl's face brightened considerably—"Dear me, dear me! I used to meet him often in the hunting field years ago. You come of a fine old stock, sir!—the Tempests of Rexmoor are well and honourably known in county chronicles."

I said nothing, feeling a trifle heated in temper, though I could not have quite explained why.

"One begins to wonder,"—said Lucio then in his soft smooth accents—"when one is the descendant of a good English county family,—a distinct cause for pride!—and moreover has the still more substantial fact of a large fortune to support that high lineage, why one should trouble to fight for merely literary honours! You are far too modest in your ambitions, Tempest!—high-seated as you are upon bank-notes and bullion, with all the glory of effulgent county chronicles behind you, you still stoop to clutch the laurel! Fie, my dear fellow! You degrade yourself by this desire to join the company of the immortals!"

His satirical tone was not lost upon the company; and I, who saw that in his own special way he was defending the claims of literature against those of mere place and money, felt soothed and grateful. The Earl looked a trifle annoyed.

"That's all very fine," he said—"But you see it isn't as if Mr. Tempest were driven by necessity to write for his living"—

"One may love work for the work's sake without any actual necessity for doing it,"—I interposed—"For example,—this Mavis Clare you speak of,—is she,—a woman,—driven by necessity?"

"Mavis Clare hasn't a penny in the world that she does not earn,"—said Lord Elton gruffly—"I suppose that if she did not write she would starve."

Diana Chesney laughed.

"I guess she's a long way off starvation just now,"—she remarked, her brown eyes twinkling—"Why, she's as proud as the proudest,—drives in the Park in her victoria and pair with the best in the land, and knows all the 'swagger' people. She's nowhere near Grub Street *I* should say. I hear she's a splendid business woman, and more than a match for the publishers all round."

"Well I should rather doubt that,"—said the Earl with a chuckle. "It needs the devil himself to match the publishers."

"You are right!"—said Lucio—"In fact I daresay that in the various 'phases' or transmigrations of the spirit into differing forms of earthy matter, the devil (should he exist at all) has frequently become a publisher,—and a particularly benevolent publisher too!—by way of diversion."

We all smiled.

"Well, I should imagine Mavis Clare to be a match for anybody or anything,"—said Lady Sibyl—"Of course she is not rich,—but she spends her money wisely and to effective advantage. I do not know her personally,—I wish I did; but I have read her books, which are quite out of the common. She is a most independent creature too; quite indifferent to opinions"—

"I suppose she must be extremely plain then"—I observed; "Plain women always try to do something more or less startling in order to attract the attention denied to their personality."

"True,—but that would not apply to Miss Clare. She is pretty, and knows how to dress besides."

"*Such* a virtue in literary women!" exclaimed Diana Chesney—"Some of them *are* such dowdies!"

"Most people of culture," went on Lady Sibyl—"in our set at any rate, are accustomed to look upon Miss Clare as quite an exception to the usual run of authors. She is charming in herself as well as in her books, and she goes everywhere. She writes with inspiration,—and always has something so new to say—"

"That of course all the critics are down upon her?" queried Lucio.

"Oh, naturally! But *we* never read reviews."

"Nor anyone else I should hope,"—said Lord Elton with a laugh—"except the fellows who write them, ha—ha—ha! I call it damned impertinence—excuse the word—on the part of a newspaper hack to presume to teach *me* what I ought to read, or what I ought to appreciate. I'm quite capable of forming my own judgment on any book that ever was written. But I avoid all the confounded 'new' poets,—avoid 'em like poison, sir—ha—ha! Anything but a 'new' poet; the old ones are good enough for me! Why sir, these reviewers who give themselves such airs with a pennorth of ink and a pen, are mostly half-grown half-educated boys who for a couple of guineas a week undertake to tell the public what *they* think of such and such a book, as if anyone cared a jot about their green opinions! Ridiculous—quite ridiculous!—what do they take the public for I wonder! Editors of responsible journals ought to know better than to employ such young coxcombs just because they can get them cheap—"

At this juncture the butler came up behind his master's chair and whispered a few words. The Earl's brow clouded,—then he addressed his sister-in-law,—

"Charlotte, Lady Elton sends word that she will come into the drawing-room to-night. Perhaps you had better go and see that she is made comfortable." And, as Miss Charlotte rose, he turned to us saying—"My wife is seldom well enough to see visitors, but this evening she feels inclined for a little change and distraction from the monotony of her sick-room. It will be very kind of you two gentlemen to entertain her,—she cannot speak much, but her hearing and sight are excellent, and she takes great interest in all that is going on. Dear dear me!" and he heaved a short troubled sigh—"She used to be one of the brightest of women!"

"The sweet Countess!" murmured Miss Chesney with patronizing tenderness—"She is quite lovely still!"

Lady Sibyl glanced at her with a sudden haughty frown which showed me plainly what a rebellious temper the young beauty held in control; and I fell straightway more in love,—according to *my* idea of love,—than ever. I confess I like a woman to have a certain amount of temper. I cannot endure your preternaturally amiable female who can find nothing in all the length or breadth of the globe to move her to any other expression than a fatuous smile. I love to see the danger-flash in bright eyes,—the delicate quiver of pride in the lines of a lovely mouth, and the warm flush of indignation on fair cheeks. It all suggests spirit, and untamed will; and rouses in a man the love of mastery that is born in his nature, urging him to conquer and subdue that which seems unconquerable. And all the desire of such conquest was strong within me, when at the close of dinner I rose and held the door open for the ladies to pass out of the room. As the fair Sibyl went, the violets she wore at her bosom dropped. I picked them up and made my first move.

"May I keep these?" I said in a low tone.

Her breath came and went quickly,—but she looked straight in my eyes with a smile that perfectly comprehended my hidden meaning.

"You may!" she answered.

I bowed,—closed the door behind her, and secreting the flowers, returned, well-satisfied, to my place at table.

MARIE CORELLI

XIII

L eft with myself and Lucio, Lord Elton threw off all reserve, and became not only familiar, but fawning in his adulation of us both. An abject and pitiable desire to please and propitiate us expressed itself in his every look and word; and I firmly believe that if I had coolly and brutally offered to buy his fair daughter by private treaty for a hundred thousand pounds, that sum to be paid down to him on the day of marriage, he would have gladly agreed to sell. Apart however from his personal covetousness, I felt and knew that my projected courtship of Lady Sibyl would of necessity resolve itself into something more or less of a market bargain, unless indeed I could win the girl's love. I meant to try and do this, but I fully realized how difficult, nay, almost impossible it would be for her to forget the fact of my unhampered and vast fortune, and consider me for myself alone. Herein is one of the blessings of poverty which the poor are frequently too apt to forget. A moneyless man if he wins a woman's love knows that such love is genuine and untainted by self-interest; but a rich man can never be truly certain of love at all. The advantages of a wealthy match are constantly urged upon all marriageable girls by both their parents and friends,— and it would have to be a very unsophisticated feminine nature indeed that could contemplate a husband possessing five millions of money, without a touch of purely interested satisfaction. A very wealthy man can never be sure even of friendship,—while the highest, strongest and noblest kind of love is nearly always denied to him, in this way carrying out the fulfilment of those strange but true words—"How hardly shall he that is a rich man, enter the Kingdom of Heaven!" The heaven of a woman's love, tried and proved true through disaster and difficulty,— of her unflinching faithfulness and devotion in days of toil and bitter anguish,—of her heroic self-abnegation, sweetness and courage through the darkest hours of doubt and disappointment;—this bright and splendid side of woman's character is reserved by Divine ordinance for the poor man. The millionaire can indeed wed whomsoever he pleases among all the beauties of the world,—he can deck his wife in gorgeous apparel, load her with jewels and look upon her in all the radiance of her richly adorned loveliness as one may look upon a perfect statue or matchless picture,—but he can never reach the deeper secrets of her soul or probe the well-springs of her finer nature. I thought this even thus early in the beginning of my admiration for Lady Sibyl Elton, though I did not then dwell upon it as I have often done since. I was too elated with the pride of wealth to count the possibilities of subtle losses amid so many solid gains; and I enjoyed to the full and with a somewhat contemptuous malice the humble prostration of a 'belted Earl' before the dazzling mine of practically unlimited cash as represented to him in the persons of my brilliant comrade and myself. I took a curious sort of pleasure in patronizing him, and addressed him with a protecting air of indulgent kindness whereat he seemed gratified. Inwardly I laughed as I thought how differently matters would have stood, supposing I had been indeed no more than 'author'! I might have proved to be one of the greatest writers of the age, but if, with that, I had been poor or only moderately well off, this same half bankrupt Earl who privately boarded an American heiress for two thousand guineas a year, would have deemed it a 'condescension' to so much as invite me to his house,—would have looked down upon me from his titled nothingness and perhaps carelessly alluded to me as 'a man who writes—er—yes—er—rather clever I believe!' and then would have thought no more about me. For this very cause as 'author' still, though millionaire, I took a fantastic pleasure in humiliating his lordship as much as possible, and I found the best way to do this was to talk about Willowsmere. I saw that he winced at the very name of his lost estate, and that notwithstanding this, he could not avoid showing his anxiety as to my intentions with regard to its occupation. Lucio, whose wisdom and foresight had suggested my becoming the purchaser of the place, assisted me in the most adroit fashion to draw him out and to make his character manifest, and by the time we had finished our cigars and coffee I knew that the 'proud' Earl of Elton, who could trace his lineage to the earliest days of the Crusaders, was as ready to bend his back and crawl in the dust for money as the veriest hotel-porter expectant of a sovereign 'tip.' I had never entertained a high opinion of the aristocracy, and on this occasion it was certainly not improved, but remembering that the spendthrift nobleman beside me was the father of Lady Sibyl, I treated him on the whole with more respect than his mean and grasping nature deserved.

On returning to the drawing-room after dinner I was struck by the chill weirdness that seemed to be imparted to it by the addition of Lady Elton's couch, which, placed near the fire, suggested a black sarcophagus in bulk and outline. It was practically a narrow bed on wheels, though partially disguised by a silk coverlet draped skilfully so as to somewhat hide its coffin-like shape. The extended figure of the paralysed Countess herself presented a death-like rigidity; but her face as she turned it towards us on our entrance, was undisfigured as yet and distinctly handsome, her eyes especially being large, clear, and almost brilliant. Her daughter introduced us both in a low tone, and she moved her head slightly by way of acknowledgment, studying us curiously the while.

"Well, my dear"—said Lord Elton briskly, "This is an unexpected pleasure! It is nearly three months since you honoured us with your company. How do you feel?"

"Better," she replied slowly, yet distinctly, her gaze now fixed with wondering intentness on Prince Rimânez.

"Mother found the room rather cold"—explained Lady Sibyl—"So we brought her as near to the fire as possible. It *is* cold"—and she shivered—"I fancy it must be freezing hard."

"Where is Diana?" asked the Earl, looking about in search of that lively young lady.

"Miss Chesney has gone to her own room to write a letter;" replied his daughter somewhat frigidly—"She will be back directly."

At this moment Lady Elton feebly raised her hand and pointed to Lucio, who had moved aside to answer some question asked of him by Miss Charlotte.

"Who is that?" she murmured.

"Why, mother dear, I told you"—said Lady Sibyl gently—"That is Prince Lucio Rimânez, Papa's great friend."

The Countess's pallid hand still remained lifted, as though it were frozen in air.

"*What* is he?" the slow voice again inquired,—and then the hand dropped suddenly like a dead thing.

"Now Helena, you must not excite yourself"—said her husband, bending over her couch with real or assumed anxiety; "Surely you remember all I have told you about the prince? And also about this gentleman, Mr. Geoffrey Tempest?"

She nodded, and her eyes, turning reluctantly away from Rimânez, regarded me fixedly.

"You are a very young man to be a millionaire,"—were her next words, uttered with evident difficulty—"Are you married?"

I smiled, and answered in the negative. Her looks wandered from me to her daughter's face,—then back to me again with a singularly intent expression. Finally, the potent magnetism of Lucio's presence again attracted her, and she indicated him by a gesture.

"Ask your friend. . . to come here. . . and speak to me."

Rimânez turned instinctively at her request, and with his own peculiar charm and gallant grace of bearing, came to the side of the paralysed lady, and taking her hand, kissed it.

"Your face seems familiar to me,"—she said, speaking now, as it seemed, with greater ease—"Have I ever met you before?"

"Dear lady, you may have done so"—he replied in dulcet tones and with a most captivating gentleness of manner—"It occurs to me, now I think of it, that years ago, I saw once, as a passing vision of loveliness, in the hey-day of youth and happiness, Helena Fitzroy, before she was Countess of Elton."

"You must have been a mere boy—a child,—at that time!" she murmured faintly smiling.

"Not so!—for you are still young, Madame, and I am old. You look incredulous? Alas, why is it I wonder, I may not look the age I am! Most of my acquaintances spend a great part of their lives in trying to look the age they are not; and I never came across a man of fifty who was not proud to be considered thirty-nine. My desires are more laudable,—yet honourable eld refuses to impress itself upon my features. It is quite a sore point with me I assure you."

"Well, how old are you really?" asked Lady Sibyl smiling at him.

"Ah, I dare not tell you!" he answered, returning the smile; "But I ought to explain that in my countings I judge age by the workings of thought and feeling, more than by the passing of years. Thus it should not surprise you to hear that I feel myself old,—old as the world!"

"But there are scientists who say that the world is young;" I observed, "And that it is only now beginning to feel its forces and put forth its vigour."

"Such optimistic wise-acres are wrong," he answered,—"The world is a veritable husk of a planet; humanity has nearly completed all its allotted phases, and the end is near."

"The end?" echoed Lady Sibyl,—"Do you believe the world will ever come to an end?"

"I do, most certainly. Or, to be more correct, it will not actually perish, but will simply change. And the change will not agree with the constitution of its present inhabitants. They will call the transformation the Day of Judgment. I should imagine it would be a fine sight."

The Countess gazed at him wonderingly,—Lady Sibyl seemed amused.

"I would rather not witness it,"—said Lord Elton gruffly.

"Oh, why?" and Rimânez looked about with quite a cheerful air— "A final glimpse of the planet ere we *a*scend or *de*scend to our future homes elsewhere, would be something to remember! Madame"—here he addressed Lady Elton; "are you fond of music?"

The invalid smiled gratefully, and bent her head in acquiescence. Miss Chesney had just entered the room and heard the question.

"Do you play?" she exclaimed vivaciously, touching him on the arm with her fan.

He bowed. "I do. In an erratic sort of fashion. I also sing. Music has always been one of my passions. When I was very young,—ages ago,—I used to imagine I could hear the angel Israfel chanting his strophes amid the golden glow of heavenly glory,—himself white-winged and wonderful, with a voice out-ringing beyond the verge of paradise!"

As he spoke, a sudden silence fell upon us all. Something in his accent touched my heart to a strange sense of sorrow and yearning, and the Countess of Elton's dark eyes, languid with long suffering, grew soft as though with repressed tears.

"Sometimes," he continued more lightly—"just at odd moments—I like to believe in Paradise. It is a relief, even to a hardened sinner like myself, to fancy that there *may* exist something in the way of a world better than this one."

"Surely sir," said Miss Charlotte Fitzroy severely—"you believe in Heaven?"

He looked at her and smiled slightly.

"Madame, forgive me! I do not believe in the clerical heaven. I know you will be angry with me for this frank confession! But I cannot picture the angels in white smocks with goose wings, or the Deity as a somewhat excitable personage with a beard. Personally I should decline to go to any heaven which was only a city with golden streets; and I should object to a sea of glass, resenting it as a want of invention on the part of the creative Intelligence. But—do not frown, dear Miss Fitzroy!—I do believe in Heaven all the same,—a different kind of heaven,—I often see it in my dreams!"

He paused, and again we were all silent, gazing at him. Lady Sibyl's eyes indeed, rested upon him with such absorbed interest, that I became somewhat irritated, and was glad, when turning towards the Countess once more, he said quietly.

"Shall I give you some music now, Madame?"

She murmured assent, and followed him with a vaguely uneasy glance as he crossed over to the grand piano and sat down. I had never heard him either play or sing; in fact so far as his accomplishments went, I knew nothing of him as yet except that he was a perfect master of the art of horsemanship. With the first few bars he struck I half started from my chair in amazement;—could a mere pianoforte produce such sounds?—or was there some witchery hidden in the commonplace instrument, unguessed by any other performer? I stared around me, bewildered,—I saw Miss Charlotte drop her knitting abstractedly,—Diana Chesney, lying lazily back in one corner of the sofa, half closed her eyelids in dreamy ecstasy,—Lord Elton stood near the fire resting one arm on the mantelpiece and shading his fuzzy brows with his hand,—and Lady Sibyl sat beside her mother, her lovely face pale with emotion, while on the worn features of the invalided lady there was an expression of mingled pain and pleasure difficult to describe. The music swelled into passionate cadence,—melodies crossed and re-crossed each other like rays of light glittering among green leaves,—voices of birds and streams and tossing waterfalls chimed in with songs of love and playful merriment;—anon came wilder strains of grief and angry clamour; cries of despair were heard echoing through the thunderous noise of some relentless storm,—farewells everlastingly shrieked amid sobs of reluctant shuddering agony;—and then, as I listened, before my eyes a black mist gathered slowly, and I thought I saw great rocks bursting asunder into flame, and drifting islands in a sea of fire,—faces, wonderful, hideous, beautiful, peered at me out of a darkness denser than night, and in the midst of this there came a tune, complete in sweetness and suggestion,—a piercing sword-like tune that plunged into my very heart and rankled there,—my breath failed me,—my senses swam,—I felt that I must move, speak, cry out, and implore that this music, this horribly insidious music should cease ere I swooned with the voluptuous poison of it,—when, with a full chord of splendid harmony that rolled out upon the air like a breaking wave, the intoxicating sounds ebbed away into silence. No one spoke,—our hearts were yet beating too wildly with the pulsations roused by that wondrous lyric storm. Diana Chesney was the first to break the spell.

MARIE CORELLI

"Well, that beats everything I've ever heard!" she murmured tremulously.

I could say nothing,—I was too occupied with my own thoughts. Something in the music had instilled itself into my blood, or so I fancied, and the clinging subtle sweetness of it, moved me to strange emotions that were neither wise, nor worthy of a man. I looked at Lady Sibyl; she was very pale,—her eyes were cast down and her hands were trembling. On a sudden impulse I rose and went to Rimânez where he still sat at the piano, his hands dumbly wandering over the keys.

"You are a great master"—I said—"A wonderful performer! But do you know what your music suggests?"

He met my fixed gaze, shrugged his shoulders, and shook his head.

"Crime!" I whispered—"You have roused in me evil thoughts of which I am ashamed. I did not think that was possible to so divine an Art."

He smiled, and his eyes glittered with the steely brightness of stars on a wintry night.

"Art takes its colours from the mind, my dear friend;"—he said—"If you discover evil suggestions in my music, the evil, I fear, must be in your own nature."

"Or in yours!" I said quickly.

"Or in mine;"—he agreed coldly—"I have often told you I am no saint."

I stood hesitatingly, looking at him. For one moment his great personal beauty appeared hateful to me, though I knew not why. Then the feeling of distrust and repulsion slowly passed, leaving me humiliated and abashed.

"Pardon me, Lucio!" I murmured regretfully—"I spoke in haste; but truly your music almost put me in a state of frenzy,—I never heard anything in the least like it—"

"Nor I,"—said Lady Sibyl, who just then moved towards the piano—"It was marvellous! Do you know, it quite frightened me?"

"I am sorry!" he answered with a penitent air—"I know I am quite a failure as a pianist—I am not sufficiently 'restrained,' as the press men would say."

"A failure? Good God!" exclaimed Lord Elton at this juncture—"Why, if you played like that in public, you'd drive everyone frantic!"

"With alarm?" queried Lucio, laughing—"Or with disgust?"

"Nonsense! you know what I mean very well. I have always had a contempt for the piano as an instrument, but by Jove! I never heard such music as yours even in a full orchestra. It is extraordinary!—it is positively magnificent! Where in the world did you study?"

"In Nature's conservatoire;"—replied Rimânez lazily. "My first 'maestro' was an amiable nightingale. He, singing on a branch of fir when the moon was full, explained with liquid-noted patience, how to construct and produce a pure roulade, cadenza and trill,—and when I had learned thus far, he showed me all the most elaborate methods of applying rhythmic tune to the upward and downward rush of the wind, thus supplying me with perfect counterpoint. Chords I learned from old Neptune, who was good enough to toss a few of his largest billows to the shore for my special benefit. He nearly deafened me with his instructions, being somewhat excitable and loud-voiced,—but on finding me an apt pupil, he drew back his waves to himself with so much delicacy among the pebbles and sand, that at once I mastered the secret of playing *arpeggi*. Once too I had a finishing lesson from a Dream,—a mystic thing with wild hair and wings—it sang one word in my ears, and the word was unpronounceable in mortal speech,—but after many efforts I discovered it lurking in the scale of sound. The best part of it all was, that my instructors asked no fees!"

"I think you are a poet as well as a musician,"—said Lady Sibyl.

"A poet! Spare me!—my dear young lady, why are you so cruel as to load me with so vile an imputation! Better be a murderer than a poet,—one is treated with much more respect and courteous consideration,—by the press at anyrate. The murderer's breakfast-menu will be given due place in many of the most estimable journals,—but the poet's lack of both breakfast and dinner will be deemed his fitting reward. Call me a live-stock producer, a horse-breeder, a timber-merchant,—anything but a poet! Why even Tennyson became an amateur milkman to somewhat conceal and excuse the shame and degradation of writing verse!"

We all laughed.

"Well, you must admit," said Lord Elton, "that we've had rather too much of poets lately. It's no wonder we're sick of them, and that poetry has fallen into disrepute. Poets are such a quarrelsome lot too—effeminate, puling, unmanly humbugs!"

"You are speaking of the newly 'discovered' ones of course," said Lucio—"Yes, they are a weedy collection. I have sometimes thought that out of pure philanthropy I would start a bon-bon manufactory, and employ them to write mottoes for the crackers. It would keep them out of mischief and provide them with a little pocket-money, for as matters stand they do not make a farthing by their books. But I do not call them 'poets' at all,—they are mere rhymers. One or two real poets do exist, but, like the prophets of Scripture, they are not 'in society,' nor can they get their logs rolled by any of their contemporaries. They are not favourites with any 'set'; that is why I am afraid my dear friend Tempest will never be accepted as the genius he is; society will be too fond of him to let him go down into dust and ashes to gather the laurel."

"It is not necessary to go down into dust and ashes for that," I said.

"I assure you it is!—" he answered gaily—"Positively imperative. The laurel flourishes best so,—it will not grow in a hot-house."

At that moment Diana Chesney approached.

"Lady Elton would like to hear you sing, prince—" she said—"Will you give us that pleasure? Do! Something quite simple, you know,—it will set our nerves straight after your terribly beautiful music! You'd hardly believe it perhaps, —but I really feel quite unstrung!"

He folded his hands with a droll air of penitence.

"Forgive me!" he said, "I'm always, as the church service says, doing those things I ought not to do."

Miss Chesney laughed, a trifle nervously.

"Oh, I forgive you!" she replied—"On condition that you sing."

"I obey!" and with that he turned again to the piano, and playing a strange wild minor accompaniment sang the following stanzas:

Sleep, my Belovëd, sleep!
Be patient!—we shall keep
Our secret closely hid
Beneath the coffin-lid,—
There is no other place in earth or air
For such a love as ours, or such despair!
And neither hell nor heaven shall care to win
Our loathëd souls, rejoicing in their sin!

Sleep!—for my hand is sure,—
The cold steel bright and pure
Strikes through thy heart and mine
Shedding our blood like wine;—

Sin's sweetness is too sweet, and if the shame
Of love must be our curse, we hurl the blame
Back on the gods who gave us love with breath
And tortured us from passion into death!

This strange song, sung in the most glorious of baritones, full and rich, and vibrating with power and sweetness, had a visibly thrilling effect upon us all. Again we were struck dumb with surprise and something like fear,—and again Diana Chesney broke the silence.

"You call that simple!" she said, half petulantly.

"Quite so. Love and Death are the simplest things in the world"— replied Lucio.—"The ballad is a mere trifle,—it is entitled 'The Last Love-Song' and is supposed to be the utterance of a lover about to kill his mistress and himself. Such events happen every day,—you know that by the newspapers,—they are perfectly common-place—"

He was interrupted by a sharp clear voice ringing imperatively across the room—

"Where did you learn that song?"

XIV

It was the paralysed Countess who spoke. She had managed to partly raise herself on her couch, and her face expressed positive terror. Her husband hurried to her side,—and, with a curiously cynical smile on his lips, Rimânez rose from the piano. Miss Charlotte, who had sat rigidly upright and silent for some time, hastened to attend upon her sister, but Lady Elton was singularly excited, and appeared to have gained a sudden access of unnatural vigour.

"Go away,—I'm not ill,"—she said impatiently—"I feel better,—much better than I have done for months. The music does me good." And addressing her husband, she added—"Ask your friend to come and sit here by me,—I want to talk to him. He has a magnificent voice,—and—I know that song he sang,—I remember reading it—in a manuscript album—long ago. I want to know where he found it—"

Rimânez here advanced with his gentle tread and courteous bearing, and Lord Elton gave him a chair beside the invalid.

"You are working miracles on my wife,"—he said—"I have not seen her so animated for years."

And leaving the two to talk, he crossed over to where Lady Sibyl, myself and Miss Chesney were all seated in a group, chatting more or less unrestrainedly.

"I have just been expressing the hope that you and your daughter will pay me a visit at Willowsmere, Lord Elton," I said.

His brows contracted a little, but he forced a smile. "We shall be delighted,"—he mumbled—"when do you take possession?"

"As soon as it is at all feasible"—I replied—"I shall wait in town till the next Levée is over, as both my friend and myself have arranged to be presented."

"Oh—ah—yes!—er—yes! That is always advisable. And it's not half such a troublesome business as a Drawing-room is for the ladies. It's soon over,—and low bodices are not *de rigeur*—ha—ha—ha! Who is your presenter?"

I named a distinguished personage, closely connected with the Court, and the Earl nodded.

"A very good man,—you could not have a better"—he said complacently—"And this book of yours,—when does it come out?"

"Next week."

"We must get it,—we must certainly get it,"—said Lord Elton, assuming interest,—"Sybil, you must put it down on your library list."

She assented, though, as I thought a trifle indifferently.

"On the contrary you must allow me to present it to you;" I said—"It will be a pleasure to me which I hope you will not deny."

"You are very kind,"—she answered, lifting her beautiful eyes to mine as she spoke—"But the librarian at Mudie's is sure to send it—he knows I read everything. Though I confess I never buy any books except those by Mavis Clare."

Again that woman's name! I felt annoyed, but took care not to show my annoyance.

"I shall be jealous of Mavis Clare," I said playfully.

"Most men are!" she replied quietly.

"You are indeed an enthusiastic partisan of hers!" I exclaimed, somewhat surprised.

"Yes, I suppose I am. I like to see any member of my sex distinguish herself as nobly as she does. I have no genius of my own, and that is one of the reasons why I honour it so much in other women."

I was about to make some suitable compliment by way of response to this remark, when we were all violently startled from our seats by a most horrible cry,—a gasping scream such as might be wrung from some tortured animal. Aghast at the sound we stood for a moment inert, staring at Rimânez, who came quickly towards us with an air of grave concern.

"I am afraid," he said softly—"that the Countess is not so well,—perhaps you had better go to her—"

Another shriek interrupted his words, and transfixed with horror we saw Lady Elton struggling in the throes of some sudden and terrific convulsion, her hands beating the air as if she were fighting with an unseen enemy. In one second her face underwent such hideous contortions as robbed it of all human semblance, and between the agonized pantings of her difficult breath, her half-choked voice could be heard uttering wild cries—

"Mercy!—mercy!—oh God—God! Tell Sibyl!—pray—pray to God,—pray—"

And with that she fell heavily back, speechless and unconscious.

All was instant confusion. Lady Sibyl rushed to her mother's side, with Miss Charlotte,—Diana Chesney hung back trembling and afraid,—Lord Elton sprang to the bell and rang it furiously.

"Fetch the doctor!" he cried to the startled servant—"Lady Elton has had another shock! She must be taken to her room at once!"

"Can I be of any service?" I inquired, with a side-glance at Rimânez, who stood gravely apart, a statuesquely composed figure of silence.

"No no,—thanks all the same!" and the Earl pressed my hand gratefully—"She should not have come downstairs,—it has been too exciting for her. Sybil, don't look at her, my dear—it will only unnerve you,—Miss Chesney, pray go to your room,—Charlotte can do all that is possible—"

As he spoke two of the men-servants came in to carry the insensible Countess upstairs,—and as they slowly bore her on her coffin-like couch past me, one of them drew the coverlet across her face to conceal it. But not so quickly that I could not see the awful change impressed upon it,—the indelible horror that was stamped on the drawn features,—horror such as surely never was seen except in a painter's idea of some lost soul in torment. The eyes were rolled up and fixed in their sockets like balls of glass, and in them also was frozen the same frenzied desperate look of fear. It was a dreadful face!—so dreadful in its ghastly immovableness that I was all at once reminded of my hideous vision of the previous night, and the pallid countenances of the three phantoms that had scared me in my sleep. Lady Elton's looks now resembled theirs! Sickened and appalled I averted my eyes, and was glad to see Rimânez taking farewell of his host, the while he expressed his regret and sympathy with him in his domestic affliction. I myself, approaching Lady Sibyl, pressed her cold and trembling hand in mine, and respectfully kissed it.

"I am deeply sorry!" I murmured—"I wish I could do anything to console you!"

She looked at me with dry calm eyes.

"Thank-you. But the doctors have always said that my mother would have another shock depriving her of speech. It is very sad; she will probably live for some years like that."

I again expressed my sympathy.

"May I come and inquire about you all to-morrow?" I asked.

"It will be very kind of you,"—she answered quietly.

"Shall I see you if I come?" I said in a lower tone.

"If you wish it,—certainly!"

Our eyes met; and I knew by instinct that she read my thoughts. I pressed her hand again and was not repulsed,—then bowing profoundly,

I left her to make my adieux to Lord Elton and Miss Chesney, who seemed terribly upset and frightened. Miss Charlotte Fitzroy had left the room in attendance on her sister, and she did not return to bid us good-night. Rimânez lingered a moment behind me to say another word or two to the Earl, and when he joined me in the hall and threw on his opera-coat, he was smiling to himself somewhat singularly.

"An unpleasant end for Helena, Countess of Elton"—he said, when we were in our brougham, driving away—"Paralysis is perhaps the worst of all the physical punishments that can befall a 'rapid' lady."

"Was she 'rapid'?"

"Well,—perhaps 'rapid' is too mild a term, but I can find no other;"—he answered—"When she was young,—she is barely fifty now,—she did everything that could be done by woman at her worst and wildest. She had scores of lovers,—and I believe one of them cleared off her husband's turf-debts,—the Earl consenting gladly,—on a rather pressing occasion."

"What disgraceful conduct!" I exclaimed.

He looked at me with an expression of cynical amusement.

"Think so? The 'upper ten' quite condone that sort of thing in their own set now-a-days. It is all right. If a lady has lovers, and her husband beams benevolence on the situation what can be said? Nothing. How very tender your conscience is, Geoffrey!"

I sat silent, thinking. My companion lit a cigarette and offered me one. I took it mechanically without lighting it.

"I made a mistake this evening,"—he went on—"I should not have sung that 'Last Love-song.' The fact is, the words were written by one of her ladyship's former admirers, a man who was something of a poet in his way,—and she had an idea that she was the only person living who had ever seen the lines. She wanted to know if I knew the man who composed them, and I was able to say that I did—very intimately. I was just explaining how it was, and why I knew him so well, when the distressing attack of convulsions came on, and finished our conversation."

"She looked horrible!" I said.

"The paralysed Helen of a modern Troy? Yes,—her countenance at the last was certainly not attractive. Beauty combined with wantonness frequently ends in the drawn twitch, fixed eye and helpless limbs of life-in-death. It is Nature's revenge on the outraged body,—and do you know, Eternity's revenge on the impure Soul is extremely similar?"

"What do you know about it?" I said, smiling in spite of myself as I looked at his fine face, expressive of perfect health and splendid intellectuality—"Your absurd fancies about the soul are the only traces of folly I discover in you."

"Really? Well I am glad I have something of the fool in my disposition,—foolishness being the only quality that makes wisdom possible. I confess I have odd, very odd notions about the soul."

"I will excuse them—" I said, laughing—God forgive me, in my own insensate blind conceit,—the while he regarded me fixedly—"In fact I will excuse anything for the sake of your voice. I do not flatter you, Lucio,—you sing like an angel."

"Don't use impossible comparisons;"—he replied—"Have you ever heard an angel sing?"

"Yes!" I answered smiling—"I have,—this very night!"

He turned deadly pale.

"A very open compliment!" he said, forcing a laugh,—and with almost rough haste, he suddenly let down the window of the carriage though the night was bitter cold—"This vehicle is suffocating me,—let us have some air. See how the stars are shining!—like great crown jewels—Deity's regalia! Hard frost, like hard times, brings noble works into prominence. Yonder, far off, is a star you can hardly perceive; red as a cinder at times and again blue as the lightning,—I can always discover it, though many cannot. It is Algol,—judged by superstitious folk to be an evil star. I love it chiefly on account of its bad reputation,—it is no doubt much maligned. It may be a cold quarter of hell where weeping spirits sit frozen in ice made of their own congealed tears,—or it may be a preparatory school for Heaven—who knows! Yonder too, shines Venus,—your star Geoffrey!—for you are in love my friend!—come confess it! are you not?"

"I am not sure;"—I answered slowly—"The phrase 'in love' scarcely describes my present feeling. . ."

"You have dropped these,"—he said suddenly, picking up a fast fading knot of violets from the floor of the brougham and holding them towards me. He smiled, as I uttered an exclamation of annoyance. They were Lady Sibyl's flowers which I had inadvertently let fall, and I saw he knew it. I took them from his hand in silence.

"My dear fellow, do not try to hide your intentions from your best friend,"—he said seriously and kindly—"You wish to marry the Earl of Elton's beautiful daughter, and you shall. Trust me!—I will do everything I can to promote your desire."

"You will?" I exclaimed with unconcealed delight, for I fully recognised the influence he had over Sibyl's father.

"I will, I promise—" he answered gravely—"I assure you that such a marriage would be one after my own heart. I'll do all I can for you,—and I have made many matches in my time!"

My heart beat high with triumph,—and when we parted that night I wrung his hand fervently and told him I was devoutly grateful to the fates for sending me such a good friend as he was.

"Grateful to—whom did you say?" he asked with a whimsical look.

"To the Fates!"

"Are you really? They are very ugly sisters I believe. Perhaps they were your ghostly visitors of last night!"

"God forbid!" I exclaimed.

"Ah! God never forbids the fulfilment of His own laws!" he answered—"To do so He would have to destroy Himself."

"If He exists at all!" I said carelessly.

"True! If—!"

And with this, we separated to our different quarters in the 'Grand.'

XV

After that evening I became a regular and welcome visitor at Lord Elton's house, and was soon on terms of the most friendly intimacy with all the members of his family, including even the severely pious Miss Charlotte Fitzroy. It was not difficult for me to see that my matrimonial aspirations were suspected,—and though the encouragement I received from Lady Sibyl herself was so slight as to make me doubtful whether after all my hopes of winning her would ever be realized, the Earl made no secret of his delight at the idea of securing me as a son-in-law. Such wealth as mine was not to be met with every day,—and even had I been a blackleg of the turf or a retired jockey, instead of an 'author,' I should, with five millions at my back, have been considered quite as desirable a suitor for the Lady Sibyl's hand. Rimânez scarcely ever went with me to the Eltons' now, pleading as excuse much pressing business and many social engagements. I was not altogether sorry for this. Greatly as I admired and honoured him, his extraordinary physical beauty and fascination of manner were in dangerous contrast to my merely 'ordinary good-looking' personality, and it seemed to me impossible that any woman, seeing much of him, could be expected to give me the preference. All the same I had no fear that he would ever voluntarily become my rival,—his antipathy to women was too deep-rooted and sincere for that. On this point indeed his feelings were so strong and passionate that I often wondered why the society sirens who eagerly courted his attention remained so blind and unconscious to the chill cynicism that lurked beneath his seeming courtesy,—the cutting satire that was coupled with apparent compliment, and the intensity of hatred that flamed under the assumed expression of admiring homage in his flashing eyes. However it was not my business to point out to those who could not, or would not, see the endless peculiarities of my friend's variable disposition. I did not pay much heed to them even so far as I myself was concerned, for I had grown accustomed to the quick changes he was wont to ring on all the gamut of human feeling, and absorbed in my own life-schemes I did not trouble myself to intimately study the man who had in a couple of months become my *fidus Achates*. I was engrossed at the moment in doing all I could to increase the Earl of Elton's appreciative sense of my value as a man and a millionaire, and to this end I paid some of his pressing debts, lent him a large sum of money without demanding interest or promise of repayment, and stocked his cellar with presents of such rare old wines as he had not been able to afford to purchase for himself for many years. Thus was confidence easily engendered between us, even to that point of affection which displayed itself in his lordship's readiness to thrust his arm through mine when we sauntered together down Piccadilly, and his calling me 'my dear boy' in public. Never shall I forget the bewildered amazement of the scrubby little editor of a sixpenny magazine who met me face to face thus accompanied in the Park one morning! That he knew the Earl of Elton by sight was evident, and that he also knew me his apoplectic stare confessed. He had pompously refused to even read any of my offered contributions on the ground that I had 'no name,'—and now—! he would have given a month's salary if I had but condescended to recognize him! I did not so condescend,—but passed him by, listening to, and laughing with my intended future father-in-law, who was retailing an extremely ancient joke for my benefit. The incident was slight, even trumpery,—yet it put me in a good humour, for one of the chiefest pleasures I had out of my wealth was the ability to repay with vengeful interest all the contempt and insult that had beaten me back from every chance of earning a livelihood while I was poor.

In all my visits to the Eltons, I never saw the paralysed Countess again. Since the last terrible visitation of her dread disease, she had not moved. She merely lived and breathed—no more. Lord Elton told me that the worst part of her illness at present, so far as it affected those who had to attend upon her, was the particularly hideous alteration of her face.

"The fact is," he said, not without a shudder—"she's dreadful to look at,—positively dreadful!—no longer human, you know. She used to be a lovely woman,—now she is literally frightful. Her eyes especially;—they are as scared and wild as if she had seen the devil. Quite an awful expression I assure you!—and it never alters. The doctors can do nothing—and of course it's very trying for Sibyl, and everybody."

I assented sympathetically; and realising that a house holding such a figure of living death within it must of necessity be more or less gloomy and depressing to a young and vigorous nature, I lost no opportunity of giving Lady Sibyl whatever slight pleasures were in my power to procure, for her distraction and entertainment. Costly flowers, boxes for the opera and 'first nights' at the play,—every sort of attention that a man can pay to a woman without being considered officious or intrusive I offered, and was not repulsed. Everything progressed well and favourably towards the easy attainment of my wishes,—I had no difficulties, no troubles of any kind,—and I voluntarily led a life of selfishly absorbed personal gratification, being commended and encouraged therein by a whole host of flatterers and interested acquaintances. Willowsmere Court was mine, and every newspaper in the kingdom had commented on the purchase, in either servile or spiteful paragraphs. My lawyers had warmly congratulated me on the possession of so admirable a property which they, in strict accordance with what they conceived to be their duty, had personally inspected and approved. The place was now in the hands of a firm of decorators and furnishers, recommended by Rimânez, and it was expected to be in perfect order for my habitation in early summer, at which time I purposed entertaining a large house-party of more or less distinguished people.

Meantime, what I had once considered would be the great event of my life, took place,—namely the publication of my book. Trumpeted forth by the most heraldic advertisements, it was at last launched on the uncertain and fluctuating tide of public favour, and special 'advance' copies were sent to the office of every magazine and journal in London. The day after this was done, Lucio, as I now familiarly called him, came in to my room with a mysterious and mischievous air.

"Geoffrey," he said—"I'm going to lend you five hundred pounds!"

I looked up with a smile.

"What for?"

He held out a cheque towards me. Glancing at it I saw that the sum he mentioned was filled in and endorsed with his signature, but that the name of the person to whom the money was to be made payable, had not yet been written.

"Well? What does it mean?"

"It means"—replied he—"that I am going to see Mr. McWhing this morning. I have an appointment with him at twelve. You, as Geoffrey Tempest, the author of the book Mr. McWhing is going to criticise and make a 'boom' of, could not possibly put your name to such a cheque. It would not be 'good form'—it might crop up afterwards and so betray 'the secrets of the prison-house.' But for me it is another affair. I am going to 'pose' as your businessman—your 'literary agent' who pockets ten per cent. of the profits and wants to make a 'big thing' out of you, and

I'm going to talk the matter over with the perfectly practical McWhing who has, like every true Scot, a keen eye for the main chance. Of course it will be in confidence,—strict confidence!" and he laughed—"It's all a question of business you know,—in these commercial days, literature has become a trade like everything else, and even critics only work for what pays them. As indeed why should they not?"

"Do you mean to tell me McWhing will take that five hundred?" I asked dubiously.

"I mean to tell you nothing of the kind. I would not put the matter so coarsely for the world! This money is not for McWhing,—it is for a literary charity."

"Indeed! I thought you had an idea perhaps of offering a bribe. . ."

"Bribe! Good Heavens! Bribe a critic! Impossible, my good Geoffrey!—such a thing was never heard of—never, never, never!" and he shook his head and rolled up his eyes with infinite solemnity—"No no! Press people never take money for anything—not even for 'booming' a new gold-mining company,—not even for putting a notice of a fashionable concert into the Morning Post. Everything in the English press is the just expression of pure and lofty sentiment, believe me! This little cheque is for a charity of which Mr. McWhing is chief patron,— you see the Civil List pensions all go by favour to the wrong persons nowadays; to the keeping of lunatic versifiers and retired actresses who never could act—the actual bona-fide 'genius' never gets anything out of Government, and moreover would scorn to take a farthing from that penurious body, which grudges him anything higher than a money-recognition. It is as great an insult to offer a beggarly pension of fifty or a hundred pounds a year to a really great writer as to give him a knighthood,—and we cannot fall much lower than to be a knight, as knights go. The present five hundred pounds will help to relieve certain 'poor and proud' but pressing literary cases known to McWhing alone!" His expression at this moment was so extraordinary, that I entirely failed to fathom it. "I have no doubt I shall be able to represent the benevolent and respectable literary agent to perfection—of course I shall insist on my ten per cent!"—and he began laughing again. "But I can't stop to discuss the matter now with you—I'm off. I promised McWhing to be with him at twelve o'clock precisely, and it's now half-past-eleven. I shall probably lunch with him, so don't wait for me. And concerning the five hundred, you needn't be in my debt an hour longer than you like—I'll take a cheque for the money back from you this evening."

"All right"—I said—"But perhaps the great oracle of the cliques will reject your proposals with scorn."

"If he does, then is Utopia realized!"—replied Lucio, carefully drawing on his gloves as he spoke—"Where's a copy of your book? Ah—here's one—smelling newly of the press," and he slipped the volume into his overcoat pocket; "Allow me, before departure, to express the opinion that you are a singularly ungrateful fellow, Geoffrey! Here am I, perfectly devoted to your interests,—and despite my princedom actually prepared to 'pose' to McWhing as your 'acting manager' *pro tem*, and you haven't so much as a thank-you to throw at me!"

He stood before me smiling, the personification of kindness and good humour. I laughed a little.

"McWhing will never take *you* for an acting manager or literary agent,"—I said—"You don't look it. If I seem churlish I'm sorry—but the fact is I am disgusted. . ."

"At what?" he inquired, still smiling.

"Oh, at the humbug of everything,"—I answered impatiently; "The stupid farce of it all. Why shouldn't a book get noticed on its own merits without any appeal to cliquism and influential wire-pulling on the press?"

"Exactly!" and he delicately flicked a grain of dust off his coat while speaking—"And why shouldn't a man get received in society on his own merits, without any money to recommend him or any influential friend to back him up?"

I was silent.

"The world is as it is made,"—he went on, regarding me fixedly—"It is moved by the lowest and pettiest motives,—it works for the most trivial, ridiculous and perishable aims. It is not a paradise. It is not a happy family of united and affectionate brethren. It is an over-populated colony of jabbering and quarrelsome monkeys, who fancy they are men. Philosophers in old days tried to teach it that the monkey-type should be exterminated for the growth and encouragement of a nobler race,— but they preached in vain—there never were enough real men alive to overcome the swarming majority of the beasts. God Himself, they say, came down from Heaven to try and set wrong things right, and to restore if possible His own defaced image to the general aspect of humanity,—and even He failed."

"There is very little of God in this world"—I said bitterly; "There is much more Devil!"

He smiled,—a musing, dreamy smile that transfigured his countenance and made him look like a fine Apollo absorbed in the thought of some new and glorious song.

"No doubt!" he said, after a little pause—"Mankind certainly prefer the devil to any other deity,—therefore if they elect him as their representative, it is scarcely to be wondered at that he governs where he is asked to govern. And yet—do you know Geoffrey—this devil,—if there is one,—can hardly, I think, be quite so bad as his detractors say. I myself don't believe he is a whit worse than a nineteenth-century financier!"

I laughed aloud at the comparison.

"After that," I said—"you had better go to McWhing. I hope you will tell him that I am the triple essence of all the newest 'discoveries' rolled into one!"

"Never fear!" returned Lucio,—"I've learned all my stock-phrases by heart—a 'star of the first magnitude' etc.,—I've read the *Athenæum* till I've got the lingo of the literary auctioneer well-nigh perfect, and I believe I shall acquit myself admirably. Au revoir!"

He was gone; and I, after a little desultory looking over my papers, went out to lunch at Arthur's, of which club I was now a member. On my way I stopped to look in at a bookseller's window to see if my 'immortal' production was yet on show. It was not,—and the volume put most conspicuously to the front among all the 'newest books' was one entitled 'Differences. By Mavis Clare.' Acting on a sudden impulse I went in to purchase it.

"Has this a good sale?" I asked, as the volume was handed to me.

The clerk at the counter opened his eyes wide.

"Sale?" he echoed—"Well, I should think so—rather! Why everybody's reading it!"

"Indeed!" and I turned over the uncut pages carelessly—"I see no allusion whatever to it in the papers."

The clerk smiled and shrugged his shoulders.

"No—and you're not likely to, sir"—he said—"Miss Clare is too popular to need reviews. Besides, a large number of the critics,—the 'log-rollers' especially, are mad against her for her success, and the public know it. Only the other day a man came in here from one of the big newspaper offices and told me he was taking a few notes on the books which had the largest sales,—would I tell him which author's works were most in demand? I said Miss Clare took the lead,—as she does,—and he got into a regular rage. Said he—'That's the answer I've had all along the line, and however true it is, it's no use to me because I dare not mention it. My editor would instantly scratch it out—he hates Miss Clare.' 'A precious editor you've got!' I said, and he looked rather queer. There's nothing like journalism, sir, for the suppression of truth!"

I smiled, and went away with my purchase, convinced that I had wasted a few shillings on a mere piece of woman's trash. If this Mavis Clare was indeed so 'popular,' then her work must naturally be of the 'penny dreadful' order, for I, like many another literary man, laboured under the ludicrous inconsistency of considering the public an 'ass' while I myself desired nothing so much as the said 'ass's' applause and approval!—and therefore I could not imagine it capable of voluntarily selecting for itself any good work of literature without guidance from the critics. Of course I was wrong; the great masses of the public in all nations are always led by some instinctive sense of right, that moves them to reject the false and unworthy, and select the true. Completely prepared, like most men of my type to sneer and cavil at the book, chiefly because it was written by a feminine hand, I sat down in a retired corner of the club reading-room, and began to cut and skim the pages. I had not read many sentences before my heart sank with a heavy sense of fear and,—jealousy!—the slow fire of an insidious envy began to smoulder in my mind. What power had so gifted this author—this mere *woman*,— that she should dare to write better than I! And that she should force me, by the magic of her pen to mentally acknowledge, albeit with wrath and shame, my own inferiority! Clearness of thought, brilliancy of style, beauty of diction, all these were hers, united to consummate ease of expression and artistic skill,—and all at once, in the very midst of reading, such a violent impulse of insensate rage possessed me that I flung the book down, dreading to go on with it. The potent, resistless, unpurchaseable quality of Genius!—ah, I was not yet so blinded by my own conceit as to be unable to recognize that divine fire when I saw it flashing up from every page as I saw it now; but, to be compelled to give that recognition to a woman's work, galled and irritated me almost beyond endurance. Women, I considered, should be kept in their places as men's drudges or toys—as wives, mothers, nurses, cooks, menders of socks and shirts, and housekeepers generally,—what right had they to intrude into the realms of art and snatch the laurels from their masters' brows! If I could but get the chance of reviewing this book, I thought to myself savagely!—I would misquote, misrepresent, and cut it to shreds with a joy too great for words! This Mavis Clare, 'unsexed,' as I at once called her in my own mind simply because she had the power I lacked,—wrote what she had to say with a gracious charm, freedom, and innate consciousness of strength,—a strength which forced me back upon myself and filled me with the bitterest humiliation. Without knowing her I hated her,—this woman who could win fame without the aid of money, and who was crowned so brightly and visibly to the world that she was beyond criticism. I took up her book again and tried to cavil at it,—over one or two dainty bits of poetic simile and sentiment I laughed,—enviously. When I left the club later in the day, I took the book with me, divided between a curious desire to read it honestly through with justice to it and its author, and an impulse to tear it asunder and fling it into the road to be crushed in the mud under rolling cab and cart wheels. In this strange humour Rimânez found me, when at about four o'clock he returned from his mission to David McWhing, smiling and—triumphant.

"Congratulate me Geoffrey!" he exclaimed as he entered my room— "Congratulate me, and yourself! I am *minus* the five hundred pound cheque I showed you this morning!"

"McWhing has pocketed it then,"—I said sullenly—"All right! Much good may it do him, and his 'charity'!"

Rimânez gave me a quick observant glance.

"Why, what has happened to you since we parted?" he inquired, throwing off his overcoat and sitting down opposite to me—"You seem out of temper! Yet you ought to be a perfectly happy man—for your highest ambition is about to be gratified. You said you wished to make your book and yourself 'the talk of London,'—well, within the next two or three weeks you will see yourself praised in a very large number of influential newspapers as the newest discovered 'genius' of the day, only a little way removed from Shakespeare himself (three of the big leading magazines are guaranteed to say that) and all this through the affability of Mr. McWhing, and the trifling sum of five hundred pounds! And are you not satisfied? Really, my friend, you are becoming difficult!—I warned you that too much good fortune spoils a man."

With a sudden movement I flung down Mavis Clare's book before him.

"Look at this"—I said—"Does *she* pay five hundred pounds to David McWhing's charity?"

He took up the volume and glanced at it.

MARIE CORELLI

"Certainly not. But then,—she gets slandered—not criticized!"

"What does that matter!" I retorted—"The man from whom I bought this book says that everybody is reading it."

"Exactly!" and Rimânez surveyed me with a curious expression, half of pity, half of amusement—"But you know the old axiom, my dear Geoffrey?—'you may lead a horse to the water but you cannot make him drink.' Which statement, interpreted for the present occasion, means that though certain log-rollers, headed by our estimable friend McWhing, may drag the horse—i.e. the public, up to their own particularly prepared literary trough, they cannot force it to swallow the mixture. The horse frequently turns tail and runs away in search of its own provender,—it has done so in the case of Miss Clare. When the public choose an author for themselves, it is a dreadful thing of course for other authors,—but it really can't be helped!"

"Why should they choose Mavis Clare?" I demanded gloomily.

"Ah, why indeed!" he echoed smiling—"McWhing would tell you they do it out of sheer idiotcy;—the public would answer that they choose her because she has genius."

"Genius!" I repeated scornfully—"The public are perfectly incapable of recognizing such a quality!"

"You think so?" he said still smiling—"you really think so? In that case it's very odd isn't it, how everything that is truly great in art and literature becomes so widely known and honoured, not only in this country but in every civilized land where people think or study? You must remember that all the very famous men and women have been steadily 'written down' in their day, even to the late English Laureate, Tennyson, who was 'criticized' for the most part in the purest Billingsgate,—it is only the mediocrities who are ever 'written up.' It seems as if the stupid public really had a hand in selecting these 'great,' for the reviewers would never stand them at any price, till driven to acknowledge them by the popular *force majeure*. But considering the barbarous want of culture and utter foolishness of the public, Geoffrey, what *I* wonder at, is that you should care to appeal to it at all!"

I sat silent,—inwardly chafing under his remarks.

"I am afraid—" he resumed, rising and taking a white flower from one of the vases on the table to pin in his button-hole—"that Miss Clare is going to be a thorn in your side, my friend! A man rival in literature is bad enough,—but a woman rival is too much to endure with any amount of patience! However you may console yourself with the certainty that *she* will never get 'boomed,'—while you—thanks to my tender fostering of the sensitive and high-principled McWhing, will be the one delightful and unique 'discovery' of the press for at least one month, perhaps two, which is about as long as any 'new star of the first magnitude' lasts in the latter-day literary skies. Shooting-stars all of them!—such as poor old forgotten Béranger sang of—

> "*les etoiles qui filent,*
> *'Qui filent,—qui filent—et disparaissent!*'"

"Except—Mavis Clare!" I said.

"True! Except Mavis Clare!" and he laughed aloud,—a laugh that jarred upon me because there was a note of mockery in it—"She is a small fixture in the vast heavens,—or so it seems—revolving very contentedly and smoothly in her own appointed orbit,—but she is not and never will be attended by the brilliant meteor-flames that will burst round *you*, my excellent fellow, at the signal of McWhing! Fie Geoffrey!—get over your sulks! Jealous of a woman! Be ashamed,—is not woman the inferior creature?, and shall the mere spectre of a feminine fame cause a five-fold millionaire to abase his lofty spirit in the dust? Conquer your strange fit of the spleen, Geoffrey, and join me at dinner!"

He laughed again as he left the room,—and again his laughter irritated me. When he had gone, I gave way to the base and unworthy impulse that had for some minutes been rankling within me, and sitting down at my writing table, penned a hasty note to the editor of a rather powerful magazine, a man whom I had formerly known and worked for. He was aware of my altered fortunes and the influential position I now occupied, and I felt confident he would be glad to oblige me in any matter if he could. My letter, marked '*private and confidential*' contained the request that I might be permitted to write for his next number, an anonymous 'slashing' review of the new novel entitled 'Differences' by Mavis Clare.

XVI

I t is almost impossible for me to describe the feverish, irritated and contradictory state of mind in which I now began to pass my days. With the absolute fixity of my fortunes, my humours became more changeful than the wind, and I was never absolutely contented for two hours together. I joined in every sort of dissipation common to men of the day, who with the usual inanity of noodles, plunged into the filth of life merely because to be morally dirty was also at the moment fashionable and much applauded by society. I gambled recklessly, solely for the reason that gambling was considered by many leaders of the 'upper ten' as indicative of 'manliness' and 'showing *grit*.'

"I hate a fellow who grudges losing a few pounds at play,"—said one of these 'distinguished' titled asses to me once—"It shows such a cowardly and currish disposition."

Guided by this 'new' morality, and wishing to avoid the possibility of being called "cowardly and currish," I indulged in baccarat and other ruinous games almost every night, willingly losing the 'few pounds' which in my case meant a few hundreds, for the sake of my occasional winnings, which placed a number of 'noble' rakes and blue-blooded blacklegs in my power for 'debts of honour,' which are supposed to be more strictly attended to and more punctually paid than any debts in the world, but which, as far as I am concerned, are still owing. I also betted heavily, on everything that could be made the subject of a bet,—and not to be behind my peers in 'style' and 'knowledge of the world' I frequented low houses and allowed a few half-nude brandy-soaked dancers and vulgar music-hall 'artistes' to get a couple of thousand pounds worth of jewels out of me, because this sort of thing was called 'seeing life' and was deemed part of a 'gentleman's' diversion. Heavens!— what beasts we all were, I and my aristocratic boon companions!—what utterly worthless, useless, callous scoundrels!—and yet,—we associated with the best and the highest in the land;—the fairest and noblest ladies in London received us in their houses with smiles and softly-worded flatteries—we—whose presence reeked with vice; we, 'young men of fashion' whom, if he had known our lives as they were, an honest cobbler working patiently for daily bread, might have spat upon, in contempt and indignation that such low rascals should be permitted to burden the earth! Sometimes, but very seldom, Rimânez joined our gambling and music-hall parties, and on such occasions I noticed that he, as it were, 'let himself go' and became the wildest of us all. But though wild he was never coarse,—as *we* were; his deep and mellow laughter had a sonorous richness in it that was totally unlike the donkey's 'hee-haw' of our 'cultured' mirth,—his manners were never vulgar; and his fluent discourse on men and things, now witty and satirical, now serious almost to pathos, strangely affected many of those who heard him talk, myself most of all. Once, I remember, when we were returning late from some foolish carouse,—I with three young sons of English peers, and Rimânez walking beside us,—we came upon a poorly clad girl sobbing and clinging to the iron railing outside a closed church door.

"Oh God!" she wailed—"Oh dear God! Do help me!"

One of my companions seized her by the arm with a lewd jest, when all at once Rimânez stepped between.

"Leave her alone!" he said sternly—"Let her find God if she can!"

The girl looked up at him terrified, her eyes streaming with tears, and he dropped two or three gold pieces into her hand. She broke out crying afresh.

"Oh God bless you!" she cried wildly—"God bless you!"

He raised his hat and stood uncovered in the moonlight, his dark beauty softened by a strangely wistful expression.

"I thank you!" he said simply—"You make me your debtor."

And he passed on; we followed, somewhat subdued and silenced, though one of my lordling friends sniggered idiotically.

"You paid dearly for that blessing, Rimânez!" he said—"You gave her three sovereigns;—by Jove! I'd have had something more than a blessing if I had been you."

"No doubt!" returned Rimânez—"You deserve more,—much more! I hope you will get it! A blessing would be of no advantage whatever to *you*;—it is, to *me*."

How often I have thought of this incident since! I was too dense to attach either meaning or importance to it then,—self-absorbed as I was, I paid no attention to circumstances which seemed to have no connection with my own life and affairs. And in all my dissipations and so-called amusements, a perpetual restlessness consumed me,—I obtained no real satisfaction out of anything except my slow and somewhat tantalizing courtship of Lady Sibyl. She was a strange girl; she knew my intentions towards her well enough; yet she affected not to know. Each time I ventured to treat her with more than the usual deference, and to infuse something of the ardour of a lover into my looks or manner, she feigned surprise. I wonder why it is that some women are so fond of playing the hypocrite in love? Their own instinct teaches them when men are amorous; but unless they can run the fox to earth, or in other words, reduce their suitors to the lowest pitch of grovelling appeal, and force them to such abasement that the poor passion-driven fools are ready to fling away life, and even honour, dearer than life, for their sakes, their vanity is not sufficiently gratified. But who, or what am I that I should judge of vanity,—I whose egregious and flagrant self-approbation was of such a character that it blinded me to the perception and comprehension of everything in which my own Ego was not represented! And yet,—with all the morbid interest I took in myself, my surroundings, my comfort, my social advancement, there was one thing which soon became a torture to me,—a veritable despair and loathing,—and this, strange to say, was the very triumph I had most looked forward to as the crown and summit of all my ambitious dreams. My book,—the book I had presumed to consider a work of genius,—when it was launched on the tide of publicity and criticism, resolved itself into a sort of literary monster that haunted my days and nights with its hateful presence; the thick, black-lettered, lying advertisements scattered broadcast by my publisher, flared at me with an offensive insistence in every paper I casually opened. And the praise of the reviewers! . . . the exaggerated, preposterous, fraudulent 'boom'! Good God!—how sickening it was!—how fulsome! Every epithet of flattery bestowed upon me filled me with disgust, and one day when I took up a leading magazine and saw a long article upon the 'extraordinary brilliancy and promise' of my book, comparing me to a new Æschylus and Shakespeare combined, with the signature of David McWhing appended to it, I could have thrashed that erudite and assuredly purchased Scot within an inch of his life. The chorus of eulogy was well-nigh universal; I was the 'genius of the day'—the 'hope of the future generation,'—I was the "Book of the Month,"—the greatest, the wittiest, most versatile, most brilliant scribbling pigmy that had ever honoured a pot of ink by using it! Of course I figured as McWhing's 'discovery,'—five hundred pounds bestowed on his mysterious 'charity' had so sharpened his eyesight that he had perceived me shining brightly on the literary horizon before anyone else had done so. The press followed his 'lead' obediently,—for though the press,—the English press at least,—is distinctly unbribable, the owners of newspapers are not insensible to the advantages of largely paying advertisements. Moreover, when Mr. McWhing announced me as his 'find' in the oracular style which distinguished him, some other literary gentlemen came forward and wrote effective articles about me, and sent me their compositions carefully marked. I took the hint,—wrote at once to thank them, and invited them to dinner. They came, and feasted royally with Rimânez and myself;—(one of them wrote an 'Ode' to me afterwards),—and at the conclusion of the revels, we sent two of the 'oracles' home, considerably overcome by champagne, in a carriage with Amiel to look after them, and help them out at their own doors. And my 'boom' expanded,—London 'talked' as I had said it should; the growling monster metropolis discussed me and my work in its own independent and peculiar fashion. The 'upper ten' subscribed to the circulating libraries, and these admirable institutions made a two or three hundred copies do for all demands, by the simple expedient of keeping subscribers waiting five or six weeks till they grew tired of asking for the book, and forgot all about it. Apart from the libraries, the public did not take me up. From the glowing criticisms that appeared in all the papers, it might have been supposed that 'everybody who was anybody' was reading my 'wonderful' production. Such however was not the case. People spoke of me as 'the great millionaire,' but they were indifferent to the bid I had made for literary fame. The remark they usually made to me wherever I went was—"You have written a novel, haven't you? What an odd thing for *you* to do!"—this, with a laugh;—"I haven't read it,—I've so little time—I must ask for it at the library." Of course a great many never did ask, not deeming it worth their while; and I whose money, combined with the resistless influence of Rimânez, had started the favourable criticisms that flooded the press, found out that the majority of the public never read criticisms at all. Hence, my anonymous review of Mavis Clare's book made no effect whatever on *her* popularity, though it appeared in the most prominent manner. It was a sheer waste of labour,—for everywhere this woman author was still looked upon as a creature of altogether finer clay than ordinary, and still her book was eagerly devoured and questioned and admired; and still it sold by thousands, despite a lack of all favourable criticism or prominent advertisement. No one guessed that I had written what I am now perfectly willing to admit was a brutally wanton misrepresentation of her work,—no one, except Rimânez. The magazine in which it appeared was a notable one, circulating in every club and library, and he, taking it up casually one afternoon, turned to that article at once.

"You wrote this!" he said, fixing his eyes upon me,—"It must have been a great relief to your mind!"

I said nothing.

He read on in silence for a little; then laying down the magazine looked at me with a curiously scrutinizing expression.

"There are some human beings so constituted," he said, "that if they had been with Noah in the ark according to the silly old legend, they would have shot the dove bearing the olive-leaf, directly it came in sight over the waste of waters. You are of that type Geoffrey."

"I do not see the force of your comparison," I murmured.

"Do you not? Why, what harm has this Mavis Clare done to you? Your positions are entirely opposed. You are a millionaire; she is a hard-working woman dependent on her literary success for a livelihood, and you, rolling in wealth do your best to deprive her of the means of existence. Does this redound to your credit? She has won her fame by her own brain and energy alone,—and even if you dislike her book need you abuse her personally as you have done in this article? You do not know her; you have never seen her, . . ."

"I hate women who write!" I said vehemently.

"Why? Because they are able to exist independently? Would you have them all the slaves of man's lust or convenience? My dear Geoffrey, you are unreasonable. If you admit that you are jealous of this woman's celebrity and grudge it to her, then I can understand your spite, for jealousy is capable of murdering a fellow-creature with either the dagger or the pen."

I was silent.

"Is the book such wretched stuff as you make it out to be?" he asked presently.

"I suppose some people might admire it,"—I said curtly, "I do not."

This was a lie; and of course he knew it was a lie. The work of Mavis Clare had excited my most passionate envy,—while the very fact that Sibyl Elton had read her book before she had thought of looking at mine, had accentuated the bitterness of my feelings.

"Well," said Rimânez at last, smiling as he finished reading my onslaught—"all I can say Geoffrey, is that this will not touch Mavis Clare in the least. You have overshot the mark, my friend! Her public will simply cry "what a shame!" and clamour for her work more than ever. And as for the woman herself,—she has a merry heart, and she will laugh at it. You must see her some day."

"I don't want to see her," I said.

"Probably not. But you will scarcely be able to avoid doing so when you live at Willowsmere Court."

"One is not obliged to know everybody in the neighbourhood,"—I observed superciliously.

Lucio laughed aloud.

"How well you carry your fortunes, Geoffrey!" he said—"For a poor devil of a Grub-street hack who lately was at a loss for a sovereign, how perfectly you follow the fashions of your time! If there is one man more than another that moves me to wondering admiration it is he who asserts his wealth strenuously in the face of his fellows, and who comports himself in this world as though he could bribe death and purchase the good-will of the Creator. It is such splendid effrontery,—such superlative pride! Now I, though over-wealthy myself, am so curiously constituted that I cannot wear my bank-notes in my countenance as it were,—I have put in a claim for intellect as well as gold,—and sometimes, do you know, in my travels round the world, I have been so far honoured as to be taken for quite a poor man! Now *you* will never have that chance again;—you are rich and you look it!"

"And you,—" I interrupted him suddenly, and with some warmth—"do you know what *you* look? You imply that I assert my wealth in my face; do you know what *you* assert in your every glance and gesture?"

"I cannot imagine!" he said smiling.

"Contempt for us all!" I said—"Immeasurable contempt,—even for me, whom you call friend. I tell you the truth, Lucio,—there are times, when in spite of our intimacy I feel that you despise me. I daresay you do; you have an extraordinary personality united to extraordinary talents; you must not however expect all men to be as self-restrained and as indifferent to human passions as yourself."

He gave me a swift, searching glance.

"Expect!" he echoed—"My good fellow, I expect nothing at all,—from men. They, on the contrary,—at least all those *I* know—expect everything from me. And they get it,—generally. As for 'despising' you, have I not said that I admire you? I do. I think there is something positively stupendous in the brilliant progress of your fame and rapid social success."

"My fame!" I repeated bitterly—"How has it been obtained? What is it worth?"

"That is not the question," he retorted with a little smile; "How unpleasant it must be for you to have these gouty twinges of conscience Geoffrey! Of course no fame is actually worth much now-a-days,—because it is not classic fame, strong in reposeful old-world dignity,—it is blatant noisy notoriety merely. But yours, such as it is, is perfectly legitimate, judged by its common-sense commercial aspect, which is the only aspect in which anyone looks at anything. You must bear in mind that no one works out of disinterestedness in the present age,—no matter how purely benevolent an action may appear on the surface, Self lies at the bottom of it. Once grasp this fact, and you will perceive that nothing could be fairer or more straightforward than the way you have obtained your fame. You have not 'bought' the incorruptible British Press; you could not do that; that is impossible, for it is immaculate, and bristles stiffly all over with honourable principles. There is no English paper existing that would accept a cheque for the insertion of a notice or a paragraph; not one!" His eyes twinkled merrily,—then he went on—"No,—it is only the Foreign Press that is corrupt, so the British Press says;—John Bull looks on virtuously aghast at journalists who, in dire stress of poverty, will actually earn a little extra pay for writing something or somebody 'up' or 'down.' Thank Heaven, *he* employs no such journalists; his pressmen are the very soul of rectitude, and will stoically subsist on a pound a week rather than take ten for a casual job 'to oblige a friend.' Do you know Geoffrey, when the Judgment Day arrives, who will be among the first saints to ascend to Heaven with the sounding of trumpets?"

I shook my head, half vexed, half amused.

"All the English (not foreign) editors and journalists!" said Lucio with an air of pious rapture—"and why? Because they are so good, so just, so unprejudiced! Their foreign brethren will be reserved for the eternal dance of devils of course—but the Britishers will pace the golden streets singing Alleluia! I assure you I consider British journalists generally the noblest examples of incorruptibility in the world—they come next to the clergy as representatives of virtue, and exponents of the three evangelical counsels,—voluntary poverty, chastity, and obedience!" Such mockery glittered in his eyes, that the light in them might have been the reflection of clashing steel. "Be consoled, Geoffrey," he resumed—"your fame is honourably won. You have simply, through me, approached one critic who writes in about twenty newspapers and influences others to write in other twenty,—that critic being a noble creature, (all critics are noble creatures) has a pet 'society' for the relief of authors in need (a noble scheme you will own) and to this charity I subscribe out of pure benevolence, five hundred pounds. Moved by my generosity and consideration, (particularly as I do not ask what becomes of the five hundred) McWhing 'obliges' me in a little matter. The editors of the papers for which he writes accept him as a wise and witty personage; *they* know nothing about the charity or the cheque,—it is not necessary for them to know. The whole thing is really quite a reasonable business arrangement;—it is only a self-tormenting analyst like you who would stop to think of such a trifle a second time."

"If McWhing really and conscientiously admired my book for itself," I began.

"Why should you imagine he does not?" asked Lucio—"Myself, I believe that he is a perfectly sincere and honorable man. I think he means all he says and writes. I consider that if he had found your work not worthy of his commendation, he would have sent me back that cheque for five hundred pounds, torn across in a noble scorn!"

And with this, throwing himself back in his chair, he laughed till the tears came into his eyes.

But I could not laugh; I was too weary and depressed. A heavy sense of despair was on my mind; I felt that the hope which had cheered me in my days of poverty,—the hope of winning real Fame, so widely different a thing to notoriety, had vanished. There was some quality in the subtle glory which could not be won by either purchase or influence. The praise of the press could not give it. Mavis Clare, working for her bread, had it,—I, with millions of money, had not. Like a fool I had thought to buy it; I had yet to learn that all the best, greatest, purest and worthiest things in life are beyond all market-value and that the gifts of the gods are not for sale.

About a fortnight after the publication of my book, we went to Court, my comrade and I, and were presented by a distinguished officer connected with the immediate and intimate surroundings of the Royal household. It was a brilliant scene enough,—but, without doubt, the most brilliant personage there was Rimânez. I was fairly startled at the stately and fascinating figure he made in his court suit of black velvet and steel ornaments; accustomed as I was to his good looks, I had never seen them so enhanced by dress as on this occasion. I had been tolerably well satisfied with my own appearance in the regulation costume till I saw him; then my personal vanity suffered a decided shock, and I realized that I merely served as a foil to show off and accentuate the superior attractions of my friend. But I was not envious of him in any way,—on the contrary I openly expressed the admiration I frankly felt.

He seemed amused. "My dear boy, it is all flunkeydom;" he said— "All sham and humbug. Look at this—" and he drew his light court rapier from its sheath—"There is no real use in this flimsy blade,—it is merely an emblem of dead chivalry. In old times, if a man insulted you, or insulted a woman you admired, out flashed a shining point of tempered Toledo steel that could lunge—so!" and he threw himself into a fencing attitude of incomparable grace and ease—"and you pricked the blackguard neatly through the ribs or arm and gave him cause to remember you. But now—" and he thrust the rapier back in its place—"men carry toys like these as a melancholy sign to show what bold fellows they were once, and what spiritless cravens they are now,— relying no more on themselves for protection, but content to go about yelling 'Police! Police!' at the least threat of injury to their worthless persons. Come, it's time we started, Geoffrey!—let us go and bow our heads before another human unit formed precisely like ourselves, and so act in defiance of Death and the Deity, who declare all men to be equal!"

We entered our carriage and were soon on our way to St James's Palace.

"His Royal Highness the Prince of Wales is not exactly the Creator of the universe;"—said Lucio suddenly, looking out of the window as we approached the line of soldiery on guard outside.

"Why no!" I answered laughing—"What do you say that for?"

"Because there is as much fuss about him as if he were,—in fact, more. The Creator does not get half as much attention bestowed upon Him as Albert Edward. We never attire ourselves in any special way for entering the presence of God; we don't put so much as a clean mind on."

"But then,"—I said indifferently—"God is *non est*,—and Albert Edward is *est*."

He smiled,—and his eyes had a scornful gleam in their dark centres.

"That is your opinion?" he queried—"Well, it is not original,—many choice spirits share it with you. There is at least one good excuse for people who make no preparation to enter the presence of God,—in going to church, which is called the 'house of God,' they do not find

God at all; they only discover the clergyman. It is somewhat of a disappointment."

I had no time to reply, as just then the carriage stopped, and we alighted at the palace. Through the intervention of the high Court official who presented us, we got a good place among the most distinguished arrivals, and during our brief wait, I was considerably amused by the study of their faces and attitudes. Some of the men looked nervous,—others conceited; one or two Radical notabilities comported themselves with an air as if they and they alone were to be honoured for allowing Royalty to hold these functions at all; a few gentlemen had evidently donned their Levée dress in haste and carelessness, for the pieces of tissue-paper in which their steel or gilt coat-buttons had been wrapped by the tailor to prevent tarnish, were still unremoved. Discovering this fortunately before it was too late, they occupied themselves by taking off these papers and casting them on the floor,—an untidy process at best, and one that made them look singularly ridiculous and undignified. Each man present turned to stare at Lucio; his striking personality attracted universal attention. When we at last entered the throne-room, and took our places in line, I was careful to arrange that my brilliant companion should go up before me, as I had a strong desire to see what sort of an effect his appearance would produce on the Royal party. I had an excellent view of the Prince of Wales from where I myself waited; he made an imposing and kingly figure enough, in full uniform with his various Orders glittering on his broad breast; and the singular resemblance discovered by many people in him to Henry VIII struck me more forcibly than I should have thought possible. His face however expressed a far greater good-humour than the pictured lineaments of the capricious but ever popular 'bluff King Hal,'—though on this occasion there was a certain shade of melancholy, even sternness on his brow, which gave a firmer character to his naturally mobile features,—a shadow, as I fancied of weariness, tempered with regret,—the look of one dissatisfied, yet resigned. A man of blunted possibilities he seemed to me,—of defeated aims, and thwarted will. Few of the other members of the Royal family surrounding him on the daïs, possessed the remarkable attraction he had for any observant student of physiognomy,—most of them were, or assumed to be, stiff military figures merely who bent their heads as each guest filed past with an automatic machine-like regularity implying neither pleasure, interest, nor good-will. But the Heir-Apparent to the greatest Empire in the world expressed in his very attitude and looks, an unaffected and courteous welcome to all,—surrounded as he was, and as such in his position must ever be, by toadies, parasites, sycophants, hypocritical self-seekers, who would never run the least risk to their own lives to serve him, unless they could get something personally satisfactory out of it, his presence impressed itself upon me as full of the suggestion of dormant but none the less resolute power. I cannot even now explain the singular excitation of mind that seized me as our turn to be presented arrived;—I saw my companion advance, and heard the Lord Chamberlain announce his name;— 'Prince Lucio Rimânez'; and then;—why then,—it seemed as if all the movement in the brilliant room suddenly came to a pause! Every eye was fixed on the stately form and noble countenance of my friend as he bowed with such consummate courtliness and grace as made all other salutations seem awkward by comparison. For one moment he stood absolutely still in front of the Royal daïs,—facing the Prince as though he sought to impress him with the fact of his presence there,— and across the broad stream of sunshine which had been pouring into the room throughout the ceremony, there fell the sudden shadow of a passing cloud. A fleeting impression of gloom and silence chilled the atmosphere,—a singular magnetism appeared to hold all eyes fixed on Rimânez; and not a man either going or coming, moved. This intense hush was brief as it was curious and impressive;—the Prince of Wales started slightly, and gazed at the superb figure before him with an expression of eager curiosity and almost as if he were ready to break the frigid bonds of etiquette and speak,—then controlling himself with an evident effort he gave his usual dignified acknowledgment of Lucio's profound reverence, whereupon my comrade passed on,—slightly smiling. I followed next,—but naturally made no impression beyond the fact of exciting a smothered whisper from some-one among the lesser Royalties who caught the name 'Geoffrey Tempest,' and at once murmured the magic words "Five millions!"—words which reached my ears and moved me to the usual weary contempt which was with me growing into a chronic malady. We were soon out of the palace, and while waiting for our carriage in the covered court-yard entrance, I touched Rimânez on the arm.

"You made a veritable sensation Lucio!"

"Did I?" He laughed. "You flatter me Geoffrey."

"Not at all. Why did you stop so long in front of the daïs?"

"To please my humour!" he returned indifferently—"And partly, to give his Royal Highness the chance of remembering me the next time he sees me."

"But he seemed to recognise you,"—I said—"Have you met him before?"

His eyes flashed. "Often! But I have never till now made a public appearance at St James's. Court costume and 'company manners' make a difference to the looks of most men,—and I doubt,—yes, I very much doubt, whether, even with his reputed excellent memory for faces, the Prince really knew me to-day for what I am!"

XVII

It must have been about a week or ten days after the Prince of Wales's Levée that I had the strange scene with Sibyl Elton I am about to relate; a scene that left a painful impression on my mind and should have been sufficient to warn me of impending trouble to come had I not been too egotistical to accept any portent that presaged ill to myself. Arriving at Lord Elton's house one evening, and ascending the stairs to the drawing-room as was now my usual custom, unannounced and without ceremony, I found Diana Chesney there alone and in tears.

"Why, what's the matter?" I exclaimed in a rallying tone, for I was on very friendly and familiar terms with the little American—"You, of all people in the world, having a private 'weep'! Has our dear railway papa 'bust up'?"

She laughed, a trifle hysterically.

"Not just yet, you bet!" she answered, lifting her wet eyes to mine and showing that mischief still sparkled brightly in them,—"There's nothing wrong with the funds as far as I know. I've only had a,—well, a sort of rumpus here with Sibyl."

"With Sibyl?"

"Yes,"—and she rested the point of her little embroidered shoe on a footstool and looked at it critically—"You see it's the Catsup's 'At Home' to-night, and I'm invited and Sibyl's invited; Miss Charlotte is knocked up with nursing the Countess, and of course I made sure that Sibyl would go. Well, she never said a word about it till she came down to dinner, and then she asked me what time I wanted the carriage. I said 'Aren't you going too?' and she looked at me in that provoking way of hers,—*you* know!—a look that takes you in from your topmost hair to your shoe-edge,—and answered 'Did you think it possible!' Well, I flared up, and said of course I thought it possible,—why shouldn't it be possible? She looked at me in the same way again and said—'To the *Catsups*? with *you*!' Now, you know, Mr. Tempest, that was real downright rudeness, and more than I could stand so I just gave way to my mind. 'Look here,' I said—'though you are the daughter of an Earl, you needn't turn up your nose at Mrs. Catsup. She isn't half bad,—I don't speak of her money,—but she's a real good sort, and has a kind heart, which it appears to me is more than you have. Mrs. Catsup would never treat me as unkindly as you do.' And then I choked,—I could have burst out in a regular yell, if I hadn't thought the footman might be outside the door listening. And Sibyl only smiled, that patent ice-refrigerator smile of hers, and asked—'would you prefer to live with Mrs. Catsup?' Of course I told her no,—nothing would induce me to live with Mrs. Catsup, and then she said—'Miss Chesney, you pay my father for the protection and guarantee of his name and position in English social circles, but the companionship of my father's daughter was not included in the bargain. I have tried to make you understand as distinctly as I can that I will not be seen in society with you,—not because I dislike you,—far from it,—but simply because people would say I was acting as your paid companion. You force me to speak plainly, and I am sorry if I offend. As for Mrs. Catsup, I have only met her once, and she seemed to me very common and ill-bred. Besides I do not care for the society of tradespeople.' And with that she got up and sailed out,—and I heard her order the carriage for me at ten. It's coming round directly, and just look at my red eyes! It's awfully hard on me,—I know old Catsup made his pile out of varnish, but varnish is as good as anything else in the general market. And—and—it's all out now, Mr. Tempest,—and you can tell Sibyl what I've said if you like; I know you're in love with her!"

I stared, bewildered by her voluble and almost breathless outburst.

"Really, Miss Chesney," I began formally.

"Oh yes, Miss Chesney, Miss Chesney—it's all very well!" she repeated impatiently, snatching up a gorgeous evening cloak which I mutely volunteered to put on, an offer she as mutely accepted—"I'm only a girl, and it isn't my fault if I've got a vulgar man for a father who wants to see me married to an English nobleman before he dies,—that's *his* look-out—*I* don't care about it. English noblemen are a ricketty lot in *my* opinion. But I've as good a heart as anyone, and I could love Sibyl if she'd let me, but she *won't*. She leads the life of an ice-berg, and doesn't care a rap for anyone. She doesn't care for you, you know!—I wish she did,—she'd be more human!"

"I'm very sorry for all this,"—I said, smiling into the piquante face of the really sweet-natured girl, and gently fastening the jewelled clasp of her cloak at her throat—"But you mustn't mind it so much. You are a dear little soul Diana,—kind and generous and impulsive and all the rest of it,—but,—well—English people are very apt to misunderstand Americans. I can quite enter into your feelings,—still you know Lady Sibyl is very proud—"

"Proud!" she interrupted—"My! I guess it must feel something splendid to have an ancestor who was piked through the body on Bosworth field, and left there for the birds to eat. It seems to give a kind of stiffness in the back to all the family ever afterwards. Shouldn't wonder if the descendants of the birds who ate him felt kinder stuck up about it too!"

I laughed,—she laughed with me, and was quite herself again.

"If I told you *my* ancestor was a Pilgrim Father, you wouldn't believe me I expect!" she said, the corners of her mouth dimpling.

"I should believe anything from *your* lips!" I declared gallantly.

"Well, believe that, then! Swallow it down if you can! I can't! He was a Pilgrim Father in the *Mayflower*, and he fell on his knees and thanked God as soon as he touched dry land in the true Pilgrim-Father way. But he couldn't hold a candle to the piked man at Bosworth."

Here we were interrupted by the entrance of a footman.

"The carriage is waiting, Miss."

"Thanks,—all right. Good-night Mr. Tempest,—you'd better send word to Sibyl you are here; Lord Elton is dining out, but Sibyl will be at home all the evening."

I offered her my arm, and escorted her to the carriage, feeling a little sorry for her as she drove off in solitary state to the festive 'crush' of the successful varnisher. She was a good girl, a bright girl, a true girl,—vulgar and flippant at times, yet on the whole sincere in her better qualities of character and sentiment,—and it was this very sincerity which, being quite unconventional and not at all *la mode*, was misunderstood, and would always be misunderstood by the higher and therefore more hypocritically polished circles of English society.

I returned to the drawing-room slowly and meditatively, telling one of the servants on my way to ask Lady Sibyl if she could see me for a few moments. I was not kept waiting long; I had only paced the room twice up and down when she entered, looking so strangely wild and beautiful that I could scarcely forbear uttering an exclamation of wonder. She wore white as was always her custom in the evenings,—her hair was less elaborately dressed than usual, and clustered over her brow in loose wavy masses,—her face was exceedingly pale, and her eyes appeared larger and darker by comparison—her smile was vague and fleeting like that of a sleep-walker. She gave me her hand; it was dry and burning.

"My father is out—" she began.

"I know. But I came to see *you*. May I stay a little?"

She murmured assent, and sinking listlessly into a chair, began to play with some roses in a vase on the table beside her.

"You look tired Lady Sibyl,"—I said gently—"Are you not well?"

"I am quite well—" she answered—"But you are right in saying I am tired. I am dreadfully tired!"

"You have been doing too much perhaps?—your attendance on your mother tries you—"

She laughed bitterly.

"Attendance on my mother!—pray do not credit me with so much devotion. I never attend on my mother. I cannot do it; I am too much of a coward. Her face terrifies me; and whenever I do venture to go near her, she tries to speak, with such dreadful, such ghastly efforts, as make her more hideous to look at than anyone can imagine. I should die of fright if I saw her often. As it is, when I do see her I can scarcely stand—and twice I have fainted with the horror of it. To think of it!— that that living corpse with the fearful fixed eyes and distorted mouth should actually be *my mother*!"

She shuddered violently, and her very lips paled as she spoke. I was seriously concerned, and told her so.

"This must be very bad for your health,"—I said, drawing my chair closer to hers—"Can you not get away for a change?"

She looked at me in silence. The expression of her eyes thrilled me strangely,—it was not tender or wistful, but fierce, passionate and commanding.

"I saw Miss Chesney for a few moments just now"—I resumed,— "She seemed very unhappy."

"She has nothing to be unhappy about—" said Sibyl coldly—"except the time my mother takes in dying. But she is young; she can afford to wait a little for the Elton coronet."

"Is not—may not this be a mistaken surmise of yours?" I ventured gently—"Whatever her faults, I think the girl admires and loves you."

She smiled scornfully.

"I want neither her love nor her admiration,"—she said—"I have few women-friends and those few are all hypocrites whom I mistrust. When Diana Chesney is my step-mother, we shall still be strangers."

I felt I was on delicate ground, and that I could not continue the conversation without the risk of giving offence.

"Where is *your* friend?" asked Sibyl suddenly, apparently to change the subject—"Why does he so seldom come here now?"

"Rimânez? Well, he is a very queer fellow, and at times takes an abhorrence for all society. He frequently meets your father at the club, and I suppose his reason for not coming here is that he hates women."

"All women?" she queried with a little smile.

"Without exception!"

"Then he hates me?"

"I did not say that—" I answered quickly—"No one could hate you, Lady Sibyl,—but truly, as far as Prince Rimânez is concerned, I expect he does not abate his aversion to womankind (which is his chronic malady) even for you."

"So he will never marry?" she said musingly.

I laughed. "Oh, never! That you may be quite sure of."

Still playing with the roses near her, she relapsed into silence. Her breath came and went quickly; I saw her long eyelashes quiver against the pale rose-leaf tint of her cheeks,—the pure outline of her delicate profile suggested to my mind one of Fra Angelico's meditative saints or angels. All at once, while I yet watched her admiringly, she suddenly sprang erect, crushing a rose in her hand,—her head thrown back, her eyes flashing, her whole frame trembling.

"Oh, I cannot bear it!" she cried wildly—"I cannot bear it!"

I started up astonished, and confronted her.

"Sibyl!"

"Oh, why don't you speak, and fill up the measure of my degradation!" she went on passionately—"Why don't you tell *me*, as you tell my father, your purpose in coming here?—why don't you say to *me*, as you say to him, that your sovereign choice has fastened upon me,—that I am the woman out of all the world you have elected to marry! Look at me!" and she raised her arms with a tragic gesture; "Is there any flaw in the piece of goods you wish to purchase? This face is deemed worthy of the fashionable photographer's pains; worthy of being sold for a shilling as one of England's 'beauties,'— this figure has served as a model for the showing-off of many a modiste's costume, purchased at half-cost on the understanding that I must state to my circle of acquaintance the name of the maker or designer,—these eyes, these lips, these arms are all yours for the buying! Why do you expose me to the shame of dallying over your bargain?—by hesitating and considering as to whether, after all, I am worthy of your gold!"

She seemed seized by some hysterical passion that convulsed her, and in mingled amazement, alarm and distress, I sprang to her and caught her hands in my own.

"Sibyl, Sibyl!" I said—"Hush—hush! You are overwrought with fatigue and excitement,—you cannot know what you are saying. My darling, what do you take me for?—what is all this nonsense in your mind about buying and selling? You know I love you,—I have made no secret of it,—you must have seen it in my face,—and if I have hesitated to speak, it is because I feared your rejection of me. You are too good for me, Sibyl,—too good for any man,—I am not worthy to win your beauty and innocence. My love, my love—do not give way in this manner"—for as I spoke she clung to me like a wild bird suddenly caged—"What can I say to you, but that I worship you with all the strength of my life,—I love you so deeply that I am afraid to think of it; it is a passion I dare not dwell upon, Sibyl,—I love you too well,—too madly for my own peace—"

I trembled, and was silent,—her soft arms clinging to me robbed me of a portion of my self-control. I kissed the rippling waves of her hair; she lifted her head and looked up at me, her eyes alit with some strange lustre that was not love as much as fear,—and the sight of her beauty thus yielded as it were to my possession, broke down the barriers of restraint I had hitherto imposed upon myself. I kissed her on the lips,—a long passionate kiss that, to my excited fancy, seemed to mingle our very beings into one,—but while I yet held her in my arms, she suddenly released herself and pushed me back. Standing apart from me she trembled so violently that I feared she would fail,—and I took her hand and made her sit down. She smiled,—a very wan smile.

"What did you feel then?" she asked.

"When, Sibyl?"

"Just now,—when you kissed me?"

"All the joys of heaven and fires of hell in a moment!" I said.

She regarded me with a curious musing frown.

"Strange! Do you know what *I* felt?"

I shook my head smiling, and pressed my lips on the soft small hand I held.

"Nothing!" she said, with a kind of hopeless gesture—"I assure you, absolutely nothing! I cannot feel. I am one of your modern women,—I can only think,—and analyse."

"Think and analyse as much as you will, my queen,"—I answered playfully—"if you will only think you can be happy with me. That is all I desire."

"Can you be happy with *me*?" she asked—"Wait—do not answer for a moment, till I tell you what I am. You are altogether mistaken in me." She was silent for some minutes, and I watched her anxiously. "I was always intended for this"—she said slowly at last,—"this, to which I have now come,—to be the property of a rich man. Many men have looked at me with a view to purchase, but they could not pay the price my father demanded. Pray do not look so distressed!—what I say is quite true and quite commonplace,—all the women of the upper classes,—the unmarried ones,—are for sale now in England as utterly as the Circassian girls in a barbarian slave-market. I see you wish to protest, and assure me of your devotion,—but there is no need of this,—I am quite sure you love me,—as much as any man can love,—and I am content. But you do not know me really,—you are attracted by my face and form,—and you admire my youth and innocence, which you think I possess. But I am not young—I am old in heart and feeling. I was young for a little while at Willowsmere, when I lived among flowers and birds and all the trustful honest creatures of the woods and fields,—but one season in town was sufficient to kill my youth in me,—one season of dinners and balls, and—fashionable novel-reading. Now *you* have written a book, and therefore you must know something about the duties of authorship,—of the serious and even terrible responsibility writers incur when they send out to the world books full of pernicious and poisonous suggestion to contaminate the minds that have hitherto been clean and undiseased. Your book has a noble motive; and for this I admire it in many parts, though to me it is not as convincing as it might have been. It is well written too; but I gained the impression while reading it, that you were not altogether sincere yourself in the thoughts you strove to inculcate,—and that therefore you just missed what you should have gained."

"I am sure you are right,"—I said, with a wholesome pang of humiliation—"The book is worthless as literature,—it is only the 'boom' of a season!"

"At any rate,"—she went on, her eyes darkening with the intensity of her feeling—"you have not polluted your pen with the vileness common to many of the authors of the day. I ask you, do you think a girl can read the books that are now freely published, and that her silly society friends tell her to read,—'because it is so dreadfully *queer*!'—and yet remain unspoilt and innocent? Books that go into the details of the lives of outcasts?—that explain and analyse the secret vices of men?—that advocate almost as a sacred duty 'free love' and universal polygamy?—that see no shame in introducing into the circles of good wives and pure-minded girls, a heroine who boldly seeks out a man, *any* man, in order that she may have a child by him, without the 'degradation' of marrying him? I have read all those books,—and what can you expect of me? Not innocence, surely! I despise men,—I despise my own sex,—I loathe myself for being a woman! You wonder at my fanaticism for Mavis Clare,—it is only because for a time her books give me back my self-respect, and make me see humanity in a nobler light,—because she restores to me, if only for an hour, a kind of glimmering belief in God, so that my mind feels refreshed and cleansed. All the same, you must not look upon me as an innocent young girl Geoffrey,—a girl such as the great poets idealized and sang of,—I am a contaminated creature, trained to perfection in the lax morals and prurient literature of my day."

I looked at her in silence, pained, startled, and with a sense of shock, as though something indefinably pure and precious had crumbled into dust at my feet. She rose and began pacing the room restlessly, moving to and fro with a slow yet fierce grace that reminded me against my wish and will of the movement of some imprisoned and savage beast of prey.

"You shall not be deceived in me,"—she said, pausing a moment and eyeing me sombrely—"If you marry me, you must do so with a full realization of the choice you make. For with such wealth as yours, you can of course wed any woman you fancy. I do not say you could find a girl better than I am; I do not think you could in *my* 'set,' because we are all alike,—all tarred with the same brush, and filled with the same merely sensual and materialistic views of life and its responsibilities as the admired heroines of the 'society' novels we read. Away in the provinces, among the middle classes it is possible you might discover a really good girl of the purest blush-rose innocence,—but then you might also find her stupid and unentertaining, and you would not care for that. My chief recommendation is that I am beautiful,—you can see that; everybody can see that,—and I am not so affected as to pretend to be unconscious of the fact. There is no sham about my external appearance; my hair is not a wig,—my complexion is natural,—my figure is not the result of the corset-maker's art,—my eyebrows and eyelashes are undyed. Oh yes,—you can be sure that the beauty of my body is quite genuine!—but it is not the outward expression of an equally beautiful soul. And this is what I want you to understand. I am passionate, resentful, impetuous,—frequently unsympathetic, and inclined to morbidness and melancholy, and I confess I have imbibed, consciously or unconsciously, that complete contempt of life and disbelief in a God, which is the chief theme of nearly all the social teachings of the time."

She ceased,—and I gazed at her with an odd sense of mingled worship and disillusion, even as a barbarian might gaze at an idol whom he still loved, but whom he could no longer believe in as divine. Yet what she said was in no way contrary to my own theories,—how then could I complain? I did not believe in a God; why should I inconsistently feel regret that she shared my unbelief? I had involuntarily clung to the old-fashioned idea that religious faith was a sacred duty in womanhood; I was not able to offer any reason for this notion, unless it was the romantic fancy of having a good woman to pray for one, if one had no time and less inclination to pray for one's self. However, it was evident Sibyl was 'advanced' enough to do without superstitious observances; *she* would never pray for me;—and if we had children, she would never teach them to make their first tender appeals to Heaven for my sake or hers. I smothered a slight sigh, and was about to speak, when she came up to me and laid her two hands on my shoulders. "You look unhappy, Geoffrey,"—she said in gentler accents—"Be consoled! it is not too late for you to change your mind!"

I met the questioning glance of her eyes,—beautiful, lustrous eyes as clear and pure as light itself.

"I shall never change, Sibyl," I answered—"I love you,—I shall always love you. But I wish you would not analyse yourself so pitilessly,—you have such strange ideas—"

"You think them strange?" she said—"You should not,—in these 'new women' days! I believe that, thanks to newspapers, magazines and 'decadent' novels, I am in all respects eminently fitted to be a wife!" and she laughed bitterly—"There is nothing in the rôle of marriage that I do not know, though I am not yet twenty. I have been prepared for a long time to be sold to the highest bidder, and what few silly notions I had about love,—the love of the poets and idealists,—when I was a dreamy child at Willowsmere, are all dispersed and ended. Ideal love is dead,—and worse than dead, being out of fashion. Carefully instructed as I have been in the worthlessness of everything but money, you can scarcely be surprised at my speaking of myself as an object of sale. Marriage for me *is* a sale, as far as my father is concerned,—for you know well enough that however much you loved me or I loved you, he would never allow me to marry you if you were not rich, and richer than most men. I want you to feel that I fully recognize the nature of the bargain struck; and I ask you not to expect a girl's fresh, confiding love from a woman as warped in heart and mind as I am!"

"Sibyl,"—I said earnestly—"You wrong yourself; I am sure you wrong yourself! You are one of those who can be in the world yet not of it; your mind is too open and pure to be sullied, even by contact with evil things. I will believe nothing you say against your own sweet and noble character,—and, Sibyl, let me again ask you not to distress me by this constant harping on the subject of my wealth, or I shall be inclined to look upon it as a curse,—I should love you as much if I were poor—"

"Oh, you might love me"—she interrupted me, with a strange smile—"but you would not dare to say so!"

I was silent. Suddenly she laughed, and linked her arms caressingly round my neck.

"There, Geoffrey!" she said—"I have finished my discourse,—my bit of Ibsenism, or whatever other ism affects me,—and we need not be miserable about it. I have said what was in my mind; I have told you the truth, that in heart I am neither young nor innocent. But I am no worse than all my 'set' so perhaps you had better make the best of me. I please your fancy, do I not?"

"My love for you cannot be so lightly expressed, Sibyl!" I answered in rather a pained tone.

"Never mind,—it is my humour so to express it"—she went on—"I please your fancy, and you wish to marry me. Well now, all I ask is, go to my father and buy me at once! Conclude the bargain! And when you have bought me,—don't look so tragic!" and she laughed again—"and when you have paid the clergyman, and paid the bridesmaids (with monogram lockets or brooches) and paid the guests (with wedding-cake and champagne) and cleared up all scores with everybody, even to the last man who shuts the door of the nuptial brougham,—will you take me away,—far away from this place—this house, where my mother's face haunts me like a ghost in the darkness; where I am tortured by terrors night and day,—where I hear such strange sounds, and dream of such ghastly things,—" here her voice suddenly broke, and she hid her face against my breast—"Oh yes, Geoffrey, take me away as quickly as possible! Let us never live in hateful London, but at Willowsmere; I may find some of the old joys there,—and some of the happy bygone days."

Touched by the appealing pathos of her accents, I pressed her to my heart, feeling that she was scarcely accountable for the strange things she said in her evidently overwrought and excitable condition.

"It shall be as you wish, my darling," I said—"The sooner I have you all to myself the better. This is the end of March,—will you be ready to marry me in June?"

"Yes," she answered, still hiding her face.

"And now Sibyl," I went on—"remember,—there must be no more talk of money and bargaining. Tell me what you have not yet told me,—that you love me,—and would love me even if I were poor."

She looked up, straightly and unflinchingly full into my eyes.

"I cannot tell you that,"—she said,—"I have told you I do not believe in love; and if you were poor I certainly should not marry you. It would be no use!"

"You are frank, Sibyl!"

"It is best to be frank, is it not?" and she drew a flower from the knot at her bosom, and began fastening it in my coat—"Geoffrey what is the good of pretence? You would hate to be poor, and so should I. I do not understand the verb 'to love,'—now and then when I read a book by Mavis Clare, I believe love may exist, but when I close the book my belief is shut up with it. So do not ask for what is not in me. I am willing—even glad to marry you; that is all you must expect."

"All!" I exclaimed, with a sudden mingling of love and wrath in my blood, as I closed my arms about her and kissed her passionately—"All!—you impassive ice-flower, it is not all!—you shall melt to my touch and learn what love *is*,—do not think you can escape its influence, you dear, foolish, beautiful child! Your passions are asleep,—they must wake!"

"For you?" she queried, resting her head back against my shoulder, and gazing up at me with a dreamy radiance in her lovely eyes.

"For me!"

She laughed.

"'Oh bid me love, and I will love!'"—she hummed softly under her breath.

"You will, you must, you shall!" I said ardently. "I will be your master in the art of loving!"

"It is a difficult art!" she said—"I am afraid it will take a life-time to complete my training, even with my 'master.'"

And a smile still lingered in her eyes, giving them a witch-like glamour, when I kissed her again and bade her good-night.

"You will tell Prince Rimânez the news?" she said.

"If you wish it."

"Of course I wish it. Tell him at once. I should like him to know."

I went down the stairs,—she leaned over the balustrade looking after me.

"Good-night Geoffrey!" she called softly.

"Good-night Sibyl!"

"Be sure you tell Prince Rimânez!"

Her white figure disappeared; and I walked out of the house in a chaotic state of mind, divided between pride, ecstasy and pain,—the engaged husband of an earl's daughter,—the lover of a woman who had declared herself incapable of love and destitute of faith.

XVIII

Looking back through the space of only three years to this particular period of my life, I can remember distinctly the singular expression of Lucio's face when I told him that Sibyl Elton had accepted me. His sudden smile gave a light to his eyes that I had never seen in them before,—a brilliant yet sinister glow, strangely suggestive of some inwardly suppressed wrath and scorn. While I spoke he was, to my vexation, toying with that uncanny favourite of his, the 'mummy-insect,'—and it annoyed me beyond measure to see the repulsive pertinacity with which the glittering bat-like creature clung to his hand.

"Women are all alike,"—he said with a hard laugh, when he had heard my news,—"Few of them have moral force enough to resist that temptation of a rich marriage."

I was irritated at this.

"It is scarcely fair of you to judge everything by the money-standard,"—I said,—then, after a little pause I added what in my own heart I knew to be a lie,—"She,—Sibyl,—loves me for myself alone."

His glance flashed over me like lightning.

"Oh!—sets the wind in that quarter! Why then, my dear Geoffrey, I congratulate you more heartily than ever. To conquer the affections of one of the proudest girls in England, and win her love so completely as to be sure she would marry you even if you had not a sou to bless yourself with—this is a victory indeed!—and one of which you may well be proud. Again and yet again I congratulate you!"

Tossing the horrible thing he called his 'sprite' off to fly on one of its slow humming circuits round the room, he shook my hand fervently, still smiling,—and I,—feeling instinctively that he was as fully aware of the truth as I was, namely, that had I been a poor author with nothing but what I could earn by my brains, the Lady Sibyl Elton would never have looked at me, much less agreed to marry me,—kept silence lest I should openly betray the reality of my position.

"You see"—he went on, with a cheerful relentlessness—"I was not aware that any old-world romance graced the disposition of one so apparently impassive as your beautiful fiancée. To love for love's sake only, is becoming really an obsolete virtue. I thought Lady Sibyl was an essentially modern woman, conscious of her position, and the necessity there was for holding that position proudly before the world at all costs,—and that the pretty pastoral sentiments of poetical Phyllises and Amandas had no place in her nature. I was wrong, it seems; and for once I have been mistaken in the fair sex!" Here he stretched out his hand to the 'sprite,' that now came winging its way back, and settled at once on its usual resting-place; "My friend, I assure you, if you have won a true woman's true love, you have a far greater fortune than your millions,—a treasure that none can afford to despise."

His voice softened,—his eyes grew dreamy and less scornful,—and I looked at him in some astonishment.

"Why Lucio, I thought you hated women?"

"So I do!" he replied quickly—"But do not forget why I hate them! It is because they have all the world's possibilities of good in their hands, and the majority of them deliberately turn these possibilities to evil. Men are influenced entirely by women, though few of them will own it,—through women they are lifted to heaven or driven to hell. The latter is the favourite course, and the one almost universally adopted."

His brow darkened, and the lines round his proud mouth grew hard and stern. I watched him for a moment,—then with sudden irrelevance I said—

"Put that abominable 'sprite' of yours away, will you? I hate to see you with it!"

"What, my poor Egyptian princess!" he exclaimed with a laugh— "Why so cruel to her Geoffrey? If you had lived in her day, you might have been one of her lovers! She was no doubt a charming person,—I find her charming still! However, to oblige you—" and here, placing the insect in its crystal receptacle he carried it away to the other end of the room. Then, returning towards me slowly, he said—"Who knows what the 'sprite' suffered as a woman, Geoffrey! Perhaps she made a rich marriage, and repented it! At anyrate I am sure she is much happier in her present condition!"

"I have no sympathy with such a ghastly fancy,"—I said abruptly—"I only know that *she* or *it* is a perfectly loathsome object to me."

"Well,—some 'transmigrated' souls *are* loathsome objects to look at;"—he declared imperturbably—"When they are deprived of their respectable two-legged fleshly covering, it is extraordinary what a change the inexorable law of Nature makes in them!"

"What nonsense you talk, Lucio!" I said impatiently—"How can you know anything about it!"

A sudden shadow passed over his face, giving it a strange pallor and impenetrability.

"Have you forgotten"—he said in deliberately measured accents—"that your friend John Carrington, when he wrote that letter of introduction I brought from him to you, told you in it, that in all matters scientific I was an 'absolute master?' In these 'matters scientific' you have not tested my skill,—yet you ask—'how can I know?' I answer that I do know—many things of which you are ignorant. Do not presume too much on your own intellectual capability my friend,—lest I prove it naught!—lest I demonstrate to you, beyond all possibility of consoling doubt, that the shreds and strippings of that change you call death, are only so many embryos of new life which you *must* live, whether you will or no!"

Somewhat abashed by his words and still more by his manner, I said—

"Pardon me!—I spoke in haste of course,—but you know my theories—"

"Most thoroughly!" and he laughed, with an immediate resumption of his old manner—"'Every man his own theory' is the fashionable motto of the hour. Each little biped tells you that he has his 'own idea' of God, and equally 'his own' idea of the Devil. It is very droll! But let us return to the theme of love. I feel I have not congratulated you half enough,—for surely Fortune favours you singularly. Out of the teeming mass of vain and frivolous femininity, you have secured a unique example of beauty, truth and purity,—a woman, who apart from all self-interest and worldly advantage, weds you, with five millions, for yourself alone! The prettiest poem in the world could be made out of such an exquisitely innocent maiden type! You are one of the luckiest men alive; in fact, you have nothing more to wish for!"

I did not contradict him, though in my own mind I felt that the circumstances of my engagement left much to be desired. I, who scoffed at religion, wished it had formed part of the character of my future wife,—I, who sneered at sentiment, craved for some expression of it in the woman whose beauty attracted my desires. However I determinedly smothered all the premonitions of my own conscience, and accepted what each day of my idle and useless life brought me without considering future consequences.

The papers soon had the news that "a marriage has been arranged and will shortly take place between Sibyl, only daughter of the Earl of Elton, and Geoffrey Tempest, the famous millionaire." Not 'famous author' mark you!—though I was still being loudly 'boomed.' Morgeson, my publisher, could offer me no consolation as to my chances of winning and keeping a steady future fame. The Tenth Edition of my book was announced, but we had not actually disposed of more than two thousand copies, including a One-Volume issue which had been hastily thrust on the market. And the work I had so mercilessly and maliciously slated,—'Differences' by Mavis Clare was in its thirtieth thousand! I commented on this with some anger to Morgeson, who was virtuously aggrieved at my complaint.

"Dear me, Mr. Tempest, you are not the only writer who has been 'boomed' by the press and who nevertheless does not sell,"— he exclaimed—"No one can account for the caprices of the public; they are entirely beyond the most cautious publisher's control or calculation. Miss Clare is a sore subject to many authors besides yourself,—she always 'takes' and no one can help it. I sympathize with you in the matter heartily, but I am not to blame. At any rate the reviewers are all with you,—their praise has been almost unanimous. Now Mavis Clare's 'Differences,' though to my thinking a very brilliant and powerful book, has been literally cut to pieces whenever it has been noticed at all,—and yet the public go for her and don't go for you. It isn't my fault. You see people have got Compulsory Education now, and I'm afraid they begin to mistrust criticism, preferring to form their own independent opinions; if this is so, of course it will be a terrible thing, because the most carefully organized clique in the world will be powerless. Everything has been done for you that can be done, Mr. Tempest,—I am sure I regret as much as yourself that the result has not been all you expected or desired. Many authors would not care so much for the public approval; the applause of cultured journalism such as you have obtained, would be more than sufficient for them."

I laughed bitterly. 'The applause of cultured journalism!' I thought I knew something of the way in which such applause was won. Almost I began to hate my millions,—golden trash that could only secure me the insincere flattery of fair-weather friends,—and that could not give me fame,—such fame as has sometimes been grasped in a moment by a starving and neglected genius, who in the very arms of death, succeeds in mastering the world. One day in a fit of disappointment and petulance I said to Lucio—

"You have not kept all your promises, my friend!—you told me you could give me fame!"

He looked at me curiously.

"Did I? Well,—and are you not famous?"

"No. I am merely notorious," I retorted.

He smiled.

"The word fame, my good Geoffrey, traced to its origin means 'a breath'—the breath of popular adulation. You have that—for your wealth."

"But not for my work!"

"You have the praise of the reviewers!"

"What is that worth!"

"Everything!" he answered smiling—"In the reviewers' own opinion!"

I was silent.

"You speak of work;" he went on—"Now the nature of work I cannot exactly express, because it is a divine thing and is judged by a divine standard. One must consider in all work two things; first, the object for which it is undertaken, and secondly the way in which it is performed. All work should have a high and unselfish intent,—without this, it perishes and is not considered work at all,—not at least by the eternal judges invisible. If it *is* work, truly and nobly done in every sense of the word, it carries with it its own reward, and the laurels descend from heaven shaped ready for wearing,—no earthly power can bestow them. I cannot give you *that* fame,—but I have secured you a very fair imitation of it."

I was obliged to acquiesce, though more or less morosely,—whereat I saw that he was somewhat amused. Unwilling to incur his contempt I said no more concerning the subject that was the nearest to my heart, and wore out many sleepless hours at night in trying to write a new book,—something novel and daring, such as should force the public to credit me with a little loftier *status* than that obtained by the possession of a huge banking account. But the creative faculty seemed dead in me,—I was crushed by a sense of impotence and failure; vague ideas were in my brain that would not lend themselves to expression in words,—and such a diseased love of hypercriticism controlled me, that after a miserably nervous analysis of every page I wrote, I tore it up as soon as it was written, thus reducing myself to a state of mind that was almost unbearable.

Early in April I made my first visit to Willowsmere, having received information from the head of the firm of decorators and furnishers employed there, that their work was close on completion, and that they would be glad of a visit of inspection from me. Lucio and I went down together for the day, and as the train rushed through a green and smiling landscape, bearing us away from the smoke, dirt and noise of the restless modern Babylon, I was conscious of a gradually deepening peace and pleasure. The first sight of the place I had recklessly purchased without so much as looking at it, filled me with delight and admiration. It was a beautiful old house, ideally English and suggestive of home-happiness. Ivy and jessamine clung to its red walls and picturesque gables,—through the long vista of the exquisitely wooded grounds, the silver gleam of the Avon river could be discerned, twisting in and out like a ribbon tied in true love-knots,—the trees and shrubs were sprouting forth in all their fresh spring beauty,—the aspect of the country was indescribably bright and soothing, and I began to feel as if a burden had been suddenly lifted from my life leaving me free to breathe and enjoy my liberty. I strolled from room to room of my future abode, admiring the taste and skill with which the whole place had been fitted and furnished, down to the smallest detail of elegance, comfort and convenience. Here my Sibyl was born, I thought, with a lover-like tenderness,—here she would dwell again as my wife, amid the lovely and beloved surroundings of her childhood,—and we should be happy—yes, we should be happy, despite all the dull and heartless social doctrines of the modern world. In the spacious and beautiful drawing-room I stopped to look out from the windows on the entrancing view of lawn and woodland that stretched before me,—and as I looked, a warm sense of gratitude and affection filled me for the friend to whose good offices I owed this fair domain. Turning, I grasped him by the hand.

"It is all your doing, Lucio!" I said—"I feel I can never thank you enough! Without you I should perhaps never have met Sibyl,—I might never have heard of her, or of Willowsmere; and I never could have been as happy as I am to-day!"

"Oh, you are happy then?" he queried with a little smile—"I fancied you were not!"

"Well—I have not been as happy as I expected to be;" I confessed,—"Something in my sudden accession to wealth seems to have dragged me down rather than lifted me up,—it is strange—"

"It is not strange at all"—he interrupted,—"on the contrary it is very natural. As a rule the most miserable people in the world are the rich."

"Are you miserable, for instance?" I asked, smiling.

His eyes rested on me with a dark and dreary pathos.

"Are you too blind to see that I am?" he answered, his accents vibrating with intense melancholy—"Can you think I am happy? Does the smile I wear,—the disguising smile men put on as a mask to hide their secret agonies from the pitiless gaze of unsympathetic fellow-creatures,—persuade you that I am free from care? As for my wealth,—I have never told you the extent of it; if I did, it might indeed amaze you, though I believe it would not now arouse your envy, considering that your trifling five millions have not been without effect in depressing your mind. But I,—I could buy up kingdoms and be none the poorer,—I could throne and unthrone kings and be none the wiser,—I could crush whole countries under the iron heel of financial speculation,—I could possess the world,—and yet estimate it at no higher value than I do now,—the value of a grain of dust circling through infinity, or a soap-bubble blown on the wind!"

His brows knitted,—his face expressed pride, scorn and sorrow.

"There is some mystery about you Lucio;"—I said—"Some grief or loss that your wealth cannot repair—and that makes you the strange being you are. One day perhaps you will confide in me. . ."

He laughed loudly,—almost fiercely;—and clapped me heavily on the shoulder.

"I will!" he said—"I will tell you my history! And you, excellent agnostic as you are, shall 'minister to a mind diseased,' and 'pluck out the memory of a rooted sorrow!' What a power of expression there was in Shakespeare, the uncrowned but actual King of England! Not the 'rooted sorrow' alone was to be 'plucked out' but the very 'memory' of it. The apparently simple line holds complex wisdom; no doubt the poet knew, or instinctively guessed the most terrible fact in all the Universe. . ."

"And what is that?"

"The eternal consciousness of Memory—" he replied—"God can not forget,—and in consequence of this, His creatures *may* not!"

I forbore to reply, but I suppose my face betrayed my thoughts, for the cynical smile I knew so well played round his mouth as he looked at me.

"I go beyond your patience, do I not!" he said, laughing again—"When I mention God,—who is declared by certain scientists to be non-existent except as a blind, indifferent natural Force or Atom-producer;—you are bored! I can see that at a glance. Pray forgive me!

Let us resume our tour of inspection through this charming abode. You will be very difficult to satisfy if you are not a very emperor of contentment here;—with a beautiful wife and plenty of cash, you can well afford to give fame the go-by."

"I may win it yet!" I said hopefully—"In this place, I feel I could write something worthy of being written."

"Good! The 'divine flutterings' of winged thoughts are in your brain! Apollo grant them strength to fly! And now let us have luncheon,—afterwards we shall have time to take a stroll."

In the dining-room I found an elegant repast prepared, which rather surprised me, as I had given no orders, having indeed forgotten to do so. Lucio however had, it appeared, not forgotten, and an advance telegram from him had placed certain caterers at Leamington on their mettle, with the result that we sat down to a feast as delicate and luxurious as any two epicures could desire.

"Now I want you to do me a favour, Geoffrey,"—said Lucio, during our luncheon—"You will scarcely need to reside here till after your marriage; you have too many engagements in town. You spoke of entertaining a big house-party down here,—I wouldn't do that if I were you,—it isn't worth while. You would have to get in a staff of servants, and leave them all afterwards to their own devices while you are on your honeymoon. This is what I propose,—give a grand fête here in honour of your betrothal to Lady Sibyl, in May—and let me be the master of the revels!"

I was in the mood to agree to anything,—moreover the idea seemed an excellent one. I said so and Rimânez went on quickly—

"You understand of course, that if I undertake to do a thing I always do it thoroughly, and brook no interference with my plans. Now as your marriage will be the signal for our parting,—at any rate for a time,—I should like to show my appreciation of your friendship, by organizing a brilliant affair of the kind I suggest,—and if you will leave it all to me, I guarantee you shall hold such a fête as has never been seen or known in England. And it will be a personal satisfaction to me if you consent to my proposal."

"My dear fellow—" I answered—"Of course I consent—willingly! I give you *carte blanche*,—do as you like; do all you like! It is most friendly and kind of you! But when are we to make this sensation?"

"You are to be married in June?" he asked.

"Yes,—in the second week of the month."

"Very well. The fête shall be held on the twenty-second of May,—that will give society time to recover from the effect of one burst of splendour in order to be ready for another,—namely the wedding. Now we need not talk of this any more—it is settled,—the rest devolves on me. We've got three or four hours to spare before we take the train back to town,—suppose we take a saunter through the grounds?"

I assented to this, and accompanied him readily, feeling in high spirits and good humour. Willowsmere and its peaceful loveliness seemed to cleanse my mind of all corroding influences;—the blessed silence of the woods and hills, after the rush and roar of town life, soothed and cheered me, and I walked beside my companion with a light heart and smiling face,—happy, and filled with a dim religious faith in the blue sky, if not in the God beyond it. We sauntered through the fair gardens which were now mine, and then out through the park into a lovely little lane,—a true Warwickshire lane, where the celandines were strewing the grass with their bright gold coinage, and the star-wort thrust up fairy bouquets of white bloom between buttercups and lover, and where the hawthorn-buds were beginning to show themselves like minute snow-pellets among the glossy young green. A thrush warbled melodiously,—a lark rose from almost our very feet and flung itself joyously into the sky with a wild outburst of song,—a robin hopped through a little hole in the hedge to look at us in blithe inquisitiveness as we passed. All at once Lucio stopped and laid his hand on my shoulder,—his eyes had the beautiful melancholy of a far-off longing which I could neither understand nor define.

"Listen, Geoffrey!" he said—"Listen to the silence of the earth while the lark sings! Have you ever observed the receptive attitude in which Nature seems to wait for sounds divine!"

I did not answer,—the silence around us was indeed impressive;—the warbling of the thrush had ceased, and only the lark's clear voice pealing over-head, echoed sweetly through the stillness of the lane.

"In the clerical Heaven," went on Lucio dreamily—"there are no birds. There are only conceited human souls braying forth 'Alleluia'! No flowers are included,—no trees; only 'golden streets.' What a poor and barbarous conception! As if a World inhabited by Deity would not contain the wonders, graces and beauties of all worlds! Even this little planet is more naturally beautiful than the clerical Heaven,—that is, it is beautiful wherever Man is not. I protest—I have always protested,—against the creation of Man!"

I laughed.

"You protest against your own existence then!" I said.

His eyes darkened slowly to a sombre brooding blackness.

"When the sea roars and flings itself in anger on the shore, it craves its prey—Mankind!—it seeks to wash the fair earth clean of the puny insect that troubles the planet's peace! It drowns the noxious creature when it can, with the aid of its sympathizing comrade the wind! When the thunder crashes down a second after the lightning, does it not seem to you that the very clouds combine in the holy war? The war against God's one mistake;—the making of humanity,—the effort to sweep it out of the universe as one erases a weak expression in an otherwise perfect Poem! You and I, for example, are the only discords in to-day's woodland harmony. We are not particularly grateful for life,—we certainly are not content with it,—we have not the innocence of a bird or a flower. We have more knowledge you will say,—but how can we be sure of that? Our wisdom came from the devil in the first place, according to the legend of the tree of knowledge,—the fruit of which taught both good and evil, but which still apparently persuades man to evil rather than good, and leads him on to a considerable amount of arrogance besides, for he has an idea he will be immortal as a god in the hereafter,—ye majestic Heavens!—what an inadequately stupendous fate for a grain of worthless dust,—a dwarfish atom such as he!"

"Well, *I* have no ideas of immortality"—I said—"I have told you that often. This life is enough for me,—I want and expect no other."

"Aye, but if there were another!" answered Lucio, fixing me with a steady look—"And—if you were not asked your opinion about it—but simply plunged headlong into a state of terrible consciousness in which you would rather not be—"

"Oh come," I said impatiently—"do not let us theorise! I am happy to-day!—my heart is as light as that of the bird singing in the sky; I am in the very best of humours, and could not say an unkind word to my worst enemy."

He smiled.

"Is that your humour?" and he took me by the arm—"Then there could be no better opportunity for showing you this pretty little corner of the world;"—and walking on a few yards, he dexterously turned me down a narrow path, leading from the lane, and brought me face to face with a lovely old cottage, almost buried in the green of the young spring

MARIE CORELLI

verdure, and surrounded by an open fence overgrown with hawthorn and sweet-briar,—"Keep firm hold over your temper Geoffrey,—and maintain the benignant tranquillity of your mind!—here dwells the woman whose name and fame you hate,—Mavis Clare!"

XIX

The blood rushed to my face, and I stopped abruptly.

"Let us go back," I said.

"Why?"

"Because I do not know Miss Clare and do not want to know her. Literary women are my abhorrence,—they are always more or less unsexed."

"You are thinking of the 'New' women I suppose,—but you flatter them,—they never had any sex to lose. The self-degrading creatures who delineate their fictional heroines as wallowing in unchastity, and who write freely on subjects which men would hesitate to name, are unnatural hybrids of no-sex. Mavis Clare is not one of them,—she is an 'old-fashioned' young woman. Mademoiselle Derino, the dancer, is 'unsexed,' but you did not object to her on that score,—on the contrary I believe you have shown your appreciation of her talents by spending a considerable amount of cash upon her."

"That's not a fair comparison"—I answered hotly—"Mademoiselle Derino amused me for a time."

"And was not your rival in art!" said Lucio with a little malicious smile—"I see! Still,—as far as the question of being 'unsexed' goes, I, personally, consider that a woman who shows the power of her intellect is more to be respected than the woman who shows the power of her legs. But men always prefer the legs,—just as they prefer the devil to the Deity. All the same, I think, as we have time to spare, we may as well see this genius."

"Genius!" I echoed contemptuously.

"Feminine twaddler, then!" he suggested, laughing—"Let us see this feminine twaddler. She will no doubt prove as amusing as Mademoiselle Derino in her way. I shall ring the bell and ask if she is at home."

He advanced towards the creeper-covered porch,—but I stood back, mortified and sullen, determined not to accompany him inside the house if he were admitted. Suddenly a blithe peal of musical laughter sounded through the air, and a clear voice exclaimed—

"Oh Tricksy! You wicked boy! Take it back directly and apologise!"

Lucio peered through the fence, and then beckoned to me energetically.

"There she is!" he whispered, "There is the dyspeptic, sour, savage

MARIE CORELLI

old blue-stocking,—there, on the lawn,—by Heaven!—she's enough to strike terror into the heart of any man—and millionaire!"

I looked where he pointed, and saw nothing but a fair-haired woman in a white gown, sitting in a low basket-chair, with a tiny toy terrier on her lap. The terrier was jealously guarding a large square dog-biscuit nearly as big as himself, and at a little distance off sat a magnificent rough-coated St Bernard, wagging his feathery tail to and fro, with every sign of good-humour and enjoyment. The position was evident at a glance,—the small dog had taken his huge companion's biscuit from him and had conveyed it to his mistress,—a canine joke which seemed to be appreciated and understood by all the parties concerned. But as I watched the little group, I did not believe that she whom I saw was Mavis Clare. That small head was surely never made for the wearing of deathless laurels, but rather for a garland of roses, (sweet and perishable) twined by a lover's hand. No such slight feminine creature as the one I now looked upon could ever be capable of the intellectual grasp and power of 'Differences,' the book I secretly admired and wondered at, but which I had anonymously striven to 'quash' in its successful career. The writer of such a work, I imagined, must needs be of a more or less strong physique, with pronounced features and an impressive personality. This butterfly-thing, playing with her dog, was no type of a 'blue-stocking,' and I said as much to Lucio.

"That cannot be Miss Clare," I said—"More likely a visitor,—or perhaps the companion-secretary. The novelist must be very different in appearance to that frivolous young person in white, whose dress is distinctly Parisian, and who seems to have nothing whatever to do but amuse herself."

"Tricksy!" said the clear voice again—"Take back the biscuit and apologise!"

The tiny terrier looked round with an innocently abstracted air, as if in the earnestness of his own thoughts, he had not quite caught the meaning of the sentence.

"Tricksy!" and the voice became more imperative—"Take it back and apologise!"

With a comical expression of resignation to circumstances, 'Tricksy' seized the large biscuit, and holding it in his teeth with gingerly care, jumped from his mistress's knee and trotting briskly up to the St Bernard who was still wagging his tail and smiling as visibly as dogs often can smile, restored his stolen goods with three short yapping barks as much as to say "There! take it!" The St Bernard rose in all his majestic bulk and sniffed at it,—then sniffed his small friend, apparently in dignified doubt as to which was terrier and which was biscuit,—then lying down again, he gave himself up to the pleasure of munching his meal, the while "Tricksy" with wild barks of delight performed a sort of mad war-dance round and round him by way of entertainment. This piece of dog-comedy was still going on, when Lucio turned away from his point of observation at the fence, and going up to the gate, rang the bell. A neat maid-servant answered the summons.

"Is Miss Clare at home?" he asked.

"Yes sir. But I am not sure whether she will receive you,—" the maid replied—"Unless you have an appointment?"

"We have no appointment,"—said Lucio,—"but if you will take these cards,—" here he turned to me—"Geoffrey, give me one of yours!" I complied, somewhat reluctantly. "If you will take these cards"—he resumed—"to Miss Clare, it is just possible she may be kind enough to see us. If not, it will be our loss."

He spoke so gently and with such an ingratiating manner that I could see the servant was at once prepossessed in his favour.

"Step in, sir, if you please,—" she said smiling and opening the gate. He obeyed with alacrity,—and I, who a moment ago had resolved not to enter the place, found myself passively following him under an archway of sprouting young leaves and early budding jessamine into 'Lily Cottage'—which was to prove one day, though I knew it not then, the only haven of peace and security I should ever crave for,—and, craving, be unable to win!

The house was much larger than it looked from the outside; the entrance-hall was square and lofty, and panelled with fine old carved oak, and the drawing-room into which we were shown was one of the most picturesque and beautiful apartments I had ever seen. There were flowers everywhere,—books,—rare bits of china,—elegant trifles that only a woman of perfect taste would have the sense to select and appreciate,—on one or two of the side-tables and on the grand piano were autograph-portraits of many of the greatest celebrities in Europe. Lucio strolled about the room, making soft comments.

"Here is the Autocrat of all the Russias," he said, pausing before a fine portrait of the Tsar—"Signed by the Imperial hand too. Now what has the 'feminine twaddler' done to deserve that honour I wonder! Here in strange contrast, is the wild-haired Paderewski,—and beside him the perennial Patti,—there is Her Majesty of Italy, and here we have the Prince of Wales,—all autographed likenesses. Upon my word, Miss Clare seems to attract a great many notabilities around her without the aid of hard cash. I wonder how she does it, Geoffrey?"—and his eyes sparkled half maliciously—"Can it be a case of genius after all? Look at those lilies!" and he pointed to a mass of white bloom in one of the windows—"Are they not far more beautiful creatures than men and women? Dumb—yet eloquent of purity!—no wonder the painters choose them as the only flowers suitable for the adornment of angels."

As he spoke the door opened, and the woman we had seen on the lawn entered, carrying her toy terrier on one arm. Was she Mavis Clare? or some-one sent to say that the novelist could not receive us? I wondered silently, looking at her in surprise and something of confusion,—Lucio advanced with an odd mingling of humility and appeal in his manner which was new to me.

"We must apologise for our intrusion, Miss Clare,"—he said—"But happening to pass your house, we could not resist making an attempt to see you. My name is—Rimânez"—he hesitated oddly for a second, then went on—"and this is my friend Mr. Geoffrey Tempest, the author,—" the young lady raised her eyes to mine with a little smile and courteous bend of her head—"he has, as I daresay you know, become the owner of Willowsmere Court. You will be neighbours, and I hope, friends. In any case if we have committed a breach of etiquette in venturing to call upon you without previous introduction, you must try and forgive us! It is difficult,—to me impossible,—to pass the dwelling of a celebrity without offering homage to the presiding genius within."

Mavis Clare,—for it was Mavis Clare,—seemed not to have heard the intended compliment.

"You are very welcome," she said simply, advancing with a pretty grace, and extending her hand to each of us in turn, "I am quite accustomed to visits from strangers. But I already know Mr. Tempest very well by reputation. Won't you sit down?"

She motioned us to chairs in the lily-decked window-corner, and rang the bell. Her maid appeared.

"Tea, Janet."

This order given, she seated herself near us, still holding her little dog curled up against her like a small ball of silk. I tried to converse, but could find nothing suitable to say,—the sight of her filled me with too great a sense of self-reproach and shame. She was such a quiet graceful creature, so slight and dainty, so perfectly unaffected and simple in manner, that as I thought of the slaughtering article I had written against her work I felt like a low brute who had been stoning a child. And yet,—after all it was her genius I hated,—the force and passion of that mystic quality which wherever it appears, compels the world's attention,—this was the gift she had that I lacked and coveted. Moved by the most conflicting sensations I gazed abstractedly out on the shady old garden,—I heard Lucio conversing on trifling matters of society and literature generally, and every now and then her bright laugh rang out like a little peal of bells. Soon I felt, rather than saw, that she was looking steadily at me,—and turning, I met her eyes,—deep dense blue eyes, candidly grave and clear.

"Is this your first visit to Willowsmere Court?" she asked.

"Yes," I answered, making an effort to appear more at my ease—"I bought the place,—on the recommendation of my friend the prince here,—without looking at it."

"So I heard,"—she said, still observing me curiously—"And you are satisfied with it?"

"More than satisfied—I am delighted. It exceeds all my best expectations."

"Mr. Tempest is going to marry the daughter of the former owner of Willowsmere,"—put in Lucio,—"No doubt you have seen it announced in the papers?"

"Yes;"—she responded with a slight smile—"I have seen it—and I think Mr. Tempest is much to be congratulated. Lady Sibyl is very lovely,—I remember her as a beautiful child when I was a child myself—I never spoke to her, but I often saw her. She must be charmed at the prospect of returning as a bride to the old home she loved so well."

Here the servant entered with the tea, and Miss Clare, putting down her tiny dog, went to the table to dispense it. I watched her move across the room with a sense of vague wonder and reluctant admiration,— she rather resembled a picture by Greuze in her soft white gown with a pale rose nestled amid the old Flemish lace at her throat,—and as she turned her head towards us, the sunlight caught her fair hair and turned it to the similitude of a golden halo circling her brows. She was not a beauty; but she possessed an undoubted individual charm,—a delicate attractiveness, which silently asserted itself, as the breath of honeysuckle hidden in the tangles of a hedge, will delight the wayfarer with sweet fragrance though the flowers be unseen.

"Your book was very clever, Mr. Tempest"—she said suddenly, smiling at me—"I read it as soon as it came out. But do you know I think your article was even cleverer?"

I felt myself growing uncomfortably red in the face.

"To what article do you allude, Miss Clare?" I stammered confusedly—"I do not write for any magazine."

"No?" and she laughed gaily—"But you did on this occasion! You 'slated' me very smartly!—I quite enjoyed it. I found out that you were the author of the philippic,—not through the editor of the journal—oh no, poor man! he is very discreet; but through quite another person who must be nameless. It is very difficult to prevent me from finding out whatever I wish to know, especially in literary matters! Why, you look quite unhappy!" and her blue eyes danced with fun as she handed me my cup of tea—"You really don't suppose I was hurt by your critique, do you? Dear me, no! Nothing of that kind ever affronts me,—I am far too busy to waste any thought on reviews or reviewers. Only your article was so exceptionally funny!"

"Funny?" I echoed stupidly, trying to smile, but failing in the effort.

"Yes, funny!" she repeated—"It was so very angry that it became amusing. My poor 'Differences'! I am really sorry it put you into such a temper,—temper does exhaust one's energies so!"

She laughed again and sat down in her former place near me, regarding me with a frankly open and half humorous gaze which I found I could not meet with any sort of composure. To say I felt foolish, would inadequately express my sense of utter bafflement. This woman with her young unclouded face, sweet voice and evidently happy nature, was not at all the creature I had imagined her to be,—and I struggled to say something,—anything,—that would furnish a reasonable and coherent answer. I caught Lucio's glance,—one of satirical amusement,—and my thoughts grew more entangled than ever. A distraction however occurred in the behaviour of the dog Tricksy, who suddenly took up a position immediately opposite Lucio, and lifting his nose in air began to howl with a desolate loudness astonishing in so small an animal. His mistress was surprised.

"Tricksy, what *is* the matter?" she exclaimed, catching him up in her arms where he hid his face shivering and moaning;—then she looked steadily at Lucio—"I never knew him do such a thing before"—she said—"Perhaps you do not like dogs, Prince Rimânez?"

"I am afraid they do not like *me*!" he replied, deferentially.

"Then pray excuse me a moment!" she murmured, and left the room, to return immediately without her canine favorite. After this I noticed that her blue eyes often rested on Lucio's handsome countenance with a bewildered and perplexed expression, as if she saw something in his very beauty that she disliked or distrusted. Meanwhile I had recovered a little of my usual self-possession, and I addressed her in a tone which I meant to be kind, but which I knew was somewhat patronizing.

"I am very glad, Miss Clare, that you were not offended at the article you speak of. It was rather strong I admit,—but you know we cannot all be of the same opinion. . ."

"Indeed no!" she said quietly and with a slight smile—"Such a state of things would make a very dull world! I assure you I was not and am not in the least offended—the critique was a smart piece of writing, and made not the slightest effect on me or on my book. You remember what Shelley wrote of critics? No? You will find the passage in his preface to 'The Revolt of Islam,' and it runs thus,—'I have sought to write as I believe that Homer, Shakespeare, and Milton wrote, with an utter disregard of anonymous censure. I am certain that calumny and misrepresentation, though it may move me to compassion cannot disturb my peace. I shall understand the expressive silence of those sagacious enemies who dare not trust themselves to speak. I shall endeavour to extract from the midst of insult and contempt and maledictions, those admonitions which may tend to correct whatever imperfections such censurers may discern in my appeal to the Public. If certain Critics were as clear-sighted as they are malignant, how great would be the benefit to be derived from their virulent writings! As it is, I fear I shall be malicious enough to be amused with their paltry tricks and lame invectives. Should the public judge that my composition is worthless, I shall indeed bow before the tribunal from which Milton received his crown of immortality, and shall seek to gather, if I live, strength from that defeat, which may nerve me to some new enterprise of thought which may *not* be worthless!'"

As she gave the quotation, her eyes darkened and deepened,—her face was lighted up as by some inward illumination,—and I discovered the rich sweetness of the voice which made the name of 'Mavis' suit her so well.

"You see I know my Shelley!" she said with a little laugh at her own emotion—"And those words are particularly familiar to me, because I have had them painted up on a panel in my study. Just to remind me, in case I should forget, what the really great geniuses of the world thought of criticism,—because their example is very encouraging and helpful to a humble little worker like myself. I am not a press-favourite—and I never get good reviews,—but—" and she laughed again—"I like my reviewers all the same! If you have finished your tea, will you come and see them?"

Come and see them! What did she mean? She seemed delighted at my visible surprise, and her cheeks dimpled with merriment.

"Come and see them!" she repeated—"They generally expect me at this hour!"

She led the way into the garden,—we followed,—I, in a bewildered confusion of mind, with all my ideas respecting 'unsexed females' and repulsive blue-stockings upset by the unaffected behaviour and charming frankness of this 'celebrity' whose fame I envied, and whose personality I could not but admire. With all her intellectual gifts she was yet a lovable woman,—ah Mavis!—how lovable and dear I was destined in misery to know! Mavis, Mavis!—I whisper your sweet name in my solitude,—I see you in my dreams, and kneeling before you I call you Angel!—my angel at the gate of a lost Paradise, whose Sword of Genius turning every way, keeps me back from all approach to my forfeited Tree of Life!

XX

S carcely had we stepped out on the lawn before an unpleasant incident occurred which might have ended dangerously. At his mistress's approach the big St Bernard dog rose from the sunny corner where he had been peacefully dozing, and prepared to greet her,—but as soon as he perceived us he stopped short with an ominous growl. Before Miss Clare could utter a warning word, he made a couple of huge bounds and sprang savagely at Lucio as though to tear him in pieces,—Lucio with admirable presence of mind caught him firmly by the throat and forced him backwards. Mavis turned deathly pale.

"Let me hold him! He will obey me!" she cried, placing her little hand on the great dog's neck—"Down, Emperor! Down! How dare you! Down sir!"

In a moment 'Emperor' dropped to the ground, and crouched abjectly at her feet, breathing heavily and trembling in every limb. She held him by the collar, and looked up at Lucio who was perfectly composed, though his eyes flashed dangerously.

"I am so very sorry!" she murmured,—"I forgot,—you told me dogs do not like you. But what a singularly marked antipathy, is it not? I cannot understand it. Emperor is generally so good-natured,—I must apologize for his bad conduct—it is quite unusual. I hope he has not hurt you?"

"Not at all!" returned Lucio affably but with a cold smile; "I hope I have not hurt *him*,—or distressed *you*!"

She made no reply, but led the St Bernard away and was absent for a few minutes. While she was gone, Lucio's brow clouded, and his face grew very stern.

"What do you think of her?" he asked me abruptly.

"I hardly know what to think," I answered abstractedly—"She is very different to what I imagined. Her dogs are rather unpleasant company!"

"They are honest animals!" he said morosely—"They are no doubt accustomed to candour in their mistress, and therefore object to personified lies."

"Speak for yourself!" I said irritably—"They object to you, chiefly."

"Am I not fully aware of that?" he retorted—"and do I not speak for myself? You do not suppose I would call you a personified lie, do you,— even if it were true! I would not be so uncivil. But I am a living lie, and knowing it I admit it, which gives me a certain claim to honesty above the ordinary run of men. This woman-wearer of laurels is a personified truth!—imagine it!—she has no occasion to pretend to be anything else than she is! No wonder she is famous!"

I said nothing, as just then the subject of our conversation returned, tranquil and smiling, and did her best, with the tact and grace of a perfect hostess, to make us forget her dog's ferocious conduct, by escorting us through all the prettiest turns and twisting paths of her garden, which was quite a bower of spring beauty. She talked to us both with equal ease, brightness and cleverness, though I observed that she studied Lucio with close interest, and watched his looks and movements with more curiosity than liking. Passing under an arching grove of budding syringas, we presently came to an open court-yard paved with blue and white tiles, having in its centre a picturesque dove-cote built in the form of a Chinese pagoda. Here pausing, Mavis clapped her hands. A cloud of doves, white, grey, brown, and opalescent answered the summons, circling round and round her head, and flying down in excited groups at her feet.

"Here are my reviewers!" she said laughing—"Are they not pretty creatures? The ones I know best are named after their respective journals,—there are plenty of anonymous ones of course, who flock in with the rest. Here, for instance, is the 'Saturday Review'"—and she picked up a strutting bird with coral-tinted feet, who seemed to rather like the attention shown to him—"He fights with all his companions and drives them away from the food whenever he can. He is a quarrelsome creature!"—here she stroked the bird's head—"You never know how to please him,—he takes offence at the corn sometimes and will only eat peas, or *vice versa*. He quite deserves his name,—go away, old boy!" and she flung the pigeon in the air and watched it soaring up and down—"He *is* such a comical old grumbler! There is the 'Speaker'"—and she pointed to a fat fussy fantail—"He struts very well, and fancies he's important, you know, but he isn't. Over there is 'Public Opinion,'—that one half-asleep on the wall; next to him is the 'Spectator,'—you see he has two rings round his eyes like spectacles. That brown creature with the fluffy wings all by himself on that flower-pot is the 'Nineteenth Century,'—the little bird with the green neck is the 'Westminster Gazette,' and the fat one sitting on the platform of the cote is the 'Pall-Mall.' He knows his name very well—see!" and she called merrily—"Pall Mall! Come boy!—come here!" The bird obeyed at once, and flying down from the cote settled on her shoulder. "There are so many others,—it is difficult to distinguish them sometimes,"—she continued,—"Whenever I get a bad review I name a pigeon,—it amuses me. That draggle-tailed one with the muddy feet is the 'Sketch,'—he is not at all a well-bred bird I must tell you!—that smart-looking dove with the purple breast is the 'Graphic,' and that bland old grey thing is the 'I. L. N.' short for 'Illustrated London News.' Those three white ones are respectively 'Daily Telegraph,' 'Morning Post,' and 'Standard.' Now see them all!" and taking a covered basket from a corner she began to scatter corn and peas and various grains in lavish quantities all over the court. For a moment we could scarcely see the sky, so thickly the birds flocked together, struggling, fighting, swooping downwards, and soaring upwards,—but the wingéd confusion soon gave place to something like order when they were all on the ground and busy, selecting their respective favourite foods from the different sorts provided for their choice.

"You are indeed a sweet-natured philosopher"—said Lucio smiling, "if you can symbolize your adverse reviewers by a flock of doves!"

She laughed merrily.

"Well, it is a remedy against all irritation,"—she returned; "I used to worry a good deal over my work, and wonder why it was that the press people were so unnecessarily hard upon me, when they showed so much leniency and encouragement to far worse writers,—but after a little serious consideration, finding that critical opinion carried no sort of conviction whatever to the public, I determined to trouble no more about it,—except in the way of doves!"

"In the way of doves, you feed your reviewers,"—I observed.

"Exactly! And I suppose I help to feed them even as women and men!" she said—"They get something from their editors for 'slashing' my work,—and they probably make a little more out of selling their 'review copies.' So you see the dove-emblem holds good throughout. But you have not seen the 'Athenæum,'—oh, you *must* see him!"

With laughter still lurking in her blue eyes, she took us out of the pigeon-court, and led the way round to a sequestered and shady corner of the garden, where, in a large aviary-cage fitted up for its special convenience, sat a solemn white owl. The instant it perceived us, it became angry, and ruffling up its downy feathers, rolled its glistening yellow eyes vindictively and opened its beak. Two smaller owls sat in the background, pressed close together,—one grey, the other brown.

"Cross old boy!" said Mavis, addressing the spiteful-looking creature in the sweetest of accents—"Haven't you found any mice to kill to-day? Oh, what wicked eyes!—what a snappy mouth!" Then turning to us, she went on—"Isn't he a lovely owl? Doesn't he look wise?—but as a matter of fact he's just as stupid as ever he can be. That is why I call him the 'Athenæum'! He looks so profound, you'd fancy he knows everything, but he really thinks of nothing but killing mice all the time,—which limits his intelligence considerably!"

Lucio laughed heartily, and so did I,—she looked so mischievous and merry.

"But there are two other owls in the cage"—I said—"What are their names?"

She held up a little finger in playful warning.

"Ah, that would be telling secrets!" she said—"They're all the 'Athenæum'—the holy Three,—a sort of literary Trinity. But why a trinity I do not venture to explain!—it is a riddle I must leave you to guess!"

She moved on, and we followed across a velvety grass-plot bordered with bright spring-flowers, such as crocuses, tulips, anemones, and hyacinths, and presently pausing she asked—"Would you care to see my work-room?"

I found myself agreeing to this proposition with an almost boyish enthusiasm. Lucio glanced at me with a slight half-cynical smile.

"Miss Clare, are you going to name a pigeon after Mr. Tempest?" he inquired—"He played the part of an adverse critic, you know—but I doubt whether he will ever do so again!"

She looked round at me and smiled.

"Oh, I have been merciful to Mr. Tempest,"—she replied; "He is among the anonymous birds whom I do not specially recognise!"

She stepped into the arched embrasure of an open window which fronted the view of the grass and flowers, and entering with her we found ourselves in a large room, octagonal in shape, where the first object that attracted and riveted the attention was a marble bust of the Pallas Athene whose grave impassive countenance and tranquil brows directly faced the sun. A desk strewn with papers occupied the left-hand side of the window-nook,—in a corner draped with olive-green velvet, the white presence of the Apollo Belvedere taught in his inscrutable yet radiant smile, the lesson of love and the triumphs of fame,—and numbers of books were about, not ranged in formal rows on shelves as if they were never read, but placed on low tables and wheeled stands, that they might be easily taken up and glanced at. The arrangement of the walls chiefly excited my interest and admiration, for these were divided into panels, and every panel had, inscribed upon it in letters of gold, some phrase from the philosophers, or some verse from the poets. The passage from Shelley which Mavis had recently quoted to us, occupied, as she had said, one panel, and above it hung a beautiful bas-relief of the drowned poet copied from the monument at Via Reggio. Another and broader panel held a fine engraving of Shakespeare, and under the picture appeared the lines—

> *"To thine own self be true,*
> *And it must follow as the night the day,*
> *Thou canst not then be false to any man."*

Byron was represented,—also Keats; but it would have taken more than a day to examine the various suggestive quaintnesses and individual charms of this 'workshop' as its owner called it, though the hour was to come when I should know every corner of it by heart, and look upon it as a haunted outlaw of bygone ages looked upon 'sanctuary.' But now time gave us little pause,—and when we had sufficiently expressed our pleasure and gratitude for the kindness with which we had been received, Lucio, glancing at his watch, suggested departure.

"We could stay on here for an indefinite period Miss Clare,"—he said with an unwonted softness in his dark eyes; "It is a place for peace and happy meditation,—a restful corner for a tired soul." He checked a slight sigh,—then went on—"But trains wait for no man, and we are returning to town to-night."

"Then I will not detain you any longer," said our young hostess, leading the way at once by a side-door, through a passage filled with flowering plants, into the drawing-room where she had first entertained us—"I hope, Mr. Tempest," she added, smiling at me,—"that now we have met, you will no longer desire to qualify as one of my pigeons! It is scarcely worth while!"

"Miss Clare," I said, now speaking with unaffected sincerity—"I assure you, on my honour, I am very sorry I wrote that article against you. If I had only known you as you are—"

"Oh, that should make no difference to a critic!" she answered merrily.

"It would have made a great difference to me"—I declared; "You are so unlike the objectionable 'literary woman,'—" I paused, and she regarded me smilingly with her bright clear candid eyes,—then I added—"I must tell you that Sibyl,—Lady Sibyl Elton—is one of your most ardent admirers."

"I am very pleased to hear that,"—she said simply—"I am always glad when I succeed in winning somebody's approval and liking."

"Does not everyone approve and admire you?" asked Lucio.

"Oh no! By no means! The 'Saturday' says I only win the applause of shop-girls!" and she laughed—"Poor old 'Saturday'!—the writers on its staff are so jealous of any successful author. I told the Prince of Wales what it said the other day, and he was very much amused."

"You know the Prince?" I asked, in a little surprise.

"Well, it would be more correct to say that he knows me," she replied—"He has been very amiable in taking some little interest in my books. He knows a good deal about literature too,—much more than people give him credit for. He has been here more than once,—and has seen me feed my reviewers—the pigeons, you know! He rather enjoyed the fun I think!"

And this was all the result of the 'slating' the press gave to Mavis Clare! Simply that she named her doves after her critics, and fed them in the presence of whatever royal or distinguished visitors she might have (and I afterwards learned she had many) amid, no doubt, much laughter from those who saw the 'Spectator'-pigeon fighting for grains of corn, or the 'Saturday Review' pigeon quarrelling over peas! Evidently no reviewer, spiteful or otherwise, could affect the vivacious nature of such a mischievous elf as she was.

"How different you are—how widely different—to the ordinary run of literary people!" I said involuntarily.

"I am glad you find me so,"—she answered—"I hope I *am* different. As a rule literary people take themselves far too seriously, and attach too much importance to what they do. That is why they become such bores. I don't believe anyone ever did thoroughly good work who was not perfectly happy over it, and totally indifferent to opinion. I should be quite content to write on, if I only had a garret to live in. I was once very poor,—shockingly poor; and even now I am not rich, but I've got just enough to keep me working steadily, which is as it should be. If I had more, I might get lazy and neglect my work,—then you know Satan might step into my life, and it would be a question of idle hands and mischief to follow, according to the adage."

"I think you would have strength enough to resist Satan,—" said Lucio, looking at her stedfastly, with sombre scrutiny in his expressive eyes.

"Oh, I don't know about that,—I could not be sure of myself!" and she smiled—"I should imagine he must be a dangerously fascinating personage. I never picture him as the possessor of hoofs and a tail,— common-sense assures me that no creature presenting himself under such an aspect would have the slightest power to attract. Milton's conception of Satan is the finest"—and her eyes darkened swiftly with the intensity of her thoughts—"A mighty Angel fallen!—one cannot but be sorry for such a fall, if the legend were true!"

There was a sudden silence. A bird sang outside, and a little breeze swayed the lilies in the window to and fro.

"Good-bye, Mavis Clare!" said Lucio very softly, almost tenderly. His voice was low and tremulous—his face grave and pale. She looked up at him in a little surprise.

"Good-bye!" she rejoined, extending her small hand. He held it a moment,—then, to my secret astonishment, knowing his aversion to women, stooped and kissed it. She flushed rosily as she withdrew it from his clasp.

"Be always as you are Mavis Clare!"—he said gently—"Let nothing change you! Keep that bright nature of yours,—that unruffled spirit of quiet contentment, and you may wear the bitter laurel of fame as sweetly as a rose! I have seen the world; I have travelled far, and have met many famous men and women,—kings and queens, senators, poets and philosophers,—my experience has been wide and varied, so that I am not altogether without authority for what I say,—and I assure you that the Satan of whom you are able to speak with compassion, can never trouble the peace of a pure and contented soul. Like consorts with like,—a fallen angel seeks the equally fallen,—and the devil,—if there be one,—becomes the companion of those only who take pleasure in his teaching and society. Legends say he is afraid of a crucifix,—but if he is afraid of anything I should say it must be of that 'sweet content' concerning which your country's Shakespeare sings, and which is a better defence against evil than the church or the prayers of the clergy! I speak as one having the right of age to speak,—I am so many many years older than you!—you must forgive me if I have said too much!"

She was quite silent; evidently moved and surprised at his words; and she gazed at him with a vaguely wondering, half-awed expression,—an expression which changed directly I myself advanced to make my adieu.

"I am very glad to have met you, Miss Clare,"—I said—"I hope we shall be friends!"

"There is no reason why we should be enemies I think," she responded frankly—"I am very pleased you came to-day. If ever you want to 'slate' me again, you know your fate!—you become a dove,—nothing more! Good-bye!"

She saluted us prettily as we passed out, and when the gate had closed behind us we heard the deep and joyous baying of the great dog 'Emperor,' evidently released from 'durance vile' immediately on our departure. We walked on for some time in silence, and it was not till we had re-entered the grounds of Willowsmere, and were making our way to the drive where the carriage which was to take us to the station already awaited us, that Lucio said—

"Well; now, what do you think of her?"

"She is as unlike the accepted ideal of the female novelist as she can well be," I answered, with a laugh.

"Accepted ideals are generally mistaken ones,"—he observed, watching me narrowly—"An accepted ideal of Divinity in some church pictures is an old man's face set in a triangle. The accepted ideal of the devil is a nondescript creature, with horns, hoofs (one of them cloven) and a tail, as Miss Clare just now remarked. The accepted ideal of beauty is the Venus de Medicis,—whereas your Lady Sibyl entirely transcends that much over-rated statue. The accepted ideal of a poet is Apollo,—he was a god,—and no poet in the flesh ever approaches the god-like! And the accepted ideal of the female novelist, is an elderly, dowdy, spectacled, frowsy fright,—Mavis Clare does not fulfil this description, yet she is the author of 'Differences.' Now McWhing, who thrashes her continually in all the papers he can command, *is* elderly, ugly, spectacled and frowsy,—and he is the author of—nothing! Women-authors are invariably supposed to be hideous,—men-authors for the most part *are* hideous. But their hideousness is not noted or insisted upon,—whereas, no matter how good-looking women-writers may be, they still pass under press-comment as frights, because the fiat of press-opinion considers they ought to be frights, even if they are not. A pretty authoress is an offence,—an incongruity,—a something that neither men nor women care about. Men don't care about her, because

being clever and independent, she does not often care about them,—
women don't care about her, because she has the effrontery to combine
attractive looks with intelligence, and she makes an awkward rival to
those who have only attractive looks without intelligence. So wags the
world!—

> O wild world!—circling through æons untold,—
> 'Mid fires of sunrise and sunset,—through flashes of silver and gold,—
> Grain of dust in a storm,—atom of sand by the sea,—
> What is your worth, O world, to the Angels of God and me!

He sang this quite suddenly, his rich baritone pealing out musically
on the warm silent air. I listened entranced.

"What a voice you have!" I exclaimed—"What a glorious gift!"

He smiled, and sang on, his dark eyes flashing—

> O wild world! Mote in a burning ray
> Flung from the spherical Heavens millions of spaces away—
> Sink in the ether or soar! Live with the planets or die!—
> What should I care for your fate, who am one with the Infinite Sky!

"What strange song is that?" I asked, startled and thrilled by the
passion of his voice—"It seems to mean nothing!"

He laughed, and took my arm.

"It does mean nothing!" he said—"All drawing-room songs mean
nothing. Mine is a drawing-room song—calculated to waken emotional
impulses in the unloved spinster religiously inclined!"

"Nonsense!" I said, smiling.

"Exactly! That is what I say. It *is* nonsense!" Here we came up to the
carriage which waited for us—"Just twenty minutes to catch the train,
Geoffrey! Off we go!"

And off we did go,—I watching the red gabled roofs of Willowsmere
Court shining in the late sunshine, till a turn in the road hid them from
view.

"You like your purchase?" queried Lucio presently.

"I do. Immensely!"

"And your rival, Mavis Clare? Do you like her?"

I paused a moment, then answered frankly,

"Yes. I like her. And I will admit something more than that to you now. I like her book. It is a noble work,—worthy of the most highly-gifted man. I always liked it—and because I liked it, I slated it."

"Rather a mysterious course of procedure!" and he smiled; "Can you not explain?"

"Of course I can explain,"—I said—"Explanation is easy. I envied her power—I envy it still. Her popularity caused me a smarting sense of injury, and to relieve it I wrote that article against her. But I shall never do anything of the kind again. I shall let her grow her laurels in peace."

"Laurels have a habit of growing without any permission,"—observed Lucio significantly—"In all sorts of unexpected places too. And they can never be properly cultivated in the forcing-house of criticism."

"I know that!" I said quickly, my thoughts reverting to my own book, and all the favourable criticisms that had been heaped upon it—"I have learned that lesson thoroughly, by heart!"

He looked at me fixedly.

"It is only one of many you may have yet to learn"—he said—"It is a lesson in fame. Your next course of instruction will be in love!"

He smiled,—but I was conscious of a certain dread and discomfort as he spoke. I thought of Sibyl and her incomparable beauty—Sibyl, who had told me she could not love,—had we both to learn a lesson? And should we master it?—or would it master us?

XXI

The preparations for my marriage now went on apace,—shoals of presents began to arrive for Sibyl as well as for myself, and I was introduced to an hitherto undemonstrated phase (as far as I personally was concerned) of the vulgarity and hypocrisy of fashionable society. Everyone knew the extent of my wealth, and how little real necessity there was for offering me or my bride-elect costly gifts; nevertheless, all our so-called 'friends' and acquaintances, strove to outvie each other in the gross cash-value, if not in the good taste, of their various donations. Had we been a young couple bravely beginning the world on true love, in more or less uncertainty as to our prospects and future income, we should have received nothing either useful or valuable,—everyone would have tried to do the present-giving in as cheap and mean a way as possible. Instead of handsome services of solid silver, we should have had a meagre collection of plated teaspoons; instead of costly editions of books sumptuously enriched with fine steel engravings, we might possibly have had to express our gratitude for a ten-shilling Family Bible. Of course I fully realized the actual nature and object of the lavish extravagance displayed on this occasion by our social 'set,'—their gifts were merely so many bribes, sent with a purpose which was easy enough to fathom. The donors wished to be invited to the wedding in the first place,—after that, they sought to be included in our visiting-list, and foresaw invitations to our dinners and house-parties;—and more than this they calculated on our influence in society, and the possible chance there might be in the dim future of our lending some of them money should pressing occasion require it. In the scant thankfulness and suppressed contempt their adulatory offerings excited, Sibyl and I were completely at one. She looked upon her array of glittering valuables with the utmost weariness and indifference, and flattered my self-love by assuring me that the only things she cared at all for were the riviére of sapphires and diamonds I had given her as a betrothal-pledge, together with an engagement-ring of the same lustrous gems. Yet I noticed she also had a great liking for Lucio's present, which was a truly magnificent masterpiece of the jeweller's art. It was a girdle in the form of a serpent, the body entirely composed of the finest emeralds, and the head of rubies and diamonds. Flexible as a reed, when Sibyl put it on, it appeared to spring and coil round her waist like a living thing, and breathe with her breathing. I did not much care for it myself as an ornament for a young bride,—it seemed to me quite unsuitable,—but as everyone else admired it and envied the possessor of such superb jewels, I said nothing of my own distaste. Diana Chesney had shown a certain amount of delicate sentiment and refinement in her offering,—it was a very exquisite marble statue of Psyche, mounted on a pedestal of solid silver and ebony. Sibyl thanked her, smiling coldly.

"You have given me an emblem of the Soul,"—she said; "No doubt you remembered I have no soul of my own!"

And her airy laugh had chilled poor Diana 'to the marrow,' as the warm-hearted little American herself, with tears, assured me.

At this period I saw very little of Rimânez. I was much occupied with my lawyers on the question of 'settlements.' Messrs Bentham and Ellis rather objected to the arrangement by which I gave the half of my fortune to my intended wife unconditionally; but I would brook no interference, and the deed was drawn up, signed, sealed and witnessed. The Earl of Elton could not sufficiently praise my 'unexampled generosity'—my 'noble character;'—and walked about, eulogising me everywhere, till he almost turned himself into a public advertisement of the virtues of his future son-in-law. He seemed to have taken a new lease of life,—he flirted with Diana Chesney openly,—and of his paralysed spouse with the fixed stare and deathly grin, he never spoke, and, I imagine, never thought. Sibyl herself was always in the hands of dressmakers and milliners,—and we only saw each other every day for a few minutes' hurried chat. On these occasions she was always charming,—even affectionate; and yet,—though I was full of passionate admiration and love for her, I felt that she was mine merely as a slave might be mine; that she gave me her lips to kiss as if she considered I had a right to kiss them because I had bought them, and for no other reason,—that her pretty caresses were studied, and her whole behaviour the result of careful forethought and not natural impulsiveness. I tried to shake off this impression, but it still remained persistently, and clouded the sweetness of my brief courtship.

Meanwhile, slowly and almost imperceptibly, my 'boomed' book dropped out of notice. Morgeson presented a heavy bill of publishing costs which I paid without a murmur; now and then an allusion to my 'literary triumphs' cropped up in one or other of the newspapers, but otherwise no one spoke of my 'famous' work, and few read it. I enjoyed the same sort of cliquey reputation and public failure attending a certain novel entitled 'Marius the Epicurean.' The journalists with whom I had come in contact began to drift away like flotsam and jetsam; I think they saw I was not likely to give many more 'reviewing' dinners or suppers, and that my marriage with the Earl of Elton's daughter would lift me into an atmosphere where Grub-street could not breathe comfortably or stretch its legs at ease. The heap of gold on which I sat as on a throne, divided me gradually from even the back courts and lower passages leading to the Temple of Fame,—and almost unconsciously to myself I retreated step by step, shading my eyes as it were from the sun, and seeing the glittering turrets in the distance, with a woman's slight figure entering the lofty portico, turning back her laurelled head to smile sorrowfully and with divinest pity upon me, ere passing in to salute the gods. Yet, if asked about it, everyone on the press would have said that I had had a great success. I—only I—realized the bitterness and truth of my failure. I had not touched the heart of the public;—I had not succeeded in so waking my readers out of the torpor of their dull and commonplace every-day lives, that they should turn towards me with outstretched hands, exclaiming—"More,—more of these thoughts which comfort and inspire us!—which make us hear God's voice proclaiming 'All's well!' above the storms of life!" I had not done it,—I could not do it. And the worst part of my feeling on this point was the idea that possibly I might have done it had I remained poor! The strongest and healthiest pulse in the composition of a man,—the necessity for hard work,—had been killed in me. I knew I need not work; that the society in which I now moved thought it ridiculous if I did work; that I was expected to spend money and 'enjoy' myself in the idiotic fashion of what the 'upper ten' term enjoyment. My acquaintances were not slow in suggesting plans for the dissipation of my surplus cash,—why did I not build for myself a marble palace on the Riviera?—or a yacht to completely outshine the Prince of Wales's 'Britannia'? Why did I not start a theatre? Or found a newspaper? Not one of my social advisers once proposed my doing any private personal good with my fortune. When some terrible case of distress was published, and subscriptions were raised to relieve the object or objects of suffering, I invariably gave Ten Guineas, and allowed myself to be thanked for my 'generous assistance.' I might as well have given ten pence, for the guineas were no more to me in comparison than the pence. When funds were started to erect a statue to some great man who had, in the usual way of the world, been a victim of misrepresentation till his death,

I produced my Ten Guineas again, when I could easily have defrayed the whole cost of the memorial, with honour to myself, and been none the poorer. With all my wealth I did nothing noteworthy; I showered no unexpected luck in the way of the patient, struggling workers in the hard schools of literature and art; I gave no 'largesse' among the poor;—and when a thin, eager-eyed curate, with a strong earnest face called upon me one day, to represent, with much nervous diffidence, the hideous sufferings of some of the sick and starving in his district down by the docks, and suggested that I might possibly care to alleviate a few of these direful sorrows as a satisfaction to myself, as well as for the sake of human brotherhood, I am ashamed to say I let him go with a sovereign, for which he heaped coals of fire on my head by his simple 'God bless you, and thank you.' I could see he was himself in the grip of poverty,—I could have made him and his poor district gloriously happy by a few strokes of my pen on a cheque for an amount I should never have missed,—and yet—I gave him nothing but that one piece of gold, and so allowed him to depart. He invited me, with earnest good-will, to go and see his starving flock,—"for, believe me Mr. Tempest," said he—"I should be sorry if you thought, as some of the wealthy are unhappily apt to do, that I seek money simply to apply it to my own personal uses. If you would visit the district yourself, and distribute whatever you pleased with your own hand, it would be infinitely more gratifying to me, and would have a far better effect on the minds of the people. For, sir, the poor will not always be patient under the cruel burdens they have to bear."

I smiled indulgently, and assured him, not without a touch of satire in my tone, that I was convinced all clergymen were honest and unselfish,—and then I sent my servant to bow him out with all possible politeness. And that very day I remember, I drank at my luncheon Chateau Yquem at twenty-five shillings a bottle.

I enter into these apparently trifling details because they all help to make up the sum and substance of the deadly consequences to follow,—and also because I wish to emphasize the fact that in my actions I only imitated the example of my compeers. Most rich men to-day follow the same course as I did,—and active personal good to the community is wrought by very few of them. No great deed of generosity illumines our annals. Royalty itself leads no fashion in this,—the royal gifts of game and cast-off clothing sent to our hospitals are too slight and conventional to carry weight. The 'entertainments for the poor' got up by some of the aristocrats at the East end, are nothing, and less than nothing. They are weak sops to our tame 'lion couchant' offered in doubtful fear and trembling. For our lion is wakeful and somewhat restive,—there is no knowing what may happen if the original ferocity of the beast is roused. A few of our over-rich men might considerably ease the load of cruel poverty in many quarters of the metropolis if they united themselves with a noble unselfishness in the strong and determined effort to do so, and eschewed red-tapeism and wordy argument. But they remain inert;—spending solely on their own personal gratification and amusement,—and meanwhile there are dark signs of trouble brooding. The poor, as the lean and anxious curate said, will not always be patient!

I must not here forget to mention, that through some secret management of Rimânez, my name, much to my own surprise, appeared on the list of competitors for the Derby. How, at so late an hour, this had been effected, I knew no more than where my horse 'Phosphor' came from. It was a superb animal, but Rimânez, whose gift to me it was, warned me to be careful as to the character of the persons admitted into the stables to view it, and to allow no one but the horse's own two attendants to linger near it long on any pretext. Speculation was very rife as to what 'Phosphor's' capabilities really were; the grooms never showed him off to advantage during exercise. I was amazed when Lucio told me his man Amiel would be the jockey.

"Good heavens!—not possible!" I exclaimed. "Can he ride?"

"Like the very devil!"—responded my friend with a smile: "He will ride 'Phosphor' to the winning-post."

I was very doubtful in my own mind of this; a horse of the Prime Minister's was to run, and all the betting was on that side. Few had seen 'Phosphor,' and those few, though keen admirers of the animal's appearance, had little opportunity of judging its actual qualities, thanks to the careful management of its two attendants, who were dark-faced, reticent-looking men, somewhat after Amiel's character and complexion. I myself was quite indifferent as to the result of the contest. I did not really care whether 'Phosphor' lost or won the race. I could afford to lose; and it would be little to me if I won, save a momentary passing triumph. There was nothing lasting, intellectual or honourable in the victory,—there *is* nothing lasting, intellectual or honourable in anything connected with racing. However, because it was 'fashionable' to be interested in this particular mode of wasting time and money, I followed the general 'lead,' for the sake of 'being talked about,' and nothing more. Meanwhile, Lucio, saying little to me concerning it, was busy planning the betrothal-fête at Willowsmere, and designing all sorts of 'surprise' entertainments for the guests. Eight hundred invitations were sent out; and society soon began to chatter volubly and excitedly on the probable magnificence of the forthcoming festival. Eager acceptances poured in; only a few of those asked were hindered from attending by illness, family deaths or previous engagements, and among these latter, to my regret, was Mavis Clare. She was going to the sea-coast to stay with some old friends, and in a prettily-worded letter explained this, and expressed her thanks for my invitation, though she found herself unable to accept it. How curious it was that when I read her little note of refusal I should experience such a keen sense of disappointment! She was nothing to me,—nothing but a 'literary' woman who, by strange chance, happened to be sweeter than most women *un*literary; and yet I felt that the fête at Willowsmere would lose something in brightness lacking her presence. I had wanted to introduce her to Sibyl, as I knew I should thus give a special pleasure to my betrothed,—however, it was not to be, and I was conscious of an inexplicable personal vexation. In strict accordance with the promise made, I let Rimânez have his own way entirely with regard to all the arrangements for what was to be the *ne plus ultra* of everything ever designed for the distraction, amusement and wonderment of listless and fastidious 'swagger' people, and I neither interfered, nor asked any questions, content to rely on my friend's taste, imagination and ingenuity. I only understood that all the plans were being carried out by foreign artists and caterers,—and that no English firms would be employed. I did venture once to inquire the reason of this, and got one of Lucio's own enigmatical replies:—

"Nothing English is good enough for the English,"—he said—"Things have to be imported from France to please the people whom the French themselves angrily designate as 'perfide Albion.' You must not have a 'Bill of Fare'; you must have a 'Menu'; and all your dishes must bear French titles, otherwise they will not be in good form. You must have French 'comediennes' and 'danseuses' to please the British taste, and your silken draperies must be woven on French looms. Lately too, it has been deemed necessary to import Parisian morality as well as Parisian fashions. It does not suit stalwart Great Britain at all, you know,—stalwart Great Britain, aping the manners of Paris, looks like a jolly open-faced, sturdy-limbed Giant, with a doll's bonnet stuck on his leonine head. But the doll's bonnet is just now *la mode*. Some day I believe the Giant will discover it looks ridiculous, and cast it off with a burst of genuine laughter at his own temporary folly. And without it, he will resume his original dignity;—the dignity that best becomes a privileged conqueror who has the sea for his standing-army."

"Evidently you like England!" I said smiling.

He laughed.

"Not in the very least! I do not like England any more than any other country on the globe. I do not like the globe itself; and England comes in for a share of my aversion as one of the spots on the trumpery ball. If I could have my way, I should like to throne myself on a convenient star for the purpose and kick out at Earth as she whirls by in space, hoping by that act of just violence to do away with her for ever!"

"But why?" I asked, amused—"Why do you hate the Earth? What has the poor little planet done to merit your abhorrence?"

He looked at me very strangely.

"Shall I tell you? You will never believe me!"

"No matter for that!" I answered smiling—"Say on!"

"What has the poor little planet done?" he repeated slowly—"The poor little planet has done—nothing. But it is what the gods have done with this same poor little planet, that awakens my anger and scorn. They have made it a living sphere of wonders,—endowed it with beauty borrowed from the fairest corners of highest Heaven,—decked it with flowers and foliage,—taught it music,—the music of birds and torrents and rolling waves and falling rains,—rocked it gently in clear ether, among such light as blinds the eyes of mortals,—guided it out of chaos, through clouds of thunder and barbèd shafts of lightning, to circle peacefully in its appointed orbit, lit on the one hand by the vivid splendours of the sun, and on the other by the sleepy radiance of the moon;—and more than all this, they have invested it with a Divine Soul in man! Oh, you may disbelieve as you will,—but notwithstanding the pigmy peeps earth takes at the vast and eternal ocean of Science, the Soul is here, and all the immortal forces with it and around it! Nay, the gods—I speak in the plural, after the fashion of the ancient Greeks— for to my thinking there are many gods emanating from the Supreme Deity,—the gods, I say, have so insisted on this fact, that One of them has walked the earth in human guise, solely for the sake of emphasizing the truth of Immortality to these frail creatures of seemingly perishable clay! For this I hate the planet;—were there not, and are there not, other and far grander worlds that a God should have chosen to dwell on than this one!"

For a moment I was silent, out of sheer surprise.

"You amaze me!" I said at last—"You allude to Christ, I suppose; but everybody is convinced by this time that He was a mere man like the rest of us; there was nothing divine about Him. What a contradiction you are! Why, I remember you indignantly denied the accusation of being a Christian."

"Of course,—and I deny it still"—he answered quickly—"I have not a fat living in the church that I should tell a lie on such a subject. I am not a Christian; nor is anyone living a Christian. To quote a very old saying 'There never was a Christian save One, and He was crucified.' But though I am not a Christian I never said I doubted the existence of Christ. That knowledge was forced upon me,—with considerable pressure too!"

"By a reliable authority?" I inquired with a slight sneer.

He made no immediate reply. His flashing eyes looked, as it were, through me and beyond me at something far away. The curious pallor that at times gave his face the set look of an impenetrable mask, came upon him then, and he smiled,—an awful smile. So might a man smile out of deadly bravado, when told of some dim and dreadful torture awaiting him.

"You touch me on a sore point,"—he said at last, slowly, and in a harsh tone—"My convictions respecting certain religious phases of man's development and progress, are founded on the arduous study of some very unpleasant truths to which humanity generally shuts its eyes, burying its head in the desert-sands of its own delusions. These truths I will not enter upon now. Some other time I will initiate you into a few of my mysteries."

The tortured smile passed from his face, leaving it intellectually composed and calm as usual,—and I hastily changed the subject, for I had made up my mind by this time that my brilliant friend had, like many exceptionally gifted persons, a 'craze' on one topic, and that topic a particularly difficult one to discuss as it touched on the superhuman and therefore (to my thinking) the impossible. My own temperament, which had, in the days of my poverty, fluctuated between spiritual striving and material gain, had, with my sudden access to fortune, rapidly hardened into the character of a man of the world worldly, for whom all speculations as to the unseen forces working in and around us, were the merest folly, not worth a moment's waste of thought. I should have laughed to scorn anyone who had then presumed to talk to me about the law of Eternal Justice, which with individuals as well as nations, works, not for a passing 'phase,' but for all time towards good, and not evil,—for no matter how much a man may strive to blind himself to the fact, he has a portion of the Divine within him, which if he wilfully corrupts by his own wickedness, he must be forced to cleanse again and yet again, in the fierce flames of such remorse and such despair as are rightly termed the quenchless fires of Hell!

XXII

On the afternoon of the twenty-first of May, I went down, accompanied by Lucio, to Willowsmere, to be in readiness for the reception of the social swarm who were to flock thither the next day. Amiel went with us,—but I left my own man, Morris, behind, to take charge of my rooms in the Grand, and to forward late telegrams and special messages. The weather was calm, warm and bright,—and a young moon showed her thin crescent in the sky as we got out at the country station and stepped into the open carriage awaiting us. The station-officials greeted us with servile humility, eyeing Lucio especially with an almost gaping air of wonderment; the fact of his lavish expenditure in arranging with the railway company a service of special trains for the use of the morrow's guests, had no doubt excited them to a speechless extent of admiration as well as astonishment. When we approached Willowsmere, and entered the beautiful drive, bordered with oak and beech, which led up to the house, I uttered an exclamation of delight at the festal decorations displayed, for the whole avenue was spanned with arches of flags and flowers, garlands of blossoms being even swung from tree to tree, and interlacing many of the lower branches. The gabled porch at the entrance of the house was draped with crimson silk and festooned with white roses,—and as we alighted, the door was flung open by a smart page in brilliant scarlet and gold.

"I think," said Lucio to me as we entered—"You will find everything as complete as this world's resources will allow. The retinue of servants here are what is vulgarly called 'on the job'; their payment is agreed upon, and they know their duties thoroughly,—they will give you no trouble."

I could scarcely find words to express my unbounded satisfaction, or to thank him for the admirable taste with which the beautiful house had been adorned. I wandered about in an ecstasy of admiration, triumphing in such a visible and gorgeous display of what great wealth could really do. The ball-room had been transformed into an elegant bijou theatre, the stage being concealed by a curtain of thick gold-coloured silk on which the oft-quoted lines of Shakespeare were embroidered in raised letters,—

"All the world's a stage,
And all the men and women merely players."

Turning out of this into the drawing-room, I found it decorated entirely round with banks of roses, red and white, the flowers forming a huge pyramid at one end of the apartment, behind which, as Lucio informed me, unseen musicians would discourse sweet harmony.

"I have arranged for a few 'tableaux vivants' in the theatre to fill up a gap of time;"—he said carelessly—"Fashionable folks now-a-days get so soon tired of one amusement that it is necessary to provide several in order to distract the brains that cannot think, or discover any means of entertainment in themselves. As a matter of fact, people cannot even converse long together because they have nothing to say. Oh, don't bother to go out in the grounds on a tour of inspection just now,—leave a few surprises for yourself as well as for your company to-morrow. Come and have dinner!"

He put his arm through mine and we entered the dining-room. Here the table was laid out with costly fruit, flowers and delicacies of every description,—four men-servants in scarlet and gold stood silently in waiting, with Amiel, in black as usual, behind his master's chair. We enjoyed a sumptuous repast served to perfection, and when it was finished, we strolled out in the grounds to smoke and talk.

"You seem to do everything by magic, Lucio;"—I said, looking at him wonderingly—"All these lavish decorations,—these servants—"

"Money, my dear fellow,—nothing but money"—he interrupted with a laugh—"Money, the devil's pass-key! you can have the retinue of a king without any of a king's responsibilities, if you only choose to pay for it. It is merely a question of cost."

"And taste!" I reminded him.

"True,—and taste. Some rich men there are who have less taste than a costermonger. I know one who has the egregious vulgarity to call the attention of his guests to the value of his goods and chattels. He pointed out for my admiration one day, an antique and hideous china plate, the only one of that kind in the world, and told me it was worth a thousand guineas. 'Break it,'—I said coolly—'You will then have the satisfaction of knowing you have destroyed a thousand guineas' worth of undesirable ugliness.' You should have seen his face! He showed me no more *curios*!"

I laughed, and we walked slowly up and down for a few minutes in silence. Presently I became aware that my companion was looking at me intently, and I turned my head quickly to meet his eyes. He smiled.

"I was just then thinking," he said, "what you would have done with your life if you had not inherited this fortune, and if,—if *I* had not come your way?"

"I should have starved, no doubt,"—I responded—"Died like a rat in a hole,—of want and wretchedness."

"I rather doubt that;" he said meditatively—"It is just possible you might have become a great writer."

"Why do you say that now?" I asked.

"Because I have been reading your book. There are fine ideas in it,—ideas that might, had they been the result of sincere conviction, have reached the public in time, because they were sane and healthy. The public will never put up for long with corrupt 'fads' and artificial 'crazes.' Now you write of God,—yet according to your own statement, you did not believe in God even when you wrote the words that imply His existence,—and that was long before I met you. Therefore the book was not the result of sincere conviction, and that's the key-note of your failure to reach the large audience you desired. Each reader can see you do not believe what you write,—the trumpet of lasting fame never sounds triumph for an author of that calibre."

"Don't let us talk about it for Heaven's sake!" I said irritably—"I know my work lacks something,—and that something may be what you say or it may not,—I do not want to think about it. Let it perish, as it assuredly will; perhaps in the future I may do better."

He was silent,—and finishing his cigar, threw the end away in the grass where it burned like a dull red coal.

"I must turn in," he then observed,—"I have a few more directions to give to the servants for to-morrow. I shall go to my room as soon as I have done,—so I'll say good-night."

"But surely you are taking too much personal trouble,"—I said—"Can't I help in any way?"

"No, you can't,"—he answered smiling. "When I undertake to do anything I like to do it in my own fashion, or not at all. Sleep well, and rise early."

He nodded, and sauntered slowly away over the dewy grass. I watched his dark tall figure receding till he had entered the house; then, lighting a fresh cigar, I wandered on alone through the grounds, noting here and there flowery arbours and dainty silk pavilions erected in picturesque nooks and corners for the morrow. I looked up at the sky; it was clear and bright,—there would be no rain. Presently I opened the wicket-gate that led into the outer by-road, and walking on slowly, almost unconsciously, I found myself in a few minutes opposite 'Lily Cottage.' Approaching the gate I looked in,—the pretty old house was dark, silent and deserted. I knew Mavis Clare was away,—and it was not strange that the aspect of her home-nest emphasized the fact of her absence. A cluster of climbing roses hanging from the wall, looked as if they were listening for the first sound of her returning footsteps; across the green breadth of the lawn where I had seen her playing with her dogs, a tall sheaf of St John's lilies stood up white against the sky, their pure hearts opened to the star-light and the breeze. The scent of honey-suckle and sweet-briar filled the air with delicate suggestions,—and as I leaned over the low fence, gazing vaguely at the long shadows of the trees on the grass, a nightingale began to sing. The sweet yet dolorous warble of the 'little brown lover of the moon,' palpitated on the silence in silver-toned drops of melody; and I listened, till my eyes smarted with a sudden moisture as of tears. Strangely enough, I never thought of my betrothed bride Sibyl then, as surely, by all the precedents of passion, I should have done at such a moment of dreamful ecstasy. It was another woman's face that floated before my memory;—a face not beautiful,—but merely sweet,—and made radiant by the light of two tender, wistful, wonderfully innocent eyes,—a face like that of some new Daphne with the mystic laurel springing from her brows. The nightingale sang on and on,—the tall lilies swayed in the faint wind as though nodding wise approval of the bird's wild music,—and, gathering one briar-rose from the hedge, I turned away with a curious heaviness at my heart,—a trouble I could not analyse or account for. I explained my feeling partly to myself as one of regret that I had ever taken up my pen to assault, with sneer and flippant jest, the gentle and brilliantly endowed owner of this little home where peace and pure content dwelt happily in student-like seclusion;—but this was not all. There was something else in my mind,—something inexplicable and sad,—which then I had no skill to define. I know now what it was,—but the knowledge comes too late!

Returning to my own domains, I saw through the trees a vivid red light in one of the upper windows of Willowsmere. It twinkled like a lurid star, and I guided my steps by its brilliancy as I made my way across the winding garden-paths and terraces back to the house. Entering the hall, the page in scarlet and gold met me, and with a respectful obeisance, escorted me to my room where Amiel was in waiting.

"Has the prince retired?" I asked him.

"Yes, sir."

"He has a red lamp in his window has he not?"

Amiel looked deferentially meditative. Yet I fancied I saw him smile.

"I think—yes,—I believe he has, sir."

I asked no more questions, but allowed him to perform his duties as valet in silence.

"Good-night sir!" he said at last, his ferret eyes fastened upon me with an expressionless look.

"Good-night!" I responded indifferently.

He left the room with his usual cat-like stealthy tread, and when he had gone, I,—moved by a sudden fresh impulse of hatred for him,—sprang to the door and locked it. Then I listened, with an odd nervous breathlessness. There was not a sound. For fully quarter of an hour I remained with my attention more or less strained, expectant of I knew not what; but the quiet of the house was absolutely undisturbed. With a sigh of relief I flung myself on the luxurious bed,—a couch fit for a king, draped with the richest satin elaborately embroidered,—and falling soundly asleep I dreamed that I was poor again. Poor,—but unspeakably happy,—and hard at work in the old lodging, writing down thoughts which I knew, by some divine intuition and beyond all doubt, would bring me the whole world's honour. Again I heard the sounds of the violin played by my unseen neighbour next door, and this time they were triumphal chords and cadences of joy, without one throb of sorrow. And while I wrote on in an ecstasy of inspiration, oblivious of poverty and pain, I heard, echoing through my visions, the round warble of the nightingale, and saw, in the far distance, an angel floating towards me on pinions of light, with the face of Mavis Clare.

XXIII

The morning broke clear, with all the pure tints of a fine opal radiating in the cloudless sky. Never had I beheld such a fair scene as the woods and gardens of Willowsmere when I looked upon them that day illumined by the unclouded sunlight of a spring half-melting into summer. My heart swelled with pride as I surveyed the beautiful domain I now owned,—and thought how happy a home it would make when Sibyl, matchless in her loveliness, shared with me its charm and luxury.

"Yes,"—I said half-aloud—"Say what philosophers will, the possession of money does insure satisfaction and power. It is all very well to talk about fame, but what is fame worth, if, like Carlyle, one is too poor to enjoy it! Besides, literature no longer holds its former high prestige,—there are too many in the field,—too many newspaper-scribblers, all believing they are geniuses,—too many ill-educated lady-paragraphists and 'new' women, who think they are as gifted as Georges Sand or Mavis Clare. With Sibyl and Willowsmere, I ought to be able to resign the idea of fame—literary fame—with a good grace."

I knew I reasoned falsely with myself,—I knew that my hankering for a place among the truly great of the world, was as strong as ever,—I knew I craved for the intellectual distinction, force, and pride which make the Thinker a terror and a power in the land, and which so sever a great poet or great romancist from the commoner throng that even kings are glad to do him or her honour,—but I would not allow my thoughts to dwell on this rapidly vanishing point of unattainable desire. I settled my mind to enjoy the luscious flavour of the immediate present, as a bee settles in the cup of honey-flowers,—and, leaving my bedroom, I went downstairs to breakfast with Lucio in the best and gayest of humours.

"Not a cloud on the day!" he said, meeting me with a smile, as I entered the bright morning-room, whose windows opened on the lawn—"The fête will be a brilliant success, Geoffrey."

"Thanks to you!" I answered—"Personally I am quite in the dark as to your plans,—but I believe you can do nothing that is not well done."

"You honour me!" he said with a light laugh—"You credit me then with better qualities than the Creator! For what He does, in the opinion of the present generation, is exceedingly ill done! Men have taken to grumbling at Him instead of praising Him,—and few have any patience with or liking for His laws."

I laughed. "Well, you must admit those laws are very arbitrary!"

"They are. I entirely acknowledge the fact!"

We sat down to table, and were waited upon by admirably-trained servants who apparently had no idea of anything else but attendance on our needs. There was no trace of bustle or excitement in the household,—no sign whatever to denote that a great entertainment was about to take place that day. It was not until the close of our meal that I asked Lucio what time the musicians would arrive. He glanced at his watch.

"About noon I should say,"—he replied—"Perhaps before. But whatever their hour, they will all be in their places at the proper moment, depend upon it. The people I employ—both musicians and 'artistes'—know their business thoroughly, and are aware that I stand no nonsense." A rather sinister smile played round his mouth as he regarded me. "None of your guests can arrive here till one o'clock,—as that is about the time the special train will bring the first batch of them from London,—and the first 'déjeuner' will be served in the gardens at two. If you want to amuse yourself there's a Maypole being put up on the large lawn,—you'd better go and look at it."

"A Maypole!" I exclaimed—"Now that's a good idea!"

"It used to be a good idea,"—he answered—"When English lads and lasses had youth, innocence, health and fun in their composition, a dance round the Maypole hand in hand, did them good and did nobody harm. But now there are no lads and lasses,—enervated old men and women in their teens walk the world wearily, speculating on the uses of life,—probing vice, and sneering down sentiment, and such innocent diversions as the Maypole no longer appeal to our jaded youth. So we have to get 'professionals' to execute the May-revels,—of course the dancing is better done by properly trained legs; but it means nothing, and *is* nothing, except a pretty spectacle."

"And are the dancers here?" I asked, rising and going towards the window in some curiosity.

"No, not yet. But the May-pole is;—fully decorated. It faces the woods at the back of the house,—go and see if you like it."

I followed his suggestion, and going in the direction indicated, I soon perceived the gaily-decked object which used to be the welcome signal of many a village holiday in Shakespeare's old-world England. The pole was already set up and fixed in a deep socket in the ground, and a dozen or more men were at work, unbinding its numerous trails of blossom and garlands of green, tied with long streamers of vari-coloured ribbon. It had a picturesque effect in the centre of the wide lawn bordered with grand old trees,—and approaching one of the men, I said something to him by way of approval and admiration. He glanced at me furtively and unsmilingly, but said nothing,—and I concluded from his dark and foreign cast of features, that he did not understand the English language. I noted, with some wonder and slight vexation that all the workmen were of this same alien and sinister type of countenance, very much after the unattractive models of Amiel and the two grooms who had my racer 'Phosphor' in charge. But I remembered what Lucio had told me,—namely, that all the designs for the fête were carried out by foreign experts and artists,—and after some puzzled consideration, I let the matter pass from my mind.

The morning hours flew swiftly by, and I had little time to examine all the festal preparations with which the gardens abounded,—so that I was almost as ignorant of what was in store for the amusement of my guests as the guests themselves. I had the curiosity to wait about and watch for the coming of the musicians and dancers, but I might as well have spared myself this waste of time and trouble, for I never saw them arrive at all. At one o'clock, both Lucio and I were ready to receive our company,—and at about twenty minutes past the hour, the first instalment of 'swagger society' was emptied into the grounds. Sibyl and her father were among these,—and I eagerly advanced to meet and greet my bride-elect as she alighted from the carriage that had brought her from the station. She looked supremely beautiful that day, and was, as she deserved to be, the cynosure of all eyes. I kissed her little gloved hand with a deeper reverence than I would have kissed the hand of a queen.

"Welcome back to your old home, my Sibyl!" I said to her in a low voice tenderly, at which words she paused, looking up at the red gables of the house with such wistful affection as filled her eyes with something like tears. She left her hand in mine, and allowed me to lead her towards the silken-draped, flower-decked porch, where Lucio waited, smiling,—and as she advanced, two tiny pages in pure white and silver glided suddenly out of some unseen hiding-place, and emptied two baskets of pink and white rose-leaves at her feet, thus strewing a fragrant pathway for her into the house. They vanished as completely and swiftly as they had appeared,—some of the guests uttered murmurs of admiration, while Sibyl gazed about her, blushing with surprise and pleasure.

"How charming of you, Geoffrey!" she said, "What a poet you are to devise so pretty a greeting!"

"I wish I deserved your praise!" I answered, smiling at her—"But the poet in question is Prince Rimânez,—he is the master and ruler of to-day's revels."

Again the rich colour flushed her cheeks, and she gave Lucio her hand. He bowed over it in courtly fashion,—but did not kiss it as he had kissed the hand of Mavis Clare. We passed into the house, through the drawing-room, and out again into the gardens, Lord Elton being loud in his praise of the artistic manner in which his former dwelling had been improved and embellished. Soon the lawn was sprinkled with gaily attired groups of people,—and my duties as host began in hard earnest. I had to be greeted, complimented, flattered, and congratulated on my approaching marriage by scores of hypocrites who nearly shook my hand off in their enthusiasm for my wealth. Had I become suddenly poor, I thought grimly, not one of them would have lent me a sovereign! The guests kept on arriving in shoals, and when there were about three or four hundred assembled, a burst of exquisite music sounded, and a procession of pages in scarlet and gold, marching two by two appeared, carrying trays full of the rarest flowers tied up in bouquets, which they offered to all the ladies present. Exclamations of delight arose on every side,—exclamations which were for the most part high-pitched and noisy,—for the 'swagger set' have long ceased to cultivate softness of voice or refinement of accent,—and once or twice the detestable slang word, 'ripping' escaped from the lips of a few dashing dames, reputed to be 'leaders' of style. Repose of manner, dignity and elegance of deportment, however, are no longer to be discovered among the present 'racing' duchesses and gambling countesses of the bluest blue blood of England, so one does not expect these graces of distinction from them. The louder they can talk, and the more slang they can adopt from the language of their grooms and stable-boys, the more are they judged to be 'in the swim' and 'up to date.' I speak, of course, of the modern scions of aristocracy. There are a few truly 'great ladies' left, whose maxim is still *noblesse oblige*,'—but they are quite in the minority and by the younger generation are voted either 'old cats' or 'bores.' Many of the 'cultured' mob that now swarmed over my grounds had come out of the sheerest vulgar curiosity to see what 'the man with five millions' could do in the way of entertaining,—others were anxious to get news, if possible, of the chances of 'Phosphor' winning the Derby, concerning which I was discreetly silent. But the bulk of the crowd wandered aimlessly about, staring impertinently or enviously at each other, and scarcely looking at the natural loveliness of the gardens or the woodland scenery around them. The brainlessness of modern society is never so flagrantly manifested as at a garden-party, where the restless trousered and petticoated bipeds move vaguely to and fro, scarcely stopping to talk civilly or intelligently to one another for five minutes, most of them hovering dubiously and awkwardly between the refreshment-pavilion and the band-stand. In my domain they were deprived of this latter harbour of refuge, for no musicians could be seen, though music was heard,—beautiful wild music which came first from one part of the grounds and then from another, and to which few listened with any attention. All were, however, happily unanimous in their enthusiastic appreciation of the excellence of the food provided for them in the luxurious luncheon tents of which there were twenty in number. Men ate as if they had never eaten in their lives before, and drank the choice and exquisite wines with equal greed and gusto. One never entirely realises the extent to which human gourmandism can go till one knows a few peers, bishops and cabinet-ministers, and watches those dignitaries feed *ad libitum*. Soon the company was so complete that there was no longer any need for me to perform the fatiguing duty of 'receiving'; and I therefore took Sibyl in to luncheon, determining to devote myself to her for the rest of the day. She was in one of her brightest and most captivating moods,—her laughter rang out as sweetly joyous as that of some happy child,—she was even kind to Diana Chesney, who was also one of my guests, and who was plainly enjoying herself with all the *verve* peculiar to pretty American women, who consider flirtation as much of a game as tennis. The scene was now one of great brilliancy, the light costumes of the women contrasting well with the scarlet and gold liveries of the seemingly innumerable servants that were now everywhere in active attendance. And, constantly through the fluttering festive crowd, from tent to tent, from table to table, and group to group, Lucio moved,—his tall stately figure and handsome face always conspicuous wherever he stood, his rich voice thrilling the air whenever he spoke. His influence was irresistible, and gradually dominated the whole assemblage,—he roused the dull, inspired the witty, encouraged the timid, and brought all the conflicting elements of rival position,

MARIE CORELLI

character and opinion into one uniform whole, which was unconsciously led by his will as easily as a multitude is led by a convincing orator. I did not know it then, but I know now, that metaphorically speaking, he had his foot on the neck of that 'society' mob, as though it were one prostrate man;—that the sycophants, liars and hypocrites whose utmost idea of good is wealth and luxurious living, bent to his secret power as reeds bend to the wind,—and that he did with them all whatsoever he chose,—as he does to this very day! God!—if the grinning, guzzling sensual fools had only known what horrors were about them at the feast!—what ghastly ministers to pleasurable appetite waited obediently upon them!—what pallid terrors lurked behind the gorgeous show of vanity and pride! But the veil was mercifully down,—and only to me has it since been lifted!

Luncheon over, the singing of mirthful voices, tuned to a kind of village roundelay, attracted the company, now fed to repletion, towards the lawn at the back of the house, and cries of delight were raised as the Maypole came into view, I myself joining in the universal applause, for I had not expected to see anything half so picturesque and pretty. The pole was surrounded by a double ring of small children,—children so beautiful in face and dainty in form, that they might very well have been taken for little fairies from some enchanted woodland. The boys were clad as tiny foresters, in doublets of green, with pink caps on their curly locks,—the girls were in white, with their hair flowing loosely over their shoulders, and wreaths of May-blossom crowning their brows. As soon as the guests appeared on the scene, these exquisite little creatures commenced their dance, each one taking a trail of blossom or a ribbon pendant from the May-pole, and weaving it with the others into no end of beautiful and fantastic designs. I looked on, as amazed and fascinated as anyone present, at the wonderful lightness and ease with which these children tripped and ran;—their tiny twinkling feet seemed scarcely to touch the turf,—their faces were so lovely,—their eyes so bright, that it was a positive enchantment to watch them. Each figure they executed was more intricate and effective than the last, and the plaudits of the spectators grew more and more enthusiastic, till presently came the *finale*, in which all the little green foresters climbed up the pole and clung there, pelting the white-robed maidens below with cowslip-balls, knots of roses, bunches of violets, posies of buttercups, daisies and clover, which the girl-children in their turn laughingly threw among the admiring guests. The air grew thick with flowers, and heavy with perfume, and resounded with song and laughter;—and Sibyl, standing at my side, clapped her hands in an ecstasy.

"Oh, it is lovely—lovely!" she cried—"Is this the prince's idea?" Then as I answered in the affirmative, she added, "Where, I wonder, did he find such exquisitely pretty little children!"

As she spoke, Lucio himself advanced a step or two in front of the other spectators and made a slight peremptory sign. The fairy-like foresters and maidens, with extraordinary activity, all sprang away from the May-pole, pulling down the garlands with them, and winding the flowers and ribbons about themselves so that they looked as if they were all tied together in one inextricable knot,—this done, they started off at a rapid run, presenting the appearance of a rolling ball of blossom, merry pipe-music accompanying their footsteps, till they had entirely disappeared among the trees.

"Oh do call them back again!" entreated Sibyl, laying her hand coaxingly on Lucio's arm,—"I should so like to speak to two or three of the prettiest!"

He looked down at her with an enigmatical smile.

"You would do them too much honour, Lady Sibyl," he replied—"They are not accustomed to such condescension from great ladies and would not appreciate it. They are paid professionals, and, like many of their class, only become insolent when praised."

At that moment Diana Chesney came running across the lawn, breathless.

"I can't see them anywhere!" she declared pantingly—"The dear little darlings! I ran after them as fast as I could; I wanted to kiss one of those perfectly scrumptious boys, but they're gone!—not a trace of them left! It's just as if they had sunk into the ground!"

Again Lucio smiled.

"They have their orders,—" he said curtly—"And they know their place."

Just then, the sun was obscured by a passing black cloud, and a peal of thunder rumbled over-head. Looks were turned to the sky, but it was quite bright and placid save for that one floating shadow of storm.

"Only summer thunder,"—said one of the guests—"There will be no rain."

And the crowd that had been pressed together to watch the 'Maypole dance' began to break up in groups, and speculate as to what diversion might next be provided for them. I, watching my opportunity, drew Sibyl away.

"Come down by the river;"—I whispered—"I must have you to myself for a few minutes." She yielded to my suggestion, and we walked away from the mob of our acquaintance, and entered a grove of trees leading to the banks of that part of the Avon which flowed through my grounds. Here we found ourselves quite alone, and putting my arm round my betrothed, I kissed her tenderly.

"Tell me," I said with a half-smile—"Do you know how to love yet?"

She looked up with a passionate darkness in her eyes that startled me.

"Yes,—I know!" was her unexpected answer.

"You do!" and I stopped to gaze intently into her fair face—"And how did you learn?"

She flushed red,—then grew pale,—and clung to me with a nervous, almost feverish force.

"Very strangely!" she replied—"And—quite suddenly! The lesson was easy, I found;—too easy! Geoffrey,"—she paused, and fixed her eyes full on mine—"I will tell you how I learnt it, . . . but not now, . . . some other day." Here she broke off, and began to laugh rather forcedly. "I will tell you. . . when we are married." She glanced anxiously about her,—then, with a sudden abandonment of her usual reserve and pride, threw herself into my arms and kissed my lips with such ardour as made my senses reel.

"Sibyl—Sibyl!" I murmured, holding her close to my heart—"Oh my darling,—you love me!—at last you love me!"

"Hush!—hush!" she said breathlessly—"You must forget that kiss,— it was too bold of me—it was wrong—I did not mean it, . . . I, . . . I was thinking of something else. Geoffrey!"—and her small hand clenched on mine with a sort of eager fierceness—"I wish I had never learned to love; I was happier before I knew!"

A frown knitted her brows.

"Now"—she went on in the same breathless hurried way—"I *want* love! I am starving, thirsting for it! I want to be drowned in it, lost in it, killed by it! Nothing else will content me!"

I folded her still closer in my arms.

"Did I not say you would change, Sibyl?" I whispered—"Your coldness and insensibility to love was unnatural and could not last,— my darling, I always knew that!"

"You always knew!" she echoed a little disdainfully—"Ah, but you do not know even now what has chanced to me. Nor shall I tell you—yet. Oh Geoffrey!—" Here she drew herself out of my embrace, and stooping, gathered some bluebells in the grass—"See these little flowers growing so purely and peacefully in the shade by the Avon!—they remind me of what I was, here in this very place, long ago. I was quite as happy, and I think as innocent as these blossoms; I had no thought of evil in my nature,—and the only love I dreamed of was the love of the fairy prince for the fairy princess,—as harmless an idea as the loves of the flowers themselves. Yes!—I was then all I should like to be now,—all that I am not!"

"You are everything that is beautiful and sweet!"—I told her, admiringly, as I watched the play of retrospective and tender expression on her perfect face.

"So you judge,—being a man who is perfectly satisfied with his own choice of a wife!" she said with a flash of her old cynicism—"But I know myself better than you know me. You call me beautiful and sweet,—but you cannot call me good! I am not good. Why, the very love that now consumes me is—"

"What?" I asked her quickly, seizing her hands with the blue-bells in them, and gazing searchingly into her eyes—"I know before you speak, that it is the passion and tenderness of a true woman!"

She was silent for a moment. Then she smiled, with a bewitching languor.

"If you know, then I need not tell you"—she said—"So, do not let us stay here any longer talking nonsense;—'society' will shake its head over us and accuse us of 'bad form,' and some lady-paragraphist will write to the papers, and, say—'Mr. Tempest's conduct as a host left much to be desired, as he and his bride-elect were "spooning" all the day.'"

"There are no lady-paragraphists here,"—I said laughing, and encircling her dainty waist with one arm as I walked.

"Oh, are there not, though!" she exclaimed, laughing also, "Why, you don't suppose you can give any sort of big entertainment without them do you? They permeate society. Old Lady Maravale, for example, who is rather reduced in circumstances, writes a guinea's worth of scandal a week for one of the papers. And *she* is here,—I saw her simply gorging herself with chicken salad and truffles an hour ago!" Here pausing, and resting against my arm, she peered through the trees. "There are the chimneys of Lily Cottage where the famous Mavis Clare lives," she said.

"Yes, I know,"—I replied readily—"Rimânez and I have visited her. She is away just now, or she would have been here to-day."

"Do you like her?" Sibyl queried.

"Very much. She is charming."

"And. . . the prince. . . does he like her?"

"Well, upon my word," I answered with a smile—"I think he likes her more than he does most women! He showed the most extraordinary deference towards her, and seemed almost abashed in her presence. Are you cold, Sibyl?" I added hastily, for she shivered suddenly and her face grew pale—"You had better come away from the river,—it is damp under these trees."

"Yes,—let us go back to the gardens and the sunshine;"—she answered dreamily—"So your eccentric friend,—the woman-hater,—finds something to admire in Mavis Clare! She must be a very happy creature I think,—perfectly free, famous, and believing in all good things of life and humanity, if one may judge from her books."

"Well, taken altogether, life isn't so very bad!" I observed playfully.

She made no reply,—and we returned to the lawns where afternoon tea was now being served to the guests, who were seated in brilliant scattered groups under the trees or within the silken pavilions, while the sweetest music,—and the strangest, if people had only had ears to hear it,—both vocal and instrumental, was being performed by those invisible players and singers whose secret whereabouts was unknown to all, save Lucio.

XXIV

Just as the sun began to sink, several little pages came out of the house, and with low salutations, distributed among the guests daintily embossed and painted programmes of the 'Tableaux Vivants,' prepared for their diversion in the extemporized bijou theatre. Numbers of people rose at once from their chairs on the lawn, eager for this new spectacle, and began to scramble along and hustle one another in that effective style of 'high-breeding' so frequently exhibited at Her Majesty's Drawing-Rooms. I, with Sibyl, hastily preceded the impatient, pushing crowd, for I wished to find a good seat for my beautiful betrothed before the room became full to over-flowing. There proved however, to be plenty of accommodation for everybody,—what space there was seemed capable of limitless expansion, and all the spectators were comfortably placed without difficulty. Soon we were all studying our programmes with considerable interest, for the titles of the 'Tableaux' were somewhat original and mystifying. They were eight in number, and were respectively headed—'Society,'—'Bravery: Ancient and Modern,'—'A Lost Angel,'—'The Autocrat,'—'A Corner of Hell,'—'Seeds of Corruption,'—'His Latest Purchase,'—and 'Faith and Materialism.' It was in the theatre that everyone became at last conscious of the weirdly beautiful character of the music that had been surging round them all day. Seated under one roof in more or less enforced silence and attention, the vague and frivolous throng grew hushed and passive,—the 'society' smirk passed off certain faces that were as trained to grin as their tongues were trained to lie,—the dreadful giggle of the unwedded man-hunter was no longer heard,—and soon the most exaggerated fashion-plate of a woman forgot to rustle her gown. The passionate vibrations of a violoncello, superbly played to a double harp accompaniment, throbbed on the stillness with a beseeching depth of sound,—and people listened, I saw, almost breathlessly, entranced, as it were, against their wills, and staring as though they were hypnotized, in front of them at the gold curtain with its familiar motto—

"All the world's a stage
And all the men and women merely players."

Before we had time to applaud the violoncello solo however, the music changed,—and the mirthful voices of violins and flutes rang out in a waltz of the giddiest and sweetest tune. At the same instant a silvery bell tinkled, and the curtain parted noiselessly in twain, disclosing the first tableau—"Society." An exquisite female figure, arrayed in evening-dress of the richest and most extravagant design, stood before us, her hair crowned with diamonds, and her bosom blazing with the same lustrous gems. Her head was slightly raised,—her lips were parted in a languid smile,—in one hand she held up-lifted a glass of foaming champagne,—her gold-slippered foot trod on an hour-glass. Behind her, catching convulsively at the folds of her train, crouched another woman in rags, pinched and wretched, with starvation depicted in her face,—a dead child lay near. And, overshadowing this group, were two Supernatural shapes,—one in scarlet, the other in black,—vast and almost beyond the stature of humanity,—the scarlet figure represented Anarchy, and its blood-red fingers were advanced to clutch the diamond crown from 'Society's' brow,—the sable-robed form was Death, and even as we looked, it slowly raised its steely dart in act to strike! The effect was weird and wonderful,—and the grim lesson the picture conveyed, was startling enough to make a very visible impression. No one spoke,—no one applauded,—but people moved restlessly and fidgetted on their seats,—and there was an audible sigh of relief as the curtain closed. Opening again, it displayed the second tableau—'Bravery—Ancient and Modern.' This was in two scenes;—the first one depicted a nobleman of Elizabeth's time, with rapier drawn, his foot on the prostrate body of a coarse ruffian who had evidently, from the grouping, insulted a woman whose slight figure was discerned shrinking timidly away from the contest. This was 'Ancient Bravery,'—and it changed rapidly to 'Modern,' showing us an enervated, narrow-shouldered, pallid dandy in opera-coat and hat, smoking a cigarette and languidly appealing to a bulky policeman to protect him from another young noodle of his own class, similarly attired, who was represented as sneaking round a corner in abject terror. We all recognised the force of the application, and were in a much better humour with this pictured satire than we had been at the lesson of 'Society.' Next followed 'A Lost Angel,' in which was shown a great hall in the palace of a king, where there were numbers of brilliantly attired people, all grouped in various attitudes, and evidently completely absorbed in their own concerns, so much so as to be entirely unconscious of the fact that in their very midst, stood a wondrous Angel, clad in dazzling white, with a halo round her fair hair, and a glory, as of the sunset, on her half drooping wings. Her eyes were wistful,—her face was pensive and expectant; she seemed to say, "Will the world ever know that I am here?" Somehow,—as the curtain slowly closed again, amid loud applause, for the picture was extraordinarily beautiful, I thought of Mavis Clare, and sighed. Sibyl looked up at me.

"Why do you sigh?" she said—"It is a lovely fancy,—but the symbol is wasted in the present audience,—no one with education believes in angels now-a-days."

"True!" I assented; yet there was a heaviness at my heart, for her words reminded me of what I would rather have forgotten,—namely her own admitted lack of all religious faith. 'The Autocrat,' was the next tableau, and represented an Emperor enthroned. At his footstool knelt a piteous crowd of the starving and oppressed, holding up their lean hands to him, clasped in anguished petition, but he looked away from them as though he saw them not. His head was turned to listen to the side-whisper of one who seemed, by the courtly bend and flattering smile, to be his adviser and confidant,—yet that very confidant held secreted behind his back, a drawn dagger, ready to strike his sovereign to the heart. "Russia!" whispered one or two of the company, as the scene was obscured; but the scarcely-breathed suggestion quickly passed into a murmur of amazement and awe as the curtain parted again to disclose "A Corner of Hell." This tableau was indeed original, and quite unlike what might have been imagined as the conventional treatment of such a subject. What we saw was a black and hollow cavern, glittering alternately with the flashings of ice and fire,—huge icicles drooped from above, and pale flames leaped stealthily into view from below, and within the dark embrasure, the shadowy form of a man was seated, counting out gold, or what seemed to be gold. Yet as coin after coin slipped through his ghostly fingers, each one was seen to change to fire,—and the lesson thus pictured was easily read. The lost soul had made its own torture, and was still at work intensifying and increasing its own fiery agony. Much as this scene was admired for its Rembrandt effect of light and shade, I, personally, was glad when it was curtained from view; there was something in the dreadful face of the doomed sinner that reminded me forcibly and unpleasantly of those ghastly Three I had seen in my horrid vision on the night of Viscount Lynton's suicide. 'Seeds of Corruption' was the next picture, and showed us a young and beautiful girl in her early teens, lying on a luxurious couch *en deshabille*, with a novel in her hand, of which the title was plainly seen by all;—a novel well-known to everyone present, and the work of a much-praised living author. Round her, on the floor, and cast carelessly on a chair at her side, were other novels of the same 'sexual' type,—all their titles turned towards us, and the names of their authors equally made manifest.

"What a daring idea!" said a lady in the seat immediately behind me—"I wonder if any of those authors are present!"

"If they are they won't mind!" replied the man next to her with a smothered laugh—"Those sort of writers would merely take it as a first-class advertisement!"

Sibyl looked at the tableau with a pale face and wistful eyes.

"That is a *true* picture!" she said under her breath—"Geoffrey, it is painfully true!"

I made no answer,—I thought I knew to what she alluded; but alas!—I did not know how deeply the 'seeds of corruption' had been sown in her own nature, or what a harvest they would bring forth. The curtain closed,—to open again almost immediately on "His Latest Purchase." Here we were shown the interior of a luxurious modern drawing-room, where about eight or ten men were assembled, in fashionable evening-dress. They had evidently just risen from a card-table,—and one of them, a dissipated looking brute, with a wicked smile of mingled satire and triumph on his face was pointing to his 'purchase,'—a beautiful woman. She was clad in glistening white like a bride,—but she was bound, as prisoners are bound, to an upright column, on which the grinning head of a marble Silenus leered above her. Her hands were tied tightly together,—with chains of diamonds; her waist was bound,—with thick ropes of pearls;—a wide collar of rubies encircled her throat;—and from bosom to feet she was netted about and tied,—with strings of gold and gems. Her head was flung back defiantly with an assumption of pride and scorn,—her eyes alone expressed shame, self-contempt, and despair at her bondage. The man who owned this white slave was represented, by his attitude, as cataloguing and appraising her 'points' for the approval and applause of his comrades, whose faces variously and powerfully expressed the differing emotions of lust, cruelty, envy, callousness, derision, and selfishness, more admirably than the most gifted painter could imagine.

"A capital type of most fashionable marriages!" I heard some-one say.

"Rather!" another voice replied—"The orthodox 'happy couple' to the life!"

I glanced at Sibyl. She looked pale,—but smiled as she met my questioning eyes. A sense of consolation crept warmly about my heart as I remembered that now, she had, as she told me 'learnt to love,'—and that therefore her marriage with me was no longer a question of material advantage alone. She was not my 'purchase,'—she was my love, my saint, my queen!—or so I chose to think, in my foolishness and vanity!

The last tableau of all was now to come,—"Faith and Materialism," and it proved to be the most startling of the series. The auditorium was gradually darkened,—and the dividing curtain disclosed a ravishingly beautiful scene by the sea-shore. A full moon cast its tranquil glory over the smooth waters, and,—rising on rainbow-wings from earth towards the skies, one of the loveliest creatures ever dreamed of by poet or painter, floated angel-like upwards, her hands holding a cluster of lilies clasped to her breast,—her lustrous eyes full of divine joy, hope, and love. Exquisite music was heard,—soft voices sang in the distance a chorale of rejoicing;—heaven and earth, sea and air,—all seemed to support the aspiring Spirit as she soared higher and higher, in ever-deepening rapture, when,—as we all watched that aerial flying form with a sense of the keenest delight and satisfaction,—a sudden crash of thunder sounded,—the scene grew dark,—and there was a distant roaring of angry waters. The light of the moon was eclipsed,—the music ceased; a faint lurid glow of red shone at first dimly, then more vividly,—and 'Materialism' declared itself,—a human skeleton, bleached white and grinning ghastly mirth upon us all! While we yet looked, the skeleton itself dropped to pieces,—and one long twining worm lifted its slimy length from the wreck of bones, another working its way through the eye-holes of the skull. Murmurs of genuine horror were heard in the auditorium,—people on all sides rose from their seats—one man in particular, a distinguished professor of sciences, pushed past me to get out, muttering crossly—"This may be very amusing to some of you, but to me, it is disgusting!"

"Like your own theories, my dear Professor!" said a rich laughing voice, as Lucio met him on his way, and the bijou theatre was again flooded with cheerful light—"They are amusing to some, and disgusting to others!—Pardon me!—I speak of course in jest! But I designed that tableau specially in your honour!"

MARIE CORELLI

"Oh, you did, did you?" growled the Professor—"Well, I didn't appreciate it."

"Yet you should have done, for it is quite scientifically correct,"—declared Lucio laughing still. "Faith,—with the wings, whom you saw joyously flying towards an impossible Heaven, is *not* scientifically correct,—have you not told us so?—but the skeleton and the worms were quite of your *cult*! No materialist can deny the correctness of that 'complexion to which we all must come at last.' Positively, some of the ladies look quite pale! How droll it is, that while everybody (to be fashionable, and in favour with the press) must accept Materialism as the only creed, they should invariably become affrighted, or let us say offended, at the natural end of the body, as completed by material agencies!"

"Well, it was not a pleasant subject, that last tableau,"—said Lord Elton, as he came out of the theatre with Diana Chesney hanging confidingly on his arm—"You cannot say it was festal!"

"It was,—for the worms!" replied Lucio gaily—"Come, Miss Chesney,—and you Tempest, come along with Lady Sibyl,—let us go out in the grounds again, and see my will-o'-the-wisps lighting up."

Fresh curiosity was excited by this remark; the people quickly threw off the gruesome and tragic impression made by the strange 'tableaux' just witnessed,—and poured out of the house into the gardens chattering and laughing more noisily than ever. It was just dusk,—and as we reached the open lawn we saw an extraordinary number of small boys, clad in brown, running about with will-o'-the-wisp lanterns. Their movements were swift and perfectly noiseless,—they leaped, jumped and twirled like little gnomes over flowerbeds, under shrubberies, and along the edges of paths and terraces, many of them climbing trees with the rapidity and agility of monkeys, and wherever they went they left behind them a trail of brilliant light. Soon, by their efforts, all the grounds were illuminated with a magnificence that could not have been equalled even by the historic fêtes at Versailles,—tall oaks and cedars were transformed to pyramids of fire-blossoms,—every branch was loaded with coloured lamps in the shape of stars,—rockets hissed up into the clear space showering down bouquets, wreaths and ribbons of flame,—lines of red and azure ran glowingly along the grass-borders, and amid the enthusiastic applause of the assembled spectators, eight huge fire-fountains of all colours sprang up in various corners of the garden, while an enormous golden balloon, dazzlingly luminous, ascended slowly into the air and remained poised above us, sending from its glittering car hundreds of gem-like birds and butterflies on fiery wings, that circled round and round for a moment and then vanished. While we were yet loudly clapping the splendid effect of this sky-spectacle, a troop of beautiful girl-dancers in white came running across the grass, waving long silvery wands that were tipped with electric stars, and to the sound of strange tinkling music, seemingly played in the distance on glass bells, they commenced a fantastic dance of the wildest yet most graceful character. Every shade of opaline colour fell upon their swaying figures from some invisible agency as they tripped and whirled,—and each time they waved their wands, ribbons and flags of fire were unrolled and tossed high in air where they gyrated for a long time like moving hieroglyphs. The scene was now so startling, so fairy-like and wonderful, that we were well-nigh struck speechless with astonishment,—too fascinated and absorbed even to applaud, we had no conception how time went, or how rapidly the night descended,— till all at once without the least warning, an appalling crash of thunder burst immediately above our heads, and a jagged fork of lightning tore the luminous fire-balloon to shreds. Two or three women began to scream,—whereupon Lucio advanced from the throng of spectators and stood in full view of all, holding up his hand.

"Stage thunder, I assure you!" he said playfully, in a clear somewhat scornful voice—"It comes and goes at my bidding. Quite a part of the game, believe me!—these sort of things are only toys for children. Again—again, ye petty elements!" he cried, laughing, and lifting his handsome face and flashing eyes to the dark heavens—"Roar your best and loudest!—roar, I say!"

Such a terrific boom and clatter answered him as baffled all description,—it was as if a mountain of rock had fallen into ruins,— but having been assured that the deafening noise was 'stage thunder' merely, the spectators were no longer alarmed, and many of them expressed their opinion that it was 'wonderfully well done.' After this, there gradually appeared against the sky a broad blaze of red light like the reflection of some great prairie fire,—it streamed apparently upward from the ground, bathing us all where we stood, in its blood-like glow. The white-robed dancing-girls waltzed on and on, their arms entwined, their lovely faces irradiated by the lurid flame, while above them now flew creatures with black wings, bats and owls, and great night-moths, that flapped and fluttered about for all the world

MARIE CORELLI

as if they were truly alive and not mere 'stage properties.' Another flash of lightning,—and one more booming thud of thunder,—and lo!—the undisturbed and fragrant night was about us, clear, dewy and calm,—the young moon smiled pensively in a cloudless heaven,—all the dancing-girls had vanished,—the crimson glow had changed to a pure silvery radiance, and an array of pretty pages in eighteenth century costumes of pale pink and blue, stood before us with lighted flaming torches, making a long triumphal avenue, down which Lucio invited us to pass.

"On, on fair ladies and gallant gentlemen!" he cried—"This extemporized path of light leads,—not to Heaven—no! that were far too dull an ending!—but to supper! On!—follow your leader!"

Every eye was turned on his fine figure and striking countenance, as with one hand he beckoned the guests,—between the double line of lit torches he stood,—a picture for a painter, with those dark eyes of his alit with such strange mirth as could not be defined, and the sweet, half-cruel, wonderfully attractive smile playing upon his lips;—and with one accord the whole company trooped pell-mell after him, shouting their applause and delight. Who could resist him!—not one in that assemblage at least;—there are few 'saints' in society! As I went with the rest, I felt as though I were in some gorgeous dream,—my senses were all in a whirl,—I was giddy with excitement and could not stop to think, or to analyse the emotions by which I was governed. Had I possessed the force or the will to pause and consider, I might possibly have come to the conclusion that there was something altogether beyond the ordinary power of man displayed in the successive wonders of this brilliant 'gala,'—but I was, like all the rest of society, bent merely on the pleasure of the moment, regardless of how it was procured, what it cost me, or how it affected others. How many I see and know to-day among the worshippers of fashion and frivolity who are acting precisely as I acted then! Indifferent to the welfare of everyone save themselves, grudging every penny that is not spent on their own advantage or amusement, and too callous to even listen to the sorrows or difficulties or joys of others when these do not in some way, near or remote, touch their own interests, they waste their time day after day in selfish trifling, wilfully blind and unconscious to the fact that they are building up their own fate in the future,—that future which will prove all the more a terrible Reality in proportion to the extent of our presumption in daring to doubt its truth.

More than four hundred guests sat down to supper in the largest pavilion,—a supper served in the most costly manner and furnished with luxuries that represented the utmost pitch of extravagance. I ate and drank, with Sybil at my side, hardly knowing what I said or did in the whirling excitement of the hour,—the opening of champagne-bottles, the clink of glasses, the clatter of plates, the loud hum of talk interspersed with monkey-like squeals or goat-like whinnies of laughter, over-ridden at intervals by the blare of trumpet-music and drums,—all these sounds were as so much noise of rushing waters in my ears,—and I often found myself growing abstracted and in a manner confused by the din. I did not say much to Sibyl,—one cannot very well whisper sentimental nothings in the ear of one's betrothed when she is eating ortolans and truffles. Presently, amid all the hubbub, a deep bell struck twelve times, and Lucio stood up at the end of one of the long tables, a full glass of foaming champagne in his hand—

"Ladies and gentlemen!"

There was a sudden silence.

"Ladies and gentlemen!" he repeated, his brilliant eyes flashing derisively, I thought, over the whole well-fed company, "Midnight has struck and the best of friends must part! But before we do so, let us not forget that we have met here to wish all happiness to our host, Mr. Geoffrey Tempest and his bride-elect, the Lady Sibyl Elton." Here there was vociferous applause. "It is said"—continued Lucio, "by the makers of dull maxims, that 'Fortune never comes with both hands full'—but in this case the adage is proved false and put to shame,—for our friend has not only secured the pleasures of wealth, but the treasures of love and beauty combined. Limitless cash is good, but limitless love is better, and both these choice gifts have been bestowed on the betrothed pair whom to-day we honour. I will ask you to give them a hearty round of cheering,—and then it must be good-night indeed, though not farewell,—for with the toast of the bride and bridegroom-elect, I shall also drink to the time,—not far distant perhaps,—when I shall see some of you, if not all of you again, and enjoy even more of your charming company than I have done to-day!"

He ceased amid a perfect hurricane of applause,—and then everyone rose and turned towards the table where I sat with Sibyl, and naming our names aloud, drank wine, the men joining in hearty shouts of "Hip, hip, hip hurrah!" Yet,—as I bowed repeatedly in response to the storm of cheering, and while Sibyl smiled and bent her graceful head to right and left, my heart sank suddenly with a sense of fear. Was it my fancy—or did I hear peals of wild laughter circling round the brilliant pavilion and echoing away, far away into distance? I listened, glass in hand. "Hip, hip, hip hurrah!" shouted my guests with gusto. "Ha—ha—! ha—ha!" seemed shrieked and yelled in my ears from the outer air. Struggling against this delusion, I got up and returned thanks for myself and my future bride in a few brief words which were received with fresh salvos of applause,—and then we all became aware that Lucio had sprung up again in his place, and was standing high above us all, with one foot on the table and the other on the chair, confronting us with a fresh glass of wine in his hand, filled to the brim. What a face he had at that moment!—what a smile!

"The parting cup, my friends!" he exclaimed—"To our next merry meeting!"

With plaudits and laughter the guests eagerly and noisily responded,—and as they drank, the pavilion was flooded by a deep crimson illumination as of fire. Every face looked blood-red!—every jewel on every woman flashed like a living flame!—for one brief instant only,—then it was gone, and there followed a general stampede of the company,—everybody hurrying as fast as they could into the carriages that waited in long lines to take them to the station, the last two 'special' trains to London being at one a.m. and one thirty. I bade Sibyl and her father a hurried good-night,—Diana Chesney went in the same carriage with them, full of ecstatic thanks and praise to me for the splendours of the day which she described in her own fashion as "knowing how to do it,—" and then the departing crowd of vehicles began to thunder down the avenue. As they went an arch of light suddenly spanned Willowsmere Court from end to end of its red gables, blazing with all the colours of the rainbow, in the middle of which appeared letters of pale blue and gold, forming what I had hitherto considered as a funereal device,

"Sic transit gloria mundi! Vale!"

But, after all, it was as fairly applicable to the ephemeral splendours of a fête as it was to the more lasting marble solemnity of a sepulchre, and I thought little or nothing about it. So perfect were all the arrangements, and so admirably were the servants trained, that the guests were not long in departing,—and the grounds were soon not only empty, but dark. Not a vestige of the splendid illuminations was left anywhere,—and I entered the house fatigued, and with a dull sense of bewilderment and fear on me which I could not explain. I found Lucio alone in the smoking-room at the further end of the oak-panelled hall, a small cosily curtained apartment with a deep bay window which opened directly on to the lawn. He was standing in this embrasure with his back to me, but he turned swiftly round as he heard my steps and confronted me with such a wild, white, tortured face that I recoiled from him, startled.

"Lucio, you are ill!" I exclaimed—"you have done too much to-day."

"Perhaps I have!" he answered in a hoarse unsteady voice, and I saw a strong shudder convulse him as he spoke,—then, gathering himself together as it were by an effort, he forced a smile—"Don't be alarmed, my friend!—it is nothing,—nothing but the twinge of an old deep-seated malady,—a troublesome disease that is rare among men, and hopelessly incurable."

"What is it?" I asked anxiously, for his death-like pallor alarmed me. He looked at me fixedly, his eyes dilating and darkening, and his hand fell with a heavy pressure on my shoulder.

"A very strange illness!" he said, in the same jarring accents. "Remorse! Have you never heard of it, Geoffrey? Neither medicine nor surgery are of any avail,—it is 'the worm that dieth not, and the flame that cannot be quenched.' Tut!—let us not talk of it,—no one can cure me,—no one will! I am past hope!"

"But remorse,—if you have it, and I cannot possibly imagine why, for you have surely nothing to regret,—is not a physical ailment!" I said wonderingly.

"And physical ailments are the only ones worth troubling about, you think?" he queried, still smiling that strained and haggard smile—"The body is our chief care,—we cosset it, and make much of it, feed it and pamper it, and guard it from so much as a pin-prick of pain if we can,—and thus we flatter ourselves that all is well,—all *must* be well! Yet it is but a clay chrysalis, bound to split and crumble with the growth of the moth-soul within,—the moth that flies with blind instinctiveness straight into the Unknown, and is dazzled by excess of light! Look out here,"—he went on with an abrupt and softer change of tone—"Look out at the dreamful shadowy beauty of your gardens now! The flowers are asleep,—the trees are surely glad to be disburdened of all the gaudy artificial lamps that lately hung upon their branches,—there is the young moon pillowing her chin on the edge of a little cloud and sinking to sleep in the west,—a moment ago there was a late nightingale awake and singing. You can feel the breath of the roses from the trellis yonder! All this is Nature's work,—and how much fairer and sweeter it is now than when the lights were ablaze and the blare of band-music startled the small birds in their downy nests!—Yet 'society' would not appreciate this cool dusk, this happy solitude;—'society' prefers a false glare to all true radiance. And what is worse it tries to make true things take a second place as adjuncts to sham ones,—and there comes in the mischief."

"It is just like you to run down your own indefatigable labours in the splendid successes of the day,"—I said laughing—"You may call it a 'false glare' if you like, but it has been a most magnificent spectacle,—and certainly in the way of entertainments it will never be equalled or excelled."

"It will make you more talked about than even your 'boomed' book could do!" said Lucio, eyeing me narrowly.

"Not the least doubt of that!" I replied—"Society prefers food and amusement to any literature,—even the greatest. By-the-by, where are all the 'artistes,'—the musicians and dancers?"

"Gone!"

"Gone!" I echoed amazedly—"Already! Good heavens! have they had supper?"

"They have had everything they want, even to their pay," said Lucio, a trifle impatiently—"Did I not tell you Geoffrey, that when I undertake to do anything, I do it thoroughly or not at all?"

I looked at him,—he smiled, but his eyes were sombre and scornful.

"All right!" I responded carelessly, not wishing to offend him,—"Have it your own way! But, upon my word, to me it is all like devil's magic!"

"What is?" he asked imperturbably.

"Everything!—the dancers,—the number of servants and pages— why, there must have been two or three hundred of them,—those wonderful 'tableaux,'—the illuminations,—the supper,—everything I tell you!—and the most astonishing part of it now is, that all these people should have cleared out so soon!"

"Well, if you elect to call money devil's magic, you are right,"—said Lucio.

"But surely in some cases, not even money could procure such perfection of detail"—I began.

"Money can procure anything!"—he interrupted, a thrill of passion vibrating in his rich voice,—"I told you that long ago. It is a hook for the devil himself. Not that the devil could be supposed to care about world's cash personally,—but he generally conceives a liking for the company of the man who possesses it;—possibly he knows what that man will do with it. I speak metaphorically of course,—but no metaphor can exaggerate the power of money. Trust no man or woman's virtue till you have tried to purchase it with a round sum in hard cash! Money, my excellent Geoffrey, has done everything for *you*,—remember that!—you have done nothing for yourself."

"That's not a very kind speech,"—I said, somewhat vexedly.

"No? And why? Because it's true? I notice most people complain of 'unkindness' when they are told a truth. It *is* true, and I see no unkindness in it. You've done nothing for yourself and you're not expected to do anything—except," and he laughed—"except just now to get to bed, and dream of the enchanting Sibyl!"

"I confess I am tired,"—I said, and an unconscious sigh escaped me—"And you?"

His gaze rested broodingly on the outer landscape.

"I also am tired," he responded slowly—"But I never get away from my fatigue, for I am tired of myself. And I always rest badly. Good-night!"

"Good-night!" I answered,—and then paused, looking at him. He returned my look with interest.

"Well?" he asked expressively.

I forced a smile.

"Well!" I echoed—"I do not know what I should say,—except—that I wish I knew you as you are. I feel that you were right in telling me once that you are not what you seem."

He still kept his eyes fixed upon me.

"As you have expressed the wish,"—he said slowly—"I promise you you *shall* know me as I am some-day! It may be well for you to know,—for the sake of others who may seek to cultivate my company."

I moved away to leave the room.

"Thanks for all the trouble you have taken to-day,"—I said in a lighter tone—"Though I shall never be able to express my full gratitude in words."

"If you wanted to thank anybody, thank God that you have lived through it!" he replied.

MARIE CORELLI

"Why?" I asked, astonished.

"Why? Because life hangs on a thread,—a society crush is the very acme of boredom and exhaustion,—and that we escape with our lives from a general guzzle and giggle is matter for thanksgiving,—that's all! And God gets so few thanks as a rule that you may surely spare Him a brief one for to-day's satisfactory ending."

I laughed, seeing no meaning in his words beyond the usual satire he affected. I found Amiel, waiting for me in my bedroom, but I dismissed him abruptly, hating the look of his crafty and sullen face, and saying I needed no attendance. Thoroughly fatigued, I was soon in bed and asleep,—and the terrific agencies that had produced the splendours of the brilliant festival at which I had figured as host, were not revealed to me by so much as a warning dream!

XXV

A few days after the entertainment at Willowsmere, and before the society papers had done talking about the magnificence and luxury displayed on that occasion, I woke up one morning, like the great poet Byron, "to find myself famous." Not for any intellectual achievement,—not for any unexpected deed of heroism,—not for any resolved or noble attitude in society or politics,—no!—I owed my fame merely to a quadruped;—'Phosphor' won the Derby. It was about a neck-and-neck contest between my racer and that of the Prime Minister, and for a second or so the result seemed doubtful,—but, as the two jockeys neared the goal, Amiel, whose thin wiry figure clad in the brightest of bright scarlet silk, stuck to his horse as though he were a part of it, put 'Phosphor' to a pace he had never yet exhibited, appearing to skim along the ground at literally flying speed, the upshot being that he scored a triumphant victory, reaching the winning-post a couple of yards or more ahead of his rival. Acclamations rent the air at the vigour displayed in the 'finish'—and I became the hero of the day,—the darling of the populace. I was somewhat amused at the Premier's discomfiture,—he took his beating rather badly. He did not know me, nor I him,—I was not of his politics, and I did not care a jot for his feelings one way or the other, but I was gratified, in a certain satirical sense, to find myself suddenly acknowledged as a greater man than he, because I was the owner of the Derby-winner! Before I well knew where I was, I found myself being presented to the Prince of Wales, who shook hands with me and congratulated me;—all the biggest aristocrats in England were willing and eager to be introduced to me;—and inwardly I laughed at this exhibition of taste and culture on the part of 'the gentlemen of England that live at home at ease.' They crowded round 'Phosphor,' whose wild eye warned strangers against taking liberties with him, but who seemed not a whit the worse for his exertions, and who apparently was quite ready to run the race over again with equal pleasure and success. Amiel's dark sly face and cruel ferret eyes were evidently not attractive to the majority of the gentlemen of the turf, though his answers to all the queries put to him, were admirably ready, respectful and not without wit. But to me the whole sum and substance of the occasion was the fact that I, Geoffrey Tempest, once struggling author, now millionaire, was simply by virtue of my ownership of the Derby-winner, 'famous' at last!—or what society considers famous,—that fame that secures for a man the attention of 'the nobility and gentry,' to quote from tradesmen's advertisements,—and also obtains the persistent adulation and shameless pursuit of all the *demi-mondaines* who want jewels and horses and yachts presented to them in exchange for a few tainted kisses from their carmined lips. Under the shower of compliments I received, I stood, apparently delighted,—smiling, affable and courteous,—entering into the spirit of the occasion, and shaking hands with my Lord That, and Sir Something Nobody, and His Serene Highness the Grand Duke So-and-So of Beer-Land, and His other Serene Lowness of Small-Principality,—but in my secret soul I scorned these people with their social humbug and hypocrisy,—scorned them with such a deadly scorn as almost amazed myself. When presently I walked off the course with Lucio, who as usual seemed to know and to be friends with everybody, he spoke in accents that were far more grave and gentle than I had ever heard him use before.

"With all your egotism, Geoffrey, there is something forcible and noble in your nature,—something which rises up in bold revolt against falsehood and sham. Why, in Heaven's name do you not give it way?"

I looked at him amazed, and laughed.

"Give it way? What do you mean? Would you have me tell humbugs that I know them as such?,—and liars that I discern their lies? My dear fellow, society would become too hot to hold me!"

"It could not be hotter—or colder—than hell, if you believed in hell, which you do not,"—he rejoined, in the same quiet voice—"But I did not assume that you should say these things straight out and bluntly, to give offence. An affronting candour is not nobleness,—it is merely coarse. To act nobly is better than to speak."

"And what would you have me do?" I asked curiously.

He was silent for a moment, and seemed to be earnestly, almost painfully considering,—then he answered,—

"My advice will seem to you singular, Geoffrey,—but if you want it, here it is. Give, as I said, the noble, and what the world would call the quixotic part of your nature full way,—do not sacrifice your higher sense of what is right and just for the sake of pandering to anyone's power or influence,—and—say farewell to *me*! I am no use to you, save to humour your varying fancies, and introduce you to those great,—or small,—personages you wish to know for your own convenience or advantage,—believe me, it would be much better for you and much more consoling at the inevitable hour of death, if you were to let all this false and frivolous nonsense go, and me with it! Leave society to its own fool's whirligig of distracted follies,—put Royalty in its true place, and show it that all its pomp, arrogance and glitter are worthless, and itself a nothing, compared to the upright standing of a brave soul in an honest man,—and, as Christ said to the rich ruler—'Sell half that thou hast and give to the poor.'"

I was silent for a minute or so out of sheer surprise, while he watched me earnestly, his face pale and expectant. A curious shock of something like compunction startled my conscience, and for a brief space I was moved to a vague regret,—regret that with all the enormous capability I possessed of doing good to numbers of my fellow-creatures with the vast wealth I owned, I had not attained to any higher moral attitude than that represented by the frivolous folk who make up what is called the 'Upper Ten' of society. I took the same egotistical pleasure in myself and my own doings as any of them,—and I was to the full as foolishly conventional, smooth-tongued and hypocritical as they. They acted their part and I acted mine,—none of us were ever our real selves for a moment. In very truth, one of the reasons why 'fashionable' men and women cannot bear to be alone is, that a solitude in which they are compelled to look face to face upon their secret selves becomes unbearable because of the burden they carry of concealed vice and accusing shame. My emotion soon passed however, and slipping my arm through Lucio's, I smiled, as I answered—

"Your advice, my dear fellow, would do credit to a Salvationist preacher,—but it is quite valueless to me, because impossible to follow. To say farewell for ever to you, in the first place, would be to make myself guilty of the blackest ingratitude,—in the second instance, society, with all its ridiculous humbug, is nevertheless necessary for the amusement of myself and my future wife,—Royalty moreover, is accustomed to be flattered, and we shall not be hurt by joining in the general inane chorus;—thirdly, if I did as the visionary Jew suggested—"

"What visionary Jew?" he asked, his eyes sparkling coldly.

"Why, Christ of course!" I rejoined lightly.

The shadow of a strange smile parted his lips.

"It is the fashion to blaspheme!" he said,—"A mark of brilliancy in literature, and wit in society! I forgot! Pray go on,—if you did as Christ suggested—"

"Yes,—if I gave half my goods to the poor, I should not be thanked for it, or considered anything but a fool for my pains."

"You would wish to be thanked?" he said.

"Naturally! Most people like a little gratitude in return for benefits."

"They do. And the Creator, who is always giving, is supposed to like gratitude also,"—he observed—"Nevertheless He seldom gets it!"

"I do not talk of hyperphysical nothingness,"—I said with impatience—"I am speaking of the plain facts of this world and the people who live in it. If one gives largely, one expects to be acknowledged as generous,—but if I were to divide my fortune, and hand half of it to the poor, the matter would be chronicled in about six lines in one of the papers, and society would exclaim 'What a fool!'"

"Then let us talk no more about it,"—said Lucio, his brows clearing, and his eyes gathering again their wonted light of mockery and mirth—"Having won the Derby, you have really done all a nineteenth-century civilization expects you to do, and for your reward, you will be in universal demand everywhere. You may hope soon to dine at Marlborough House,—and a little back-stair influence and political jobbery will work you into the Cabinet if you care for it. Did I not tell you I would set you up as successfully as the bear who has reached the bun on the top of the slippery pole, a spectacle for the envy of men and the wonder of angels? Well, there you are!—triumphant!—a great creature Geoffrey!—in fact, you are the greatest product of the age, a man with five millions and owner of the Derby-winner! What is the glory of intellect compared to such a position as yours! Men envy you,— and as for angels,—if there are any,—you may be sure they *do* wonder! A man's fame guaranteed by a horse, is something indeed to make an angel stare!"

He laughed uproariously, and from that day he never spoke again of his singular proposition that I should 'part with him,' and let the "nobler" nature in me have its way. I was not to know then that he had staked a chance upon my soul and lost it,—and that from henceforward he took a determined course with me, implacably on to the appalling end.

My marriage took place on the appointed day in June with all the pomp and extravagant show befitting my position, and that of the woman I had chosen to wed. It is needless to describe the gorgeousness of the ceremony in detail,—any fashionable 'ladies paper' describing the wedding of an Earl's daughter to a five-fold millionaire, will give an idea, in hysterical rhapsody, of the general effect. It was an amazing scene,—and one in which costly millinery completely vanquished all considerations of solemnity or sacredness in the supposed 'divine' ordinance. The impressive command: "I require and charge ye both, as ye will answer at the dreadful day of judgment,"—did not obtain half so much awed attention as the exquisite knots of pearls and diamonds which fastened the bride's silver-embroidered train to her shoulders. 'All the world and his wife' were present,—that is, the social world, which imagines no other world exists, though it is the least part of the community. The Prince of Wales honoured us by his presence: two great dignitaries of the church performed the marriage-rite, resplendent in redundant fulness of white sleeve and surplice, and equally imposing in the fatness of their bodies and unctuous redness of their faces; and Lucio was my 'best man.' He was in high, almost wild spirits,—and, during our drive to the church together, had entertained me all the way with numerous droll stories, mostly at the expense of the clergy. When we reached the sacred edifice, he said laughingly as he alighted—

"Did you ever hear it reported, Geoffrey, that the devil is unable to enter a church, because of the cross upon it, or within it?"

"I have heard some such nonsense,"—I replied, smiling at the humour expressed in his sparkling eyes and eloquent features.

"It *is* nonsense,—for the makers of the legend forgot one thing;" he continued, dropping his voice to a whisper as we passed under the carved gothic portico—"The cross may be present,—but—so is the clergyman! And wherever a clergyman is, the devil may surely follow!"

I almost laughed aloud at his manner of making this irreverent observation, and the look with which he accompanied it. The rich tones of the organ creeping softly on the flower-scented silence however, quickly solemnized my mood,—and while I leaned against the altar-rails waiting for my bride, I caught myself wondering for the hundredth time or more, at my comrade's singularly proud and kingly aspect, as with folded arms and lifted head, he contemplated the lily-decked altar and the gleaming crucifix upon it, his meditative eyes bespeaking a curious mingling of reverence and contempt.

One incident I remember, as standing out particularly in all the glare and glitter of the brilliant scene, and this occurred at the signing of our names in the register. When Sibyl, a vision of angelic loveliness in all her bridal white, affixed her signature to the entry, Lucio bent towards her,—

"As 'best man' I claim an old-fashioned privilege!" he said, and kissed her lightly on the cheek. She blushed a vivid red,—then suddenly grew ghastly pale,—and with a kind of choking cry, reeled back in a dead faint in the arms of one of her bridesmaids. It was some minutes before she was restored to consciousness,—but she made light both of my alarm and the consternation of her friends,—and assuring us that it was nothing but the effect of the heat of the weather and the excitement of the day, she took my arm and walked down the aisle smilingly, through the brilliant ranks of her staring and envious 'society' friends, all of whom coveted her good fortune, not because she had married a worthy or gifted man,—that would have been no special matter for congratulation,—but simply because she had married five millions of money! I was the appendage to the millions—nothing further. She held her head high and haughtily, though I felt her tremble as the thundering strains of the 'Bridal March' from Lohengrin poured sonorous triumph on the air. She trod on roses all the way,—I remembered that too, . . . afterwards! Her satin slipper crushed the hearts of a thousand innocent things that must surely have been more dear to God than she;—the little harmless souls of flowers, whose task in life, sweetly fulfilled, had been to create beauty and fragrance by their mere existence, expired to gratify the vanity of one woman to whom nothing was sacred. But I anticipate,—I was yet in my fool's dream,—and imagined that the dying blossoms were happy to perish thus beneath her tread!

A grand reception was held at Lord Elton's house after the ceremony,—and in the midst of the chattering, the eating and the drinking, we,—my newly made wife and I,—departed amid the profuse flatteries and good wishes of our 'friends' who, primed with the very finest champagne, made a very decent show of being sincere. The last person to say farewell to us at the carriage-door was Lucio,—and the sorrow I felt at parting with him was more than I could express in words. From the very hour of the dawning of my good fortune we had been almost inseparable companions,—I owed my success in society,—everything, even my bride herself,—to his management and tact,—and though I had now won for my life's partner the most beautiful of women, I could not contemplate even the temporary breaking of the association between myself and my gifted and brilliant comrade, without a keen pang of personal pain amid my nuptial joys. Leaning his arms on the carriage-window, he looked in upon us both, smiling.

"My spirit will be with you both in all your journeyings!" he said—"And when you return, I shall be one of the first to bid you welcome home. Your house-party is fixed for September, I believe?"

"Yes,—and you will be the most eagerly desired guest of all invited!" I replied heartily, pressing his hand.

"Fie, for shame!" he retorted laughingly—"Be not so disloyal of speech, Geoffrey! Are you not going to entertain the Prince of Wales?—and shall anyone be more 'eagerly-desired' than he? No,—I must play a humble third or even fourth on your list where Royalty is concerned,—*my* princedom is alas! not that of Wales,—and the throne I might claim (if I had anyone to help me, which I have not) is a long way removed from that of England!"

Sibyl said nothing,—but her eyes rested on his handsome face and fine figure with an odd wonder and wistfulness, and she was very pale.

"Good-bye Lady Sibyl!" he added gently—"All joy be with you! To us who are left behind, your absence will seem long,—but to *you*,—ah!—Love gives wings to time, and what would be to ordinary folks a month of mere dull living, will be for you nothing but a moment's rapture! Love is better than wealth,—you have found that out already I know!—but I think—and hope—that you are destined to make the knowledge more certain and complete! Think of me sometimes! Au revoir!"

The horses started,—a handful of rice flung by the society idiot who is always at weddings, rattled against the door and on the roof of the brougham, and Lucio stepped back, waving his hand. To the last we saw him,—a tall stately figure on the steps of Lord Elton's mansion,—surrounded by an ultra-fashionable throng, . . . bridesmaids in bright attire and picture-hats,—young girls all eager and excited-looking, each of them no doubt longing fervently for the day to come when they might severally manage to secure as rich a husband as myself, . . . match-making mothers and wicked old dowagers, exhibiting priceless lace on their capacious bosoms, and ablaze with diamonds, . . . men with white button-hole bouquets in their irreproachably fitting frock-coats,—servants in gay liveries, and the usual street-crowd of idle sight-seers;—all this cluster of faces, costumes and flowers, was piled against the grey background of the stone portico,—and in the midst, the dark beauty of Lucio's face and the luminance of his flashing eyes made him the conspicuous object and chief centre of attraction, . . . then, . . . the carriage turned a sharp corner,—the faces vanished,—and Sibyl and I realised that from henceforward we were left alone,—alone to face the future and ourselves,—and to learn the lesson of love. . . or hate. . . for evermore together!

XXVI

I cannot now trace the slow or swift flitting by of phantasmal events, . . . wild ghosts of days or weeks that drifted past, and brought me gradually and finally to a time when I found myself wandering, numb and stricken and sick at heart, by the shores of a lake in Switzerland,—a small lake, densely blue, with apparently a thought in its depths such as is reflected in a child's earnest eye. I gazed down at the clear and glistening water almost unseeingly,—the snow-peaked mountains surrounding it were too high for the lifting of my aching sight,—loftiness, purity, and radiance were unbearable to my mind, crushed as it was beneath a weight of dismal wreckage and ruin. What a fool was I ever to have believed that in this world there could be such a thing as happiness! Misery stared me in the face,—life-long misery,—and no escape but death. Misery!—it was the word which like a hellish groan, had been uttered by the three dreadful phantoms that had once, in an evil vision, disturbed my rest. What had I done, I demanded indignantly of myself, to deserve this wretchedness which no wealth could cure?—why was fate so unjust? Like all my kind, I was unable to discern the small yet strong links of the chain I had myself wrought, and which bound me to my own undoing,—I blamed fate, or rather God,—and talked of injustice, merely because *I* personally suffered, never realizing that what I considered unjust was but the equitable measuring forth of that Eternal Law which is carried out with as mathematical an exactitude as the movement of the planets, notwithstanding man's pigmy efforts to impede its fulfilment. The light wind blowing down from the snow peaks above me ruffled the placidity of the little lake by which I aimlessly strolled,—I watched the tiny ripples break over its surface like the lines of laughter on a human face, and wondered morosely whether it was deep enough to drown in! For what was the use of living on,—knowing what I knew! Knowing that she whom I had loved, and whom I loved still in a way that was hateful to myself, was a thing viler and more shameless in character than the veriest poor drab of the street who sells herself for current coin,—that the lovely body and angel-face were but an attractive disguise for the soul of a harpy,—a vulture of vice, . . . my God!—an irrepressible cry escaped me as my thoughts went on and on in the never-ending circle and problem of incurable, unspeakable despair,—and I threw myself down on a shelving bank of grass that sloped towards the lake and covered my face in a paroxysm of tearless agony.

Still inexorable thought worked in my brain, and forced me to consider my position. Was she,—was Sibyl—more to blame than I myself for all the strange havoc wrought? I had married her of my own free will and choice,—and she had told me beforehand—"I am a contaminated creature, trained to perfection in the lax morals and prurient literature of my day." Well,—and so it had proved! My own blood burned with shame as I reflected how ample and convincing were the proofs!—and, starting up from my recumbent posture I paced up and down again restlessly in a fever of self-contempt and disgust. What could I do with a woman such as she to whom I was now bound for life? Reform her? She would laugh me to scorn for the attempt. Reform myself? She would sneer at me for an effeminate milksop. Besides, was not I as willing to be degraded as she was to degrade me?—a very victim to my brute passions? Tortured and maddened by my feelings I roamed about wildly, and started as if a pistol-shot had been fired near me when the plash of oars sounded on the silence and the keel of a small boat grated on the shore, the boatman within it respectfully begging me in mellifluous French to employ him for an hour. I assented, and in a minute or two was out on the lake in the middle of the red glow of sunset which turned the snow-summits to points of flame, and the waters to the hue of ruby wine. I think the man who rowed me saw that I was in no very pleasant humour, for he preserved a discreet silence,—and I, pulling my hat partly over my eyes, lay back in the stern, still busy with my wretched musings. Only a month married!—and yet,—a sickening satiety had taken the place of the so-called 'deathless' lover's passion. There were moments even, when my wife's matchless physical beauty appeared hideous to me. I knew her as she was,—and no exterior charm could ever again cover for me the revolting nature within. And what puzzled me from dawn to dusk was her polished, specious hypocrisy,—her amazing aptitude for lies! To look at her,—to hear her speak,—one would have deemed her a very saint of purity,—a delicate creature whom a coarse word would startle and offend,—a very incarnation of the sweetest and most gracious womanhood,—all heart and feeling and sympathy. Everyone thought thus of her,—and never was there a greater error. Heart she had none; that fact was borne in upon me two days after our marriage while we were in Paris, for there a telegram reached us announcing her mother's death. The paralysed

Countess of Elton had, it appeared, expired suddenly on our wedding-day, or rather our wedding night,—but the Earl had deemed it best to wait forty-eight hours before interrupting our hymeneal happiness with the melancholy tidings. He followed his telegram by a brief letter to his daughter, in which the concluding lines were these—"As you are a bride and are travelling abroad, I should advise you by no means to go into mourning. Under the circumstances it is really not necessary."

And Sibyl had readily accepted his suggestion, keeping generally however to white and pale mauve colourings in her numerous and wonderful toilettes, in order not to outrage the proprieties too openly in the opinions of persons known to her, whom she might possibly meet casually in the foreign towns we visited. No word of regret passed her lips, and no tears were shed for her mother's loss. She only said,

"What a good thing her sufferings are over!"

Then, with a little sarcastic smile, she had added—

"I wonder when we shall receive the Elton-Chesney wedding cards!"

I did not reply, for I was pained and grieved at her lack of all gentle feeling in the matter, and I was also, to a certain extent, superstitiously affected by the fact of the death occurring on our marriage-day. However this was now a thing of the past; a month had elapsed,—a month in which the tearing-down of illusions had gone on daily and hourly,—till I was left to contemplate the uncurtained bare prose of life and the knowledge that I had wedded a beautiful feminine animal with the soul of a shameless libertine. Here I pause and ask myself,—Was not I also a libertine? Yes,—I freely admit it,—but the libertinage of a man, while it may run to excess in hot youth, generally resolves itself, under the influence of a great love, into a strong desire for undefiled sweetness and modesty in the woman beloved. If a man has indulged in both folly and sin, the time comes at last, when, if he has any good left in him at all, he turns back upon himself and lashes his own vices with the scorpion-whip of self-contempt till he smarts with the rage and pain of it,—and then, aching in every pulse with his deserved chastisement, he kneels in spirit at the feet of some pure, true-hearted woman whose white soul, like an angel, hovers compassionately above him, and there lays down his life, saying "Do what you will with it,—it is yours!" And woe to her who plays lightly with such a gift, or works fresh injury upon it! No man, even if he has in his day, indulged in 'rapid' living, should choose a 'rapid' woman for his wife,—he had far better put a loaded pistol to his head and make an end of it!

The sunset-glory began to fade from the landscape as the little boat glided on over the tranquil water, and a great shadow was on my mind, like the shadow of that outer darkness which would soon be night. Again I asked myself—Was there no happiness possible in all the world? Just then the Angelus chimed from a little chapel on the shore, and as it rang, a memory stirred in my brain moving me well-nigh to tears. Mavis Clare was happy!—Mavis, with her frank fearless eyes, sweet face and bright nature,—Mavis, wearing her crown of Fame as simply as a child might wear a wreath of may-blossom,—she, with a merely moderate share of fortune which even in its slight proportion was only due to her own hard incessant work,—she was happy. And I,—with my millions,—was wretched! How was it? Why was it? What had I done? I had lived as my compeers lived,—I had followed the lead of all society,—I had feasted my friends and effectually 'snubbed' my foes,—I had comported myself exactly as others of my wealth comport themselves,—and I had married a woman whom most men, looking upon once, would have been proud to win. Nevertheless there seemed to be a curse upon me. What had I missed out of life? I knew,—but was ashamed to own it, because I had previously scorned what I called the dream-nothings of mere sentiment. And now I had to acknowledge the paramount importance of those 'dream-nothings' out of which all true living must come. I had to realize that my marriage was nothing but the mere mating of the male and female animal,—a coarse bodily union, and no more;—that all the finer and deeper emotions which make a holy thing of human wedlock, were lacking,—the mutual respect, the trusting sympathy,—the lovely confidence of mind with mind,—the subtle inner spiritual bond which no science can analyse, and which is so much closer and stronger than the material, and knits immortal souls together when bodies decay—these things had no existence, and never would exist between my wife and me. Thus, as far as I was concerned, there was a strange blankness in the world,—I was thrust back upon myself for comfort and found none. What should I do with my life, I wondered drearily! Win fame,—true fame,—after all? With Sibyl's witch-eyes mocking my efforts?—never! If I had ever had any gifts of creative thought within me, *she* would have killed it!

The hour was over,—the boatman rowed me in to land, and I paid and dismissed him. The sun had completely sunk,—there were dense purple shadows darkening over the mountains, and one or two small stars faintly discernible in the east. I walked slowly back to the villa where we were staying,—a 'dépendance' belonging to the large hotel of the district, which we had rented for the sake of privacy and independence, some of the hotel-servants being portioned off to attend upon us, in addition to my own man Morris, and my wife's maid. I found Sibyl in the garden, reclining in a basket-chair, her eyes fixed on the after-glow of the sunset, and in her hands a book,—one of the loathliest of the prurient novels that have been lately written by women to degrade and shame their sex. With a sudden impulse of rage upon me which I could not resist, I snatched the volume from her and flung it into the lake below. She made no movement of either surprise or offence,—she merely turned her eyes away from the glowing heavens, and looked at me with a little smile.

"How violent you are to-day, Geoffrey!" she said.

I gazed at her in sombre silence. From the light hat with its pale mauve orchids that rested on her nut-brown hair, to the point of her daintily embroidered shoe, her dress was perfect,—and *she* was perfect. *I* knew that,—a matchless piece of womanhood. . . outwardly! My heart beat,—there was a sense of suffocation in my throat,—I could have killed her for the mingled loathing and longing which her beauty roused in me.

"I am sorry!" I said hoarsely, avoiding her gaze—"But I hate to see you with such a book as that!"

"You know its contents?" she queried, with the same slight smile.

"I can guess."

"Such things have to be written, they say nowadays,"—she went on—"And, certainly, to judge from the commendation bestowed on these sort of books by the press, it is very evident that the wave of opinion is setting in the direction of letting girls know all about marriage before they enter upon it, in order that they may do so with their eyes wide open,—*very* wide open!" She laughed, and her laughter hurt me like a physical wound. "What an old-fashioned idea the bride of the poets and sixty-years-ago romancists seems now!" she continued—"Imagine her!—a shrinking tender creature, shy of beholders, timid of speech, . . . wearing the emblematic veil, which in former days, you know, used to cover the face entirely, as a symbol that the secrets of marriage were as yet hidden from the maiden's innocent and ignorant eyes. Now the veil is worn flung back from the bride's brows, and she stares unabashed at everybody,—oh yes, indeed we know quite well what we are doing now when we marry, thanks to the 'new' fiction!"

"The new fiction is detestable,"—I said hotly—"Both in style and morality. Even as a question of literature I wonder at your condescending to read any of it. The woman whose dirty book I have just thrown away—and I feel no compunction for having done it,—is destitute of grammar as well as decency."

"Oh, but the critics don't notice that,"—she interrupted, with a delicate mockery vibrating in her voice—"It is apparently not their business to assist in preserving the purity of the English language. What they fall into raptures over is the originality of the 'sexual' theme, though I should have thought all such matters were as old as the hills. I never read reviews as a rule, but I did happen to come across one on the book you have just drowned,—and in it, the reviewer stated he had cried over it!"

She laughed again.

"Beast!" I said emphatically—"He probably found in it some glozing-over of his own vices. But you, Sibyl—why do you read such stuff?— how can you read it?"

"Curiosity moved me in the first place,"—she answered listlessly—"I wanted to see what makes a reviewer cry! Then when I began to read, I found that the story was all about the manner in which men amuse themselves with the soiled doves of the highways and bye-ways,—and as I was not very well instructed in that sort of thing, I thought I might as well learn! You know these unpleasant morsels of information on unsavoury subjects are like the reputed suggestions of the devil,—if you listen to one, you are bound to hear more. Besides, literature is supposed to reflect the time we live in,—and that kind of literature being more prevalent than anything else, we are compelled to accept and study it as the mirror of the age."

With an expression on her face that was half mirth and half scorn, she rose from her seat, and looked down into the lovely lake below her.

"The fishes will eat that book,—" she observed—"I hope it will not poison them! If they could read and understand it, what singular ideas they would have of us human beings!"

"Why don't you read Mavis Clare's books?" I asked suddenly—"You told me you admired her."

"So I do,—immensely!" she answered,—"I admire her and wonder at her, both together. How that woman can keep her child's heart and child's faith in a world like this, is more than I can understand. It is always a perfect marvel to me,—a sort of supernatural surprise. You ask me why don't I read her books,—I do read them,—I've read them all over and over again,—but she does not write many, and one has to wait for her productions longer than for those of most authors. When I want to feel like an angel, I read Mavis Clare,—but I more often am inclined to feel the other way, and then her books are merely so many worries to me."

"Worries?" I echoed.

"Yes. It is worrying to find somebody believing in a God when *you* can't believe in Him,—to have beautiful faiths offered to you which *you* can't grasp,—and to know that there is a creature alive, a woman like yourself in everything except mind, who is holding fast a happiness which you can never attain,—no, not though you held out praying hands day and night and shouted wild appeals to the dull heavens!"

At that moment she looked like a queen of tragedy,—her violet eyes ablaze,—her lips apart,—her breast heaving;—I approached her with a strange nervous hesitation and touched her hand. She gave it to me passively,—I drew it through my arm, and for a minute or two we paced silently up and down the gravel walk. The lights from the monster hotel which catered for us and our wants, were beginning to twinkle from basement to roof,—and just above the châlet we rented, a triad of stars sparkled in the shape of a trefoil.

"Poor Geoffrey!" she said presently, with a quick upward glance at me,—"I am sorry for you! With all my vagaries of disposition I am not a fool, and at anyrate I have learned how to analyse myself as well as others. I read you as easily as I read a book,—I see what a strange tumult your mind is in! You love me—and you loathe me!—and the contrast of emotion makes a wreck of you and your ideals. Hush,—don't speak; I know,—I know! But what would you have me be? An angel? I cannot realize such a being for more than a fleeting moment of imagination. A saint? They were all martyred. A good woman? I never met one. Innocent?—ignorant? I told you before we married that I was neither; there is nothing left for me to discover as far as the relations between men and women are concerned,—I have taken the measure of the inherent love of vice in both sexes. There is not a pin to choose between them,—men are no worse than women,—women no worse than men. I have discovered everything—except God!—and I conclude no God could ever have designed such a crazy and mean business as human life."

While she thus spoke, I could have fallen at her feet and implored her to be silent. For she was, unknowingly, giving utterance to some

MARIE CORELLI

of the many thoughts in which I myself had frequently indulged,—
and yet, from her lips they sounded cruel, unnatural, and callous to
a degree that made me shrink from her in fear and agony. We had
reached a little grove of pines,—and here in the silence and shadow
I took her in my arms and stared disconsolately upon the beauty of
her face.

"Sibyl!" I whispered—"Sibyl, what is wrong with us both? How is
it that we do not seem to find the loveliest side of love?—why is it
that even in our kisses and embraces, some impalpable darkness comes
between us, so that we anger or weary each other when we should be
glad and satisfied? What is it? Can you tell? For you know the darkness
is there!"

A curious look came into her eyes,—a far-away strained look of
hungry yearning, mingled, as I thought, with compassion for me.

"Yes, it is there!" she answered slowly—"And it is of our own mutual
creation. I believe you have something nobler in your nature, Geoffrey,
than I have in mine,—an indefinable something that recoils from me
and my theories despite your wish and will. Perhaps if you had given
way to that feeling in time, you would never have married me. You
speak of the loveliest side of love,—to me there is no lovely side,—it
is all coarse and horrible! You and I for instance,—cultured man and
woman,—we cannot, in marriage, get a flight beyond the common
emotions of Hodge and his girl!" She laughed violently, and shuddered
in my arms. "What liars the poets are, Geoffrey! They ought to be
sentenced to life-long imprisonment for their perjuries! They help to
mould the credulous beliefs of a woman's heart;—in her early youth she
reads their delicious assurances, and imagines that love will be all they
teach,—a thing divine and lasting beyond earthly countings;—then
comes the coarse finger of prose on the butterfly-wing of poesy, and the
bitterness and hideousness of complete disillusion!"

I held her still in my arms with the fierce grasp of a man clinging to
a spar ere he drowns in mid-ocean.

"But I love you Sibyl!—my wife, I love you!" I said, with a passion
that choked my utterance.

"You love me,—yes, I know, but how? In a way that is abhorrent
to yourself!" she replied—"It is not poetic love,—it is man's love, and
man's love is brute love. So it is,—so it will be,—so it must be. Moreover
the brute-love soon tires,—and when it dies out from satiety there is
nothing left. Nothing, Geoffrey,—absolutely nothing but a blank and

civil form of intercourse, which I do not doubt we shall be able to keep up for the admiration and comment of society!"

She disengaged herself from my embrace, and moved towards the house.

"Come!" she added, turning her exquisite head back over her shoulder with a feline caressing grace that she alone possessed, "You know there is a famous lady in London who advertises her saleable charms to the outside public by means of her monogram worked into the lace of all her window-blinds, thinking it no doubt good for trade! I am not quite so bad as that! You have paid dearly for me I know;—but remember I as yet wear no jewels but yours, and crave no gifts beyond those you are generous enough to bestow,—and my dutiful desire is to give you as much full value as I can for your money."

"Sibyl, you kill me!" I cried, tortured beyond endurance, "Do you think me so base—"

I broke off with almost a sob of despair.

"You cannot help being base," she said, steadily regarding me,—"because you are a man. I am base because I am a woman. If we believed in a God, either of us, we might discover some different way of life and love—who knows?—but neither you nor I have any remnant of faith in a Being whose existence all the scientists of the day are ever at work to disprove. We are persistently taught that we are animals and nothing more,—let us therefore not be ashamed of animalism. Animalism and atheism are approved by the scientists and applauded by the press,—and the clergy are powerless to enforce the faith they preach. Come Geoffrey, don't stay mooning like a stricken Parsifal under those pines,—throw away that thing which troubles you, your conscience,—throw it away as you have thrown the book I was lately reading, and consider this,—that most men of your type take pride and rejoice in being the prey of a bad woman!—so you should really congratulate yourself on having one for a wife!—one who is so broad-minded too, that she will always let you have your own way in everything you do, provided you let her have hers! It is the way all marriages are arranged nowadays,—at any rate in *our* set,—otherwise the tie would be impossible of endurance. Come!"

"We cannot live together on such an understanding, Sibyl!" I said hoarsely, as I walked slowly by her side towards the villa.

"Oh yes, we can!" she averred, a little malign smile playing round her lips—"We can do as others do,—there is no necessity for us to stand out from the rest like quixotic fools, and pose as models to other married people,—we should only be detested for our pains. It is surely better to be popular than virtuous,—virtue never pays! See, there is our interesting German waiter coming to inform us that dinner is ready; please don't look so utterly miserable, for we have not quarrelled, and it would be foolish to let the servants think we have."

I made no answer. We entered the house, and dined,—Sibyl keeping up a perfect fire of conversation, to which I replied in mere monosyllables,—and after dinner we went as usual to sit in the illuminated gardens of the adjacent hotel, and hear the band. Sibyl was known, and universally admired and flattered by many of the people staying there,—and, as she moved about among her acquaintances, chatting first with one group and then with another, I sat in moody silence, watching her with increasing wonderment and horror. Her beauty seemed to me like the beauty of the poison-flower, which, brilliant in colour and perfect in shape, exhales death to those who pluck it from its stem. And that night, when I held her in my arms, and felt her heart beating against my own in the darkness, an awful dread arose in me,—a dread as to whether I might not at some time or other be tempted to strangle her as she lay on my breast—strangle her as one would strangle a vampire that sucked one's blood and strength away!

XXVII

We concluded our wedding-tour rather sooner than we had at first intended, and returned to England and Willowsmere Court, about the middle of August. I had a vague notion stirring in me that gave me a sort of dim indefinable consolation, and it was this,—I meant to bring my wife and Mavis Clare together, believing that the gentle influence of the gracious and happy creature, who, like a contented bird in its nest, dwelt serene in the little domain so near my own, might have a softening and wholesome effect upon Sibyl's pitiless love of analysis and scorn of all noble ideals. The heat in Warwickshire was at this time intense,—the roses were out in their full beauty, and the thick foliage of the branching oaks and elms in my grounds afforded grateful shade and repose to the tired body, while the tranquil loveliness of the woodland and meadow scenery, comforted and soothed the equally tired mind. After all, there is no country in the world so fair as England,—none so richly endowed with verdant forests and fragrant flowers,—none that can boast of sweeter nooks for seclusion and romance. In Italy, that land so over-praised by hysterical *poseurs* who foolishly deem it admirable to glorify any country save their own, the fields are arid and brown, and parched by the too fervent sun,—there are no shady lanes such as England can boast of in all her shires,—and the mania among Italians for ruthlessly cutting down their finest trees, has not only actually injured the climate, but has so spoilt the landscape that it is difficult to believe at all in its once renowned, and still erroneously reported charm. Such a bower of beauty as Lily Cottage was in that sultry August, could never have been discovered in all the length and breadth of Italy. Mavis superintended the care of her gardens herself,—she had two gardeners, who under her directions, kept the grass and trees continually watered,—and nothing could be imagined more lovely than the picturesque old-fashioned house, covered with roses and tufts of jessamine that seemed to tie up the roof in festal knots and garlands, while around the building spread long reaches of deep emerald lawn, and bosky arbours of foliage where all the most musical song-birds apparently found refuge and delight, and where at evening a perfect colony of nightingales kept up a bubbling fountain of delicious melody. I remember well the afternoon, warm, languid and still, when I took Sibyl to see the woman-author she had so long admired. The heat was so great that in our own grounds all the birds were silent, but when we approached Lily Cottage the first thing we heard was the piping of a thrush up somewhere among the roses,—a mellow liquid warble expressing 'sweet content,' and mingling with the subdued coo-cooings of the dove 'reviewers' who were commenting on whatever pleased or displeased them in the distance.

"What a pretty place it is!" said my wife, as she peeped over the gate, and through the odorous tangles of honeysuckle and jessamine—"I really think it is prettier than Willowsmere. It has been wonderfully improved."

We were shown in,—and Mavis, who had expected our visit did not keep us waiting long. An she entered, clad in some gossamer white stuff that clung softly about her pretty figure and was belted in by a simple ribbon, an odd sickening pang went through my heart. The fair untroubled face,—the joyous yet dreamy student eyes,—the sensitive mouth, and above all, the radiant look of happiness that made the whole expression of her features so bright and fascinating, taught me in one flash of conviction all that a woman might be, and all that she too frequently is not. And I had hated Mavis Clare!—I had even taken up my pen to deal her a wanton blow through the medium of anonymous criticism, . . . but this was before I knew her,—before I realized that there could be any difference between her and the female scarecrows who so frequently pose as 'novelists' without being able to write correct English, and who talk in public of their 'copy' with the glibness gained from Grub Street and the journalists' cheap restaurant. Yes—I had hated her,—and now—now, almost I loved her! Sibyl, tall, queenly and beautiful, gazed upon her with eyes that expressed astonishment as well as admiration.

"To think that you are the famous Mavis Clare!" she said, smiling, as she held out her hand—"I always heard and knew that you did not look at all literary, but I never quite realized that you could be exactly what I see you are!"

"To look literary does not always imply that you *are* literary!" returned Mavis, laughing a little—"Too often I am afraid you will find that the women who take pains to *look* literary are ignorant of literature! But how glad I am to see you, Lady Sibyl! Do you know I used to watch you playing about on the lawns at Willowsmere when I was quite a little girl?"

"And I used to watch you,"—responded Sibyl—"You used to make daisy-chains and cowslip-balls in the fields opposite on the other side of the Avon. It is a great pleasure to me to know we are neighbours. You must come and see me often at Willowsmere."

Mavis did not answer immediately,—she busied herself in pouring out tea and dispensing it to both of us. Sibyl, who was always on the alert for glimpses of character, noticed that she did not answer, and repeated her words coaxingly.

"You will come, will you not? As often as you like,—the oftener the better. We must be friends, you know!"

Mavis looked up then, a frank sweet smile in her eyes.

"Do you really mean it?" she asked.

"Mean it!" echoed Sibyl—"Why, of course I do!"

"How can you doubt it!" I exclaimed.

"Well, you must both forgive me for asking such a question"—said Mavis still smiling—"But you see you are now among what are called the 'county magnates,' and county magnates consider themselves infinitely above all authors!" She laughed outright, and her blue eyes twinkled with fun. "I think many of them estimate writers of books as some sort of strange outgrowth of humanity that is barely decent. It is deliciously funny and always amuses me,—nevertheless, among my many faults, the biggest one is, I fancy, pride, and a dreadfully obstinate spirit of independence. Now, to tell you the truth, I have been asked by many so-called 'great' people to their houses, and when I *have* gone, I have generally been sorry for it afterwards."

"Why?" I asked—"They honour themselves by inviting you."

"Oh, I don't think they take it in that way at all!" she replied, shaking her fair head demurely—"They fancy they have performed a great act of condescension,—whereas it is really I who condescend, for it is very good of me, you know, to leave the society of the Pallas Athene in my study for that of a flounced and frizzled lady of fashion!" Her bright smile again irradiated her face and she went on—"Once I was asked to luncheon with a certain baron and baroness who invited a few guests "to meet me," so they said. I was not introduced to more than one or two of these people,—the rest sat and stared at me as if I were a new kind of fish or fowl. Then the baron showed me his house, and told me the prices of his pictures and his china,—he was even good enough to explain which was Dresden and which was Delft ware, though I believe, benighted author as I am, I could have instructed him equally on these, and other matters. However I managed to smile amicably through the whole programme, and professed myself charmed and delighted in the usual way;—but they never asked me to visit them again,—and, (unless indeed they wanted me to be impressed with their furniture-catalogue) I can never make out what I did to be asked at all, and what I have done never to be asked any more!"

"They must have been *parvenus*,"—said Sibyl indignantly—"No well-bred people would have priced their goods to you, unless they happened to be Jews."

Mavis laughed—a merry little laugh like a peal of bells,—then she continued—

"Well, I will not say who they were,—I must keep something for my 'literary reminiscences' when I get old! Then all these people will be named, and go down to posterity as Dante's enemies went down to Dante's hell! I have only told you the incident just to show you why I asked you if you meant it, when you invited me to visit you at Willowsmere. Because the baron and baroness I have spoken of 'gushed' over me and my poor books to such an extent that you would have fancied I was to be for evermore one of their dearest friends,— and they *didn't* mean it! Other people I know embrace me effusively and invite me to their houses, and *they* don't mean it! And when I find out these shams, I like to make it very clear on my own side that I do not seek to be embraced or invited, and that if certain great folks deem it a 'favour' to ask me to their houses, I do not so consider it, but rather think the 'favour' is entirely on my part if I accept the invitation. And I do not say this for my own self at all,—self has nothing to do with it,—but I do say it and strongly assert it for the sake of the dignity of Literature as an art and profession. If a few other authors would maintain this position, we might raise the standard of letters by degrees to what it was in the old days of Scott and Byron. I hope you do not think me too proud?"

"On the contrary, I think you are quite right"—said Sibyl earnestly— "And I admire you for your courage and independence. Some of the aristocracy are, I know, such utter snobs that often I feel ashamed to belong to them. But as far as we are concerned, I can only assure you that if you will honour us by becoming our friend as well as neighbour, you shall not regret it. Do try and like me if you can!"

She bent forward with a witching smile on her fair face. Mavis looked at her seriously and admiringly.

"How beautiful you are!" she said frankly—"Everybody tells you this of course,—still, I cannot help joining in the general chorus. To me, a lovely face is like a lovely flower,—I must admire it. Beauty is quite a divine thing, and though I am often told that the plain people are always the good people, I never can quite believe it. Nature is surely bound to give a beautiful face to a beautiful spirit."

Sibyl, who had smiled with pleasure at the first words of the open compliment paid her by one of the most gifted of her own sex, now flushed deeply.

"Not always, Miss Clare,"—she said, veiling her brilliant eyes beneath the droop of her long lashes—"One can imagine a fair fiend as easily as a fair angel."

"True!" and Mavis looked at her musingly,—then suddenly laughing in her blithe bright way, she added—"Quite true! Really I cannot picture an ugly fiend,—for the fiends are supposed to be immortal, and I am convinced that immortal ugliness has no part in the universe. Downright hideousness belongs to humanity alone,—and an ugly face is such a blot on creation that we can only console ourselves by the reflection that it is fortunately perishable, and that in course of time the soul behind it will be released from its ill-formed husk, and will be allowed to wear a fairer aspect. Yes, Lady Sibyl, I will come to Willowsmere; I cannot refuse to look upon such loveliness as yours as often as I may!"

"You are a charming flatterer!" said Sibyl, rising and putting an arm round her in that affectionate coaxing way of hers which seemed so sincere, and which so frequently meant nothing—"But I confess I prefer to be flattered by a woman rather than by a man. Men say the same things to all women,—they have a very limited répertoire of compliments,—and they will tell a fright she is beautiful, if it happens to serve their immediate purpose. But women themselves can so hardly be persuaded to admit that any good qualities exist either inwardly or outwardly in one another, that when they do say a kind or generous thing of their own sex it is a wonder worth remembering. May I your study?"

Mavis willingly assented,—and we all three went into the peaceful sanctum where the marble Pallas presided, and where the dogs Tricksy and Emperor were both ensconced,—Emperor sitting up on his haunches and surveying the prospect from the window, and Tricksy with a most absurd air of importance, imitating the larger animal's attitude precisely, at a little distance off. Both creatures were friendly to my wife and to me, and while Sibyl was stroking the St Bernard's massive head, Mavis said suddenly,

"Where is the friend who came with you here first, Prince Rimânez?"

"He is in St Petersburg just now,"—I answered—"But we expect him in two or three weeks to stay with us on a visit for some time."

"He is surely a very singular man,"—said Mavis thoughtfully—"Do you remember how strangely my dogs behaved to him? Emperor was quite restless and troublesome for two or three hours after he had gone."

And in a few words, she told Sibyl the incident of the St Bernard's attack upon Lucio.

"Some people have a natural antipathy to dogs,"—said Sibyl, as she heard—"And the dogs always find it out, and resent it. But I should not have thought Prince Rimânez had an antipathy to any creatures except—women!"

And she laughed, a trifle bitterly.

"Except women!" echoed Mavis surprisedly—"Does he hate women? He must be a very good actor then,—for to me he was wonderfully kind and gentle."

Sibyl looked at her intently, and was silent for a minute. Then she said—

"Perhaps it is because he knows you are unlike the ordinary run of women and have nothing in common with their usual trumpery aims. Of course he is always courteous to our sex,—but I think it is easy to see that his courtesy is often worn as a mere mask to cover a very different feeling."

"You have perceived that, then, Sibyl?" I said with a slight smile.

"I should be blind if I had not perceived it"—she replied; "I do not however blame him for his pet aversion,—I think it makes him all the more attractive and interesting."

"He is a great friend of yours?" inquired Mavis, looking at me as she put the question.

"The very greatest friend I have,"—I replied quickly—"I owe him more than I can ever repay,—indeed I have to thank him even for introducing me to my wife!"

I said the words unthinkingly and playfully, but as I uttered them, a sudden shock affected my nerves,—a shock of painful memory. Yes, it was true!—I owed to him, to Lucio, the misery, fear, degradation and shame of having such a woman as Sibyl was, united to me till death should us part. I felt myself turning sick and giddy,—and I sat down in one of the quaint oak chairs that helped to furnish Mavis Clare's study, allowing the two women to pass out of the open French window into the sunlit garden together, the dogs following at their heels. I watched them as they went,—my wife, tall and stately, attired in the newest and most fashionable mode,—Mavis, small and slight, with her soft white gown and floating waist-ribbon,—the one sensual, the other spiritual,—the one base and vicious in desire,—the other pure-souled and aspiring to noblest ends,—the one, a physically magnificent animal,—the other merely sweet-faced and ideally fair like a sylph of the woodlands,—and looking, I clenched my hands as I thought with bitterness of spirit what a mistaken choice I had made. In the profound egotism which had always been part of my nature I now actually allowed myself to believe that I might, had I chosen, have wedded Mavis Clare,—never for one moment imagining that all my wealth would have been useless to me in such a quest, and that I might as well have proposed to pluck a star from the sky as to win a woman who was able to read my nature thoroughly, and who would never have come down to my money-level from her intellectual throne,—no, not though I had been a monarch of many nations. I stared at the large tranquil features of the Pallas Athene,—and the blank eyeballs of the marble goddess appeared to regard me in turn with impassive scorn. I glanced round the room, and at the walls adorned with the wise sayings of poets and philosophers,—sayings that reminded me of truths which I knew, yet never accepted as practicable; and presently my eyes were attracted to a corner near the writing-desk which I had not noticed before, where there was a small dim lamp burning. Above this lamp an ivory crucifix gleamed white against draperies of dark purple velvet,—below it, on a silver bracket, was an hour-glass through which the sand was running in glistening grains, and round the entire little shrine was written in letters of gold "Now is the acceptable time!"—the word 'Now' being in larger characters than the rest. 'Now' was evidently Mavis's motto,—to lose no moment, but to work, to pray, to love, to hope, to thank God and be glad for life, all in the 'Now'—and neither to regret the past nor forebode the future, but simply do the best that could be done, and leave all else in child-like confidence to the Divine Will. I got up restlessly,—the sight of the crucifix curiously annoyed me;—and I followed the path my wife and Mavis had taken through the garden. I found them looking in at the cage of the 'Athenæum' owls,—the owl-in-chief being as usual puffed out with his own importance, and swelling visibly with indignation and excess of feather. Sibyl turned as she saw me,—her face was bright and smiling.

MARIE CORELLI

"Miss Clare has very strong opinions of her own, Geoffrey," she said—"She is not as much captivated by Prince Rimânez as most people are,—in fact, she has just confided to me that she does not quite like him."

Mavis blushed, but her eyes met mine with fearless candour.

"It is wrong to say what one thinks, I know,—" she murmured in somewhat troubled accents—"And it is a dreadful fault of mine. Please forgive me Mr. Tempest! You tell me the prince is your greatest friend,—and I assure you I was immensely impressed by his appearance when I first saw him, . . . but afterwards, . . . after I had studied him a little, the conviction was borne in upon me that he was not altogether what he seemed."

"That is exactly what he says of himself,"—I answered, laughing a little—"He has a mystery I believe,—and he has promised to clear it up for me some day. But I'm sorry you don't like him, Miss Clare,—for he likes you."

"Perhaps when I meet him again my ideas may be different"—said Mavis gently—"at present, . . . well,—do not let us talk of it any more,—indeed I feel I have been very rude to express any opinion at all concerning one for whom you and Lady Sibyl have so great a regard. But somehow I seemed impelled, almost against my will, to say what I did just now."

Her soft eyes looked pained and puzzled, and to relieve her and change the subject, I asked if she was writing anything new.

"Oh yes,"—she replied—"It would never do for me to be idle. The public are very kind to me,—and no sooner have they read one thing of mine than they clamour for another, so I am kept very busy."

"And what of the critics?" I asked, with a good deal of curiosity.

She laughed.

"I never pay the least attention to them," she answered, "except when they are hasty and misguided enough to write lies about me,—then I very naturally take the liberty to contradict those lies, either through my own statement or that of my lawyers. Apart from refusing to allow the public to be led into a false notion of my work and aims, I have no grudge whatever against the critics. They are generally very poor hard-working men, and have a frightful struggle to live. I have often, privately, done some of them a good turn without their knowledge. A publisher of mine sent me an MS. the other day by one of my deadliest enemies on the press, and stated that my opinion would decide its rejection or acceptance,—I read it through, and though it was not very brilliant work, it was good enough, so I praised it as warmly as I could, and urged its publication, with the stipulation that the author should never be told I had had the casting vote. It has just come out I see,—and I'm sure I hope it will succeed." Here she paused to gather a few deep damask roses, which she handed to Sibyl. "Yes,—critics are very badly, even cruelly paid,"—she went on musingly—"It is not to be expected that they should write eulogies of the successful author, while they continue unsuccessful,—such work could not be anything but gall and wormwood to them. I know the poor little wife of one of them,—and settled her dressmaker's bill for her because she was afraid to show it to her husband. The very week afterwards he slashed away at my last book in the most approved style in the paper on which he is employed, and got, I suppose, about a guinea for his trouble. Of course he didn't know about his little wife and her dunning dressmaker; and he never will know, because I have bound her over to secrecy."

"But why do you do such things?" asked Sibyl astonished; "I would have let his wife get into the County Court for her bill, if I had been you!"

"Would you?" and Mavis smiled gravely—"Well, I could not. You know Who it was that said 'Bless them that curse you, and do good to them that hate you'? Besides, the poor little woman was frightened to death at her own expenditure. It is pitiful, you know, to see the helpless agonies of people who *will* live beyond their incomes,—they suffer much more than the beggars in the street who make frequently more than a pound a day by merely whining and snivelling. The critics are much more in evil case than the beggars—few of them make even a pound a day, and of course they regard as their natural enemies the authors who make thirty to fifty pounds a week. I assure you I am very sorry for critics all round,—they are the least-regarded and worst-rewarded of all the literary community. And I never bother myself at all about what they say of me, except as I before observed, when in their haste they tell lies,—then of course it becomes necessary for me to state the truth in simple self-defence as well as by way of duty to my public. But as a rule I hand over all my press-notices to Tricksy there,"—indicating the minute Yorkshire terrier who followed closely at the edge of her white gown,—"and he tears them to indistinguishable shreds in about three minutes!"

She laughed merrily, and Sibyl smiled, watching her with the same wonder and admiration that had been expressed in her looks more or less since the beginning of our interview with this light-hearted possessor of literary fame. We were now walking towards the gate, preparatory to taking our departure.

"May I come and talk to you sometimes?" my wife said suddenly, in her prettiest and most pleading voice—"It would be such a privilege!"

"You can come whenever you like in the afternoons,"—replied Mavis readily—"The mornings belong to a goddess more dominant even than Beauty;—Work!"

"You never work at night?" I asked.

"Indeed no! I never turn the ordinances of Nature upside down, as I am sure I should get the worst of it if I made such an attempt. The night is for sleep—and I use it thankfully for that blessed purpose."

"Some authors can only write at night though," I said.

"Then you may be sure they only produce blurred pictures and indistinct characterization," said Mavis—"Some I know there are, who invite inspiration through gin or opium, as well as through the midnight influences, but I do not believe in such methods. Morning, and a freshly rested brain are required for literary labour,—that is, if one wants to write a book that will last for more than one 'season.'"

She accompanied us to the gate and stood under the porch, her big dog beside her, and the roses waving high over her head.

"At any rate work agrees with you,"—said Sibyl fixing upon her a long, intent, almost envious gaze—"You look perfectly happy."

"I *am* perfectly happy,"—she answered, smiling—"I have nothing in all the world to wish for, except that I may die as peacefully as I have lived."

"May that day be far distant!" I said earnestly.

She raised her soft meditative eyes to mine.

"Thank you!" she responded gently—"But I do not mind when it comes, so long as it finds me ready."

She waved her hand to us as we left her and turned the corner of the lane,—and for some minutes we walked on slowly in absolute silence. Then at last Sibyl spoke—

"I quite understand the hatred there is in some quarters for Mavis Clare,"—she said—"I am afraid I begin to hate her myself!"

I stopped and stared at her, astonished and confounded.

"You begin to hate her—you?—and why?"

"Are you so blind that you cannot perceive why?" she retorted, the little malign smile I knew so well playing round her lips—"Because she is happy! Because she has no scandals in her life, and because she dares to be content! One longs to make her miserable! But how to do it? She believes in a God,—she thinks all He ordains is right and good. With such a firm faith as that, she would be happy in a garret earning but a few pence a day. I see now perfectly how she has won her public,—it is by the absolute conviction she has herself of the theories of life she tries to instil. What can be done against her? Nothing! But I understand why the critics would like to 'quash' her,—if I were a critic, fond of whiskey-and-soda, and music-hall women, I should like to quash her myself for being so different to the rest of her sex!"

"What an incomprehensible woman you are, Sibyl!" I exclaimed with real irritation,—"You admire Miss Clare's books,—you have always admired them,—you have asked her to become your friend,— and almost in the same breath you aver you would like to 'quash' her or to make her miserable! I confess I cannot understand you!"

"Of course you cannot!" she responded tranquilly, her eyes resting upon me with a curious expression, as we paused for an instant under the deep shade of a chestnut tree before entering our own grounds—"I never supposed you could, and unlike the ordinary *femme incomprise*, I have never blamed you for your want of comprehension. It has taken me some time to understand myself, and even now I am not quite sure that I have gauged the depths or shallownesses of my own nature correctly. But on this matter of Mavis Clare, can you not imagine that badness may hate goodness? That the confirmed drunkard may hate the sober citizen? That the outcast may hate the innocent maiden? And that it is possible that I,—reading life as I do, and finding it loathsome in many of its aspects,—distrusting men and women utterly,—and being destitute of any faith in God,—may hate,—yes *hate*,"—and she clenched her hand on a tuft of drooping leaves and scattered the green fragments at her feet—"a woman who finds life beautiful, and God existent,—who takes no part in our social shams and slanders,— and who in place of my self-torturing spirit of analysis, has secured an enviable fame and the honour of thousands, allied to a serene content? Why it would be something worth living for, to make such a woman wretched for once in her life!—but, as she is constituted, it is impossible to do it."

She turned from me and walked slowly onward,—I following in a pained silence.

"If you do not mean to be her friend, you should tell her so,"—I said presently—"You heard what she said about pretended protestations of regard?"

"I heard,"—she replied morosely—"She is a clever woman, Geoffrey, and you may trust her to find me out without any explanation!"

As she said this, I raised my eyes and looked full at her,—her exceeding beauty was becoming almost an agony to my sight, and in a sudden fool's paroxysm of despair I exclaimed—

"O Sibyl, Sibyl! Why were you made as you are!"

"Ah, why indeed!" she rejoined, with a faint mocking smile—"And why, being made as I am, was I born an Earl's daughter? If I had been a drab of the street, I should have been in my proper place,—and novels would have been written about me, and plays,—and I might have become such a heroine as should cause all good men to weep for joy because of my generosity in encouraging their vices! But as an Earl's daughter, respectably married to a millionaire, am a mistake of nature. Yet nature does make mistakes sometimes Geoffrey, and when she does they are generally irremediable!"

We had now reached our own grounds, and I walked, in miserable mood, beside her across the lawn towards the house.

"Sibyl,"—I said at last—"I had hoped you and Mavis Clare might be friends."

She laughed.

"So we shall be friends I daresay,—for a little while"—she replied—"But the dove does not willingly consort with the raven, and Mavis Clare's way of life and studious habits would be to me insufferably dull. Besides, as I said before, she, as a clever woman and a thinker, is too clear-sighted not to find me out in the course of time. But I will play humbug as long as I can. If I perform the part of 'county lady' or 'patron,' of course she won't stand me for a moment. I shall have to assume a much more difficult rôle,—that of an honest woman!"

Again she laughed,—a cruel little laugh that chilled my blood, and paced slowly into the house through the open windows of the drawing-room. And I, left alone in the garden among the nodding roses and waving trees, felt that the beautiful domain of Willowsmere had suddenly grown hideous and bereft of all its former charm, and was nothing but a haunted house of desolation,—haunted by an all-dominant and ever victorious Spirit of Evil.

XXVIII

One of the strangest things in all the strange course of our human life is the suddenness of certain unlooked-for events, which, in a day or even an hour, may work utter devastation where there has been more or less peace, and hopeless ruin where there has been comparative safety. Like the shock of an earthquake, the clamorous incidents thunder in on the regular routine of ordinary life, crumbling down our hopes, breaking our hearts, and scattering our pleasures into the dust and ashes of despair. And this kind of destructive trouble generally happens in the midst of apparent prosperity, without the least warning, and with all the abrupt fierceness of a desert-storm. It is constantly made manifest to us in the unexpected and almost instantaneous downfall of certain members of society who have held their heads proudly above their compeers and have presumed to pose as examples of light and leading to the whole community; we see it in the capricious fortunes of kings and statesmen, who are in favour one day and disgraced the next, and vast changes are wrought with such inexplicable quickness that it is scarcely wonderful to hear of certain religious sects who, when everything is prospering more than usually well with them, make haste to put on garments of sackcloth, and cast ashes on their heads, praying aloud "Prepare us, O Lord, for the evil days which are at hand!" The moderation of the Stoics, who considered it impious either to rejoice or grieve, and strove to maintain an equable middle course between the opposing elements of sorrow and joy, without allowing themselves to be led away by over-much delight or over-much melancholy, was surely a wise habit of temperament. I, who lived miserably as far as my inner and better consciousness was concerned, was yet outwardly satisfied with the material things of life and the luxuries surrounding me,—and I began to take comfort in these things, and with them endeavoured to quell and ignore my more subtle griefs, succeeding so far in that I became more and more of a thorough materialist every day, loving bodily ease, appetizing food, costly wine, and personal indulgence to a degree that robbed me gradually of even the desire for mental effort. I taught myself moreover, almost insensibly, to accept and tolerate what I knew of the wanton side of my wife's character,—true, I respected her less than the Turk respects the creature of his harem,—but like the Turk, I took a certain savage satisfaction in being the possessor of her beauty, and with this feeling, and the brute passion it engendered, I was fain to be content. So that for a short time at least, the drowsy satisfaction of a well-fed, well-mated animal was mine,—I imagined that nothing short of a stupendous financial catastrophe to the country itself could exhaust my stock of cash,—and that therefore there was no necessity for me to exert myself in any particular branch of usefulness, but simply to 'eat drink and be merry' as Solomon advised. Intellectual activity was paralysed in me,—to take up my pen and write, and make another and higher bid for fame, was an idea that now never entered my mind; I spent my days in ordering about my servants, and practising the petty pleasures of tyranny on gardeners and grooms, and in generally giving myself airs of importance, mingled with an assumption of toleration and benevolence, for the benefit of all those in my employ. I knew the proper thing to do, well enough!—I had not studied the ways of the over-wealthy for nothing,—I was aware that the rich man never feels so thoroughly virtuous as when he has inquired after the health of his coachman's wife, and has sent her a couple of pounds for the outfit of her new-born baby. The much prated-of 'kindness of heart' and 'generosity' possessed by millionaires, generally amounts to this kind of thing,—and when, if idly strolling about my parklands, I happened to meet the small child of my lodge-keeper, and then and there bestowed sixpence upon it, I almost felt as if I deserved a throne in Heaven at the right hand of the Almighty, so great was my appreciation of my own good-nature. Sibyl, however, never affected this sort of county-magnate beneficence. She did nothing at all among our poor neighbours;—the clergyman of the district unfortunately happened to let slip one day a few words to the effect that "there was no great want of anything among his parishioners, owing to the continual kindness and attention of Miss Clare,"—and Sibyl never from that moment proffered any assistance. Now and then she took her graceful person into Lily Cottage and sat with its happy and studious occupant for an hour,—and occasionally the fair author herself came and dined with us, or had 'afternoon tea' under the branching elms on the lawn,—but even I, intense egotist as I was, could see that Mavis was scarcely herself on these occasions. She was always charming and bright of course,—indeed the only times in which I was able to partially forget myself and the absurdly increasing importance of my personality in my own esteem, were when she, with her sweet voice and animated manner, brought her wide knowledge of books, men, and things, to bear on the conversation, thus raising it to a higher level than was ever reached by my wife or me. Yet I now and then noticed a certain vague constraint about her,—and her frank eyes had frequently a pained and questioning look of trouble when they rested for any length of time on the enchanting beauty of Sibyl's face and form. I, however, paid little heed to these trifling matters, my whole care being to lose myself more and more utterly in the enjoyment of purely physical ease and comfort, without troubling myself as to what such self-absorption might lead in the future. To be completely without a conscience, without a heart and without sentiment was, I perceived, the best way to keep one's appetite, and preserve one's health;—to go about worrying over the troubles of other people, or put one's self out to do any good in the world, would involve such an expenditure of time and trouble as must inevitably spoil one's digestion,—and I saw that no millionaire or even moderately rich man cares to run the risk of injuring his digestion for the sake of performing a kindness to a poorer fellow-creature. Profiting by the examples presented to me everywhere in society, I took care of *my* digestion, and was particular about the way in which my meals were cooked and served,—particular too, as to the fashion in which my wife dressed for those meals,—for it suited my supreme humour to see her beauty bedecked as suitably and richly as possible, that I might have the satisfaction of considering her 'points' with the same epicurean fastidiousness as I considered a dish of truffles or specially prepared game. I never thought of the stern and absolute law—"Unto whom much is given, even from him should much be required;"—I was scarcely aware of it in fact,—the New Testament was of all books in the world the most unfamiliar to me. And while I wilfully deafened myself to the voice of conscience,—that voice which ever and anon urged me in vain to a nobler existence,—the clouds were gathering, ready to burst above me with that terrific suddenness such as always seems to us who refuse to study the causes of our calamities, as astonishing and startling as death itself. For we are always more or less startled at death notwithstanding that it is the commonest occurrence known.

Towards the middle of September my 'royal and distinguished' house-party arrived and stayed at Willowsmere Court for a week. Of course it is understood that whenever the Prince of Wales honours any private residence with a visit, he selects, if not all, at any rate the greater part of those persons who are to be invited to meet him. He did so in the present instance, and I was placed in the odd position of having to entertain certain people whom I had never met before, and who, with the questionable taste frequently exhibited among the 'upper ten,' looked upon me merely as "the man with the millions," the caterer for their provisions, and no more,—directing their chief attention to Sibyl, who was by virtue of her birth and associations one of their 'set,' and pushing me, their host, more or less into the background. However the glory of entertaining Royalty more than sufficed for my poor pride at that time, and with less self-respect than an honest cur, I was content to be snubbed and harassed and worried a hundred times a day by one or the other of the 'great' personages who wandered at will all over my house and grounds, and accepted my lavish hospitality. Many people imagine that it must be an 'honour' to entertain a select party of aristocrats, but I, on the contrary, consider that it is not only a degradation to one's manlier and more independent instincts, but also a bore. These highly-bred, highly-connected individuals, are for the most part unintelligent, and devoid of resources in their own minds,—they are not gifted as conversationalists or wits,—one gains no intellectual advantage from their society,—they are simply dull folk, with an exaggerated sense of their own importance, who expect wherever they go, to be amused without trouble to themselves. Out of all the visitors at Willowsmere the only one whom it was really a pleasure to serve was the Prince of Wales himself,—and amid the many personal irritations I had to suffer from others, I found it a positive relief to render him any attention, however slight, because his manner was always marked by that tact and courtesy which are the best attributes of a true gentleman whether he be prince or peasant. In his own affable way, he went one afternoon to see Mavis Clare, and came back in high good-humour, talking for some time of nothing but the author of 'Differences,' and of the success she had achieved in literature. I had asked Mavis to join our party before the Prince came, as I felt pretty sure he would not have erased her name from the list of guests submitted to him,—but she would not accept, and begged me very earnestly not to press the point.

"I like the Prince,"—she had said—"Most people like him who know him,—but I do not always like those who surround him,—pardon me for my frankness! The Prince of Wales is a social magnet,—he draws a number of persons after him who by dint of wealth, if not intelligence, can contrive to 'push' into his set. Now I am not an advocate of 'push'—moreover I do not care to be seen with 'everybody';—this is my sinful pride you will say, or as our American cousins would put it, my 'cussedness.' But I assure you, Mr. Tempest, the best possession I have, and one which I value a great deal more even than my literary success, is my absolute independence, and I would not have it thought, even erroneously, that I am anxious to mix with the crowd of sycophants and time-servers who are only too ready to take advantage of the Prince's good-nature."

And, acting upon her determination, she had remained more than ever secluded in her cottage-nest of foliage and flowers during the progress of the week's festivities,—the result being, as I have stated, that the Prince 'dropped in' upon her quite casually one day, accompanied by his equerry, and probably for all I knew, had the pleasure of seeing the dove 'reviewers' fed, and squabbling over their meal.

Much as we had desired and expected the presence of Rimânez at our gathering, he did not appear. He telegraphed his regrets from Paris, and followed the telegram by a characteristic letter, which ran thus:—

My dear Tempest

You are very kind to wish to include me, your old friend, in the party you have invited to meet His Royal Highness, and I only hope you will not think me churlish for refusing to come. I am sick to death of Royalties,—I have known so many of them in the course of my existence that I begin to find their society monotonous. Their positions are all so exactly alike too,—and moreover have always been alike from the days of Solomon in all his glory, down to the present blessed era of Victoria, Queen and Empress. One thirsts for a change; at least I do. The only monarch that ever fascinated my imagination particularly was Richard Coeur de Lion; there was something original and striking about that man, and I presume he would have been well worth talking to. And Charlemagne was doubtless, as the slangy young man of the day would observe, 'not half bad.' But for the rest,—*un fico!*Much talk is there made about Her Majesty Elizabeth, who was a shrew and a vixen and blood-thirsty withal,—the chief glory of her reign was Shakespeare, and he made kings and queens the dancing puppets of his thought. In this, though in nothing else, I resemble him. You will have enough to do in the entertainment of your distinguished guests, for I suppose there is no amusement they have not tried, and found more or less unsatisfactory, and I am sorry I can suggest nothing particularly new for you to do. Her Grace the Duchess of Rapidryder is very fond of being tossed in a strong table-cloth between four able-bodied gentlemen of good birth and discretion, before going to bed o' nights,—she cannot very well appear on a music-hall stage you know, owing to her exalted rank,—and this is a child-like, pretty and harmless method of managing to show her legs, which she rightly considers, are too shapely to be hidden. Lady Bouncer, whose name I see in your list, always likes to cheat at cards,—I would aid and abet her in her aim if I were you, as if she can only clear her dressmaker's bill by her winnings at Willowsmere, she will bear it in mind, and be a useful social friend to you. The Honourable Miss Fitz-Gander who has a great reputation for virtue, is anxious, for pressing and particular reasons, to marry Lord Noodles,—if you can move on matters between them into a definite engagement of marriage before her lady-mother returns from her duty-visits in Scotland, you will be doing her a good turn, and saving society a scandal. To amuse the men I suggest plenty of shooting, gambling, and unlimited smoking. To entertain the Prince, do little,—for he is clever enough to entertain himself privately with the folly and humbug of those he sees around him, without actually sharing in the petty comedy. He is a keen observer,—and must derive infinite gratification from his constant study of men and manners, which is sufficiently deep and searching to fit him for the occupation of even the throne of England. I say 'even,' for at present, till Time's great hour-glass turns, it is the grandest throne in the world. The Prince reads, understands, and secretly laughs to scorn the table-cloth vagaries of the Duchess of Rapidryder, the humours of my Lady Bouncer and the nervous pruderies of the Honourable Miss Fitz-Gander. And there is nothing he will appreciate so much in his reception as a lack of toadyism, a sincere demeanour, an unostentatious hospitality, a simplicity of speech, and a total absence of affectation. Remember this, and take my advice for what it is worth. Of all the Royalties at present flourishing on this paltry planet, I have the greatest respect for the Prince of Wales, and it is by reason of this very respect that I do not intend, on this occasion at any rate, to thrust myself upon his notice. I shall arrive at Willowsmere when your 'royal' festivities are over. My homage to your fair spouse, the Lady Sibyl, and believe me,

Yours as long as you desire it
Lucio Rimânez

I laughed over this letter and showed it to my wife, who did not laugh. She read it through with a closeness of attention that somewhat surprised me, and when she laid it down there was a strange look of pain in her eyes.

"How he despises us all!" she said slowly—"What scorn underlies his words! Do you not recognise it?"

"He was always a cynic,—" I replied indifferently—"I never expect him to be anything else."

"He seems to know some of the ways of the women who are coming here—" she went on in the same musing accents; "It is as if he read their thoughts, and perceived their intentions at a distance."

Her brows knitted frowningly, and she seemed for some time absorbed in gloomy meditation. But I did not pursue the subject,—I was too intent on my own fussy preparations for the Prince's arrival to care about anything else.

And, as I have said, Royalty, in the person of one of the most genial of men, came and went through the whole programme devised for his entertainment, and then departed again with his usual courteous acknowledgments for the hospitality offered and accepted,—leaving us, as he generally leaves everybody, charmed with his good-humour and condescension, provided his temper has not been ruffled. When, with his exit from the scene, the whole party broke up, leaving my wife and me to our own two selves once more, there came a strange silence and desolation over the house that was like the stealthy sense of some approaching calamity. Sibyl seemed to feel it as much as I did,—and though we said nothing to each other concerning our mutual sensations, I could see that she was under the same cloud of depression as myself. She went oftener to Lily Cottage, and always from these visits to the fair-haired student among the roses, came back, I hopefully fancied in softer mood,—her very voice was gentler,—her eyes more thoughtful and tender. One evening she said—

"I have been thinking, Geoffrey, that perhaps there is some good in life after all, if I could only find it out and *live* it. But you are the last person to help me in such a matter."

I was sitting in an arm-chair near the open window, smoking, and I turned my eyes upon her with some astonishment and a touch of indignation.

"What do you mean, Sibyl?" I asked—"Surely you know that I have the greatest desire to see you always in your best aspect,—many of your ideas have been most repugnant to me. . ."

"Stop there!" she said quickly, her eyes flashing as she spoke—"My ideas have been repugnant to you, you say? What have *you* done, you as my husband, to change those ideas? Have you not the same base passions as I?—and do you not give way to them as basely? What have I seen in you from day to day that I should take you as an example? You are master here, and you rule with all the arrogance wealth can give,—you eat, drink and sleep,—you entertain your acquaintances simply that you may astonish them by the excess of luxury in which you indulge,—you read and smoke, shoot and ride, and there an end,—you are an ordinary, not an exceptional man. Do you trouble to ask what is wrong with *me*?—do you try, with the patience of a great love, to set before me nobler aims than those I have consciously or unconsciously imbibed?—do you try to lead me, an erring, passionate, misguided woman, into what I dream of as the light,—the light of faith and hope which alone gives peace?"

And suddenly, burying her head in the pillows of the couch on which she leaned, she broke into a fit of smothered weeping.

I drew my cigar from my mouth and stared at her helplessly. It was about an hour after dinner, and a warm soft autumnal evening,—I had eaten and drunk well, and I was drowsy and heavy-brained.

"Dear me!" I murmured—"you seem very unreasonable, Sibyl! I suppose you are hysterical. . ."

She sprang up from the couch,—her tears dried on her cheeks as though by sheer heat of the crimson glow that flushed them, and she laughed wildly.

"Yes, that is it!" she exclaimed—"Hysteria!—nothing else! It is accountable for everything that moves a woman's nature. A woman has no right to have any emotions that cannot be cured by smelling-salts! Heart-ache?—pooh!—cut her stay-lace! Despair and a sense of sin and misery?—nonsense!—bathe her temples with vinegar! An uneasy conscience?—ah!—for an uneasy conscience there is nothing better than sal volatile! Woman is a toy,—a breakable fool's toy;—and when she *is* broken, throw her aside and have done with her,—don't try to piece together the fragile rubbish!"

She ceased abruptly, panting for breath,—and before I could collect my thoughts or find any words wherewith to reply, a tall shadow suddenly darkened the embrasure of the window, and a familiar voice enquired—

"May I, with the privilege of friendship, enter unannounced?"

I started up.

"Rimânez!" I cried, seizing him by the hand.

"Nay, Geoffrey, my homage is due here first,"—he replied, shaking off my grasp, and advancing to Sibyl, who stood perfectly still where she had risen up in her strange passion—"Lady Sibyl, am I welcome?"

"Can you ask it!" she said, with an enchanting smile, and in a voice from which all harshness and excitement had fled; "More than welcome!" Here she gave him both her hands which he respectfully kissed. "You cannot imagine how much I have longed to see you again!"

"I must apologise for my sudden appearance, Geoffrey,"—he then observed, turning to me—"But as I walked here from the station and came up your fine avenue of trees, I was so struck with the loveliness of this place and the exquisite peace of its surroundings, that, knowing my way through the grounds, I thought I would just look about and see if you were anywhere within sight before I presented myself at the conventional door of entrance. And I was not disappointed,—I found you, as I expected, enjoying each other's society!—the happiest and most fortunate couple existent,—people whom, out of all the world I should be disposed to envy, if I envied worldly happiness at all, which I do not!"

I glanced at him quickly;—he met my gaze with a perfectly unembarrassed air, and I concluded that he had not overheard Sibyl's sudden melodramatic outburst.

"Have you dined?" I asked, with my hand on the bell.

"Thanks, yes. The town of Leamington provided me with quite a sumptuous repast of bread and cheese and ale. I am tired of luxuries you know,—that is why I find plain fare delicious. You are looking wonderfully well, Geoffrey!—shall I offend you if I say you are growing—yes—positively stout?—with the stoutness befitting a true county gentleman, who means to be as gouty in the future as his respectable ancestors?"

I smiled, but not altogether with pleasure; it is never agreeable to be called 'stout' in the presence of a beautiful woman to whom one has only been wedded a matter of three months.

"*You* have not put on any extra flesh;—" I said, by way of feeble retort.

"No"—he admitted, as he disposed his slim elegant figure in an armchair near my own—"The necessary quantity of flesh is a bore to me always,—extra flesh would be a positive infliction. I should like, as the irreverent though reverend Sidney Smith said, on a hot day, 'to sit in my bones,' or rather, to become a spirit of fine essence like Shakespeare's Ariel, if such things were possible and permissible. How admirably married life agrees with *you*, Lady Sibyl!"

His fine eyes rested upon her with apparent admiration,—she flushed under his gaze I saw, and seemed confused.

"When did you arrive in England?" she inquired.

"Yesterday,"—he answered,—"I ran over Channel from Honfleur in my yacht,—you did not know I had a yacht, did you Tempest?—oh, you must come for a trip in her some day. She is a quick vessel, and the weather was fair."

"Is Amiel with you?" I asked.

"No. I left him on board the yacht. I can, as the common people say, 'valet myself' for a day or two."

"A day or two?" echoed Sibyl—"But you surely will not leave us so soon? You promised to make a long visit here."

"Did I?" and he regarded her steadily, with the same languorous admiration in his eyes—"But, my dear Lady Sibyl, time alters our ideas, and I am not sure whether you and your excellent husband are of the same opinion as you were when you started on your wedding-tour. You may not want me now!"

He said this with a significance to which I paid no heed whatever.

"Not want you!" I exclaimed—"I shall always want you Lucio,—you are the best friend I ever had, and the only one I care to keep. Believe me!—there's my hand upon it!"

He looked at me curiously for a minute,—then turned his head towards my wife.

"And what does Lady Sibyl say?" he asked in a gentle, almost caressing tone.

"Lady Sibyl says," she answered with a smile, and the colour coming and going in her cheeks—"that she will be proud and glad if you will consider Willowsmere your home as long as you have leisure to make it so,—and that she hopes,—though you are reputed to be a hater of women,—" here she raised her beautiful eyes and fixed them full upon him—"you will relent a little in favour of your present châtelaine!"

With these words, and a playful salutation, she passed out of the room into the garden, and stood on the lawn at a little distance from us, her white robes shimmering in the mellow autumnal twilight,—and Lucio, springing up from his seat, looked after her, clapping his hand down heavily on my shoulder.

"By Heaven!" he said softly, "A perfect woman! I should be a churl to withstand her,—or you, my good Geoffrey,"—and he regarded me earnestly—"I have led a very devil of a life since I saw you last,—it's time I reformed,—upon my soul it is! The peaceful contemplation of virtuous marriage will do me good!—send for my luggage to the station, Geoffrey, and make the best of me,—*I've come to stay!*"

XXIX

A tranquil time now ensued; a time which, though I knew it not, was just that singular pause so frequently observed in nature before a storm, and in human life before a crushing calamity. I put aside all troublesome and harassing thoughts, and became oblivious of everything save my own personal satisfaction in the renewal of the comradeship between myself and Lucio. We walked together, rode together, and passed most of our days in each other's company,— nevertheless though I gave my friend much of my closest confidence I never spoke to him of the moral obliquities and perversions I had discovered in Sibyl's character,—not out of any consideration for Sibyl, but simply because I knew by instinct what his reply would be. He would have no sympathy with my feelings. His keen sense of sarcasm would over-rule his friendship, and he would retort upon me with the question—What business had I, being imperfect myself, to expect perfection in my wife? Like many others of my sex I had the notion that I, as man, could do all I pleased, when I pleased and how I pleased; I could sink to a level lower than that of the beasts if I chose,—but all the same I had the right to demand from my wife the most flawless purity to mate with my defilement. I was aware how Lucio would treat this form of arrogant egoism,—and with what mocking laughter he would receive any expression of ideas from me on the subject of morality in woman. So I was careful to let no hint of my actual position escape me,—and I comported myself on all occasions to Sibyl with special tenderness and consideration, though she, I thought, appeared rather to resent my playing the part of lover-husband too openly. She was herself, in Lucio's presence, strangely erratic of humour, by turns brilliant and mournful,—sometimes merry and anon depressed: yet never had she displayed a more captivating grace and charm of manner. How foolish and blind I was all the while!—how dead to any perception of the formation and sequence of events! Absorbed in gross material pleasures, I ignored all the hidden forces that make the history of an individual life no less than of a whole nation, and looked upon each day that dawned almost as if it had been my own creation and possession, to waste as I thought fit,—never considering that days are but so many white leaflets from God's chronicle of human life, whereon we place our mark, good or bad, for the just and exact summing-up of our thoughts and deeds here after. Had any one dared to say this truth to me then, I should have bade him go and preach nonsense to children,—but *now*,—when I recall those white leaves of days that were unrolled before me fresh and blank with every sunrise, and with which I did nothing save scrawl my own Ego in a foul smudge across each one, I tremble, and inwardly pray that I may never be forced to send back my self-written record! Yet of what use is it to pray against eternal Law? It is eternal Law that we shall ourselves count up our own misdeeds at the final reckoning,—hence it is no wonder that many are found who prefer not to believe in a future after death. Rightly do such esteem it better to die utterly, than be forced to live again and look back upon the wilful evil they have done!

October ripened slowly and almost imperceptibly towards its end, and the trees put on their gorgeous autumnal tints of burning crimson and gold. The weather remained fine and warm, and what the French Canadians poetically term the 'Summer of all Saints' gave us bright days and cloudless moonlit evenings. The air was so mild that we were always able to take our coffee after dinner on the terrace overlooking the lawn in front of the drawing-room,—and it was on one of these balmy nights that I was the interested spectator of a strange scene between Lucio and Mavis Clare,—a scene I should have thought impossible of occurrence had I not myself witnessed it. Mavis had dined at Willowsmere; she very rarely so honoured us; and there were a few other guests besides. We had lingered over the coffee longer than usual, for Mavis had given an extra charm to the conversation by her eloquent vivacity and bright humour, and all present were anxious to hear, see and know as much of the brilliant novelist as possible. But when a full golden moon rose in mellow splendour over the tree-tops, my wife suggested a stroll in the grounds, and everyone agreeing to the proposal with delight, we started,—more or less together,—some in couples, some in groups of three or four. After a little desultory rambling however, the party got separated in the rose-gardens and adjacent shrubberies, and I found myself alone. I turned back to the house to get my cigar-case which I had left on a table in the library, and passing out again in another direction I strolled slowly across the grass, smoking as I went, towards the river, the silver gleam of which could clearly be discerned through the fast-thinning foliage overhanging its banks. I had almost reached the path that followed the course of the winding water, when I was brought to a standstill by the sound of voices—one, a man's, low and persuasive,—

the other a woman's, tender, grave and somewhat tremulous. Neither voice could be mistaken; I recognized Lucio's rich penetrating tones, and the sweet *vibrante* accents of Mavis Clare. Out of sheer surprise I paused,—had Lucio fallen in love, I wondered, half-smiling?—was I about to discover that the supposed 'woman-hater' had been tamed and caught at last? By Mavis too!—little Mavis, who was not beautiful according to accepted standards, but who had something more than beauty to enravish a proud and unbelieving soul,—here, as my thoughts ran on, I was conscious of a foolish sense of jealousy,—why should he choose Mavis, I thought, out of all women in the world? Could he not leave her in peace with her dreams, her books and her flowers?—safe under the pure, wise, impassive gaze of Pallas Athene, whose cool brows were never fevered by a touch of passion? Something more than curiosity now impelled me to listen, and I cautiously advanced a step or two towards the shadow of a broad elm where I could see without being seen. Yes, there was Rimânez,—standing erect with folded arms, his dark, sad, inscrutable eyes fixed on Mavis, who stood opposite to him a few paces off, looking at him in her turn with an expression of mingled fascination and fear.

"I have asked you Mavis Clare,"—said Lucio slowly—"to let me serve you. You have genius—a rare quality in a woman,—and I would advance your fortunes. I should not be what I am if I did not try to persuade you to let me help on your career. You are not rich,—I could show you how to become so. You have a great fame—that I grant; but you have many enemies and slanderers who are for ever trying to pull you down from the throne you have won. I could bring these to your feet, and make them your slaves. With your intellectual power, your personal grace and gifts of temperament, I could, if you would let me guide you, give you such far-reaching influence as no woman has possessed in this century. I am no boaster,—I can do what I say and more; and I ask nothing from you in return except that you should follow my advice implicitly. My advice, let me tell you is not difficult to follow; most people find it easy!"

His expression of face, I thought, was very singular as he spoke,—it was so haggard, dreary and woe-begone that one might have imagined he was making some proposal that was particularly repugnant to him, instead of offering to perform the benevolent action of helping a hard-working literary woman to achieve greater wealth and distinction. I waited expectantly for Mavis to reply.

"You are very good, Prince Rimânez," she said, after a little pause—"to take any thought for me at all. I cannot imagine why you should do so; for I am really nothing to you. I have of course heard from Mr. Tempest of your great wealth and influence, and I have no doubt you mean kindly. But I have never owed anything to any one,—no one has ever helped me,—I have helped myself, and still prefer to do so. And really I have nothing to wish for,—except—when the time comes—a happy death. It is true I am not rich,—but then I do not want to be rich. I would not be the possessor of wealth for all the world! To be surrounded with sycophants and flatterers,—never to be able to distinguish false friends from true,—to be loved for what you *have* and not for what you *are*!—oh no, it would be misery to me. And I have never craved for power,—except perhaps the power to win love. And that I have,—many people love my books, and through my books love me,—I feel their love, though I may never see or know them personally. But I am so conscious of their sympathy that I love them in return without the necessity of personal acquaintance. They have hearts which respond to *my* heart,—that is all the power I care about."

"You forget your numerous enemies!" said Lucio, still morosely regarding her.

"No, I do not forget them,"—she returned,—"But—I forgive them! They can do me no harm. As long as I do not lower myself, no one else can lower me. If my own conscience is clear, no reproaches can wound. My life is open to all,—people can see how I live, and what I do. I try to do well,—but if there are those who think I do ill, I am sorry,—and if my faults can be amended I shall be glad to amend them. One must have enemies in this world,—that is, if one makes any sort of position,—people without enemies are generally nonentities. All who succeed in winning some little place of independence must expect the grudging enmity of hundreds who cannot find even the smallest foothold, and are therefore failures in the battle of life,—I pity these sincerely, and when they say or write cruel things of me, I know it is only spleen and disappointment that moves both their tongues and pens, and freely pardon them. They cannot hurt or hinder me,—in fact, no one can hurt or hinder me but myself."

I heard the trees rustle slightly,—a branch cracked,—and peering through the leaves, I saw that Lucio had advanced a step closer to where Mavis stood. A faint smile was on his face, softening it wonderfully and giving an almost supernatural light to his beautiful dark features.

"Fair philosopher, you are almost a feminine Marcus Aurelius in your estimate of men and things!"—he said; "But—you are still a woman—and there is one thing lacking to your life of sublime and calm contentment—a thing at whose touch philosophy fails, and wisdom withers at its root. Love, Mavis Clare!—lover's love,—devoted love, blindly passionate,—this has not been yours as yet to win! No heart beats against your own,—no tender arms caress you,—you are alone. Men are for the most part afraid of you,—being brute fools themselves, they like their women to be brute fools also,—and they grudge you your keen intellect,—your serene independence. Yet which is best?—the adoration of a brute fool, or the loneliness pertaining to a spirit aloft on some snowy mountain-peak, with no companions but the stars? Think of it!—the years will pass, and you must needs grow old,—and with the years will come that solitary neglect which makes age bitter. Now, you will doubtless wonder at my words—yet believe me I speak the truth when I say that I can give you love,—not *my* love, for I love none,—but I can bring to your feet the proudest men in any country of the world as suitors for your hand. You shall have your choice of them, and your own time for choosing,—and whomsoever you love, him you shall wed, . . . why—what is wrong with you that you shrink from me thus?"

For she had retreated, and was gazing at him in a kind of horror.

"You terrify me!" she faltered,—and as the moonlight fell upon her I could see that she was very pale—"Such promises are incredible—impossible! You speak as if you were more than human! I do not understand you, Prince Rimânez,—you are different to anyone I ever met, and. . . and. . . something in me stronger than myself warns me against you. What are you?—why do you talk to me so strangely? Pardon me if I seem ungrateful. . . , oh, let us go in—it is getting quite late I am sure, and I am cold. . ."

She trembled violently, and caught at the branch of a tree to steady herself,—Rimânez stood immovably still, regarding her with a fixed and almost mournful gaze.

"You say my life is lonely,"—she went on reluctantly and with a note of pathos in her sweet voice—"and you suggest love and marriage as the only joys that can make a woman happy. You may be right. I do not presume to assert that you are wrong. I have many married women-friends—but I would not change my lot with any one of them. I have dreamed of love,—but because I have not realized my dream I am not the less content. If it is God's will that I should be alone all my days,

I shall not murmur, for *my* solitude is not actual loneliness. Work is a good comrade,—then I have books, and flowers and birds—I am never really lonely. And that I shall fully realize my dream of love one day I am sure,—if not here, then hereafter. I can wait!"

As she spoke, she looked up to the placid heavens where one or two stars twinkled through the arching boughs,—her face expressed angelic confidence and perfect peace,—and Rimânez advancing a step or two, fully confronted her with a strange light of exultation in his eyes.

"True,—you can wait, Mavis Clare!" he said in deep clear tones from which all sadness had fled—"You can afford to wait! Tell me,—think for a moment!—can you remember me? Is there a time on which you can look back, and looking, see my face, not here but elsewhere? Think! Did you ever see me long ago—in a far sphere of beauty and light, when you were an Angel, Mavis,—and I was—not what I am now! How you tremble! You need not fear me,—I would not harm you for a thousand worlds! I talk wildly at times I know;—I think of things that are past,—long long past,—and I am filled with regrets that burn my soul with fiercer heat than fire! And so neither world's wealth, world's power, nor world's love will tempt you, Mavis!—and you,—a woman! You are a living miracle then,—as miraculous as the drop of undefiled dew which reflects in its tiny circumference all the colours of the sky, and sinks into the earth sweetly, carrying moisture and refreshment where it falls. I can do nothing for you—you will not have my aid—you reject my service? Then as I may not help you, you must help *me*!"—and dropping before her, he reverently took her hand and kissed it—"I ask a very little thing of you,—pray for me! I know you are accustomed to pray, so it will be no trouble to you,—*you* believe God hears you,—and when I look at you, *I* believe it too. Only a pure woman can make faith possible to man. Pray for me then, as one who has fallen from his higher and better self,—who strives, but who may not attain,—who labours under heavy punishment,—who would fain reach Heaven, but who by the cursëd will of man, and man alone, is kept in Hell! Pray for me, Mavis Clare! promise it!—and so shall you lift me a step nearer the glory I have lost!"

I listened, petrified with amazement. Could this be Lucio?—the mocking, careless, cynical scoffer I knew, as I thought, so well?—was it really he who knelt thus like a repentant sinner, abasing his proud head before a woman? I saw Mavis release her hand from his, the while she stood looking down upon him in alarm and bewilderment. Presently she spoke in sweet yet tremulous accents—

"Since you desire it so earnestly, I promise,"—she said—"I will pray that the strange and bitter sorrow which seems to consume you may be removed from your life—"

"Sorrow!" he echoed, interrupting her and springing to his feet with an impassioned gesture—"Woman,—genius,—angel, whatever you are, do not speak of *one* sorrow for me! I have a thousand thousand sorrows!—aye a million million, that are as little flames about my heart, and as deeply seated as the centres of the universe! The foul and filthy crimes of men,—the base deceits and cruelties of women,—the ruthless, murderous ingratitude of children,—the scorn of good, the martyrdom of intellect, the selfishness, the avarice, the sensuality of human life, the hideous blasphemy and sin of the creature to the Creator—these are *my* endless sorrows!—these keep me wretched and in chains, when I would fain be free. These create hell around me, and endless torture,—these bind and crush me and pervert my being till I become what I dare not name to myself, or to others. And yet, . . . as the eternal God is my witness, . . . I do not think I am as bad as the worst man living! I may tempt—but I do not pursue,—I take the lead in many lives, yet I make the way I go so plain that those who follow me do so by their own choice and free will more than by my persuasion!" He paused,—then continued in a softer tone—"You look afraid of me,—but be assured you never had less cause for terror. You have truth and purity—I honour both. You will have none of my advice or assistance in the making of your life's history,—to-night therefore we part, to meet no more on earth. Never again, Mavis Clare!—no, not through all your quiet days of sweet and contented existence will I cross your path,—before Heaven I swear it!"

"But why?" asked Mavis gently, approaching him now as she spoke, with a soft grace of movement, and laying her hand on his arm—"Why do you speak with such a passion of self-reproach? What dark cloud is on your mind? Surely you have a noble nature,—and I feel that I have wronged you in my thoughts, . . . you must forgive me—I have mistrusted you—"

"You do well to mistrust me!" he answered, and with these words he caught both her hands and held them in his own, looking at her full in the face with eyes that flashed like jewels, "Your instinct teaches you rightly. Would there were many more like you to doubt me and repel me! One word,—if, when I am gone, you ever think of me, think that I am more to be pitied than the veriest paralysed and starving wretch that ever crawled on earth,—for he, perchance, has hope—and I have none. And when you pray for me—for I hold you to this promise,—pray for one who dares not pray for himself! You know the words, 'Lead us not into temptation but deliver us from evil'? To-night you have been led into temptation, though you knew it not, but you have delivered yourself from evil as only a true soul can. And now farewell! In life I shall see you no more:—in death,—well! I have attended many death-beds in response to the invitations of the moribund,—but I shall not be present at yours! Perhaps, when your parting spirit is on the verge between darkness and light, you may know who I was, and am!—and you may thank God with your last breath that we parted to-night—as we do now—forever!"

He loosened his grasp of her,—she fell back from him pale and terrified,—for there was something now in the dark beauty of his face that was unnatural and appalling. A sombre shadow clouded his brows,—his eyes had gleams in them as of fire,—and a smile was on his lips, half tender, half cruel. His strange expression moved even me to a sense of fear, and I shivered with sudden cold, though the air was warm and balmy. Slowly retreating, Mavis moved away, looking round at him now and then as she went, in wistful wonder and alarm,—till in a minute or two her slight figure in its shimmering silken white robe, had vanished among the trees. I lingered, hesitating and uncertain what to do,—then finally determining to get back to the house if possible without being noticed, I made one step, when Lucio's voice, scarcely raised, addressed me—

"Well, eavesdropper! Why did you not come out of the shadow of that elm-tree and see the play to a better advantage?"

Surprised and confused, I advanced, mumbling some unintelligible excuse.

"You saw a pretty bit of acting here," he went on, striking a match and lighting a cigar the while he regarded me coolly, his eyes twinkling with their usual mockery—"you know my theory, that all men and all women are purchaseable for gold? Well, I wanted to try Mavis Clare. She rejected all my advantageous offers, as you must have heard, and I could only make matters smooth by asking her to pray for me. That I did this very melodramatically I hope you will admit? A woman of that dreamy idealistic temperament always likes to imagine that there is a man who is grateful for her prayers!"

"You seemed very much in earnest about it!" I said, vexed with myself that he had caught me spying.

"Why, of course!" he responded, thrusting his arm familiarly through mine—"I had an audience! Two fastidious critics of dramatic art heard me rant my rantings,—I had to do my best!"

"Two critics?" I repeated perplexedly.

"Yes. You on one side,—Lady Sibyl on the other. Lady Sibyl rose, after the custom of fashionable beauties at the opera, before the last scene, in order to get home in good time for supper!"

He laughed wildly and discordantly, and I felt desperately uncomfortable.

"You must be mistaken Lucio—" I said—"That *I* listened I admit,—and it was wrong of me to do so,—but my wife would never condescend. . ."

"Ah, then it must have been a sylph of the woods that glided out of the shadow with a silken train behind her and diamonds in her hair!" he retorted gaily—"Tut Geoffrey!—don't look so crestfallen. I have done with Mavis Clare, and she with me. I have not been making love to her,—I have simply, just to amuse myself, tested her character,—and I find it stronger than I thought. The combat is over. She will never go my way,—nor, I fear, shall I ever go hers!"

"Upon my word, Lucio," I said with some irritation—"Your disposition seems to grow more and more erratic and singular every day!"

"Does it not!" he answered with a droll affectation of interested surprise in himself—"I am a curious creature altogether! Wealth is mine and I care not a jot for it,—power is mine and I loathe its responsibility;—in fact I would rather be anything but what I am! Look at the lights of your 'home, sweet home' Geoffrey!" this he said as we emerged from among the trees on to the moonlit lawn, from whence could be seen the shining of the electric lamps in the drawing-room— "Lady Sibyl is there,—an enchanting and perfect woman, who lives but to welcome you to her embracing arms! Fortunate man!—who would not envy you! Love!—who would, who could exist without it—save me! Who, in Europe at least, would forego the delights of kissing,— (which the Japanese by-the-by consider a disgusting habit),—without embraces,—and all those other endearments which are supposed to dignify the progress of true love! One never tires of these things,—there is no satiety! I wish I could love somebody!"

"So you can, if you like,"—I said, with a little uneasy laugh.

"I cannot. It is not in me. You heard me tell Mavis Clare as much. I have it in my power to make other people fall in love, somewhat after the dexterous fashion practised by match-making mothers,—but for myself, love on this planet is too low a thing—too brief in duration. Last night, in a dream,—I have strange dreams at times,—I saw one whom possibly I could love,—but she was a Spirit, with eyes more lustrous than the morning, and a form as transparent as flame;—she could sing sweetly, and I watched her soaring upward, and listened to her song. It was a wild song, and to many mortal ears meaningless,—it was something like this. . ." and his rich baritone pealed lusciously forth in melodious tune—

Into the Light,
Into the heart of the fire!
To the innermost core of the deathless flame
I ascend,—I aspire!
Under me rolls the whirling Earth
With the noise of a myriad wheels that run
Ever round and about the sun,—
Over me circles the splendid heaven
Strewn with the stars of morn and even,
And I a queen
Of the air serene,
Float with my flag-like wings unfurled,
Alone—alone—'twixt God and the world!

Here he broke off with a laugh. "She was a strange Spirit,"—he said—"because she could see nothing but herself ''twixt God and the world.' She was evidently quite unaware of the numerous existing barriers put up by mankind between themselves and their Maker. I wonder what unenlightened sphere she came from!"

I looked at him in mingled wonder and impatience.

"You talk wildly,"—I said—"And you sing wildly. Of things that mean nothing, and *are* nothing."

He smiled, lifting his eyes to the moon, now shining her fullest and brightest.

"True!" he replied—"Things which have meaning and are valuable, have all to do with money or appetite, Geoffrey! There is no wider outlook evidently! But we were speaking of love, and I hold that love should be eternal as hate. Here you have the substance of my religious creed if I have any,—that there are two spiritual forces ruling the universe—love and hate,—and that their incessant quarrel creates the general confusion of life. Both contend one against the other,—and only at Judgment-Day will it be proved which is the strongest. I am on the side of Hate myself,—for at present Hate has scored all the victories worth winning, while Love has been so often martyred that there is only the poor ghost of it left on earth."

At that moment my wife's figure appeared at the drawing-room window, and Lucio threw away his half-smoked cigar.

"Your guardian-angel beckons!" he said, looking at me an odd expression of something like pity mingled with disdain,—"Let us go in."

XXX

The very next night but one after Lucio's strange interview with Mavis Clare, the thunderbolt destined to wreck my life and humiliate me to the dust, fell with appalling suddenness. No warning given!—it came at a moment when I had dared to deem myself happy. All that day,—the last day I was ever to know of pride or self-gratulation,—I had enjoyed life to the full; it was a day too in which Sibyl had seemed transformed to a sweeter, gentler woman than I had hitherto known her,—when all her attractions of beauty and manner were apparently put forth to captivate and enthrall me as though she were yet to be wooed and won. Or,—did she mean to bewitch and subjugate Lucio? Of this I never thought,—never dreamed:—I only saw in my wife an enchantress of the most voluptuous and delicate loveliness,—a woman whose very garments seemed to cling to her tenderly as though proud of clothing so exquisite a form,—a creature whose every glance was brilliant, whose every smile was a ravishment,— and whose voice, attuned to the softest and most caressing tones appeared in its every utterance to assure me of a deeper and more lasting love than I had yet enjoyed. The hours flew by on golden wings,—we all three,—Sibyl, myself and Lucio,—had attained, as I imagined, to a perfect unity of friendship and mutual understanding,—we had passed that last day together in the outlying woods of Willowsmere, under a gorgeous canopy of autumn leaves, through which the sun shed mellow beams of rose and gold,—we had had an *al fresco* luncheon in the open air,—Lucio had sung for us wild old ballads and love-madrigals till the very foliage had seemed to tremble with joy at the sound of such entrancing melody,—and not a cloud had marred the perfect peace and pleasure of the time. Mavis Clare was not with us,—and I was glad. Somehow I felt that of late she had been more or less a discordant element whenever she had joined our party. I admired her,—in a sort of fraternal half-patronizing way I even loved her,—nevertheless I was conscious that her ways were not as our ways,—her thoughts not as our thoughts. I placed the fault on her of course; I concluded that it was because she had what I elected to call 'literary egoism,' instead of by its rightful name, the spirit of honourable independence. I never considered the inflated quality of my own egoism,—the poor pride of a 'cash and county' position, which is the pettiest sort of vain-glory anyone can indulge in,—and after turning the matter over in my mind, I decided that Mavis was a very charming young woman with great literary gifts, and an amazing pride, which made it totally impossible for her to associate with many 'great' people, so-called,—as she would never descend to the necessary level of flunkeyish servility which they expected, and which *I* certainly demanded. I should almost have been inclined to relegate her to 'Grub Street,' had not a faint sense of justice as well as shame held me back from doing her that indignity even in my thoughts. However I was too much impressed with my own vast resources of unlimited wealth, to realize the fact that anyone who, like Mavis, earns independence by intellectual work and worth alone, is entitled to feel a far greater pride than those who by mere chance of birth or heritage become the possessors of millions. Then again, Mavis Clare's literary position was, though I liked her personally, always a kind of reproach to me when I thought of my own abortive efforts to win the laurels of fame. So that on the whole I was glad she did not spend that day with us in the woods;—of course, if I had paid any attention to the "trifles which make up the sum of life" I should have remembered that Lucio had told her he would "meet her no more on earth,"—but I judged this to be a mere trifle of hasty and melodramatic speech, without any intentional meaning.

So my last twenty-four hours of happiness passed away in halcyon serenity,—I felt a sense of deepening pleasure in existence, and I began to believe that the future had brighter things in store for me than I had lately ventured to expect. Sibyl's new phase of gentleness and tenderness towards me, combined with her rare beauty, seemed to augur that the misunderstandings between us would be of short duration, and that her nature, too early rendered harsh and cynical by a 'society' education would soften in time to that beautiful womanliness which is, after all, woman's best charm. Thus I thought, in blissful and contented reverie, reclining under the branching autumnal foliage, with my fair wife beside me, and listening to the rich tones of my friend Lucio's magnificent voice pealing forth sonorous, wild melodies, as the sunset deepened in the sky and the twilight shadows fell. Then came the night—the night which dropped only for a few hours over the quiet landscape, but for ever over me!

We had dined late, and, pleasantly fatigued with our day in the open air, had retired early. I had latterly grown a heavy sleeper, and I suppose I must have slumbered some hours, when I was awakened suddenly as though by an imperative touch from some unseen hand. I started up in my bed,—the night-lamp was burning dimly, and by its glimmer I saw that Sibyl was no longer at my side. My heart gave one bound against my ribs and then almost stood still—a sense of something unexpected and calamitous chilled my blood. I pushed aside the embroidered silken hangings of the bed and peered into the room,—it was empty. Then I rose hastily, put on my clothes and went to the door,—it was carefully shut, but not locked as it had been when we retired for the night. I opened it without the least noise, and looked out into the long passage,—no one there! Immediately opposite the bedroom door there was a winding oak staircase leading down to a broad corridor, which in former times had been used as a music-room or picture-gallery,—an ancient organ, still sweet of tone, occupied one end of it with dull golden pipes towering up to the carved and embossed ceiling,—the other end was lit by a large oriel window like that of a church, filled with rare old stained glass, representing in various niches the lives of the saints, the centre subject being the martyrdom of St Stephen. Advancing with soft caution to the balustrade overlooking this gallery, I gazed down into it, and for a moment could see nothing on the polished floor but the criss-cross patterns made by the moonlight falling through the great window,—but presently, as I watched breathlessly, wondering where Sibyl could have gone to at this time of night, I saw a dark tall Shadow waver across the moonlit network of lines, and I heard the smothered sound of voices. With my pulses beating furiously, and a sensation of suffocation in my throat,—full of strange thoughts and suspicions which I dared not define, I crept slowly and stealthily down the stair, till as my foot touched the last step I saw—what nearly struck me to the ground with a shock of agony—and I had to draw back and bite my lips hard to repress the cry that nearly escaped them. There,—there before me in the full moonlight, with the colours of the red and blue robes of the painted saints on the window glowing blood-like and azure about her, knelt my wife,—arrayed in a diaphanous garment of filmy white which betrayed rather than concealed the outline of her form,—her wealth of hair falling about her in wild disorder,—her hands clasped in supplication,— her pale face upturned; and above her towered the dark imposing figure of Lucio! I stared at the twain with dry burning eyes,—what did this portend? Was she—my wife—false? Was he—my friend—a traitor?

"Patience—patience!—" I muttered to myself—"This is a piece of acting doubtless—such as chanced the other night with Mavis Clare!—

patience!—let us hear this—this comedy!" And, drawing myself close up against the wall, I leaned there, scarcely drawing breath, waiting for *her* voice,—for *his*;—when they spoke I should know,—yes, I should know all! And I fastened my looks on them as they stood there,—vaguely wondering even in my tense anguish, at the fearful light on Lucio's face,—a light which could scarcely be the reflection of the moon, as he backed the window,—and at the scorn of his frowning brows. What terrific humour swayed him?—why did he, even to my stupefied thought appear more than human?—why did his very beauty seem hideous at that moment, and his aspect fiendish? Hush—hush! *She* spoke,—my wife,—I heard her every word—heard all and endured all, without falling dead at her feet in the extremity of my dishonour and despair!

"I love you!" she wailed—"Lucio, I love you, and my love is killing me! Be merciful!—have pity on my passion!—love me for one hour, one little hour!—it is not much to ask, and afterwards,—do with me what you will,—torture me, brand me an outcast in the public sight, curse me before Heaven—I care nothing—I am yours body and soul—I love you!"

Her accents vibrated with mad idolatrous pleading,—I listened infuriated, but dumb. "Hush,—hush!" I told myself "This is a comedy—not yet played out!" And I waited, with every nerve strained, for Lucio's reply. It came, accompanied by a laugh, low and sarcastic.

"You flatter me!" he said—"I regret I am unable to return the compliment!"

My heart gave a throb of relief and fierce joy,—almost I could have joined in his ironical laughter. She—Sibyl—dragged herself nearer to him.

"Lucio—Lucio!" she murmured—"Have you a heart? Can you reject me when I pray to you thus?—when I offer you all myself,—all that I am, or ever hope to be? Am I so repugnant to you? Many men would give their lives if I would say to them what I say to you,—but they are nothing to me—you alone are my world,—the breath of my existence!—ah, Lucio, can you not believe, will you not realize how deeply I love you!"

He turned towards her with a sudden fierce movement that startled me,—and the cloud of scorn upon his brows grew darker.

"I know you love me!" he said, and from where I stood I saw the cold derisive smile flash from his lips to his eyes in lightning-like mockery—

"I have always known it! Your vampire soul leaped to mine at the first glance I ever gave you,—you were a false foul thing from the first, and you recognized your master! Yes—your Master!" for she had uttered a faint cry as if in fear,—and he, stooping, snatched her two hands and grasped them hard in his own—"Listen to the truth of yourself for once from one who is not afraid to speak it!—you love me,—and truly your body and soul are mine to claim, if I so choose! You married with a lie upon your lips; you swore fidelity to your husband before God, with infidelity already in your thoughts, and by your own act made the mystical blessing a blasphemy and a curse! Wonder not then that the curse has fallen! I knew it all!—the kiss I gave you on your wedding-day put fire in your blood and sealed you mine!—why, you would have fled to me that very night, had I demanded it,—had I loved you as you love me,—that is, if you choose to call the disease of vanity and desire that riots in your veins, by such a name as love! But now hear *me*!" and as he held her two wrists he looked down upon her with such black wrath depicted in his face as seemed to create a darkness round him where he stood,—"I hate you! Yes—I hate you, and all such women as you! For you corrupt the world,—you turn good to evil,—you deepen folly into crime,—with the seduction of your nude limbs and lying eyes, you make fools, cowards and beasts of men! When you die, your bodies generate foulness,—things of the mould and slime are formed out of the flesh that was once fair for man's delight,—you are no use in life— you become poison in death,—I hate you all! I read your soul—it is an open book to me—and it is branded with a name given to those who are publicly vile, but which should, of strict right and justice, be equally bestowed on women of your position and type, who occupy pride and place in this world's standing, and who have not the excuse of poverty for selling themselves to the devil!"

He ceased abruptly and with passion, making a movement as though to fling her from him,—but she clung to his arm,—clung with all the pertinacity of the loathly insect he had taken from the bosom of the dead Egyptian woman and made a toy of to amuse his leisure! And I, looking on and listening, honoured him for his plain speaking, for his courage in telling this shameless creature what she was in the opinion of an honest man, without glozing over her outrageous conduct for the sake of civility or social observance. My friend,—my more than friend! He was true,—he was loyal—he had neither desire nor intent to betray or dishonour me. My heart swelled with gratitude to him, and also with a curious sense of feeble self-pity,—compassionating myself intensely, I could have sobbed aloud in nervous fury and pain, had not my desire to hear more, repressed my personal excitement and emotion. I watched my wife wonderingly—what had become of her pride that she still knelt before the man who had taunted her with such words as should have been beyond all endurance?

"Lucio! . . . Lucio!" she whispered, and her whisper sounded through the long gallery like the hiss of a snake—"Say what you will—say all you will of me,—you can say nothing that is not true. I am vile—I own it. But is it of much avail to be virtuous? What pleasure comes from goodness?—what gratification from self-denial? There is no God to care! A few years, and we all die, and are forgotten even by those who loved us,—why should we lose such joys as we may have for the mere asking? Surely it is not difficult to love even me for an hour?—am I not fair to look upon?—and is all this beauty of my face and form worthless in your sight, and you no more than man? Murder me as you may with all the cruelty of cruel words, I care nothing!—I love you—love you!"— and in a perfect passion of self-abandonment she sprang to her feet, tossing back her rich hair over her shoulders, and stood erect, a very bacchante of wild loveliness—"Look at me! You shall not,—you dare not spurn such a love as mine!"

Dead silence followed her outburst,—and I stared in fascinated awe at Lucio as he turned more fully round and confronted her. The expression of his countenance struck me then as quite unearthly,—his beautiful broad brows were knitted in a darkling line of menace,—his eyes literally blazed with scorn, and yet he laughed,—a low laugh, resonant with satire.

"Shall not!—dare not!" he echoed disdainfully—"Woman's words,— woman's ranting!—the shriek of the outraged feminine animal who fails to attract, as she thinks, her chosen mate. Such a love as yours!—what is it? Degradation to whosoever shall accept it,—shame to whosoever shall rely upon it! You make a boast of your beauty; your mirror shows you a pleasing image,—but your mirror lies!—as admirably as you do! You see within it not the reflection of yourself, for that would cause you to recoil in horror, . . . you merely look upon your fleshly covering, a garment of tissues, shrinkable, perishable, and only fit to mingle with the dust from which it sprang. Your beauty! I see none of it,—I see You! and to me you are hideous, and will remain hideous for ever. I hate you!—I hate you with the bitterness of an immeasurable and unforgiving hatred,—for you have done me a wrong,—you have wrought an injury upon me,—you have added another burden to the load of punishment I carry!"

She made a forward movement with outstretched arms,—he repulsed her by a fierce gesture.

"Stand back!" he said—"Be afraid of me, as of an unknown Terror! O pitiless Heaven!—to think of it!—but a night ago I was lifted a step nearer to my lost delight!—and now this woman drags me back, and down!—and yet again I hear the barring of the gates of Paradise! O infinite torture! O wicked souls of men and women!—is there no touch of grace or thought of God left in you!—and will ye make my sorrows eternal!"

He stood, lifting his face to the light where it streamed through the oriel window, and the moonbeams colouring themselves faintly roseate as they filtered through the painted garments of St Stephen, showed a great and terrible anguish in his eyes. I heard him with amazement and awe,—I could not imagine what he meant by his strange words,—and it was evident by her expression, that my reckless and abandoned wife was equally mystified.

"Lucio,"—she murmured—"Lucio, . . . what is it. . . what have I done?—I who would not wound you for the world?—I who but seek your love, Lucio, to repay it in full with such fond passion and tenderness as you have never known! For this and this only, I married Geoffrey,—I chose your friend as husband because he was your friend!" (O perfidious woman!) "and because I saw his foolish egotism—his pride in himself and his riches,—his blind confidence in me and in you;—I knew that I could, after a time, follow the fashion of many another woman in my set and choose my lover,—ah, my lover!—I had chosen him already,—I have chosen you, Lucio!—yes, though you hate me you cannot hinder me from loving you,—I shall love you till I die!"

He turned his gaze upon her steadily,—the gloom deepening on his brows.

"And after you die?" he said—"Will you love me then?"

There was a stern derision in his tone which appeared to vaguely terrify her.

"After death! . . ." she stammered.

"Yes,—after death!" he repeated sombrely—"There *is* an after;—as your mother knows!" A faint exclamation escaped her,—she fixed her eyes upon him affrightedly. "Fair lady," he went on—"your mother was, like yourself, a voluptuary. She, like you, made up her mind to 'follow the fashion' as you put it, as soon as her husband's 'blind' or willing confidence was gained. She chose, not one lover but many. You know her end. In the written but miscomprehended laws of Nature, a diseased body is the natural expression of a diseased mind,—her face in her last days was the reflex of her soul. You shudder?—the thought of her hideousness is repellent to your self-conscious beauty? Yet the evil that was in her is also in you,—it festers in your blood slowly but surely, and as you have no faith in God to cure the disease, it will have its way—even at the final moment when death clutches at your throat and stops your breathing. The smile upon your frozen lips then will not be the smile of a saint, believe me, but of a sinner! Death is never deceived, though life may be. And afterwards. . . I ask again, will you love me, do you think? . . . when you know WHO I am?"

I was myself startled at his manner of putting this strange question;—I saw her lift her hands beseechingly towards him, and she seemed to tremble.

"When I know who you are!" she repeated wonderingly—"Do I not know? You are Lucio,—Lucio Rimânez—my love,—my love!—whose voice is my music,—whose beauty I adore,—whose looks are my heaven" . . .

"And Hell!" he interposed, with a low laugh—"Come here!"

She went towards him eagerly, yet falteringly. He pointed to the ground,—I saw the rare blue diamond he always wore on his right hand, flash like a flame in the moonrays.

"Since you love me so well,"—he said—"Kneel down and worship me!"

She dropped on her knees—and clasped her hands,—I strove to move,—to speak,—but some resistless force held me dumb and motionless;—the light from the stained glass window fell upon her face, and showed its fairness illumined by a smile of perfect rapture.

"With every pulse of my being I worship you!" she murmured passionately—"My king!—my god! The cruel things you say but deepen my love for you,—you can kill, but you can never change me! For one kiss of your lips I would die,—for one embrace from you I would give my soul! . . ."

"Have you one to give?" he asked derisively—"Is it not already disposed of? You should make sure of that first! Stay where you are and let me look at you! So!—a woman, wearing a husband's name, holding a husband's honour, clothed in the very garments purchased with a husband's money, and newly risen from a husband's side, steals forth thus in the night, seeking to disgrace him and pollute herself by the vulgarest unchastity! And this is all that the culture and training of nineteenth-century civilization can do for you? Myself, I prefer the barbaric fashion of old times, when rough savages fought for their women as they fought for their cattle, treated them as cattle, and kept them in their place, never dreaming of endowing them with such strong virtues as truth and honour! If women were pure and true, then the lost happiness of the world might return to it,—but the majority of them are like you, liars, ever pretending to be what they are not. I may do what I choose with you, you say? torture you, kill you, brand you with the name of outcast in the public sight, and curse you before Heaven—if I will only love you!—all this is melodramatic speech, and I never cared for melodrama at any time. I shall neither kill you, brand you, curse you, nor love you;—I shall simply—call your husband!"

I stirred from my hiding-place,—then stopped. She sprang to her feet in an insensate passion of anger and shame.

"You dare not!" she panted—"You dare not so. . . disgrace me!"

"Disgrace you!" he echoed scornfully—"That remark comes rather late, seeing you have disgraced yourself!"

But she was now fairly roused. All the savagery and obstinacy of her nature was awakened, and she stood like some beautiful wild animal at bay, trembling from head to foot with the violence of her emotions.

"You repulse me,—you scorn me!" she muttered in hurried fierce accents that scarcely rose above an angry whisper—"You make a mockery of my heart's anguish and despair, but you shall suffer for it! I am your match,—nay your equal! You shall not spurn me a second time! You ask, will I love you when I know who you are,—it is your pleasure to deal in mysteries, but I have no mysteries—I am a woman who loves you with all the passion of a life,—and I will murder myself and you, rather than live to know that I have prayed you for your love in vain. Do you think I came unprepared?—no!" and she suddenly drew from her bosom a short steel dagger with a jewelled hilt, a *curio* I recognized as one of the gifts to her on her marriage; "Love me, I say!—or I will stab myself dead here at your feet, and cry out to Geoffrey that you have murdered me!"

She raised the weapon aloft,—I almost sprang forward—but I drew

　　　　　　　　　　　　　　　　MARIE CORELLI

back again quickly as I saw Lucio seize the hand that held the dagger and drag it firmly down,—while, wresting the weapon from her clutch he snapped it asunder and flung the pieces on the floor.

"Your place was the stage, Madam!" he said—"You should have been the chief female mime at some 'high-class' theatre! You would have adorned the boards, drawn the mob, had as many lovers, stagey and private as you pleased, been invited to act at Windsor, obtained a payment-jewel from the Queen, and written your name in her autograph album. That should undoubtedly have been your 'great' career—you were born for it—made for it! You would have been as brute-souled as you are now,—but that would not have mattered,—mimes are exempt from chastity!"

In the action of breaking the dagger, and in the intense bitterness of his speech he had thrust her back a few paces from him, and she stood breathless and white with rage, eyeing him in mingled passion and terror. For a moment she was silent,—then advancing slowly with the feline suppleness of movement which had given her a reputation for grace exceeding that of any woman in England, she said in deliberately measured accents—

"Lucio Rimâncz, I have borne your insults as I would bear my death at your hands, because I love you. You loathe me, you say—you repulse me,—I love you still! You cannot cast me off—I am yours! You shall love me, or I will die,—one of the two. Take time for thought,—I leave you to-night,—I give you all to-morrow to consider,—love me,—give me yourself,—be my lover,—and I will play the comedy of social life as well as any other woman,—so well that my husband shall never know. But refuse me again as you have refused me now, and I will make away with myself. I am not 'acting,'—I am speaking calmly and with conviction; I mean what I say!"

"Do you?" queried Lucio coldly—"Let me congratulate you! Few women attain to such coherence!"

"I will put an end to this life of mine;" she went on, paying no sort of heed to his words—"I cannot endure existence without your love, Lucio!" and a dreary pathos vibrated in her voice—"I hunger for the kisses of your lips,—the clasp of your arms! Do you know—do you ever think of your own power?—the cruel, terrible power of your eyes, your speech, your smile,—the beauty which makes you more like an angel than a man,—and have you no pity? Do you think that ever a man was born like you?" he looked at her as she said this, and a faint smile rested on his lips—"When you speak, I hear music—when you sing, it seems to me that I understand what the melodies of a poet's heaven must be;—surely, surely you know that your very looks are a snare to the warm weak soul of a woman! Lucio!—" and emboldened by his silence, she stole nearer to him—"Meet me to-morrow in the lane near the cottage of Mavis Clare. . ."

He started as if he had been stung—but not a word escaped him.

"I heard all you said to her the other night;" she continued, advancing yet a step closer to his side—"I followed you,—and I listened. I was well-nigh mad with jealousy—I thought—I feared—you loved her,—but I was wrong. I never do thank God for anything,—but I thanked God that night that I was wrong! She was not made for you—I am! Meet me outside her house, where the great white rose-tree is in bloom—gather one,—one of those little autumnal roses and give it to me—I shall understand it as a signal—a signal that I may come to you to-morrow night and not be cursed or repulsed, but loved,—loved!—ah Lucio! promise me!—one little rose!—the symbol of an hour's love!—then let me die; I shall have had all I ask of life!"

With a sudden swift movement, she flung herself upon his breast, and circling her arms about his neck, lifted her face to his. The moonbeams showed me her eyes alit with rapture, her lips trembling with passion, her bosom heaving, . . . the blood surged up to my brain, and a red mist swam before my sight, . . . would Lucio yield? Not he!—he loosened her desperate hands from about his throat, and forced her back, holding her at arm's length.

"Woman, false and accurséd!" he said in tones that were sonorous and terrific—"You know not what you seek! All that you ask of life shall be yours in death!—this is the law,—therefore beware what demands you make lest they be too fully granted! A rose from the cottage of Mavis Clare?—a rose from the garden of Eden!—they are one and the same to me! Not for my gathering or yours! Love and joy? For the unfaithful there is no love,—for the impure there is no joy. Add no more to the measure of my hatred and vengeance!—Go while there is yet time,—go and front the destiny you have made for yourself—for nothing can alter it! And as for me, whom you love,—before whom you have knelt in idolatrous worship—" and a low fierce laugh escaped him—"why,—restrain your feverish desires, fair fiend!—have patience!—we shall meet ere long!"

I could not bear the scene another moment, and springing from

　　　　　　　　　　　　　　　　MARIE CORELLI

my hiding-place, I dragged my wife away from him and flung myself between them.

"Let me defend you, Lucio, from the pertinacities of this wanton!" I cried with a wild burst of laughter—"An hour ago I thought she was my wife,—I find her nothing but a purchased chattel, who seeks a change of masters!"

XXXI

For one instant we all three stood facing each other,—I breathless and mad with fury,—Lucio calm and disdainful,—my wife staggering back from me, half-swooning with fear. In an access of black rage, I rushed upon her and seized her in my arms.

"I have heard you!" I said—"I have seen you! I have watched you kneel before my true friend, my loyal comrade there, and try your best to make him as vile as yourself! I am that poor fool, your husband,—that blind egoist whose confidence you sought to win—and to betray! I am the unhappy wretch whose surplus of world's cash has bought for him in marriage a shameless courtezan! You dare to talk of love? You profane its very name! Good God!—what are such women as you made of? You throw yourselves into our arms,—you demand our care—you exact our respect—you tempt our senses—you win our hearts,—and then you make fools of us all! Fools, and worse than fools,—you make us men without feeling, conscience, faith, or pity! If we become criminals, what wonder! If we do things that shame our sex, is it not because you set us the example? God—God! I, who loved you,—yes, loved you in spite of all that my marriage with you taught me,—I, who would have died to save you from a shadow of suspicion,—I am the one out of all the world you choose to murder by your treachery!"

I loosened my grasp of her,—she recovered her self-possession by an effort, and looked at me straightly with cold unfeeling eyes.

"What did you marry me for?" she demanded—"For my sake or your own?"

I was silent,—too choked with wrath and pain to speak. All I could do was to hold out my hand to Lucio, who grasped it with a cordial and sympathetic pressure. Yet. . . I fancied he smiled!

"Was it because you desired to make me happy out of pure love for me?" pursued Sibyl—"Or because you wished to add dignity to your own position by wedding the daughter of an Earl? Your motives were not unselfish,—you chose me simply because I was the 'beauty' of the day whom London men stared at and talked of,—and because it gave you a certain 'prestige' to have me for your wife, in the same way as it gave you a footing with Royalty to be the owner of the Derby-winner. I told you honestly what I was before our marriage,—it made no effect upon your vanity and egoism. I never loved you,—I could not love you, and I told you so. You have heard, so you say, all that has passed between me and Lucio,—therefore you know why I married you. I state it boldly to your face,—it was that I might have your intimate friend for my lover. That you should pretend to be scandalized at this is absurd; it is a common position of things in France, and is becoming equally common in England. Morality has always been declared unnecessary for men,—it is becoming equally unnecessary for women!"

I stared at her, amazed at the glibness of her speech, and the cool convincing manner in which she spoke, after her recent access of passion and excitement.

"You have only to read the 'new' fiction,"—she went on, a mocking smile lighting up her pale face, "and indeed all 'new' literature generally, to be assured that your ideas of domestic virtue are quite out of date. Both men and women are, according to certain accepted writers of the day, at equal liberty to love when they will, and where they may. Polygamous purity is the 'new' creed! Such love, in fact, so we are taught, constitutes the only 'sacred' union. If you want to alter this 'movement,' and return to the old-fashioned types of the modest maiden and the immaculate matron, you must sentence all the 'new' writers of profitable pruriency to penal servitude for life, and institute a Government censorship of the modern press. As matters stand, your attitude of the outraged husband is not only ridiculous,—it is unfashionable. I assure you I do not feel the slightest prick of conscience in saying I love Lucio,—any woman might be proud of loving him;—he, however, will not, or cannot love me,—we have had a 'scene,' and you have completed the dramatic effect by witnessing it,—there is no more to be said or done in the affair. I do not suppose you can divorce me,—but if you can, you may—I shall make no defence."

She turned, as if to go;—I still stared dumbly at her, finding no words to cope with her effrontery,—when Lucio's voice, attuned to a grave and soothing suavity, interposed,—

"This is a very painful and distressing state of things,"—he said, and the strange half-cynical, half contemptuous smile still rested on his lips—"but I must positively protest against the idea of divorce, not only for her ladyship's sake, but my own. I am entirely innocent in the matter!"

"Innocent!" I exclaimed, grasping him again by the hand; "You are nobility itself, Lucio!—as loyal a friend as ever man had! I thank you for your courage,—for the plain and honest manner in which you have spoken. I heard all you said! Nothing was too strong,—nothing could be too strong to awaken this misguided woman to a sense of her outrageous conduct,—her unfaithfulness—"

"Pardon me!" he interrupted delicately—"The Lady Sibyl can scarcely be called unfaithful, Geoffrey. She suffers,—from—let us call it, a little exaltation of nerves! In thought she may be guilty of infidelity, but society does not know that,—and in act she is pure,—pure as the newly-driven snow,—and as the newly-driven snow, will society, itself immaculate, regard her!"

His eyes glittered,—I met his chill derisive glance.

"You think as I do, Lucio!" I said hoarsely—"You feel with me, that a wife's unchaste thought is as vile as her unchaste act. There is no excuse,—no palliative for such cruel and abominable ingratitude. Why,"—and my voice rose unconsciously as I turned fiercely again towards Sibyl—"Did I not free you and your family from the heavy pressure of poverty and debt? Have I grudged you anything? Are you not loaded with jewels?—have you not greater luxuries and liberties than a queen? And do you not owe me at least some duty?"

"I owe you nothing!" she responded boldly—"I gave you what you paid for,—my beauty and my social position. It was a fair bargain!"

"A dear and bitter one!" I cried.

"Maybe so. But such as it was, you struck it,—not I. You can end it when you please,—the law. . ."

"The law will give you no freedom in such a case,"—interposed Lucio with a kind of satirical urbanity—"A judicial separation on the ground of incompatibility of temper might be possible certainly—but would not that be a pity? Her ladyship is unfortunate in her tastes,—that is all!—she selected me as her *cavaliere servente*, and I refused the situation,—hence there is nothing for it but to forget this unpleasant incident, and try to live on a better understanding for the future—"

"Do you think"—said my wife, advancing with her proud head uplifted in scorn, the while she pointed at me—"Do you think I will live with him after what he has seen and heard to-night? What do you take me for?"

"For a very charming woman of hasty impulses and unwise reasoning,"—replied Lucio, with an air of sarcastic gallantry—"Lady Sibyl, you are illogical,—most of your sex are. You can do no good by prolonging this scene,—a most unpleasant and trying one to us poor men. You know how we hate 'scenes'! Let me beg of you to retire!

Your duty is to your husband; pray heaven he may forget this midnight delirium of yours, and set it down to some strange illness rather than to any evil intention."

For all answer she came towards him, stretching out her arms in wild appeal.

"Lucio!" she cried—"Lucio, my love! Good-night!—Good-bye!"

I sprang between him and her advancing form.

"Before my very face!" I exclaimed—"O infamous woman! Have you no shame?"

"None!" she said, with a wild smile—"I glory in my love for such a king of worth and beauty! Look at him!—and then look at yourself in the nearest mirror that reflects so poor and mean a picture of a man! How, even in your egoism, could you deem it possible for a woman to love *you* when *he* was near! Stand out of the light!—you interpose a shadow between my god and me!"

As she uttered these mad words, her aspect was so strange and unearthly, that out of sheer stupefied wonder, I mechanically did as she bade me, and stood aside. She regarded me fixedly.

"I may as well say good-bye to you also,"—she observed—"For I shall never live with you again."

"Nor I with you!" I said fiercely.

"Nor I with you—nor I with you!" she repeated like a child saying a lesson—"Of course not!—if I do not live with you, you cannot live with me!" She laughed discordantly; then turned her beseeching gaze once more upon Lucio—"Good-bye!" she said.

He looked at her with a curious fixity, but returned no word in answer. His eyes flashed coldly in the moonlight like sharp steel, and he smiled. She regarded him with such passionate intentness that it seemed as though she sought to draw his very soul into herself by the magnetism of her glance,—but he stood unmoved, a very statue of fine disdain and intellectual self-repression. My scarcely controlled fury broke out again at the sight of her dumb yearning, and I gave vent to a shout of scornful laughter.

"By heaven, a veritable new Venus and reluctant Adonis!" I cried deliriously—"A poet should be here to immortalize so touching a scene! Go—go!"—and I motioned her away with a furious gesture—"Go, if you do not want me to murder you! Go, with the proud consciousness that you have worked all the mischief and ruin that is most dear to the heart of a woman,—you have spoilt a life and dishonoured a name,—

you can do no more,—your feminine triumph is complete! Go!—would to God I might never see your face again!—would to God I had been spared the misery of having married you!"

She paid no attention whatever to my words, but kept her eyes fixed on Lucio. Retreating slowly, she seemed to feel rather than see her way to the winding stair, and there, turning, she began to ascend. Half way up she paused—looked back and fully confronted us once more,—with a wild wicked rapture on her face she kissed her hands to Lucio, smiling like a spectral woman in a dream,—then she went onward and upward step by step, till the last white fold of her robe had vanished,—and we two,—my friend and I,—were alone. Facing one another we stood, silently,—I met his sombre eyes and thought I read an infinite compassion in them!—then,—while I yet looked upon him, something seemed to clutch my throat and stop my breathing,—his dark and beautiful countenance appeared to me to grow suddenly lurid as with fire,—a coronal of flame seemed to tremble above his brows,— the moonlight glistened blood-red!—a noise was in my ears of mingled thunder and music as though the silent organ at the end of the gallery were played by hands invisible;—struggling against these delusive sensations, I involuntarily stretched out my hands. . .

"Lucio! . . ." I gasped—"Lucio. . . my friend! I think, . . . I am, . . . dying! My heart is broken!"

As I spoke, a great blackness closed over me,—and I fell senseless.

XXXII

Oh, the blessedness of absolute unconsciousness! It is enough to make one wish that death were indeed annihilation! Utter oblivion,—complete destruction,—surely this would be a greater mercy to the erring soul of man than the terrible God's-gift of Immortality,— the dazzling impress of that divine 'Image' of the Creator in which we are all made, and which we can never obliterate from our beings. I, who have realized to the full the unalterable truth of eternal life,— eternal regeneration for each individual spirit in each individual human creature,—look upon the endless futures through which I am compelled to take my part with something more like horror than gratitude. For I have wasted my time and thrown away priceless opportunities,—and though repentance may retrieve these, the work of retrieval is long and bitter. It is easier to lose a glory than to win it; and if I could have died the death that positivists hope for at the very moment when I learned the full measure of my heart's desolation, surely it would have been well! But my temporary swoon was only too brief,—and when I recovered I found myself in Lucio's own apartment, one of the largest and most sumptuously furnished of all the guest-chambers at Willowsmere,— the windows were wide open, and the floor was flooded with moonlight. As I shuddered coldly back to life and consciousness, I heard a tinkling sound of tune, and opening my eyes wearily I saw Lucio himself seated in the full radiance of the moon with a mandoline on his knee from which he was softly striking delicate impromptu melodies. I was amazed at this,—astounded that while I personally was overwhelmed with a weight of woe, *he* should still be capable of amusing himself. It is a common idea with us all that when we ourselves are put out, no one else should dare to be merry,—in fact we expect Nature itself to wear a miserable face if our own beloved Ego is disturbed by any trouble,— such is the extent of our ridiculous self-consciousness. I moved in my chair and half rose from it,—when Lucio, still thrumming the strings of his instrument *piano pianissimo*, said—

"Keep still, Geoffrey! You'll be all right in a few minutes. Don't worry yourself."

"Worry myself!" I echoed bitterly—"Why not say don't kill yourself!"

"Because I see no necessity to offer you that advice at present—" he responded coolly—"and if there were necessity, I doubt if I should give it,—because I consider it better to kill one's self than worry one's self. However opinions differ. I want you to take this matter lightly."

"Lightly!—take my own dishonour and disgrace lightly!" I exclaimed, almost leaping from my chair—"You ask too much!"

"My good fellow, I ask no more than is asked and expected of a hundred 'society' husbands to-day. Consider!—your wife has been led away from her soberer judgment and reasoning by an exalted and hysterical passion for me on account of my looks,—not for myself at all—because she really does not know *Me*,—she only sees me as I appear to be. The love of handsome exterior personalities is a common delusion of the fair sex—and passes in time like other women's diseases. No actual dishonour or disgrace attaches to her or to you,—nothing has been seen, heard, or done, *in public*. This being so, I can't understand what you are making a fuss about. The great object of social life, you know, is to hide all savage passions and domestic differences from the gaze of the vulgar crowd. You can be as bad as you like in private—only God sees—and that does not matter!"

His eyes had a mocking lustre in them,—twanging his mandoline, he sang under his breath,

> *"If she be not fair for me*
> *What care I how fair she be!"*

"That is the true spirit, Geoffrey,"—he went on—"It sounds flippant to you no doubt in your present tragic frame of mind,—but it is the only way to treat women, in marriage or out of it. Before the world and society, your wife is like Cæsar's, above suspicion. Only you and I (we will leave God out) have been the witnesses of her attack of hysteria. . ."

"Hysteria, you call it! She loves you!" I said hotly—"And she has always loved you. She confessed it,—and you admitted that you always knew it!"

"I always knew she was hysterical—yes—if that is what you mean;"—he answered—"The majority of women have no real feelings, no serious emotions—except one—vanity. They do not know what a great love means,—their chief desire is for conquest,—and failing in this, they run up the gamut of baffled passion to the pitch of frenetic hysteria, which with some becomes chronic. Lady Sibyl suffers in this way. Now listen to me. I will go off to Paris or Moscow or Berlin at once,—after what has happened, of course I cannot stay here,—and I give you my word I will not intrude myself into your domestic circle again. In a few days you will tide over this rupture, and learn the wisdom of supporting the differences that occur in matrimony, with composure—"

"Impossible! I will not part with you!" I said vehemently—"Nor will I live with her! Better the companionship of a true friend than that of a false wife!"

He raised his eyebrows with a puzzled half humorous expression— then shrugged his shoulders, as one who gives up a difficult argument. Rising, he put aside his mandoline and came over to me, his tall imposing figure casting a gigantic shadow in the brilliant moonbeams.

"Upon my word, you put me in a very awkward position Geoffrey,— what is to be done? You can get a judicial separation if you like, but I think it would be an unwise course of procedure after barely four months of marriage. The world would be set talking at once. Really it is better to do anything than give the gossips a chance for floating scandal. Look here—don't decide anything hastily,—come up to town with me for a day, and leave your wife alone to meditate upon her foolishness and its possible consequences,—then you will be better able to judge as to your future movements. Go to your room, and sleep till morning."

"Sleep!" I repeated with a shudder—"In that room where she—" I broke off with a cry and looked at him imploringly—"Am I going mad, I wonder! My brain seems on fire! If I could forget! . . . if I could forget! Lucio—if you, my loyal friend, had been false to me I should have died,—your truth, your honour have saved me!"

He smiled—an odd, cynical little smile.

"Tut—I make no boast of virtue"—he rejoined—"If the lady's beauty had been any temptation to me I might have yielded to her charms,—in so doing I should have been no more than man, as she herself suggested. But perhaps I *am* more than man!—at anyrate bodily beauty in woman makes no sort of effect on me, unless it is accompanied by beauty of soul,—then it does make an effect, and a very extraordinary one. It provokes me to try how deep the beauty goes—whether it is impervious or vulnerable. As I find it, so I leave it!"

I stared wearily at the moonlight patterns on the floor.

"What am I to do?" I asked—"What would you advise?"

"Come up to town with me,"—he replied—"You can leave a note for your wife, explaining your absence,—and at one of the clubs we will talk over the matter quietly, and decide how best to avoid a social scandal. Meanwhile, go to bed. If you won't go back to your own room, sleep in the spare one next to mine."

I rose mechanically and prepared to obey him. He watched me furtively.

"Will you take a composing draught if I mix it for you?" he said—"It is harmless, and will give you a few hours' sleep."

"I would take poison from your hand!" I answered recklessly—"Why don't you mix *that* for me?—and then, . . . then I should sleep indeed,— and forget this horrible night!"

"No,—unfortunately you would not forget!" he said, going to his dressing-case and taking out a small white powder which he dissolved gradually in a glass of water—"That is the worst of what people call dying. I must instruct you in a little science by-and-by, to distract your thoughts. The scientific part of death,—the business that goes on behind the scenes you know—will interest you very much—it is highly instructive, particularly that section of it which I am entitled to call the regeneration of atoms. The brain-cells are atoms, and within these, are other atoms called memories, curiously vital and marvellously prolific! Drink this,"—and he handed me the mixture he had prepared—"For temporary purposes it is much better than death—because it does numb and paralyse the conscious atoms for a little while, whereas death only liberates them to a larger and more obstinate vitality."

I was too self-absorbed to heed or understand his words, but I drank what he gave me submissively and returned the glass,—he still watched me closely for about a minute. Then he opened the door of the apartment which adjoined his own.

"Throw yourself on that bed and close your eyes,"—he continued in somewhat peremptory accents—"Till morning breaks I give you a respite,—" and he smiled strangely—"both from dreams and memories! Plunge into Oblivion, my friend!—brief as it is and as it must ever be, it is sweet!—even to a millionaire!"

The ironical tone of his voice vexed me,—I looked at him half reproachfully, and saw his proud beautiful face, pale as marble, clear-cut as a cameo, soften as I met his eyes,—I felt he was sorry for me despite his love of satire,—and grasping his hand I pressed it fervently without offering any other reply. Then, going into the next room as he bade me, I lay down, and falling asleep almost instantly, I remembered no more.

MARIE CORELLI

XXXIII

With the morning came full consciousness; I realized bitterly all that had happened, but I was no longer inclined to bemoan my fate. My senses were stricken, as it seemed, too numb and rigid for any further outbreak of passion. A hard callousness took the place of outraged feeling; and though despair was in my heart, my mind was made up to one stern resolve,—I would look upon Sibyl no more. Never again should that fair face, the deceitful mask of a false nature, tempt my sight and move me to pity or forgiveness,—that I determined. Leaving the room in which I had passed the night, I went to my study and wrote the following letter;—

Sibyl

After the degrading and disgraceful scene of last night you must be aware that any further intercourse between us is impossible. Prince Rimânez and I are leaving for London; we shall not return. You can continue to reside at Willowsmere,—the house is yours,—and the half of my fortune unconditionally settled upon you on our marriage-day will enable you to keep up the fashions of your 'set,' and live with that luxury and extravagance you deem necessary to an 'aristocratic' position. I have decided to travel,—and I intend to make such arrangements as may prevent, if possible, our ever meeting again,—though I shall of course do my best for my own sake, to avoid any scandal. To reproach you for your conduct would be useless; you are lost to all sense of shame. You have abased yourself in the humiliation of a guilty passion before a man who despises you,—who, in his own loyal and noble nature, hates you for your infidelity and hypocrisy,—and I can find no pardon for the wrong you have thus done to me, and the injury you have brought upon my name. I leave you to the judgment of your own conscience,—if you have one,—which is doubtful. Such women as you, are seldom troubled with remorse. It is not likely you will ever see me or the man to whom you have offered your undesired love again,—make of your life what you can or will, I am indifferent to your movements, and for my own part, shall endeavour as much as may be, to forget that you exist.

Your husband,
Geoffrey Tempest

This letter, folded and sealed, I sent to my wife in her own apartments by her maid,—the girl came back and said she had delivered it, but that there was no answer. Her ladyship had a severe headache and meant to keep her room that morning. I expressed just as much civil regret as a confidential maid would naturally expect from the newly-wedded husband of her mistress,—and then, giving instructions to my man Morris to pack my portmanteau, I partook of a hurried breakfast with Lucio in more or less silence and constraint, for the servants were in attendance, and I did not wish them to suspect that anything was wrong. For their benefit, I gave out that my friend and I were called suddenly to town on urgent business,—that we might be absent a couple of days, perhaps longer,—and that any special message or telegram could be sent on to me at Arthur's Club. I was thankful when we at last got away,—when the tall, picturesque red gables of Willowsmere vanished from my sight,—and when finally, seated in a railway smoking-carriage reserved for our two selves, we were able to watch the miles of distance gradually extending between us and the beautiful autumnal woods of poet-haunted Warwickshire. For a long time we kept silence, turning over and pretending to read the morning's papers,—till presently flinging down the dull and wearisome 'Times' sheet, I sighed heavily, and leaning back, closed my eyes.

"I am truly very much distressed about all this;" said Lucio then, with extreme gentleness and suavity—"It seems to me that *I* am the adverse element in the affair. If Lady Sibyl had never seen *me*,—"

"Why, then I should never have seen *her*!" I responded bitterly—"It was through you I met her first."

"True!" and he eyed me thoughtfully—"I am very unfortunately placed!—it is almost as if I were to blame, though no-one could be more innocent or well-intentioned than myself!" He smiled,—then went on very gravely—"I really should avoid scandalous gossip if I were you,—I do not speak of my own involuntary share in the disaster,—what people say of me is quite immaterial; but for the lady's sake—"

"For my own sake I shall try to avoid it;" I said brusquely, whereat his eyes glittered strangely—"It is myself I have to consider most of all. I shall, as I hinted to you this morning, travel for a few years."

"Yes,—go on a tiger-hunting expedition in India,"—he suggested—"Or kill elephants in Africa. It is what a great many men do when their wives forget themselves. Several well-known husbands are abroad just now!"

Again the brilliant enigmatical smile flashed over his face,—but I could not smile in answer. I stared moodily out of the window at the bare autumnal fields, past which the train flew,—bare of harvest,—stripped of foliage—like my own miserable life.

"Come and winter with me in Egypt,"—he continued—"Come in my yacht 'The Flame,'—we will take her to Alexandria,—and then do the Nile in a dahabeah, and forget that such frivolous dolls as women exist except to be played with by us 'superior' creatures and thrown aside."

"Egypt—the Nile!" I murmured,—somehow the idea pleased me—"Yes,—why not?"

"Why not indeed!" he echoed—"The proposal is agreeable to you I am sure. Come and see the land of the old gods,—the land where my princess used to live and torture the souls of men!—perhaps we may discover the remains of her last victim,—who knows!"

I avoided his gaze;—the recollection of the horrible winged thing he persisted in imagining to be the transmigrated soul of an evil woman, was repugnant to me. Almost I felt as if there were some subtle connection between that hateful creature and my wife Sibyl. I was glad when the train reached London, and we, taking a hansom, were plunged into the very vortex of human life. The perpetual noise of traffic, the motley crowds of people, the shouting of news-boys and omnibus-conductors,—all this hubbub was grateful to my ears, and for a time at least, distracted my thoughts. We lunched at the Savoy, and amused ourselves with noting the town noodles of fashion,—the inane young man in the stocks of the stiff high collar, and wearing the manacles of equally stiff and exaggerated cuffs, a veritable prisoner in the dock of silly custom,—the frivolous fool of a woman, painted and powdered, with false hair and dyed eyebrows, trying to look as much like a paid courtezan as possible,—the elderly matron, skipping forward on high heels, and attempting by the assumption of juvenile airs and graces to cover up and conceal the obtrusive facts of a too obvious paunch and overlapping bosom,—the would-be dandy and 'beau' of seventy, strangely possessed by youthful desires, and manifesting the same by goat-like caperings at the heels of young married women;— these and such-like contemptible units of a contemptible social swarm, passed before us like puppets at a country fair, and aroused us in turn to laughter or disdain. While we yet lingered over our wine, a man came in alone, and sat down at the table next to ours;—he had with him a book, which, after giving his orders for luncheon, he at once opened at a marked place and began to read with absorbed attention,—I recognised the cover of the volume and knew it to be Mavis Clare's "Differences." A haze floated before my sight,—a sensation of rising tears was in my throat,—I saw the fair face, earnest eyes, and sweet smile of Mavis,— that woman-wearer of the laurel-crown,—that keeper of the lilies of purity and peace. Alas, those lilies!—they were for me

> "*des fleurs étranges,*[3]
> *Avec leurs airs de sceptres d'anges;*
> *De thyrses lumineux pour doigts de séraphins,—*
> *Leurs parfums sont trop forts, tout ensemble, et trop fins!*"

I shaded my eyes with one hand,—yet under that shade I felt that Lucio watched me closely. Presently he spoke softly, just as if he had read my thoughts.

"Considering the effect a perfectly innocent woman has on the mind of even an evil man, it's strange, isn't it that there are so few of them!"

I did not answer.

"In the present day," he went on—"there are a number of females clamouring like unnatural hens in a barn-yard about their 'rights' and 'wrongs.' Their greatest right, their highest privilege, is to guide and guard the souls of men. This, they for the most part, throw away as worthless. Aristocratic women, royal women even, hand over the care of their children to hired attendants and inferiors, and then are surprised and injured if those children turn out to be either fools or blackguards. If I were controller of the State, I would make it a law that every mother should be bound to nurse and guard her children herself as nature intended, unless prevented by ill-health, in which case she would have to get a couple of doctor's certificates to certify the fact. Otherwise, any woman refusing to comply with the law should be

---

3. *Edmond Rostand.* '*La Princesse Lointaine.*'

sentenced to imprisonment with hard labour. This would bring them to their senses. The idleness, wickedness, extravagance and selfishness of women, make men the boors and egotists they are."

I looked up.

"The devil is in the whole business;"—I said bitterly—"If women were good, men would have nothing to do with them. Look round you at what is called 'society'! How many men there are who deliberately choose tainted women for their wives, and leave the innocent uncared for! Take Mavis Clare—"

"Oh, you were thinking of Mavis Clare, were you?" he rejoined, with a quick glance at me—"But she would be a difficult prize for any man to win. She does not seek to be married,—and she is not uncared for, since the whole world cares for her."

"That is a sort of impersonal love;"—I answered—"It does not give her the protection such a woman needs, and ought to obtain."

"Do you want to become her lover?" he asked with a slight smile—"I'm afraid you've no chance!"

"I! Her lover! Good God!" I exclaimed, the blood rushing hotly to my face at the mere suggestion—"What a profane idea!"

"You are right,—it *is* profane;"—he agreed, still smiling—"It is as though I should propose your stealing the sacramental cup from a church, with just this difference,—you might succeed in running off with the cup because it is only the church's property, but you would never succeed in winning Mavis Clare, inasmuch as she belongs to God. You know what Milton says:

> 'So dear to Heaven is saintly chastity
> That when a soul is found sincerely so,
> A thousand liveried angels lacquey her,
> Driving far off each thing of sin and guilt,
> And in clear dream and solemn vision
> Tell her of things which no gross ear can hear,
> Till oft converse with heavenly habitants
> Begin to cast a beam on th'outward shape
> The unpolluted temple of the mind,
> And turns it by degrees to the soul's essence
> Till all be made immortal!'

He quoted the lines softly and with an exquisite gravity.

"That is what you see in Mavis Clare,"—he continued—"that 'beam on the outward shape' which 'turns it by degrees to the soul's essence,'—and which makes her beautiful, without what is called beauty by lustful men."

I moved impatiently, and looked out from the window near which we were seated, at the yellow width of the flowing Thames below.

"Beauty, according to man's ordinary standard," pursued Lucio, "means simply good flesh,—nothing more. Flesh, arranged prettily and roundly on the always ugly skeleton beneath,—flesh, daintily coloured and soft to the touch, without scar or blemish. Plenty of it too, disposed in the proper places. It is the most perishable sort of commodity,—an illness spoils it,—a trying climate ruins it,—age wrinkles it,—death destroys it,—but it is all the majority of men look for in their bargains with the fair sex. The most utter *roué* of sixty that ever trotted jauntily down Piccadilly pretending to be thirty, expects like Shylock his 'pound' or several pounds of youthful flesh. The desire is neither refined nor intellectual, but there it is,—and it is solely on this account that the 'ladies' of the music-hall become the tainted members and future mothers of the aristocracy."

"It does not need the ladies of the music-hall to taint the already tainted!" I said.

"True!" and he looked at me with kindly commiseration—"Let us put the whole mischief down to the 'new' fiction!"

We rose then, having finished luncheon, and leaving the Savoy we went on to Arthur's. Here we sat down in a quiet corner and began to talk of our future plans. It took me very little time to make up my mind,—all quarters of the world were the same to me, and I was really indifferent as to where I went. Yet there is always something suggestive and fascinating about the idea of a first visit to Egypt, and I willingly agreed to accompany Lucio thither, and remain the winter.

"We will avoid society"—he said—"The well-bred, well-educated 'swagger' people who throw champagne-bottles at the Sphinx, and think a donkey-race 'ripping fun' shall not have the honour of our company. Cairo is full of such dancing dolls, so we will not stay there. Old Nile has many attractions; and lazy luxury on a dahabeah will soothe your overwrought nerves. I suggest our leaving England within a week."

I consented,—and while he went over to a table and wrote some letters in preparation for our journey, I looked through the day's papers. There was nothing to read in them,—for though all the world's news palpitates into Great Britain on obediently throbbing electric wires, each editor of each little pennyworth, being jealous of every other editor of every other pennyworth, only admits into his columns exactly what suits his politics or personally pleases his taste, and the interests of the public at large are scarcely considered. Poor, bamboozled, patient public!—no wonder it is beginning to think that a halfpenny spent on a newspaper which is only purchased to be thrown away, enough and more than enough. I was still glancing up and down the tedious columns of the Americanized Pall Mall Gazette, and Lucio was still writing, when a page-boy entered with a telegram.

"Mr. Tempest?"

"Yes." And I snatched the yellow-covered missive and tore it open,— and read the few words it contained almost uncomprehendingly. They ran thus—

"Return at once. Something alarming has happened. Afraid to act without you. Mavis Clare."

A curious chill came over me,—the telegram fell from my hands on the table. Lucio took it up and glanced at it. Then, regarding me stedfastly, he said—

"Of course you must go. You can catch the four-forty train if you take a hansom."

"And you?" I muttered. My throat was dry and I could scarcely speak.

"I'll stay at the Grand, and wait for news. Don't delay a moment,— Miss Clare would not have taken it upon herself to send this message, unless there had been serious cause."

"What do you think—what do you suppose—" I began.

He stopped me by a slight imperative gesture.

"I think nothing—I suppose nothing. I only urge you to start immediately. Come!"

And almost before I realized it, he had taken me with him out into the hall of the club, where he helped me on with my coat, gave me my hat, and sent for a cab to take me to the railway station. We scarcely exchanged farewells,—stupefied with the suddenness of the unexpected summons back to the home I had left in the morning, as I thought, for ever, I hardly knew what I was doing or where I was going, till I found myself alone in the train, returning to Warwickshire as fast as steam would bear me, with the gloom of the deepening dusk around me, and such a fear and horror at my heart as I dared not think of or define. What was the 'something alarming' that had happened? How was it that Mavis Clare had telegraphed to me? These, and endless other questions tormented my brain,—and I was afraid to suggest answers to any of them. When I arrived at the familiar station, there was no one waiting to receive me, so I hired a fly, and was driven up to my own house just as the short evening deepened into night. A low autumnal wind was sighing restlessly among the trees like a wandering soul in torment; not a star shone in the black depths of the sky. Directly the carriage stopped, a slim figure in white came out under the porch to meet me,—it was Mavis, her angel's face grave and pale with emotion.

"It is you at last!" she said in a trembling voice—"Thank God you have come!"

XXXIV

I grasped her hands hard.

"What is it?"—I began;—then, looking round I saw that the hall was full of panic-stricken servants, some of whom came forward, confusedly murmuring together about being 'afraid,' and 'not knowing what to do.' I motioned them back by a gesture and turned again to Mavis Clare.

"Tell me,—quick—what is wrong?"

"We fear something has happened to Lady Sibyl,"—she replied at once—"Her rooms are locked, and we cannot make her hear. Her maid got alarmed, and ran over to my house to ask me what was best to be done,—I came at once, and knocked and called, but could get no response. You know the windows are too high to reach from the ground,—there is no ladder on the premises long enough for the purpose,—and no one can climb up that side of the building. I begged some of the servants to break open the door by force,—but they would not,—they were all afraid; and I did not like to act on my own responsibility, so I telegraphed for you—"

I sprang away from her before she had finished speaking and hurried upstairs at once,—outside the door of the ante-room which led into my wife's luxurious 'suite' of apartments, I paused breathless.

"Sibyl!" I cried.

There was not a sound. Mavis had followed me, and stood by my side, trembling a little. Two or three of the servants had also crept up the stairs, and were clinging to the banisters, listening nervously.

"Sibyl!" I called again. Still absolute silence. I turned round upon the waiting and anxious domestics with an assumption of calmness.

"Lady Sibyl is probably not in her rooms at all;"—I said; "She may have gone out unobserved. This door of the ante-chamber has a spring-lock,—it can easily get fast shut by the merest accident. Bring a strong hammer,—or a crowbar,—anything that will break it open,—if you had had sense you would have obeyed Miss Clare, and done this a couple of hours ago."

And I waited with enforced composure, while my instructions were carried out as rapidly as possible. Two of the men-servants appeared with the necessary tools, and very soon the house resounded with clamour,—blow after blow was dealt upon the solid oaken door for some time without success,—the spring lock would not yield,—neither would the strong hinges give way. Presently however, after ten minutes' hard labour, one of the finely carved panels was smashed in,—then another,—and, springing over the débris I rushed through the ante-room into the boudoir,—then paused, listening, and calling again, "Sibyl!" No one followed me,—some indefinable instinct, some nameless dread, held the servants back, and Mavis Clare as well. I was alone, . . . and in complete darkness. Groping about, with my heart beating furiously, I sought for the ivory button in the wall which would, at pressure, flood the rooms with electric light, but somehow I could not find it. My hand came in contact with various familiar things which I recognised by touch,—rare bits of china, bronzes, vases, pictures,—costly trifles that were heaped up as I knew, in this particular apartment with a lavish luxury and disregard of cost befitting a wanton eastern empress of old time,—cautiously feeling my way along, I started with terror to see, as I thought, a tall figure outline itself suddenly against the darkness,—white, spectral and luminous,—a figure that, as I stared at it aghast, raised a pallid hand and pointed me forward with a menacing air of scorn! In my dazed horror at this apparition, or delusion, I stumbled over the heavy trailing folds of a velvet *portiére*, and knew by this that I had passed from the boudoir into the adjoining bedroom. Again I stopped,—calling "Sibyl!" but my voice had scarcely strength enough to raise itself above a whisper. Giddy and confused as I was, I remembered that the electric light in this room was fixed at the side of the toilet-table, and I stepped hurriedly in that direction, when all at once in the thick gloom I touched something clammy and cold like dead flesh, and brushed against a garment that exhaled faint perfume, and rustled at my touch with a silken sound. This alarmed me more thoroughly than the spectre I fancied I had just seen,—I drew back shudderingly against the wall,—and in so doing, my fingers involuntarily closed on the polished ivory stud which, like a fairy talisman in modern civilization, emits radiance at the owner's will. I pressed it nervously,—the light blazed forth through the rose-tinted shells which shaded its dazzling clearness, and showed me where I stood, . . . within an arm's length of a strange, stiff white creature that sat staring at itself in the silver-framed mirror with wide-open, fixed and glassy eyes!

"Sibyl!" I gasped—"My wife. . . ! . . ." but the words died chokingly in my throat. Was it indeed my wife?—this frozen statue of a woman, watching her own impassive image thus intently? I looked upon her wonderingly,—doubtingly,—as if she were some stranger;—it took me time to recognize her features, and the bronze-gold darkness of her long hair which fell loosely about her in a lavish wealth of rippling waves, . . . her left hand hung limply over the arm of the chair in which, like some carven ivory goddess, she sat enthroned,—and tremblingly, slowly, reluctantly, I advanced and took that hand. Cold as ice it lay in my palm much as though it were a waxen model of itself;—it glittered with jewels,—and I studied every ring upon it with a curious, dull pertinacity, like one who seeks a clue to identity. That large turquoise in a diamond setting was a marriage-gift from a duchess,—that opal her father gave her,—the lustrous circle of sapphires and brilliants surmounting her wedding-ring was my gift,—that ruby I seemed to know,—well, well! what a mass of sparkling value wasted on such fragile clay! I peered into her face,—then at the reflection of that face in the mirror,—and again I grew perplexed,—was it, could it be Sibyl after all? Sibyl was beautiful,—*this* dead thing had a devilish smile on its blue, parted lips, and frenzied horror in its eyes! Suddenly something tense in my brain seemed to snap and give way,—dropping the chill fingers I held, I cried aloud—

"Mavis! Mavis Clare!"

In a moment she was with me,—in a glance she comprehended all. Falling on her knees by the dead woman she broke into a passion of weeping.

"Oh, poor girl!" she cried—"Oh, poor, unhappy, misguided girl!"

I stared at her gloomily. It seemed to me very strange that she should weep for sorrows not her own. There was a fire in my brain,—a confused trouble in my thoughts,—I looked at my dead wife with her fixed gaze and evil smile, sitting rigidly upright, and robed in the mocking sheen of her rose-silk peignoir, showered with old lace, after the costliest of Paris fashions,—then at the living, tender-souled, earnest creature, famed for her genius throughout the world, who knelt on the ground, sobbing over the stiffening hand on which so many rare gems glistened derisively,—and an impulse rose in me stronger than myself, moving me to wild and clamorous speech.

"Get up, Mavis!" I cried—"Do not kneel there! Go,—go out of this room,—out of my sight! You do not know what she was—this woman whom I married,—I deemed her an angel, but she was a fiend,—yes, Mavis, a fiend! Look at her, staring at her own image in the glass,—you cannot call her beautiful—*now*! She smiles, you see,—just as she smiled last night when, . . . ah, you know nothing of last night! I tell you, go!" and I stamped my foot almost furiously,—"This air is contaminated,— it will poison you! The perfume of Paris and the effluvia of death intermingled are sufficient to breed a pestilence! Go quickly,—inform the household their mistress is dead,—have the blinds drawn down,— show all the exterior signs of decent and fashionable woe!"—and I began laughing deliriously—"Tell the servants they may count upon expensive mourning,—for all that money can do shall be done in homage to King Death! Let everyone in the place eat and drink as much as they can or will,—and sleep, or chatter as such menials love to do, of hearses, graves and sudden disasters;—but let *me* be left alone,—alone with *her*;—we have much to say to one another!"

White and trembling, Mavis rose up and stood gazing at me in fear and pity.

"Alone? . . ." she faltered—"You are not fit to be alone!"

"No, I am not fit to be, but I must be,"—I rejoined quickly and harshly—"This woman and I loved—after the manner of brutes, and were wedded or rather mated in a similar manner, though an archbishop blessed the pairing, and called upon Heaven to witness its sanctity! Yet we parted ill friends,—and dead though she is, I choose to pass the night with her,—I shall learn much knowledge from her silence! To-morrow the grave and the servants of the grave may claim her, but to-night she is mine!"

The girl's sweet eyes brimmed over with tears.

"Oh you are too distracted to know what you are saying," she murmured—"You do not even try to discover how she died!"

"That is easy enough to guess,"—I answered quickly, and I took up a small dark-coloured bottle labelled 'Poison' which I had already perceived on the toilet-table—"This is uncorked and empty. What it contained I do not know,—but there must be an inquest of course,— people must be allowed to make money for themselves out of her ladyship's rash act! And see there,—" here I pointed to some loose sheets of note-paper covered with writing, and partially concealed by a filmy lace handkerchief which had evidently been hastily thrown across them, and a pen and inkstand close by—"There is some admirable reading prepared for me doubtless!—the last message from the beloved dead is sacred, Mavis Clare; surely you, a writer of tender romances, can realize this!—and realizing it, you will do as I ask you,—leave me!"

She looked at me in deep compassion, and slowly turned to go.

"God help you!" she said sobbingly—"God console you!"

At this, some demon in me broke loose, and springing to her side I caught her hands in mine.

"Do not dare to talk of God!" I said in passionate accents; "Not in this room,—not in *that* presence! Why should you call curses down upon me? The help of God means punishment,—the consolations of God are terrible! For strength must acknowledge itself weak before He will help it,—and a heart must be broken before He will console it! But what do I say!—I believe in *no* God—! I believe in an unknown Force that encompasses me and hunts me down to the grave, but nothing more. *She* thought as I do,—and with reason,—for what has God done for her? She was made evil from the first,—a born snare of Satan. . ."

Something caught my breath here,—I stopped, unable to utter another word. Mavis stared at me affrighted, and I stared back again.

"What is it?" she whispered alarmedly. I struggled to speak,—finally, with difficulty I answered her—

"Nothing!"

And I motioned her away with a gesture of entreaty. The expression of my face must have startled or intimidated her I fancy, for she retreated hastily and I watched her disappearing as if she were the phantom of a dream,—then, as she passed out through the boudoir, I drew close the velvet portiére behind her and locked the intermediate door. This done I went slowly back to the side of my dead wife.

"Now Sibyl,"—I said aloud—"we are alone, you and I—alone with our own reflected images,—you dead, and I living! You have no terrors for me in your present condition,—your beauty has gone. Your smile, your eyes, your touch cannot stir me to a throb of the passion you craved, yet wearied of! What have you to say to me?—I have heard that the dead can speak at times,—and you owe me reparation,—reparation for the wrong you did me,—the lie on which you based our marriage,— the guilt you cherished in your heart! Shall I read your petition for forgiveness here?"

And I gathered up the written sheets of note-paper in one hand, feeling them rather than seeing them, for my eyes were fixed on the pallid corpse in its rose-silk 'negligée' and jewels, that gazed at itself so pertinaciously in the shining mirror. I drew a chair close to it, and sat down, observing likewise the reflection of my own haggard face in the glass beside that of the self-murdered woman. Turning presently, I began to scrutinize my immovable companion more closely—and perceived that she was very lightly clothed,—under the silk peignoir there was only a flowing white garment of soft fine material lavishly embroidered, through which the statuesque contour of her rigid limbs could be distinctly seen. Stooping, I felt her heart,—I knew it was pulseless; yet I half imagined I should feel its beat. As I withdrew my hand, something scaly and glistening caught my eye, and looking I perceived Lucio's marriage-gift circling her waist,—the flexible emerald snake with its diamond crest and ruby eyes. It fascinated me,— coiled round that dead body it seemed alive and sentient,—if it had lifted its glittering head and hissed at me I should scarcely have been surprised. I sat back for a moment in my chair, almost as rigid as the corpse beside me,—I stared again, as the corpse stared always, into the mirror which pictured us both, we 'twain in one,' as the sentimentalists aver of wedded folk, though in truth it often happens that there are no two creatures in the world more widely separated than husband and wife. I heard stealthy movements and suppressed whisperings in the passage outside, and guessed that some of the servants were there watching and waiting,—but I cared nothing for that. I was absorbed in the ghastly night interview I had planned for myself, and I so entered into the spirit of the thing, that I turned on all the electric lamps in the room, besides lighting two tall clusters of shaded candles on either side of the toilet-table. When all the surroundings were thus rendered as brilliant as possible, so that the corpse looked more livid and ghastly by comparison, I seated myself once more, and prepared to read the last message of the dead.

"Now Sibyl,"—I muttered, leaning forward a little, and noting with a morbid interest that the jaws of the corpse had relaxed a little within the last few minutes, and that the smile on the face was therefore more hideous—"Confess your sins!—for I am here to listen. Such dumb, impressive eloquence as yours deserves attention!"

A gust of wind fled round the house with a wailing cry,—the windows shook, and the candles flickered. I waited till every sound had died away, and then—with a glance at my dead wife, under the sudden impression that she had heard what I said, and knew what I was doing, I began to read.

XXXV

Thus ran the 'last document,' commencing abruptly and without prefix;—

"I have made up my mind to die. Not out of passion or petulance,—but from deliberate choice, and as I think, necessity. My brain is tired of problems,—my body is tired of life; it is best to make an end. The idea of death,—which means annihilation,—is very sweet to me. I am glad to feel that by my own will and act I can silence this uneasy throbbing of my heart, this turmoil and heat of my blood,—this tortured aching of my nerves. Young as I am, I have no delight now in existence,—I see nothing but my love's luminous eyes, his god-like features, his enthralling smile,—and these are lost to me. For a brief while he has been my world, life and time,—he has gone,—and without him there is no universe. How could I endure the slow, wretched passing of hours, days, weeks, months and years alone?—though it is better to be alone than in the dull companionship of the self-satisfied, complacent and arrogant fool who is my husband. He has left me for ever, so he says in a letter the maid brought to me an hour ago. It is quite what I expected of him,—what man of his type could find pardon for a blow to his own *amour propre*! If he had studied my nature, entered into my emotions, or striven in the least to guide and sustain me,—if he had shown me any sign of a great, true love such as one sometimes dreams of and seldom finds,—I think I should be sorry for him now,—I should even ask his forgiveness for having married him. But he has treated me precisely as he might treat a paid mistress,—that is, he has fed me, clothed me, and provided me with money and jewels in return for making me the toy of his passions,—but he has not given me one touch of sympathy,—one proof of self-denial or humane forbearance. Therefore, I owe him nothing. And now he, and my love who will not be my lover, have gone away together; I am free to do as I will with this small pulse within me called life, which is after all, only a thread, easily broken. There is no one to say me nay, or to hold my hand back from giving myself the final *quietus*. It is well I have no friends; it is good for me that I have probed the hypocrisy and social sham of the world, and that I have mastered the following hard truths of life,—that there is no love without lust,—no friendship without self-interest,—no religion without avarice,—and no so-called virtue without its accompanying stronger vice. Who, knowing these things, would care to take part in them! On the verge of the grave I look back along the short vista of my years, and I see myself a child in this very place, this wooded Willowsmere; I can note how that life began to which I am about to put an end. Pampered, petted and spoilt, told that I must 'look pretty' and take pleasure in my clothes, I was even at the age of ten, capable of a certain amount of coquetry. Old *roués*, smelling of wine and tobacco, were eager to take me on their knees and pinch my soft flesh;—they would press my innocent lips with their withered ones,—withered and contaminated by the kisses of *cocottes* and 'soiled doves' of the town!—I have often wondered how it is these men can dare to touch a young child's mouth, knowing in themselves what beasts they are! I see my nurse,—a trained liar and time-server, giving herself more airs than a queen, and forbidding me to speak to this child or that child, because they were 'beneath' me;—then came my governess, full of a prurient prudery, as bad a woman in morals as ever lived, yet 'highly recommended' and with excellent references, and wearing an assumption of the strictest virtue, like many equally hypocritical clergymen's wives I have known. I soon found her out,—for even as a child I was painfully observant,—and the stories she and my mother's French maid used to tell, in lowered voices now and then broken by coarse laughter, were sufficient to enlighten me as to her true character. Yet, beyond having a supreme contempt for the woman who practised religious austerity outwardly, and was at heart a rake, I gave small consideration to the difficult problem such a nature suggested. I lived,—how strange it seems that I should be writing now of myself, as past and done with!—yes, I lived in a dreamy, more or less idyllic state of mind, thinking without being conscious of thought, full of fancies concerning the flowers, trees and birds,—wishing for things of which I knew nothing,— imagining myself a queen at times, and again, a peasant. I was an omnivorous reader,—and I was specially fond of poetry. I used to pore over the mystic verse of Shelley, and judged him then as a sort of demi-god;—and never, even when I knew all about his life, could I realize him as a man with a thin, shrieking falsetto voice and 'loose' notions concerning women. But I am quite sure it was good for his fame that he was drowned in early youth with so many melancholy and dramatic surroundings,—it saved him, I consider, from a possibly vicious and repulsive old age. I adored Keats till I knew he had wasted his passion on a Fanny Brawn,— and then the glamour of him vanished. I can offer no reason for this,—I merely set down the fact. I made a hero of Lord Byron,— in fact he has always formed for me the only heroical type of poet. Strong in himself and pitiless in his love for women, he treated them for the most part as they merited, considering the singular and unworthy specimens of the sex it was his misfortune to encounter. I used to wonder, when reading these men's amorous lines, whether love would ever come my way, and what beatific state of emotion I should then enjoy. Then came the rough awakening from all my dreams,—childhood melted into womanhood,—and at sixteen I was taken up to town with my parents to "know something of the ways and manners of society," before finally 'coming out.' Oh, those ways and manners! I learnt them to perfection! Astonished at first, then bewildered, and allowed no time to form any judgment on what I saw, I was hurried through a general vague 'impression' of things such as I had never imagined or dreamed of. While I was yet lost in wonderment, and kept constantly in companionship with young girls of my own rank and age, who nevertheless seemed much more advanced in knowledge of the world than I, my father suddenly informed me that Willowsmere was lost to us,—that he could not afford to keep it up,—and that we should return there no more. Ah, what tears I shed!—what a fury of grief consumed me!—I did not then comprehend the difficult entanglements of either wealth or poverty;—all I could realize was that the doors of my dear old home were closed upon me for ever. After that, I think I grew cold and hard in disposition; I had never loved my mother very dearly,—in fact I had seen very little of her, as she was always away visiting, if not entertaining visitors, and she seldom had me with her,—so that when she was suddenly struck down by a first shock of paralysis, it affected me but little. She had her doctors and nurses,—I had my governess still with me; and my mother's sister, Aunt Charlotte, came to keep house for us,—so I began to analyse society for myself, without giving any expression of my opinions on what I observed. I was not yet 'out,' but I went everywhere where girls of my age were invited, and perceived things without showing that I had any faculty of perception. I cultivated a passionless and cold exterior,—a listless, uninterested and frigid demeanor,—for I discovered that this was accepted by many people as dullness or stupidity, and that by assuming such a character, certain otherwise crafty persons would talk more readily before me, and betray themselves and their vices unawares. Thus my 'social education' began in grim earnest;—women of title and renown would ask me to their 'quiet teas,' because I was what they were pleased to call a 'harmless girl—' 'rather pretty, but dull,'—and allow me to assist them in entertaining the lovers who called upon them while their husbands were out. I remember that on one occasion, a great lady famous for two things, her diamonds and her intimacy with the Queen, kissed her 'cavaliere servente,' a noted sporting earl, with considerable *abandon* in my presence. He muttered something about me,—I heard it;—but his amorous mistress merely answered in a whisper—"Oh, it's only Sibyl Elton,—she understands nothing." Afterwards however, when he had gone, she turned to me with a grin and remarked— "You saw me kiss Bertie, didn't you? I often do; he's quite like my brother!" I made no reply,—I only smiled vaguely; and the next day she sent me a valuable diamond ring, which I at once returned to her with a prim little note, stating that I was much obliged, but that my father considered me too young as yet to wear diamonds. Why do I think of these trifles now I wonder!— now when I am about to take my leave of life and all its lies! . . . There is a little bird singing outside my bedroom window,—such a pretty creature! I suppose it is happy?—it should be, as it is not human. . . The tears are in my eyes as I listen to its sweet warbling, and think that it will be living and singing still to-day at sunset when I am dead!

That last sentence was mere sentiment, for I am not sorry to die. If I felt the least regret about it I should not carry out my intention. I must resume my narrative,—for it is an analysis I am trying to make of myself, to find out if I can whether there are no excuses to be found for my particular disposition,—whether it is not after all, the education and training I have had that have made me what I am, or whether indeed I was born evil from the first. The circumstances that surrounded me, did not, at any rate, tend to soften or improve my character. I had just passed my seventeenth birthday, when one morning my father called me into his library and told me the true position of his affairs. I learned that he was crippled on all sides with debt,—that he lived on advances made to him by Jew usurers,—and that these advances were trusted to him solely on the speculation that I, his only daughter, would make a sufficiently rich marriage to enable him to repay all loans with heavy interest. He went on to say that he hoped I would act sensibly,—and that when any men showed indications of becoming suitors for my hand, I would, before encouraging them, inform him, in order that he might make strict enquiries as to their actual extent of fortune. I then understood, for the first time, that I was for sale. I listened in silence till he had finished,—then I asked him—'Love, I suppose, is not to be considered in the matter?' He laughed, and assured me it was much easier to love a rich man than a poor one, as I would find out after a little experience. He added, with some hesitation, that to help make both ends meet, as the expenses of town life were considerable, he had arranged to take a young American lady under his charge, a Miss Diana Chesney, who wished to be introduced into English society, and who would pay two thousand guineas a year to him for that privilege, and for Aunt Charlotte's services as chaperône. I do not remember now what I said to him when I heard this,—I know that my long suppressed feelings broke out in a storm of fury, and that for the moment he was completely taken aback by the force of my indignation. An American boarder in *our* house!—it seemed to me as outrageous and undignified as the conduct of a person I once heard of, who, favoured by the Queen's patronage with 'free' apartments in Kensington Palace, took from time to time on the sly, an American or Colonial 'paying-guest,' who adopted forthwith the address of Her Majesty's birthplace as her own, thus lowering the whole prestige of that historic habitation. My wrath however was useless;—the bargain was arranged,—my father, regardless of his proud lineage and the social dignity of his position, had degraded himself, in my opinion, to the level of a sort of superior lodging-house keeper,—and from that time I lost all my former respect for him. Of course it can be argued that I was wrong,—that I ought to have honoured him for turning his name to monetary account by loaning it out as a protective shield and panoply for an American woman without anything but the dollars of a vulgar 'railway-king' to back her up in society,—but I could not see it in that light. I retreated into myself more than ever,—and became more than pleasantly known for my coldness, reserve and hauteur. Miss Chesney came, and strove hard to be my friend,—but she soon found that impossible. She is a good-hearted creature I believe,—but she is badly bred and badly trained as all her compatriots are, more or less, despite their smattering of an European education; I disliked her from the first, and have spared no pains to show it. Yet I know she will be Countess of Elton as soon as it is decently possible,—say, after the year's ceremonious mourning for my mother has expired, and perhaps three months' hypocritical wearing of black for me,— my father believes himself to be still young and passably good-looking, and he is quite incapable of resisting the fortune she will bring him. When she took up her fixed abode in our house and Aunt Charlotte became her paid chaperône, I seldom went out to any social gatherings, for I could not endure the idea of being seen in her companionship. I kept to my own room a great deal, and thus secluded, read many books. All the fashionable fiction of the day passed through my hands, much to my gradual enlightenment, if not to my edification. One day,—a day that is stamped on my memory as a kind of turning-point in my life,—I read a novel by a woman which I did not at first entirely understand,—but on going over some of its passages a second time, all at once its horrible lasciviousness flashed upon me, and filled me with such genuine disgust that I flung it on the ground in a fit of loathing and contempt. Yet I had seen it praised in all the leading journals of the day; its obscenities were hinted at as 'daring,'—its vulgarities were quoted as 'brilliant wit,'—in fact so many laudatory columns were written about it in the press that I resolved to read it again. Encouraged by the 'literary censors' of the time, I did so, and little by little the insidious abomination of it filtered into my mind and *stayed there*. I began to think about it,—and by-and-by found pleasure in thinking about it. I sent for other books by the same tainted hand, and my appetite for that kind of prurient romance grew keener. At this particular juncture as chance or fate would have it, an acquaintance of mine, the daughter of a Marchioness, a girl with large black eyes, and those full protruding lips which remind one unconsciously of a swine's snout, brought me two or three odd volumes of the poems of Swinburne. Always devoted to poetry, and considering it to be the highest of the arts, and up to that period having been ignorant of this writer's work, I turned over the books with eagerness, expecting to enjoy the usual sublime emotions which it is the privilege and glory of the poet to inspire in mortals less divinely endowed than himself, and who turn to him

"for help to climb
Beyond the highest peaks of time."

Now I should like, if I could do so, to explain clearly the effect of this satyr-songster upon my mind,—for I believe there are many women to whom his works have been deadlier than the deadliest poison, and far more soul-corrupting than any book of Zola's or the most pernicious of modern French writers. At first I read the poems quickly, with a certain pleasure in the musical swing and jangle of rhythm, and without paying much attention to the subject-matter of the verse,—but presently, as though a lurid blaze of lightning had stripped a fair tree of its adorning leaves, my senses suddenly perceived the cruelty and sensuality concealed under the ornate language and persuasive rhymes,—and for a moment I paused in my reading, and closed my eyes, shuddering and sick at heart. Was human nature as base and abandoned as this man declared it to be? Was there no God but Lust? Were men and women lower and more depraved in their passions and appetites than the very beasts? I mused and dreamed,—I pored over the 'Laus Veneris'—'Faustine' and 'Anactoria,' till I felt myself being dragged down to the level of the mind that conceived such outrages to decency,—I drank in the poet's own fiendish contempt of God, and I read over and over again his verses 'Before a Crucifix' till I knew them by heart;—till they rang in my brain as persistently as any nursery jingle, and drove my thoughts into as haughty a scorn of Christ and His teachings, as any unbelieving Jew. It is nothing to me now,—now, when without hope, or faith or love, I am about to take the final plunge into eternal darkness and silence,—but for the sake of those who *have* the comfort of a religion I ask, why, in a so-called Christian country, is such a hideous blasphemy as 'Before a Crucifix' allowed to circulate among the people without so much as one reproof from those who elect themselves judges of literature? I have seen many noble writers condemned unheard,—many have been accused of blasphemy, whose works tend quite the other way,—but these lines are permitted to work their cruel mischief unchecked, and the writer of them is glorified as though he were a benefactor to mankind. I quote them here, from bitter memory, that I may not be deemed as exaggerating their nature—

> "So when our souls look back to thee,
> They sicken, seeing against thy side,
> Too foul to speak of or to see,
> The leprous likeness of a bride,
> Whose kissing lips through his lips grown
> Leave their God rotten to the bone.
>
> When we would see thee man, and know
> What heart thou had'st towards man indeed,
> Lo, thy blood-blackened altars; lo,
> The lips of priests that pray and feed,
> While their own hell's worm curls and licks
> The poison of the crucifix.
>
> Thou had'st the children come to thee,—
> What children now but curses come,
> What manhood in that God can be
> Who sees their worship and is dumb?—
> No soul that lived, loved, wrought, and died
> Is this, their Carrion Crucified!
>
> Nay, if their God and thou be one
> If thou and this thing be the same,

Thou should'st not look upon the sun,
The sun grows haggard at thy name!
Come down, be done with, cease, give o'er,
Hide thyself, strive not, be no more!"

From the time of reading this, I used to think of Christ as 'carrion crucified';—if I ever thought at all. I found out that no one had ever reproached Swinburne for this term,—that it did not interfere with his chances for the Laureateship,—and that not even a priest of the church had been bold-spoken or zealous enough in his Master's cause to publicly resent the shameless outrage. So I concluded that Swinburne must, after all, be right in his opinions, and I followed the lazy and unthinking course of social movement, spending my days with such literature as stored my brain with a complete knowledge of things evil and pernicious. Whatever soul I had in me was killed; the freshness of my mind was gone,—Swinburne, among others, had helped me to live mentally, if not physically, through such a phase of vice as had poisoned my thoughts for ever. I understand there is some vague law in existence about placing an interdiction on certain books considered injurious to public morals,—if there is such a rule, it has been curiously lax concerning the author of 'Anactoria'—who, by virtue of being a poet, passes unquestioned into many a home, carrying impure suggestion into minds that were once cleanly and simple. As for me, after I had studied his verse to my heart's content, nothing remained sacred,—I judged men as beasts and women as little better,—I had no belief in honour, virtue or truth,—and I was absolutely indifferent to all things save one, and that was my resolve to have my own way as far as love was concerned. I might be forced to marry without love for purely money-considerations,—but all the same, love I would have, or what I called love;—not an 'ideal' passion by any means, but precisely what Mr. Swinburne and a few of the most-praised novelists of the day had taught me to consider as love. I began to wonder when and how I should meet my lover,—such thoughts as I had at this time indeed would have made moralists stare and uplift their hands in horror,—but to the exterior world I was the very pink and pattern of maidenly decorum, reserve and pride. Men desired, but feared me; for I never gave them any encouragement, seeing as yet none among them whom I deemed worthy of such love as I could give. The majority resembled carefully trained baboons,—respectably clothed and artistically shaven,—but nevertheless all with the spasmodic grin, the leering eye and the uncouth gestures of the hairy woodland monster. When I was just eighteen I 'came out' in earnest—that is, I was presented at Court with all the foolish and farcical pomp practised on such occasions. I was told before going that it was a great and necessary thing to be 'presented,'—that it was a guarantee of position, and above all of reputation,—the Queen received none whose conduct was not rigidly correct and virtuous. What humbug it all was!—I laughed then, and I can smile now to think of it,—why, the very woman who presented me had two illegitimate sons, unknown to her lawful husband, and she was not the only playful sinner in the Court comedy! Some women were there that day whom since even *I* would not receive—so openly infamous are their lives and characters, yet they make their demure curtseys before the Throne at stated times, and assume to be the very patterns of virtue and austerity. Now and then, it chances in the case of an exceedingly beautiful woman, of whom all the others are jealous, that for her little slips she is selected as an 'example' and excluded from Court, while her plainer sisters, though sinning seventy times seven against all the laws of decency and morality, are still received,—but otherwise, there is very little real care exercised as to the character and prestige of the women whom the Queen receives. If any one of them *is* refused, it is certain she adds to her social enormities, the greater crime of being beautiful, otherwise there would be no one to whisper away her reputation! I was what is called a 'success' on my presentation day. That is, I was stared at, and openly flattered by certain members of my sex who were too old and ugly to be jealous, and treated with insolent contempt by those who were young enough to be my rivals. There was a great crush to get into the Throne-Room; and some of the ladies used rather strong language. One duchess, just in front of me, said to her companion—'Do as I do,—*kick out*! Bruise their shins for them— as hard as you can,—we shall get on faster then!' This choice remark was accompanied by the grin of a fishwife and the stare of a drab. Yet it was a 'great' lady who spoke,—not a Transatlantic importation, but a woman of distinguished lineage and connection. Her observation however was only one out of many similar speeches which I heard on all sides of me during the 'distinguished' mélée,—a thoroughly ill-mannered 'crush,' which struck me as supremely vulgar and totally unfitting the dignity of our Sovereign's court. When I curtsied before the Throne at last, and saw the majesty of the Empire represented by a kindly faced old lady, looking very tired and bored, whose hand was as cold as ice when I kissed it, I was conscious of an intense feeling of pity for her in her high estate. Who would be a Monarch, to be doomed to the perpetual receiving of a company of fools! I got through my duties quickly, and returned home more or less wearied out and disgusted with the whole ceremony,—and next day I found that my 'debût' had given me the position of a 'leading beauty'; or in other words that I was now formally put up for sale. That is really what is meant by being 'presented' and 'coming out,'—these are the fancy terms of one's parental auctioneer. My life was now passed in dressing, having my photograph taken, giving 'sittings' to aspiring fashionable painters, and being 'inspected' by men with a view to matrimony. It was distinctly understood in society that I was not to be sold under a certain figure per annum,—and the price was too high for most would-be purchasers. How sick I grew of my constant exhibition in the marriage-market! What contempt and hatred was fostered in me for the mean and pitiable hypocrisies of my set! I was not long in discovering that money was the chief-motive power of all social success,—that the proudest and highest personages in the world could be easily gathered together under the roof of any vulgar plebeian who happened to have enough cash to feed and entertain them. As an example of this, I remember a woman, ugly, passée and squint-eyed, who during her father's life was only allowed about half-a-crown a week as pocket-money up to her fortieth year,—and who, when that father died, leaving her in possession of half his fortune, (the other half going to illegitimate children of whom she had never heard, he having always posed as a pattern of immaculate virtue) suddenly blossomed out as a 'leader' of fashion, and succeeded, through cautious scheming and ungrudging toadyism, in assembling some of the highest people in the land under her roof.

Ugly and passée though she was, and verging towards fifty, with neither grace, wit, nor intelligence, through the power of her cash alone she invited Royal dukes and 'titles' generally to her dinners and dances,—and it is to their shame that they actually accepted her invitations. Such voluntary degradations on the part of really well-connected people I have never been able to understand,—it is not as if they were actually in want of food or amusement, for they have a surfeit of both every season,—and it seems to me that they ought to show a better example than to flock in crowds to the entertainments of a mere uninteresting and ugly nobody just because she happens to have money. I never entered her house myself though she had the audacity to invite me,—I learned moreover, that she had promised a friend of mine a hundred guineas if she could persuade me to make one appearance in her rooms. For my renown as a 'beauty' combined with my pride and exclusiveness, would have given her parties a *prestige* greater than even Royalty could bestow,—*she* knew that and *I* knew that,—and knowing it, never condescended to so much as notice her by a bow. But though I took a certain satisfaction in thus revenging myself on the atrocious vulgarity of *parvenus* and social interlopers, I grew intensely weary of the monotony and emptiness of what fashionable folks call 'amusement,' and presently falling ill of a nervous fever, I was sent down to the seaside for a few weeks' change of air with a young cousin of mine, a girl I rather liked because she was so different to myself. Her name was Eva Maitland—she was but sixteen and extremely delicate—poor little soul! she died two months before my marriage. She and I, and a maid to attend us, went down to Cromer,—and one day, sitting on the cliffs together, she asked me timidly if I knew an author named Mavis Clare? I told her no,—whereupon she handed me a book called 'The Wings of Psyche.'

"Do read it!" she said earnestly—"It will make you feel so happy!"

I laughed. The idea of a modern author writing anything to make one feel happy, seemed to me quite ludicrous, the aim of most of them being to awaken a disgust of life, and a hatred of one's fellow-creatures. However, to please Eva, I read the 'Wings of Psyche,'—and if it did not make me actually happy, it moved me to a great wonder and deep reverence for the woman-writer of such a book. I found out all about her,—that she was young, good-looking, of a noble character and unblemished reputation, and that her only enemies were the press-critics. This last point was so much in her favour with me that I at once bought everything she had ever written, and her works became, as it were, my haven of rest. Her theories of life are strange, poetic, ideal and beautiful;—though I have not been able to accept them or work them out in my own case, I have always felt soothed and comforted for a while in the very act of wishing they were true. And the woman is like her books,—strange, poetic, ideal and beautiful,—how odd it is to think that she is within ten minutes walk of me now!—I could send for her if I liked, and tell her all,—but she would prevent me carrying out my resolve. She would cling to me woman-like and kiss me, and hold my hands and say 'No, Sibyl, no! You are not yourself,—you must come to me and rest!' An odd fancy has seized me, . . . I will open my window and call her very gently,—she might be in the garden coming here to see me,—and if she hears and answers, who knows!—why, perhaps my ideas may change, and fate itself may take a different course!

Well, I have called her. I have sent her name 'Mavis!' softly out on the sunshine and still air three times, and only a little brown namesake of hers, a thrush, swinging on a branch of fir, answered me with his low autumnal piping. Mavis! She will not come,— to-day God will not make her His messenger. She cannot guess—she does not know this tragedy of my heart, greater and more poignant than all the tragedies of fiction. If she did know me as I am, I wonder what she would think of me!

Let me go back to the time when love came to me,—love, ardent, passionate, and eternal! Ah, what wild joy thrilled through me! what mad ecstasy fired my blood!—what delirious dreams possessed my brain!—I saw Lucio,—and it seemed as if the splendid eyes of some great angel had flashed a glory in my soul! With him came his friend, the foil to his beauty,—the arrogant, self-satisfied fool of a millionaire, Geoffrey Tempest,—he who bought me, and who by virtue of his purchase, is entitled by law to call himself my husband. . ."

Here I paused in my reading and looked up. The dead woman's eyes appeared now to regard me as steadily as herself in the opposite mirror,—the head was a little more dropped forward on the breast, and the whole face very nearly resembled that of the late Countess of Elton when the last shock of paralysis had rendered her hideous disfigurement complete.

"To think I loved *that*!" I said aloud, pointing at the corpse's ghastly reflection—"Fool that I was indeed!—as great a fool as all men are who barter their lives for the possession of a woman's mere body! Why if there were any life after death,—if such a creature had a soul that at all resembled this poisoned clay, the very devils might turn away aghast from such a loathly comrade!"

The candles flickered and the dead face seemed to smile,—a clock chimed in the adjoining room, but I did not count the hour,—I merely arranged the manuscript pages I held more methodically, and read on with renewed attention.

XXXVI

"From the moment I saw Lucio Rimânez"—went on Sibyl's 'dying speech'—"I abandoned myself to love and the desire of love. I had heard of him before from my father who had (as I learned to my shame) been indebted to him for monetary assistance. On the very night we met, my father told me quite plainly that now was my chance to get 'settled' in life. 'Marry Rimânez or Tempest, whichever you can most easily catch,' he said—'The prince is fabulously wealthy—but he keeps up a mystery about himself and no one knows where he actually comes from,—besides which he dislikes women;—now Tempest has five millions and seems an easy-going fool,—I should say you had better go for Tempest.' I made no answer and gave no promise either way. I soon found out however that Lucio did not intend to marry,—and I concluded that he preferred to be the lover of many women, instead of the husband of one. I did not love him any the less for this,—I only resolved that I would at least be one of those who were happy enough to share his passion. I married the man Tempest, feeling that like many women I knew, I should when safely wedded, have greater liberty of action,—I was aware that most modern men prefer an amour with a married woman to any other kind of *liaison*,—and I thought Lucio would have readily yielded to the plan I had pre-conceived. But I was mistaken,—and out of this mistake comes all my perplexity, pain and bewilderment I cannot understand why my love,—beloved beyond all word or thought,—should scorn me and repulse me with such bitter loathing! It is such a common thing now-a-days for a married woman to have her own lover, apart from her husband *de convenance*! The writers of books advise it,—I have seen the custom not only excused but advocated over and over again in long and scientific articles that are openly published in leading magazines. Why then should I be blamed or my desires considered criminal? As long as no public scandal is made, what harm is done? I cannot see it,—it is not as if there were a God to care,—the scientists say there is no God!

I was very startled just now. I thought I heard Lucio's voice calling me. I have walked through the rooms looking everywhere, and I opened my door to listen, but there is no one. I am alone. I have told the servant not to disturb me till I ring; . . . I shall never ring! Now I come to think of it, it is singular that I have never known who Lucio really is. A prince, he says—and that I can well believe,—though truly princes now-a-days are so plebeian and common in look and bearing that he seems too great to belong to so shabby a fraternity. From what kingdom does he come?—to what nation does he belong? These are questions which he never answers save equivocally.

I pause here, and look at myself in the mirror. How beautiful I am! I note with admiration the deep and dewy lustre of my eyes and their dark silky fringes,—I see the delicate colouring of my cheeks and lips,—the dear rounded chin with its pretty dimple,— the pure lines of my slim throat and snowy neck,—the glistening wealth of my long hair. All this was given to me for the attraction and luring of men, but my love, whom I love with all this living, breathing, exquisite being of mine, can see no beauty in me, and rejects me with such scorn as pierces my very soul. I have knelt to him,—I have prayed to him,—I have worshipped him,—in vain! Hence it comes that I must die. Only one thing he said that had the sound of hope, though the utterance was fierce, and his looks were cruel,—'Patience!' he whispered—'we shall meet ere long!' What did he mean?—what possible meeting can there be now, when death must close the gate of life, and even love would come too late!

I have unlocked my jewel-case and taken from it the deadly thing secreted there,—a poison that was entrusted to me by one of the physicians who lately attended my mother. 'Keep this under lock and key,' he said, 'and be sure that it is used only for external purposes. There is sufficient in this flask to kill ten men, if swallowed by mistake.' I look at it wonderingly. It is colourless,—and there is not enough to fill a teaspoon, . . . yet. . . it will bring down upon me an eternal darkness, and close up for ever the marvellous scenes of the universe! So little!—to do so much! I have fastened Lucio's wedding-gift round my waist,—the beautiful snake of jewels that clings to me as though it were charged with an embrace from him,—ah! would I could cheat myself into so pleasing a fancy! . . . I am trembling, but not with cold or fear,—it is simply an excitation of the nerves,—an instinctive recoil of flesh and blood at the near prospect of death. . . How brilliantly the sun shines through my window!—its callous golden stare has watched so many tortured creatures die without so much as a cloud to dim its radiance by way of the suggestion of pity! If there were a God I fancy He would be like the sun,—glorious, changeless, unapproachable, beautiful, but pitiless!

Out of all the various types of human beings I think I hate the class called poets most. I used to love them and believe in them; but I know them now to be mere weavers of lies,—builders of cloud castles in which no throbbing life can breathe, no weary heart find rest. Love is their chief motive,—they either idealize or degrade it,—and of the love we women long for most, they have no conception. They can only sing of brute passion or ethical impossibilities,—of the mutual great sympathy, the ungrudging patient tenderness that should make love lovely, they have no sweet things to say. Between their strained æstheticism and unbridled sensualism, my spirit has been stretched on the rack and broken on the wheel, . . . I should think many a wretched woman wrecked among love's disillusions must curse them as I do!

I am ready now, I think. There is nothing more to say. I offer no excuses for myself. I am as I was made,—a proud and rebellious woman, self-willed and sensual, seeing no fault in free love, and no crime in conjugal infidelity;—and if I am vicious, I can honestly declare that my vices have been encouraged and fostered in me by most of the literary teachers of my time. I married, as most women of my set marry, merely for money,—I loved, as most women of my set love, for mere bodily attraction,—I die, as most women of my set will die, either naturally or self-slain, in utter atheism, rejoicing that there is no God and no Hereafter!

I had the poison in my hand a moment ago, ready to take, when I suddenly felt someone approaching me stealthily from behind, and glancing up quickly at the mirror I saw. . . my mother! Her face, hideous and ghastly as it had been in her last illness, was reflected in the glass, peering over my shoulder! I sprang up and confronted her,—she was gone! And now I am shivering with cold, and I feel a chill dampness on my forehead,—mechanically I have soaked a handkerchief with perfume from one of the silver bottles on the dressing table, and have passed it across my temples to help me recover from this sick swooning sensation. To *recover*!—how foolish of me, seeing I am about to die. I do not believe in ghosts,—yet I could have sworn my mother was actually present just now,—of course it was an optical delusion of my own feverish brain. The strong scent on my handkerchief reminds me of Paris—I can see the shop where I bought this particular perfume, and the well-dressed doll of a man who served me, with his little waxed moustache, and his indefinable French manner of conveying a speechless personal compliment while making out a bill. . . Laughing at this recollection, I see my face radiate in the glass,—my eyes flash into vivid lustre, and the dimples near my lips come and go, giving my expression an enchanting sweetness. Yet in a few hours this loveliness will be destroyed,—and in a few days, the worms will twine where the smile is now!

An idea has come upon me that perhaps I ought to say a prayer. It would be hypocritical,—but conventional. To die fashionably, one ought to concede a few words to the church. And yet. . . to kneel down with clasped hands and tell an inactive, unsympathetic, selfish, paid community called the church, that I am going to kill myself for the sake of love and love's despair, and that therefore I humbly implore its forgiveness for the act seems absurd,—as absurd as to tell the same thing to a non-existent Deity. I suppose the scientists do not think what a strange predicament their advanced theories put the human mind in at the hour of death. They forget that on the brink of the grave, thoughts come that will not be gainsaid, and that cannot be appeased by a learned thesis. . . However I will not pray,—it would seem to myself cowardly that I who have never said my prayers since I was a child, should run over them now in a foolish babbling attempt to satisfy the powers invisible,—I could not, out of sheer association, appeal to Mr. Swinburne's 'crucified carrion'! Besides I do not believe in the powers invisible at all,—I feel that once outside this life, 'the rest' as Hamlet said 'is silence.'

I have been staring dreamily and in a sort of stupefaction at the little poison-flask in my hand. *It is quite empty now.* I have swallowed every drop of the liquid it contained,—I took it quickly and determinately as one takes nauseous medicine, without allowing myself another moment of time for thought or hesitation. It tasted acrid and burning on my tongue,—but at present I am not conscious of any strange or painful result. I shall watch my face in the mirror and trace the oncoming of death,— this will be at any rate a new sensation not without interest!

My mother is here,—here with me in this room! She is moving about restlessly, making wild gestures with her hands and trying to speak. She looks as she did when she was dying,—only more alive, more sentient. I have followed her up and down, but am unable to touch her,—she eludes my grasp. I have called her 'Mother! Mother!' but no sound issues from her white lips. Her face is so appalling that I was seized with a convulsion of terror a moment ago and fell on my knees before her imploring her to leave me,—and then she paused in her gliding to and fro and—smiled! What a hideous smile it was! I think I lost consciousness, . . . for I found myself lying on the ground. A sharp and terrible pain running through me made me spring to my feet, . . . and I bit my lips till they bled, lest I should scream aloud with the agony I suffered and so alarm the house. When the paroxysm passed I saw my mother standing quite near to me, dumbly watching me with a strange expression of wonder and remorse. I tottered past her and back to this chair where I now sit,—I am calmer now, and I am able to realize that she is only the phantom of my own brain—that I *fancy* she is here while *knowing* she is dead.

Torture indescribable has made of me a writhing, moaning, helpless creature for the past few minutes. Truly that drug was deadly;—the pain is horrible. . . horrible! . . . it has left me quivering in every limb and palpitating in every nerve. Looking at my face in the glass I see that it has already altered. It is drawn and livid,—all the fresh rose-tint of my lips has gone,—my eyes protrude unnaturally, . . . there are dull blue marks at the corners of my mouth and in the hollows of my temples, and I observe a curious quick pulsation in the veins of my throat. Be my torment what it will, now there is no remedy,—and I am resolved to sit here and study my own features to the end. 'The reaper whose name is Death' must surely be near, ready to gather my long hair in his skeleton hand like a sheaf of ripe corn, . . . my poor beautiful hair!—how I have loved its glistening ripples, and brushed it, and twined it round my fingers, . . . and how soon it will lie like a dank weed in the mould!

A devouring fire is in my brain and body,—I am burning with heat and parched with thirst,—I have drunk deep draughts of cold water, but this has not relieved me. The sun glares in upon me like an open furnace,—I have tried to rise and close the blind against it, but find I have no force to stand upright. The strong radiance blinds me:—the silver toilet boxes on my table glitter like so many points of swords. It is by a powerful effort of will that I am able to continue writing,—my head is swimming round,—and there is a choking sensation in my throat.

A moment since I thought I was dying. Torn asunder as it were by the most torturing pangs, I could have screamed for help,—and would have done so, had voice been left me. But I cannot speak above a whisper,—I mutter my own name to myself 'Sibyl! Sibyl!' and can scarcely hear it. My mother stands beside me,—apparently waiting;—a little while ago I thought I heard her say 'Come, Sibyl! Come to your chosen lover!' Now I am conscious of a great silence everywhere,—a numbness has fallen upon me, and a delicious respite from pain,—but I see my face in the glass and know it is the face of the dead. It will soon be all over,—a few more uneasy breathings,—and I shall be at rest. I am glad,—for the world and I were never good friends;—I am sure that if we could know, before we were born, what life really is, we should never take the trouble to live!

A horrible fear has suddenly beset me. What if death were not what the scientists deem it,—suppose it were another form of life?

Can it be that I am losing reason and courage together? . . . or what is this terrible misgiving that is taking possession of me? . . . I begin to falter. . . a strange sense of horror is creeping over me. . . I have no more physical pain, but something worse than pain oppresses me. . . a feeling that I cannot define. I am dying. . . dying!—I repeat this to myself for comfort, . . . in a little while I shall be deaf and blind and unconscious, . . . why then is the silence around me now broken through by sound? I listen,—and I hear distinctly the clamour of wild voices mingled with a sullen jar and roll as of distant thunder! . . . My mother stands closer to me, . . . she is stretching out her hand to touch mine!

Oh God! . . . Let me write—write—while I can! Let me yet hold fast the thread which fastens me to earth,—give me time— time before I drift out, lost in yonder blackness and flame! Let me write for others the awful Truth, as I see it,—there is No death! None—none!—*I cannot die.* I am passing out of my body,—I am being wrenched away from it inch by inch in inexplicable mystic torture,—but I am not dying,—I am being carried forward into a new life, vague and vast! . . . I see a new world full of dark forms, half shaped yet shapeless!—they float towards me, beckoning me on. I am actively conscious—I hear, I think, I know! Death is a mere human dream,—a comforting fancy; it has no real existence,—there is nothing in the Universe but life! O hideous misery!—*I cannot die!* In my mortal body I can scarcely breathe,—the pen I try to hold writes of itself rather than through my shaking hand,—but these pangs are the throes of birth—not death! . . . I hold back,—with all the force of my soul I strive not to plunge into that black abyss I see before me— but—*my mother drags me with her,*—I cannot shake her off! I hear her voice now;—she speaks distinctly, and laughs as though she wept; 'Come Sibyl! Soul of the child I bore, come and meet your lover! Come and see upon WHOM you fixed your faith! Soul of the woman I trained, return to that from whence you came!' Still I hold back,—nude and trembling I stare into a dark void— and now there are wings about me,—wings of fiery scarlet!— they fill the space,—they enfold me,—they propel me,—they rush past and whirl around me, stinging me as with flying arrows and showers of hail!

Let me write on,—write on, with this dead fleshly hand, . . . one moment more time, dread God! . . . one moment more to write the truth,—the terrible truth of Death whose darkest secret, Life, is unknown to men! I live!—a new, strong, impetuous vitality possesses me, though my mortal body is nearly dead. Faint gasps and weak shudderings affect it still,—and I, outside it and no longer of it, propel its perishing hand to write these final words—*I live!* To my despair and horror,—to my remorse and agony, I live!—oh the unspeakable misery of this new life! And worst of all,—God whom I doubted, God whom I was taught to deny, this wronged, blasphemed, and outraged God Exists! And I could have found Him had I chosen,—this knowledge is forced upon me as I am torn from hence,—it is shouted at me by a thousand wailing voices! . . . too late!—too late!—the scarlet wings beat me downward,—these strange half-shapeless forms close round and drive me onward. . . to a further darkness, . . . amid wind and fire!

Serve me, dead hand, once more ere I depart, . . . my tortured spirit must seize and compel you to write down this thing unnameable, that earthly eyes may read, and earthly souls take timely warning! . . . I know at last Whom I have loved!—whom I have chosen, whom I have worshipped! . . . Oh God, have mercy! . . . I know Who claims my worship now, and drags me into yonder rolling world of flame! . . . his name is. . ."

Here the manuscript ended,—incomplete and broken off abruptly,—and there was a blot on the last sentence as though the pen had been violently wrenched from the dying fingers and hastily flung down.

The clock in the west room again chimed the hour. I rose stiffly from my chair, trembling,—my self-possession was giving way, and I began to feel at last unnerved. I looked askance at my dead wife,—she, who with a superhuman dying effort had declared herself to be yet alive,—who, in some imaginable strange way had seemingly written *after* death, in a frantic desire to make some appalling declaration which nevertheless remained undeclared. The rigid figure of the corpse had now real terrors for me,—I dared not touch it,—I scarcely dared look at it, . . . in some dim inscrutable fashion I felt as if "scarlet wings" environed it, beating me down, yet pressing me on,—me too, in my turn! With the manuscript gathered close in my hand, I bent nervously forward to blow out the wax lights on the toilet table, . . . I saw on the floor the handkerchief odorous with the French perfume the dead woman had written of,—I picked it up and placed it near her where she sat, grinning hideously at her own mirrored ghastliness. The flash of the jewelled serpent round her waist caught my eyes anew as I did this, and I stared for a moment at its green glitter, dumbly fascinated,—then, moving stealthily, with the cold sweat pouring down my back and every pulse in me rendered feeble by sheer horror, I turned to leave the room. As I reached the portiére and lifted it, some instinct made me look back at the dread picture of the leading "society" beauty sitting stark and livid pale before her own stark and livid-pale image in the glass,—what a "fashion-plate" she would make now, I thought, for a frivolous and hypocritical "ladies' paper!"

"You say you are not dead, Sibyl!" I muttered aloud—"Not dead, but living! Then, if you are alive, where are you, Sibyl?—where are you?"

The heavy silence seemed fraught with fearful meaning,—the light of the electric lamps on the corpse and on the shimmering silk garment wrapped round it appeared unearthly,—and the perfume in the room had a grave-like earthy smell. A panic seized me, and dragging frantically at the portiére till all its velvet folds were drawn thickly together, I made haste to shut out from my sight the horrible figure of the woman whose bodily fairness I had loved in the customary way of sensual men,—and left her without so much as a pardoning or pitying kiss of farewell on the cold brow. For, . . . after all I had Myself to think of, . . . and She was dead!

XXXVII

I pass over all the details of polite "shock," affected sorrow, and feigned sympathy of society at my wife's sudden death. No one was really grieved about it,—men raised their eyebrows, shrugged their shoulders, lit extra cigarettes and dismissed the subject as too unpleasant and depressing to dwell upon,—women were glad of the removal of a too beautiful and too much admired rival, and the majority of fashionable folk delighted in having something "thrilling" to talk about in the tragic circumstances of her end. As a rule, people are seldom or never unselfish enough to be honestly sorry for the evanishment of some leading or brilliant figure from their midst,—the vacancy leaves room for the pushing in of smaller fry. Be sure that if you are unhappily celebrated for either beauty, wit, intellect, or all three together, half society wishes you dead already, and the other half tries to make you as wretched as possible while you are alive. To be missed at all when you die, some one must love you very deeply and unselfishly; and deep unselfish love is rarer to find among mortals than a pearl in a dust-bin.

Thanks to my abundance of cash, everything concerning Sibyl's suicide was admirably managed. In consideration of her social position as an Earl's daughter, two doctors certified (on my paying them very handsome fees) that hers was a 'death by misadventure,'—namely, through taking an accidental overdose of a powerful sleeping draught. It was the best report to make,—and the most respectable. It gave the penny press an opportunity of moralizing on the dangers that lurked in sleeping draughts generally,—and Tom, Dick, and Harry all wrote letters to their favorite periodicals (signing their names in full) giving *their* opinions as to the nature of sleeping draughts, so that for a week at least the ordinary dullness of the newspapers was quite enlivened by ungrammatical *gratis* 'copy.' The conventionalities of law, decency and order were throughout scrupulously observed and complied with,—everybody was paid (which was the chief thing), and everybody was, I believe, satisfied with what they managed to make out of the death-payment. The funeral gave joy to the souls of all undertakers,—it was so expensive and impressive. The florist's trade gained something of an impetus by the innumerable orders received for wreaths and crosses made of the costliest flowers. When the coffin was carried to the grave, it could not be seen for the load of blossoms that covered it. And amid all the cards and 'loving tokens' and 'farewell dearests' and 'not-lost-but-gone-befores'—that ticketed the white masses of lilies, gardenias and roses which were supposed to symbolize the innocence and sweetness of the poisoned corpse they were sent to adorn, there was not one honest regret,—not one unfeigned expression of true sorrow. Lord Elton made a sufficiently striking figure of dignified parental woe, but on the whole I think he was not sorry for his daughter's death, since the only opposing obstacle to his marriage with Diana Chesney was now removed. I fancy Diana herself was sorry, so far as such a frivolous little American could be sorry for anything,—perhaps, however it would be more correct to say that she was frightened. Sibyl's sudden end startled and troubled her,—but I am not sure that it grieved her. There is such a difference between unselfish grief, and the mere sense of nervous personal shock! Miss Charlotte Fitzroy took the news of her niece's death with that admirable fortitude which frequently characterizes religious spinsters of a certain age. She put by her knitting,—said 'God's will be done!' and sent for her favorite clergyman. He came, stayed with her some hours drinking strong tea,—and the next morning at church administered to her communion. This done, Miss Fitzroy went on the blameless and even tenor of her way, wearing the same virtuously distressed expression as usual, and showed no further sign of feeling. I, as the afflicted millionaire-husband, was no doubt the most interesting figure on the scene; I was, I know very well got up, thanks to my tailor, and to the affectionate care of the chief undertaker who handed me my black gloves on the day of the funeral with servile solicitude, but in my heart I felt myself to be a far better actor than Henry Irving, and if only for my admirable mimicry of heart-break, more fully worthy of the accolade. Lucio did not attend the obsequies,—he wrote me a brief note of sympathy from town, and hinted that he was sure I could understand his reasons for not being present. I did understand, of course,—and appreciated his respect, as I thought, for me and my feelings,—yet strange and incongruous as it may seem, I never longed so much for his company as I did then! However,—we had a glorious burial of my fair and false lady,—prancing horses drew coroneted carriages in a long defile down the pretty Warwickshire lanes to the grey old church, picturesque and peaceful, where the clergyman and his assistants in newly-washed surplices, met the flower-laden coffin, and with the usual conventional mumblings, consigned it to the dust. There were even press-reporters present, who not only described the scene as it did *not* happen, but who also sent fancy sketches, to their respective journals, of the church as it did *not* exist. I mention this simply to show how thoroughly all "proper forms" were carried out and conceded to. After the ceremony all we "mourners" went back to Willowsmere to luncheon, and I well remember that Lord Elton told me a new and *risqué* joke over a glass of port before the meal was finished. The undertakers had a sort of festive banquet in the servants' hall,—and taking everything into due consideration, my wife's death gave a great deal of pleasure to many people, and put useful money into several ready pockets. She had left no blank in society that could not be easily filled up,—she was merely one butterfly out of thousands, more daintily coloured perhaps and more restless in flight,—but never judged as more than up to the butterfly standard. I said no one gave her an honest regret, but I was wrong. Mavis Clare was genuinely, almost passionately grieved. She sent no flowers for the coffin, but she came to the funeral by herself, and stood a little apart waiting silently till the grave was covered in,—and then, just as the "fashionable" train of mourners were leaving the churchyard, she advanced and placed a white cross of her own garden-lilies upon the newly-turned brown mould. I noticed her action, and determined that before I left Willowsmere for the East with Lucio (for my journey had only been postponed a week or two on account of Sibyl's death) she should know all.

The day came when I carried out this resolve. It was a rainy and chill afternoon, and I found Mavis in her study, sitting beside a bright log fire with her small terrier in her lap and her faithful St Bernard stretched at her feet. She was absorbed in a book,—and over her watched the marble Pallas inflexible and austere. As I entered she rose, and putting down the volume and her pet dog together, she advanced to meet me with an intense sympathy in her clear eyes, and a wordless pity in the tremulous lines of her sweet mouth. It was charming to see how sorry she felt for me,—and it was odd that I could not feel sorry for myself. After a few words of embarrassed greeting I sat down and watched her silently, while she arranged the logs in the fire to make them burn brighter, and for the moment avoided my gaze.

"I suppose you know,"—I began with harsh abruptness—"that the sleeping-draught story is a polite fiction? You know that my wife poisoned herself intentionally?"

Mavis looked at me with a troubled and compassionate expression.

"I feared it was so—" . . . she began nervously.

"Oh there is nothing either to fear or to hope"—I said with some violence—"*She did it.* And can you guess why she did it? Because she was mad with her own wickedness and sensuality,—because she loved with a guilty love, my friend Lucio Rimânez."

Mavis gave a little cry as of pain, and sat down white and trembling.

"You can read quickly, I am sure,"—I went on. "Part of the profession of literature is the ability to skim books and manuscripts rapidly, and grasp the whole gist of them in a few minutes;—read *this*—" and I handed her the rolled-up pages of Sibyl's dying declaration—"Let me stay here, while you learn from that what sort of a woman she was, and judge whether, despite her beauty, she is worth a regret!"

"Pardon me,—" said Mavis gently—"I would rather not read what was not meant for my eyes."

"But it *is* meant for your eyes,"—I retorted impatiently—"It is meant for everybody's eyes apparently,—it is addressed to nobody in particular. There is a mention of you in it. I beg—nay I command you to read it!— I want your opinion on it,—your advice; you may possibly suggest, after perusal, the proper sort of epitaph I ought to inscribe on the monument I am going to build to her sacred and dear memory!"

I covered my face with one hand to hide the bitter smile which I knew betrayed my thoughts, and pushed the manuscript towards her. Very reluctantly she took it,—and slowly unrolling it, began to read. For several minutes there was a silence, broken only by the crackling of the logs on the fire, and the regular breathing of the dogs who now both lay stretched comfortably in front of the wood blaze. I looked covertly at the woman whose fame I had envied,—at the slight figure, the coronal of soft hair,—the delicate, drooping sensitive face,—the small white classic hand that held the written sheets of paper so firmly, yet so tenderly,—the very hand of the Greek marble Psyche;—and I thought what short-sighted asses some literary men are who suppose they can succeed in shutting out women like Mavis Clare from winning everything that fame or fortune can offer. Such a head as hers, albeit covered with locks fair and caressable, was not meant, in its fine shape and compactness, for submission to inferior intelligences whether masculine or feminine,—that determined little chin which the firelight delicately outlined, was a visible declaration of the strength of will and the indomitably high ambition of its owner,—and yet, . . . the soft eyes,—the tender mouth,—did not these suggest the sweetest love, the purest passion that ever found place in a woman's heart? I lost myself in dreamy musing,—I thought of many things that had little to do with either my own past or present. I realized that now and then at rare intervals God makes a woman of genius with a thinker's brain and an angel's soul,—and that such an one is bound to be a destiny to all mortals less divinely endowed, and a glory to the world in which she dwells. So considering, I studied Mavis Clare's face and form,—I saw her eyes fill with tears as she read on;—why should she weep, I wondered, over that 'last document' which had left me unmoved and callous? I was startled almost as if from sleep when her voice, thrilling with pain, disturbed the stillness,—she sprang up, gazing at me as if she saw some horrible vision.

"Oh, are you so blind," she cried, "as not to see what this means? Can you not understand? Do you not know your worst enemy?"

"My worst enemy?" I echoed amazed—"You surprise me, Mavis,— what have I, or my enemies or friends to do with my wife's last confession? She raved,—between poison and passion, she could not tell, as you see by her final words, whether she was dead or alive,—and her writing at all under such stress of circumstances was a phenomenal effort,—but it has nothing to do with me personally."

"For God's sake do not be so hard-hearted!"—said Mavis passionately—"To me these last words of Sibyl's,—poor, tortured, miserable girl!—are beyond all expression horrible and appalling. Do you mean to tell me you have no belief in a future life?"

"None." I answered with conviction.

"Then this is nothing to you?—this solemn assurance of hers that she is not dead, but living again,—living too, in indescribable misery!—you do not believe it?"

"Does anyone believe the ravings of the dying!" I answered—"She was, as I have said, suffering the torments of poison and passion,—and in those torments wrote as one tormented. . ."

"Is it impossible to convince you of the truth?" asked Mavis solemnly,—"Are you so diseased in your spiritual perceptions as not to *know*, beyond a doubt, that this world is but the shadow of the Other Worlds awaiting us? I assure you, as I live, you will have that terrible knowledge forced upon you some day! I am aware of your theories,— your wife had the same beliefs or rather non-beliefs as yourself,—yet *she* has been convinced at last! I shall not attempt to argue with you. If this last letter of the unhappy girl you wedded cannot open your eyes to the eternal facts you choose to ignore, nothing will ever help you. You are in the power of your enemy!"

"Of whom are you speaking, Mavis?" I asked astonished, observing that she stood like one suddenly appalled in a dream, her eyes fixed musingly on vacancy, and her lips trembling apart.

"Your Enemy—your Enemy!" she repeated with energy—"It seems to me as if his Shadow stood near you now! Listen to this voice from the dead—Sibyl's voice!—what does she say?—'*Oh God, have mercy!—I know who claims my worship now and drags me into yonder rolling world of flame. . . his name is—*'" . . .

"Well!" I interrupted eagerly—"She breaks off there; his name is—"

"Lucio Rimânez!" said Mavis in a thrilling tone—"I do not know from whence he came,—but I take God to witness my belief that he is a worker of evil,—a fiend in beautiful human shape,—a destroyer and a corrupter! The curse of him fell on Sibyl the moment she met him,—the same curse rests on you! Leave him if you are wise,—take your chance of escape while it remains to you,—and never let him see your face again!"

She spoke with a kind of breathless haste as though impelled by a force not her own,—I stared at her amazed, and in a manner irritated.

"Such a course of action would be impossible to me, Mavis,"—I said somewhat coldly—"The Prince Rimânez is my best friend—no man ever had a better;—and his loyalty to me has been put to a severe test under which most men would have failed. I have not told you all."

And I related in a few words the scene I had witnessed between my wife and Lucio in the music-gallery at Willowsmere. She listened,—but with an evident effort,—and pushing back her clustering hair from her brows she sighed heavily.

"I am sorry,—but it does not alter my conviction!"—she said—"I look upon your best friend as your worst foe. And I feel you do not realize the awful calamity of your wife's death in its true aspect. Will you forgive me if I ask you to leave me now?—Lady Sibyl's letter has affected me terribly—I feel I cannot speak about it any more. . . I wish I had not read it. . ."

She broke off with a little half-suppressed sob,—I saw she was unnerved, and taking the manuscript from her hand, I said half-banteringly—

"You cannot then suggest an epitaph for my wife's monument?"

She turned upon me with a grand gesture of reproach.

"Yes I can!"—she replied in a low indignant voice—"Inscribe it as— 'From a pitiless hand to a broken heart!' That will suit the dead girl,— and you, the living man!"

Her rustling gown swept across my feet,—she passed me and was gone. Stupefied by her sudden anger, and equally sudden departure, I stood inert,—the St Bernard rose from the hearth-rug and glowered at me suspiciously, evidently wishing me to take my leave,—Pallas Athene stared, as usual, through me and beyond me in a boundless scorn,—all the various objects in this quiet study seemed silently to eject me as an undesired occupant. I looked round it once longingly as a tired outcast may look on a peaceful garden and wish in vain to enter.

"How like her sex she is after all!" I said half aloud—"She blames *me* for being pitiless,—and forgets that Sibyl was the sinner,—not I! No matter how guilty a woman may be, she generally manages to secure a certain amount of sympathy,—a man is always left out in the cold."

A shuddering sense of loneliness oppressed me as my eyes wandered round the restful room. The odour of lilies was in the air, exhaled, so I fancied, from the delicate and dainty personality of Mavis herself.

"If I had only known her first,—and loved her!" I murmured, as I turned away at last and left the house.

But then I remembered I had hated her before I ever met her,—and not only had I hated her, but I had vilified and misrepresented her work with a scurrilous pen under the shield of anonymity, and out of sheer malice,—thus giving her in the public sight, the greatest proof of her own genius a gifted woman can ever win,—man's envy!

XXXVIII

Two weeks later I stood on the deck of Lucio's yacht 'The Flame,'—a vessel whose complete magnificence filled me, as well as all other beholders, with bewildered wonderment and admiration. She was a miracle of speed, her motive power being electricity; and the electric engines with which she was fitted were so complex and remarkable as to baffle all would-be inquirers into the secret of their mechanism and potency. A large crowd of spectators gathered to see her as she lay off Southampton, attracted by the beauty of her shape and appearance,—some bolder spirits even came out in tugs and row-boats, hoping to be allowed to make a visit of inspection on board, but the sailors, powerfully-built men of a foreign and somewhat unpleasing type, soon intimated that the company of such inquisitive persons was undesirable and unwelcome. With white sails spread, and a crimson flag flying from her mast, she weighed anchor at sunset on the afternoon of the day her owner and I joined her, and moving through the waters with delicious noiselessness and incredible rapidity, soon left far behind her the English shore, looking like a white line in the mist, or the pale vision of a land that might once have been. I had done a few quixotic things before departing from my native country,—for example, I had made a free gift of his former home Willowsmere, to Lord Elton, taking a sort of sullen pleasure in thinking that he, the spendthrift nobleman, owed the restoration of his property to *me*,—to me who had never been either a successful linen-draper or furniture-man, but simply an author, one of 'those sort of people' whom my lord and my lady imagine they can 'patronize' and neglect again at pleasure without danger to themselves. The arrogant fools invariably forget what lasting vengeance can be taken for an unmerited slight by the owner of a brilliant pen! I was glad too, in a way, to realize that the daughter of the American railway-king would be brought to the grand old house to air her 'countess-ship,' and look at her prettily pert little physiognomy in the very mirror where Sibyl had watched herself die. I do not know why this idea pleased me, for I bore no grudge against Diana Chesney,—she was vulgar but harmless, and would probably make a much more popular châtelaine at Willowsmere Court than my wife had ever been. Among other things, I dismissed my man Morris, and made him miserable,—with the gift of a thousand pounds, to marry and start a business on. He was miserable because he could not make up his mind what business to adopt, his anxiety being to choose the calling that would 'pay' best,—and also, because though he 'had his eye' upon several young women, he could not tell which among them would be likely to be least extravagant, and the most serviceable as a cook and housekeeper. The love of money and the pains of taking care of it, embittered his days as it embitters the days of most men, and my unexpected munificence towards him burdened him with such a weight of trouble as robbed him of natural sleep and appetite. I cared nothing for his perplexities however, and gave him no advice, good or bad. My other servants I dismissed, each with a considerable gift of money, not that I particularly wished to benefit *them*, but simply because I desired them to speak well of *me*. And in this world it is very evident that the only way to get a good opinion is to pay for it! I gave orders to a famous Italian sculptor for Sibyl's monument, English sculptors having no conception of sculpture,—it was to be of exquisite design, wrought in purest white marble, the chief adornment being the centre-figure of an angel ready for flight, with the face of Sibyl faithfully copied from her picture. Because, however devilish a woman may be in her life-time, one is bound by all the laws of social hypocrisy to make an angel of her as soon as she is dead! Just before I left London I heard that my old college-friend 'Boffles,' John Carrington, had met with a sudden end. Busy at the 'retorting' of his gold, he had been choked by the mercurial fumes and had died in hideous torment. At one time this news would have deeply affected me, but now, I was scarcely sorry. I had heard nothing of him since I had come into my fortune,—he had never even written to congratulate me. Always full of my own self-importance, I judged this as great neglect on his part, and now that he was dead I felt no more than any of us feel now-a-days at the loss of friends. And that is very little,—we have really no time to be sorry,—so many people are always dying!—and we are in such a desperate hurry to rush on to death ourselves! Nothing seemed to touch me that did not closely concern my own personal interest,—and I had no affections left, unless I may call the vague tenderness I had for Mavis Clare an affection. Yet, to be honest, this very emotion was after all nothing but a desire to be consoled, pitied and loved by her,—to be able to turn upon the world and say "This woman whom you have lifted on your shield of honour and crowned with laurels,—she loves *me*—she is not yours, but *mine*!" Purely interested and purely selfish was the longing,—and it deserved no other name than selfishness.

My feelings for Rimânez too began at this time to undergo a curious change. The fascination I had for him, the power he exercised over me remained as great as ever, but I found myself often absorbed in a close study of him, strangely against my own will. Sometimes his every look seemed fraught with meaning,—his every gesture suggestive of an almost terrific authority. He was always to me the most attractive of beings,—nevertheless there was an uneasy sensation of doubt and fear growing up in my mind regarding him,—a painful anxiety to know more about him than he had ever told me,—and on rare occasions I experienced a sudden shock of inexplicable repulsion against him which like a tremendous wave threw me back with violence upon myself and left me half-stunned with a dread of I knew not what. Alone with him, as it were, on the wide sea, cut off for a time from all other intercourse than that which we shared together, these sensations were very strong upon me. I began to note many things which I had been too blind or too absorbed in my own pursuits to observe before; the offensive presence of Amiel, who acted as chief steward on board the yacht, filled me now not only with dislike, but nervous apprehension,—the dark and more or less repulsive visages of the crew haunted me in my dreams;— and one day, leaning over the vessel's edge and gazing blankly down into the fathomless water below, I fell to thinking of strange sorceries of the East, and stories of magicians who by the exercise of unlawful science did so make victims of men and delude them that their wills were entirely perverted and no longer their own. I do not know why this passing thought should have suddenly overwhelmed me with deep depression,—but when I looked up, to me the sky had grown dark, and the face of one of the sailors who was near me polishing the brass hand-rail, seemed singularly threatening and sinister. I moved to go to the other side of the deck, when a hand was gently laid on my shoulder from behind, and turning, I met the sad and splendid eyes of Lucio.

"Are you growing weary of the voyage Geoffrey?" he asked—"Weary of those two suggestions of eternity—the interminable sky, the interminable sea? I am afraid you are!—man easily gets fatigued with his own littleness and powerlessness when he is set afloat on a plank between air and ocean. Yet we are travelling as swiftly as electricity will bear us,—and, as worked in this vessel, it is carrying us at a far greater speed than you perhaps realize or imagine."

I made no immediate answer, but taking his arm strolled slowly up and down. I felt he was looking at me, but I avoided meeting his gaze.

"You have been thinking of your wife?" he queried softly and, as I thought, sympathetically—"I have shunned,—for reasons you know of,—all allusion to the tragic end of so beautiful a creature. Beauty is, alas!—so often subject to hysteria! Yet—if you had any faith, you would believe she is an angel now!"

I stopped short at this, and looked straight at him. There was a fine smile on his delicate mouth.

"An angel!" I repeated slowly—"or a devil? Which would you say she is?—you, who sometimes declare that you believe in Heaven,—and Hell?"

He was silent, but the dreamy smile remained still on his lips.

"Come, speak!" I said roughly—"You can be frank with me, you know,—angel or devil—which?"

"My dear Geoffrey!" he remonstrated gently and with gravity—"A woman is always an angel,—both here and hereafter!"

I laughed bitterly. "If that is part of your faith I am sorry for you!"

"I have not spoken of my faith,"—he rejoined in colder accents, lifting his brilliant eyes to the darkening heaven—"I am not a Salvationist, that I should bray forth a creed to the sound of trump and drum."

"All the same, you *have* a creed;"—I persisted—"And I fancy it must be a strange one! If you remember, you promised to explain it to me—"

"Are you ready to receive such an explanation?" he asked in a somewhat ironical tone—"No, my dear friend!—permit me to say you are *not* ready—not yet! My beliefs are too positive to be brought even into contact with your contradictions,—too frightfully real to submit to your doubts for a moment. You would at once begin to revert to the puny, used-up old arguments of Voltaire, Schopenhauer and Huxley,—little atomic theories like grains of dust in the whirlwind of My knowledge! I can tell you I believe in God as a very Actual and Positive Being,—and that is presumably the first of the Church articles."

"You believe in God!" I echoed his words, staring at him stupidly. He seemed in earnest. In fact he had always seemed in earnest on the subject of Deity. Vaguely I thought of a woman in society whom I slightly knew,—an ugly woman, unattractive and mean-minded, who passed her time in entertaining semi-Royalties and pushing herself amongst them,—she had said to me one day—[4] "I hate people who believe in God, don't you? The idea of a God makes me *sick*!"

---

4. Said in the author's hearing by one of the 'lady leaders' of 'smart' society.

"You believe in God!" I repeated again dubiously.

"Look!" he said, raising his hand towards the sky—"There a few drifting clouds cover millions of worlds, impenetrable, mysterious, yet *actual*;—down there—" and he pointed to the sea, "lurk a thousand things of which, though the ocean is a part of earth, human beings have not yet learned the nature. Between these upper and lower spaces of the Incomprehensible yet Absolute, you, a finite atom of limited capabilities stand, uncertain how long the frail thread of your life shall last, yet arrogantly balancing the question with your own poor brain, as to whether you,—*you* in your utter littleness and incompetency shall condescend to accept a God or not! I confess, that of all astonishing things in the Universe, this particular attitude of modern mankind is the most astonishing to me!"

"Your own attitude is?—"

"The reluctant acceptance of such terrific knowledge as is forced upon me,—" he replied with a dark smile—"I do not say I have been an apt or a willing pupil,—I have had to suffer in learning what I know!"

"Do you believe in hell?" I asked him suddenly—"And in Satan, the Arch-Enemy of mankind?"

He was silent for so long that I was surprised, the more so as he grew pale to the lips, and a curious, almost deathlike rigidity of feature gave his expression something of the ghastly and terrible. After a pause he turned his eyes upon me,—an intense burning misery was reflected in them, though he smiled.

"Most assuredly I believe in hell! How can I do otherwise if I believe in heaven? If there is an Up there must be a Down; if there is Light, there must also be Darkness! And, . . . concerning the Arch-Enemy of mankind,—if half the stories reported of him be true, he must be the most piteous and pitiable figure in the Universe! What would be the sorrows of a thousand million worlds, compared to the sorrows of Satan!"

"Sorrows!" I echoed—"He is supposed to rejoice in the working of evil!"

"Neither angel nor devil can do that,"—he said slowly—"To rejoice in the working of evil is a temporary mania which affects man only. For actual joy to come out of evil, Chaos must come again, and God must extinguish Himself." He stared across the dark sea,—the sun had sunk, and one faint star twinkled through the clouds. "And so I again say—the sorrows of Satan! Sorrows immeasurable as eternity itself,—

imagine them! To be shut out of Heaven!—to hear all through the unending æons, the far-off voices of angels whom once he knew and loved!—to be a wanderer among deserts of darkness, and to pine for the light celestial that was formerly as air and food to his being,—and to know that Man's folly, Man's utter selfishness, Man's cruelty, keep him thus exiled, an outcast from pardon and peace! Man's nobleness may lift the Lost Spirit almost within reach of his lost joys,—but Man's vileness drags him down again,—easy was the torture of Sisyphus compared with the torture of Satan! No wonder that he loathes Mankind!—small blame to him if he seeks to destroy the puny tribe eternally,—little marvel that he grudges them their share of immortality! Think of it as a legend merely,"—and he turned upon me with a movement that was almost fierce—"Christ redeemed Man,—and by his teaching, showed how it was possible for Man to redeem the Devil!"

"I do not understand you—" I said feebly, awed by the strange pain and passion of his tone.

"Do you not? Yet my meaning is scarcely obscure! If men were true to their immortal instincts and to the God that made them,—if they were generous, honest, fearless, faithful, reverent, unselfish, . . . if women were pure, brave, tender and loving,—can you not imagine that in the strong force and fairness of such a world, 'Lucifer, son of the Morning' would be moved to love instead of hate?—that the closed doors of Paradise would be unbarred—and that he, lifted towards his Creator on the prayers of pure lives, would wear again his Angel's crown? Can you not realize this, even by way of a legendary story?"

"Why yes, as a legendary story the idea is beautiful,"—I admitted—"And to me, as I told you once before, quite new. Still, as men are never likely to be honest or women pure, I'm afraid the poor devil stands a bad chance of ever getting redeemed!"

"I fear so too!" and he eyed me with a curious derision—"I very much fear so! And his chances being so slight, I rather respect him for being the Arch-Enemy of such a worthless race!" He paused a moment, then added—"I wonder how we have managed to get on such an absurd subject of conversation? It is dull and uninteresting as all 'spiritual' themes invariably are. My object in bringing you out on this voyage is not to indulge in psychological argument, but to make you forget your troubles as much as possible, and enjoy the present while it lasts."

There was a vibration of compassionate kindness in his voice which at once moved me to an acute sense of self-pity, the worst enervator of moral force that exists. I sighed heavily.

"Truly I have suffered"—I said—"More than most men!"

"More even than most millionaires deserve to suffer!" declared Lucio, with that inevitable touch of sarcasm which distinguished some of his friendliest remarks—"Money is supposed to make amends to a man for everything,—and even the wealthy wife of a certain Irish 'patriot' has not found it incompatible with affection to hold her moneybags close to herself while her husband has been declared a bankrupt. How she has 'idolized' him, let others say! Now, considering *your* cash-abundance, it must be owned the fates have treated you somewhat unkindly!"

The smile that was half-cruel and half-sweet radiated in his eyes as he spoke,—and again a singular revulsion of feeling against him moved me to dislike and fear. And yet,—how fascinating was his company! I could not but admit that the voyage with him to Alexandria on board 'The Flame' was one of positive enchantment and luxury all the way. There was nothing in a material sense left to wish for,—all that could appeal to the intelligence or the imagination had been thought of on board this wonderful yacht which sped like a fairy ship over the sea. Some of the sailors were skilled musicians, and on tranquil nights or at sunset, would bring stringed instruments and discourse to our ears the most dulcet and ravishing melodies. Lucio himself too would often sing,—his luscious voice resounding, as it seemed, over all the visible sea and sky, with such passion as might have drawn an angel down to listen. Gradually my mind became impregnated with these snatches of mournful, fierce, or weird minor tunes,—and I began to suffer in silence from an inexplicable depression and foreboding sense of misery, as well as from another terrible feeling to which I could scarcely give a name,—a dreadful *uncertainty of myself*, as of one lost in a wilderness and about to die. I endured these fits of mental agony alone,—and in such dreary burning moments, believed I was going mad. I grew more and more sullen and taciturn, and when we at last arrived at Alexandria I was not moved to any particular pleasure. The place was new to me, but I was not conscious of novelty,—everything seemed flat, dull, and totally uninteresting. A heavy almost lethargic stupor chained my wits, and when we left the yacht in harbour and went on to Cairo, I was not sensible of any personal enjoyment in the journey, or interest in what I saw. I was only partially roused when we took possession of a luxurious dahabeah, which, with a retinue of attendants, had been specially chartered for us, and commenced our lotus-like voyage up the Nile. The reed-edged, sluggish yellow river fascinated me,—I used to spend long hours reclining at full length in a deck-chair, gazing at the flat shores, the blown sand-heaps, the broken columns and mutilated temples of the dead kingdoms of the past. One evening, thus musing, while the great golden moon climbed languidly up into the sky to stare at the wrecks of earthly ages I said—

"If one could only see these ancient cities as they once existed, what strange revelations might be made! Our modern marvels of civilization and progress might seem small trifles after all,—for I believe in our days we are only re-discovering what the peoples of old time knew."

Lucio drew his cigar from his mouth and looked at it meditatively. Then he glanced up at me with a half-smile—

"Would you like to see a city resuscitated?" he inquired—"Here, in this very spot, some six thousand years ago, a king reigned, with a woman not his queen but his favourite, (quite a lawful arrangement in those days) who was as famous for her beauty and virtue, as this river is for its fructifying tide. Here civilization had progressed enormously,— with the one exception that it had not outgrown faith. Modern France and England have beaten the ancients in their scorn of God and creed, their contempt for divine things, their unnameable lasciviousness and blasphemy. This city"—and he waved his hand towards a dreary stretch of shore where a cluster of tall reeds waved above the monster fragment of a fallen column,—"was governed by the strong pure faith of its people more than anything,—and the ruler of social things in it was a woman. The king's favourite was something like Mavis Clare in that she possessed genius,—she had also the qualities of justice, intelligence, love, truth and a most noble unselfishness,—she made this place happy. It was a paradise on earth while she lived,—when she died, its glory ended. So much can a woman do if she chooses,—so much does she *not* do, in her usual cow-like way of living!"

"How do you know all this you tell me of?" I asked him.

"By study of past records"—he replied—"I read what modern men declare they have no time to read. You are right in the idea that all 'new' things are only old things re-invented or re-discovered,—if you had gone a step further and said that some of men's present lives are only the continuation of their past, you would not have been wrong. Now, if you like, I can by my science, show you the city that stood here long ago,— the 'City Beautiful' as its name is, translated from the ancient tongue."

I roused myself from my lounging attitude and looked at him amazedly. He met my gaze unmoved.

"You can show it to me!" I exclaimed—"How can you do such an impossible thing?"

"Permit me to hypnotize you,"—he answered smiling,—"My system of hypnotism is, very fortunately, not yet discovered by meddlesome inquirers into occult matters,—but it never fails of its effect,—and I promise you, you shall, under my influence, see not only the place, but the people."

My curiosity was strongly excited, and I became more eager to try the suggested experiment than I cared to openly show. I laughed however, with affected indifference.

"I am perfectly willing!" I said—"All the same, I don't think you can hypnotize me,—I have much too strong a will of my own—" at which remark I saw a smile, dark and saturnine, hover on his lips—"But you can make the attempt."

He rose at once, and signed to one of our Egyptian servants.

"Stop the dahabeah, Azimah," he said—"We will rest here for the night."

Azimah, a superb-looking Eastern in picturesque white garments, put his hands to his head in submission and retired to give the order. In another few moments the dahabeah had stopped. A great silence was around us,—the moonlight fell like yellow wine on the deck,—in the far distance across the stretches of dark sand, a solitary column towered so clear-cut against the sky that it was almost possible to discern upon it the outline of a monstrous face. Lucio stood still, confronting me,— saying nothing, but looking me steadily through and through, with those wonderful mystic, melancholy eyes that seemed to penetrate and burn my very flesh. I was attracted as a bird might be by the basilisk eyes of a snake,—yet I tried to smile and say something indifferent. My efforts were useless,—personal consciousness was slipping from me fast,—the sky, the water and the moon whirled round each other in a giddy chase for precedence;—I could not move, for my limbs seemed fastened to my chair with weights of iron, and I was for a few minutes absolutely powerless. Then suddenly my vision cleared (as I thought)— my senses grew vigorous and alert, . . . I heard the sound of solemn marching music, and there,—there in the full radiance of the moon, with a thousand lights gleaming forth from high cupolas, shone the 'City Beautiful'!

XXXIX

A vision of majestic buildings, vast, stately and gigantic!—of streets crowded with men and women in white and coloured garments adorned with jewels,—of flowers that grew on the roofs of palaces and swung from terrace to terrace in loops and garlands of fantastic bloom,—of trees, broad-branched and fully leafed,—of marble embankments overlooking the river,—of lotus-lilies growing thickly below, by the water's edge,—of music that echoed in silver and brazen twangings from the shelter of shady gardens and covered balconies,— every beautiful detail rose before me more distinctly than an ivory carving mounted on an ebony shield. Just opposite where I stood or seemed to stand, on the deck of a vessel in the busy harbour, a wide avenue extended, opening up into huge squares embellished with strange figures of granite gods and animals,—I saw the sparkling spray of many fountains in the moonlight, and heard the low persistent hum of the restless human multitudes that thronged the place as thickly as bees clustered in a hive. To the left of the scene I could discern a huge bronze gate guarded by sphinxes; there was a garden beyond it, and from that depth of shade a girl's voice, singing a strange wild melody, came floating towards me on the breeze. Meanwhile the marching music I had first of all caught the echo of, sounded nearer and nearer,—and presently I perceived a great crowd approaching with lighted torches and garlands of flowers. Soon I saw a band of priests in brilliant robes that literally blazed with sun-like gems,—they were moving towards the river, and with them came young boys and little children, while on either side, maidens white-veiled and rose-wreathed, paced demurely, swinging silver censers to and fro. After the priestly procession walked a regal figure between ranks of slaves and attendants,—I knew it for the King of this 'City Beautiful,' and was almost moved to join in the thundering acclamations which greeted his progress. And that snowy palanquin, carried by lily-crowned girls, that followed his train,—who occupied it? . . . what gem of his land was thus tenderly enshrined? I was consumed by an extraordinary longing to know this,—I watched the white burden coming nearer to my point of vantage,—I saw the priests arrange themselves in a semi-circle on the river-embankment, the King in their midst, and the surging shouting multitude around,—then came the brazen clangour of many bells, intermixed with the rolling of drums and the shrilling sound of reed-pipes lightly blown upon,—and, amid the blaze of the flaring torches, the White Palanquin was set down upon the ground. A woman, clad in some silvery glistening tissue, stepped forth from it like a sylph from the foam of the sea, but—she was veiled,—I could not discern so much as the outline of her features,—and the keen disappointment of this was a positive torture to me. If I could but see her, I thought, I should know something I had never hitherto guessed! "Lift, oh lift the shrouding veil, Spirit of the City Beautiful!" I inwardly prayed—"For I feel I shall read in your eyes the secret of happiness!"

But the veil was not withdrawn, . . . the music made barbaric clamour in my ears, . . . the blaze of strong light and colour blinded me, . . . and I felt myself reeling into a dark chaos, where as I imagined, I chased the moon, as she flew before me on silver wings,—then. . . the sound of a rich baritone trolling out a light song from a familiar modern *opera bouffe* confused and startled me,—and in another second I found myself staring wildly at Lucio, who, lying easily back in his deck-chair, was carolling joyously to the silent night and the blank expanse of sandy shore, in front of which our dahabeah rested motionless. With a cry I flung myself upon him.

"Where is she?" I exclaimed—"*Who* is she?"

He looked at me without replying, and smiling quizzically, released himself from my sudden grasp. I drew back shuddering and bewildered.

"I saw it all!" I murmured—"The city—the priests,—the people— the King!—all but Her face! Why was that hidden from me!"

And actual tears rose to my eyes involuntarily,—Lucio surveyed me with evident amusement.

"What a 'find' you would be to a first-class 'spiritual' impostor playing his tricks in cultured and easily-gulled London society!" he observed— "You seem most powerfully impressed by a passing vision!"

"Do you mean to tell me," I said earnestly "that what I saw just now was the mere thought of your brain conveyed to mine?"

"Precisely!" he responded—"I know what the 'City Beautiful' was like, and I was able to draw it for you on the canvas of my memory and present it as a complete picture to your inward sight. For you *have* an inward sight,—though like most people, you live unconscious of that neglected faculty."

"But—who was She?" I repeated obstinately.

"'She' was, I presume, the King's favourite. If she kept her face hidden from you as you complain, I am sorry!—but I assure you it was not my fault! Get to bed, Geoffrey,—you look dazed. You take visions badly,—yet they are better than realities, believe me!"

Somehow I could not answer him. I left him abruptly and went below to try and sleep, but my thoughts were all cruelly confused, and I began to be more than ever overwhelmed with a sense of deepening terror,—a feeling that I was being commanded, controlled and, as it were, driven along by a force that had in it something unearthly. It was a most distressing sensation,—it made me shrink at times, from the look of Lucio's eyes,—now and then indeed I almost cowered before him, so increasingly great was the indefinable dread I had of his presence. It was not so much the strange vision of the 'City Beautiful' that had inspired this in me,—for after all, that was only a trick of hypnotism, as he had said, and as I was content to argue it with myself,—but it was his whole manner that suddenly began to impress me as it had never impressed me before. If any change was slowly taking place in my sentiments towards him, so surely it seemed was he changing equally towards me. His imperious ways were more imperial,—his sarcasm more sarcastic,— his contempt for mankind more openly displayed and more frequently pronounced. Yet I admired him as much as ever,—I delighted in his conversation, whether it were witty, philosophical or cynical,—I could not imagine myself without his company. Nevertheless the gloom on my mind deepened,—our Nile trip became infinitely wearisome to me, so much so, that almost before we had got half-way on our journey up the river, I longed to turn back again and wished the voyage at an end. An incident that occurred at Luxor was more than sufficient to strengthen this desire. We had stayed there for several days exploring the district and visiting the ruins of Thebes and Karnac, where they were busy excavating tombs. One afternoon they brought to light a red granite sarcophagus intact,—in it was a richly painted coffin which was opened in our presence, and was found to contain the elaborately adorned mummy of a woman. Lucio proved himself an apt reader of hieroglyphs, and he translated in brief, and with glib accuracy the history of the corpse as it was pictured inside the sepulchral shell.

"A dancer at the court of Queen Amenartes;" he announced for the benefit of several interested spectators who with myself, stood round the sarcophagus—"Who because of her many sins, and secret guilt which made her life unbearable, and her days full of corruption, died of poison administered by her own hand, according to the King's command, and in presence of the executioners of law. Such is the lady's story,—condensed;—there are a good many other details of course. She appears to have been only in her twentieth year. Well!" and he smiled as he looked round upon his little audience,—"We may congratulate ourselves on having progressed since the days of these over-strict ancient Egyptians! The sins of dancers are not, with us, taken *au grand serieux*! Shall we see what she is like?"

No objection was raised by the authorities concerned in the discoveries,—and I, who had never witnessed the unrolling of a mummy before, watched the process with great interest and curiosity. As one by one of the scented wrappings were removed, a long tress of nut-brown hair became visible,—then, those who were engaged in the task, used more extreme and delicate precaution, Lucio himself assisting them to uncover the face. As this was done, a kind of sick horror stole over me,— brown and stiff as parchment though the features were, their contour was recognisable,—and when the whole countenance was exposed to view I could almost have shrieked aloud the name of '*Sibyl!*' For it was like her!—dreadfully like!—and as the faint, half aromatic half-putrid odours of the unrolled cerements crept towards me on the air, I reeled back giddily and covered my eyes. Irresistibly I was reminded of the subtle French perfume exhaled from Sibyl's garments when I found her dead,—that, and this sickly effluvia were similar! A man standing near me saw me swerve as though about to fall, and caught me on his arm.

"The sun is too strong for you I fear?" he said kindly—"This climate does not suit everybody."

I forced a smile and murmured something about a passing touch of vertigo,—then, recovering myself I gazed fearfully at Lucio, who was studying the mummy attentively with a curious smile. Presently stooping over the coffin he took out of it a piece of finely wrought gold in the shape of a medallion.

"This, I imagine must be the fair dancer's portrait,"—he said, holding it up to the view of all the eager and exclaiming spectators—"Quite a treasure-trove! An admirable piece of ancient workmanship, besides being the picture of a very lovely woman. Do you not think so, Geoffrey?"

He handed me the medallion,—and I examined it with deadly and fascinated interest,—the face was exquisitely beautiful,—but assuredly it was the face of Sibyl!

I never remember how I lived through the rest of that day. At night, as soon as I had an opportunity of speaking to Rimânez alone, I asked him. . .

"Did you see,—did you not recognize? . . ."

"That the dead Egyptian dancer resembled your late wife?" he quietly continued—"Yes,—I noticed it at once. But that should not affect you. History repeats itself,—why should not lovely women repeat themselves? Beauty always has its double somewhere, either in the past or future."

I said no more,—but next morning I was very ill,—so ill that I could not rise from my bed, and passed the hours in restless moaning and irritable pain that was not so much physical as mental. There was a physician resident at the hotel at Luxor, and Lucio, always showing himself particularly considerate for my personal comfort, sent for him at once. He felt my pulse, shook his head, and after much dubious pondering, advised my leaving Egypt immediately. I heard his mandate given with a joy I could scarcely conceal. The yearning I had to get quickly away from this 'land of the old gods' was intense and feverish,—I loathed the vast and awful desert silences, where the Sphinx frowns contempt on the puny littleness of mankind,—where the opened tombs and coffins expose once more to the light of day, faces that are the very semblances of those we ourselves have known and loved in our time,—and where painted history tells us of just such things as our modern newspapers chronicle, albeit in different form. Rimânez was ready and willing to carry out the doctor's orders,—and arranged our return to Cairo and from thence to Alexandria, with such expedition as left me nothing to desire, and filled me with gratitude for his apparent sympathy. In as short a time as abundance of cash could make possible, we had rejoined 'The Flame,' and were *en route*, as I thought, for France or England. We had not absolutely settled our destination, having some idea of coasting along the Riviera,—but my old confidence in Rimânez being now almost restored, I left this to him for decision, sufficiently satisfied in myself that I had not been destined to leave my bones in terror-haunted Egypt. And it was not till I had been about a week or ten days on board, and had made good progress in the recovery of my health, that the beginning of the end of this never-to-be-forgotten voyage was foreshadowed to me in such terrific fashion as nearly plunged me into the darkness of death,—or rather let me now say, (having learned my bitter lesson thoroughly) into the fell brilliancy of that Life beyond the tomb which we refuse to recognise or realize till we are whirled into its glorious or awful vortex!

One evening, after a bright day of swift and enjoyable sailing over

MARIE CORELLI

a smooth and sunlit sea, I retired to rest in my cabin, feeling almost happy. My mind was perfectly tranquil,—my trust in my friend Lucio was again re-established,—and I may add, so was my old arrogant and confident trust in myself. My access to fortune had not, so far, brought me either much joy or distinction,—but it was not too late for me yet to pluck the golden apples of Hesperides. The various troubles I had endured, though of such recent occurrence, began to assume a blurred indistinctness in my mind, as of things long past and done with,—I considered the strength of my financial position again with satisfaction, to the extent of contemplating a second marriage—and that marriage with—Mavis Clare! No other woman should be my wife, I mentally swore,—she, and she only should be mine! I foresaw no difficulties in the way,—and full of pleasant dreams and self-delusions I settled myself in my berth, and dropped easily off to sleep. About midnight I awoke, vaguely terrified, to see the cabin full of a strong red light and fierce glare. My first dazed impression was that the yacht was on fire,— the next instant I became paralysed and dumb with horror. Sibyl stood before me! . . . Sibyl, a wild, strange, tortured writhing figure, half nude, waving beckoning arms, and making desperate gestures,—her face was as I had seen it last in death, livid and hideous, . . . her eyes blazed mingled menace, despair, and warning upon me! Round her a living wreath of flame coiled upwards like a twisted snake, . . . her lips moved as though she strove to speak, but no sound came from them,—and while I yet looked at her, she vanished! I must have lost consciousness then,—for when I awoke it was broad day. But this ghastly visitation was only the first of many such,—and at last, *every night* I saw her thus, sheeted in flame, till I grew well-nigh mad with fear and misery. My torment was indescribable,—yet I said nothing to Lucio, who watched me, as I imagined, narrowly,—I took sleeping-draughts in the hope to procure unbroken rest, but in vain,—always I woke at one particular moment, and always I had to face this fiery phantom of my dead wife, with despair in her eyes and an unuttered warning on her lips. This was not all. One day in the full sunlight of a quiet afternoon, I entered the saloon of the yacht alone, and started back amazed to see my old friend John Carrington seated at the table, pen in hand, casting up accounts. He bent over his papers closely,—his face was furrowed and very pale,—but so life-like was he, so seemingly substantial that I called him by name, whereat he looked up,—smiled drearily, and was gone! Trembling in every limb I realized that here was another spectral terror added to the burden of my days; and sitting down, I tried to rally my scattered forces and reason out what was best to be done. There was no doubt I was very ill;—these phantoms were the warning of brain-disease. I must endeavour, I thought, to keep myself well under control till I got to England,—there I determined to consult the best physicians, and put myself under their care till I was thoroughly restored.

"Meanwhile"—I muttered to myself—"I will say nothing, . . . not even to Lucio. He would only smile, . . . and I should hate him! . . ."

I broke off, wondering at this. For was it possible I should ever hate him? Surely not!

That night by way of a change, I slept in a hammock on deck, hoping to dispel midnight illusions by resting in the open air. But my sufferings were only intensified. I woke as usual, . . . to see, not only Sibyl, but also to my deadly fear, the Three Phantoms that had appeared to me in my room in London on the evening of Viscount Lynton's suicide. There they were,—the same, the very same!—only this time all their livid faces were lifted and turned towards me, and though their lips never moved, the word 'Misery!' seemed uttered, for I heard it tolling like a funeral bell on the air and across the sea! . . . And Sibyl, with her face of death in the coils of a silent flame, . . . Sibyl smiled at me!—a smile of torture and remorse! . . . God!—I could endure it no longer! Leaping from my hammock, I ran towards the vessel's edge, . . . one plunge into the cool waves, . . . ha!—there stood Amiel, with his impenetrable dark face and ferret eyes!

"Can I assist you sir?" he inquired deferentially.

I stared at him,—then burst into a laugh.

"Assist me? Why no!—you can do nothing. I want rest, . . . and I cannot sleep here, . . . the air is too close and sulphureous,—the very stars are burning hot! . . ." I paused,—he regarded me with his usual gravely derisive expression. "I am going down to my cabin"—I continued, trying to speak more calmly—"I shall be *alone* there. . . perhaps!" Again I laughed wildly and involuntarily, and staggered away from him down the deck-stairs, afraid to look back lest I should see those Three Figures of fate following me.

Once safe in my cabin I shut to the door violently, and in feverish haste, seized my case of pistols. I took out one and loaded it. My heart was beating furiously,—I kept my eyes fixed on the ground, lest they should encounter the dead eyes of Sibyl.

"One click of the trigger—" I whispered—"and all is over! I shall be at peace,—senseless,—sightless and painless. Horrors can no longer haunt me, . . . I shall sleep!"

I raised the weapon steadily to my right temple, . . . when suddenly my cabin-door opened, and Lucio looked in.

"Pardon me!" he said, as he observed my attitude—"I had no idea you were busy! I will go away. I would not disturb you for the world!"

His smile had something fiendish in its fine mockery;—moved with a quick revulsion of feeling I turned the pistol downwards and held its muzzle firmly against the table near me.

"*You* say that!" I exclaimed in acute anguish,—"*you* say it—seeing me thus! I thought you were my friend!"

He looked full at me, . . . his eyes grew large and luminous with a splendour of scorn, passion and sorrow intermingled.

"Did you?" and again the terrific smile lit up his pale features,—"You were mistaken! *I am your Enemy!*"

A dreadful silence followed. Something lurid and unearthly in his expression appalled me, . . . I trembled and grew cold with fear. Mechanically I replaced the pistol in its case,—then I gazed up at him with a vacant wonder and wild piteousness, seeing that his dark and frowning figure seemed to increase in stature, towering above me like the gigantic shadow of a storm-cloud! My blood froze with an unnameable sickening terror, . . . then, thick darkness veiled my sight, and I dropped down senseless!

XL

Thunder and wild tumult,—the glare of lightning,—the shattering roar of great waves leaping mountains high and hissing asunder in mid-air,—to this fierce riot of savage elements let loose in a whirling boisterous dance of death, I woke at last with a convulsive shock. Staggering to my feet I stood in the black obscurity of my cabin, trying to rally my scattered forces,—the electric lamps were extinguished, and the lightning alone illumined the sepulchral darkness. Frantic shoutings echoed above me on deck,—fiend-like yells that sounded now like triumph, now like despair, and again like menace,—the yacht leaped to and fro like a hunted stag amid the furious billows, and every frightful crash of thunder threatened, as it seemed, to split her in twain. The wind howled like a devil in torment,—it screamed and moaned and sobbed as though endowed with a sentient body that suffered acutest agony,—anon it rushed downwards with an angry swoop as of wide-flapping wings, and at each raging gust I thought the vessel must surely founder. Forgetting everything but immediate personal danger, I tried to open my door. It was locked outside!—I was a prisoner! My indignation at this discovery exceeded every other feeling, and beating with both hands on the wooden panels, I called, I shouted, I threatened, I swore,—all in vain! Thrown down twice by the topsy-turvey lurching of the yacht, I still kept up a desperate hammering and calling, striving to raise my voice above the distracting pandemonium of noise that seemed to possess the ship from end to end, but all to no purpose,—and finally, hoarse and exhausted, I stopped and leaned against the unyielding door to recover breath and strength. The storm appeared to be increasing in force and clamour,—the lightning was well-nigh incessant, and the clattering thunder followed each flash so instantaneously as to leave no doubt but that it was immediately above us. I listened,—and presently heard a frenzied cry—

"Breakers ahead!" This was followed by peals of discordant laughter. Terrified, I strained my ears for every sound,—and all at once some-one spoke to me quite closely, as though the very darkness around me had found a tongue.

"Breakers ahead! Throughout the world, storm and danger and doom! Doom and Death!—but afterwards—Life!"

A certain intonation in these words filled me with such frantic horror that I fell on my knees in abject misery, and almost prayed to the God I had through all my life disbelieved in and denied. But I was too mad with fear to find words;—the dense blackness,—the horrid uproar of the wind and sea,—the infuriated and confused shouting,—all this was to my mind as though hell itself had broken loose, and I could only kneel dumbly and tremble. Suddenly a swirling sound as of an approaching monstrous whirlwind made itself heard above all the rest of the din,—a sound that gradually resolved itself into a howling chorus of thousands of voices sweeping along on the gusty blast,—fierce cries were mingled with the jarring thunder, and I leapt erect as I caught the words of the clangorous shout—

"AVE SATHANAS! AVE!"

Rigidly upright, with limbs stiffening for sheer terror, I stood listening,—the waves seemed to roar "AVE SATHANAS!"—the wind shrieked it to the thunder,—the lightning wrote it in a snaky line of fire on the darkness "AVE SATHANAS!" My brain swam round and grew full to bursting,—I was going mad,—raving mad surely!—or why should I thus distinctly hear such unmeaning sounds as these? With a sudden access of superhuman force I threw the whole weight of my body against the door of my cabin in a delirious effort to break it open,—it yielded slightly,—and I prepared myself for another rush and similar attempt,— when all at once it was flung widely back, admitting a stream of pale light, and Lucio, wrapped in heavy shrouding garments, confronted me.

"Follow me, Geoffrey Tempest,—" he said in low clear tones—"Your time has come!"

As he spoke, all self-possession deserted me,—the terrors of the storm, and now the terror of his presence, overwhelmed my strength, and I stretched out my hands to him appealingly, unknowing what I did or said.

"For God's sake. . . !" I began wildly.

He silenced me by an imperious gesture.

"Spare me your prayers! For God's sake, for your own sake, and for mine! Follow!"

He moved before me like a black phantom in the pale strange light surrounding him,—and I, dazzled, dazed and terror-stricken, trod in his steps closely, moved, as it seemed by some volition not my own, till I found myself alone with him in the saloon of the yacht, with the waves hissing up against the windows like live snakes ready to sting. Trembling and scarcely able to stand I sank on a chair,—he turned round and looked at me for a moment meditatively. Then he threw open one of the windows,—a huge wave dashed in and scattered its bitter salt spray upon me where I sat,—but I heeded nothing,—my agonised looks were fixed on Him,—the Being I had so long made the companion of my days. Raising his hand with a gesture of authority he said—

"Back, ye devils of the sea and wind!—ye which are not God's elements but My servants, the unrepenting souls of men! Lost in the waves, or whirled in the hurricane, whichever ye have made your destiny, get hence and cease your clamour! This hour is Mine!"

Panic-stricken I heard,—aghast I saw the great billows that had shouldered up in myriads against the vessel, sink suddenly,—the yelling wind dropped, silenced,—the yacht glided along with a smooth even motion as though on a tranquil inland lake,—and almost before I could realize it, the light of the full moon beamed forth brilliantly and fell in a broad stream across the floor of the saloon. But in the very cessation of the storm the words "AVE SATHANAS!" trembled as it were upwards to my ears from the underworld of the sea, and died away in distance like a parting echo of thunder. Then Lucio faced me,—with what a countenance of sublime and awful beauty!

"Do you know Me now, man whom my millions of dross have made wretched?—or do you need me to tell you WHO I am?"

My lips moved,—but I could not speak; the dim and dreadful thought that was dawning on my mind seemed as yet too frenzied, too outside the boundaries of material sense for mortal utterance.

"Be dumb,—be motionless!—but hear and feel!" he continued—"By the supreme power of God,—for there is no other power in any world or any heaven,—I control and command you at this moment, your own will being set aside for once as naught! I choose you as one out of millions to learn in this life the lesson that all must learn hereafter;—let every faculty of your intelligence be ready to receive that which I shall impart,—and teach it to your fellow-men if you have a conscience as you have a Soul!"

Again I strove to speak,—he seemed so human,—so much my friend still, though he had declared himself my Enemy,—and yet. . . what was that lambent radiance encircling his brows?—that burning glory steadily deepening and flashing from his eyes?

"You are one of the world's 'fortunate' men,—" he went on, surveying me straightly and pitilessly—"So at least this world judges you, because you can buy its good-will. But the Forces that govern all worlds, do not judge you by such a standard,—you cannot buy *their* good-will, not though all the Churches should offer to sell it you! They regard you as you *are*, stripped soul-naked,—not as you *seem*! They behold in you a shameless egoist, persistently engaged in defacing their divine Image of Immortality,—and for that sin there is no excuse and no escape but Punishment. Whosoever prefers Self to God, and in the arrogance of that Self, presumes to doubt and deny God, invites another Power to compass his destinies,—the power of Evil, made evil and kept evil by the disobedience and wickedness of Man alone,—that power whom mortals call Satan, Prince of Darkness,—but whom once the angels knew as Lucifer, Prince of Light!" . . . He broke off,—paused,—and his flaming regard fell full upon me. "Do you know Me, . . . now?"

I sat a rigid figure of fear, dumbly staring, . . . was this man, for he seemed man, mad that he should thus hint at a thing too wild and terrible for speech?

"If you do not know Me,—if you do not feel in your convicted soul that you are aware of Me,—it is because you will not know! Thus do I come upon men, when they rejoice in their wilful self-blindness and vanity!—thus do I become their constant companion, humouring them in such vices as they best love!—thus do I take on the shape that pleases *them*, and fit myself to their humours! *They* make me what I am;—they mould my very form to the fashion of their flitting time. Through all their changing and repeating eras, they have found strange names and titles for me,—and their creeds and churches have made a monster of me,—as though imagination could compass any worse monster than the Devil in Man!"

Frozen and mute I heard, . . . the dead silence, and his resonant voice vibrating through it, seemed more terrific than the wildest storm.

"You,—God's work,—endowed as every conscious atom of His creation is endowed,—with the infinite germ of immortality;—you, absorbed in the gathering together of such perishable trash as you conceive good for yourself on this planet,—you dare, in the puny reach of your mortal intelligence to dispute and question the everlasting things invisible! You, by the Creator's will, are permitted to see the Natural Universe,—but in mercy to you, the veil is drawn across the Super-natural! For such things as exist there, would break your puny earth-brain as a frail shell is broken by a passing wheel,—and because you cannot see, you doubt! You doubt not only the surpassing Love and Wisdom that keeps you in ignorance till you shall be strong enough to bear full knowledge, but you doubt the very fact of such another universe itself. Arrogant fool!—your hours are counted by Super-natural time!—your days are compassed by Super-natural law!—your every thought, word, deed and look must go to make up the essence and shape of your being in Super-natural life hereafter!—and what you *have been* in your Soul *here*, must and shall be the aspect of your Soul *there*! That law knows no changing!"

The light about his face deepened,—he went on in clear accents that vibrated with the strangest music.

"Men make their own choice and form their own futures," he said— "And never let them dare to say they are not *free* to choose! From the uttermost reaches of high Heaven the Spirit of God descended to them as Man,—from the uttermost depths of lowest Hell, I, the Spirit of Rebellion, come,—equally as Man! But the God-in-Man was rejected and slain,—I, the Devil-in-Man live on, forever accepted and adored! Man's choice this is—not God's or mine! Were this self-seeking human race once to reject me utterly, I should exist no more as I am,—nor would they exist who are with me. Listen, while I trace your career!—it is a copy of the lives of many men;—and judge how little the powers of Heaven can have to do with you!—how much the powers of Hell!"

I shuddered involuntarily;—dimly I began to realize the awful nature of this unearthly interview.

"You, Geoffrey Tempest, are a man in whom a Thought of God was once implanted,—that subtle fire or note of music out of heaven called Genius. So great a gift is rarely bestowed on any mortal,—and woe betide him, who having received it, holds it as of mere personal value, to be used for Self and not for God! Divine laws moved you gently in the right path of study,—the path of suffering, of disappointment, of self-denial and poverty,—for only by these things is humanity made noble and trained in the ways of perfection. Through pain and enduring labour the soul is armed for battle, and strengthened for conquest. For it is more difficult to bear a victory well, than to endure many buffetings of war! But you,—you resented Heaven's good-will towards you,—the Valley of Humiliation suited you not at all. Poverty maddened you,—starvation sickened you. Yet poverty is better than arrogant wealth,—and starvation is healthier than self-indulgence! You could not wait,—your own troubles seemed to you enormous,—

your own efforts laudable and marvellous,—the troubles and efforts of others were nothing to you;—you were ready to curse God and die. Compassionating yourself, admiring yourself and none other, with a heart full of bitterness, and a mouth full of cursing, you were eager to make quick havoc of both your genius and your soul. For this cause, your millions of money came—and,—*so did I*!"

Standing now full height he confronted me,—his eyes were less brilliant, but, they reflected in their dark splendour a passionate scorn and sorrow.

"O fool!—in my very coming I warned you!—on the very day we met I told you I was not what I seemed! God's elements crashed a menace when we made our compact of friendship! And I,—when I saw the faint last struggle of the not quite torpid soul in you to resist and distrust me, did I not urge you to let that better instinct have its way? You,—jester with the Supernatural!—you,—base scoffer at Christ! A thousand hints have been given you,—a thousand chances of doing such good as must have forced me to leave you,—as would have brought me a welcome respite from sorrow,—a moment's cessation of torture!"

His brows contracted in a sombre frown,—he was silent a moment,— then he resumed—

"Now learn from me the weaving of the web you so willingly became entangled in! Your millions of money were Mine!—the man that left you heir to them, was a wretched miser, evil to the soul's core! By virtue of his own deeds he and his dross were Mine! and maddened by the sheer accumulation of world's wealth, he slew himself in a fit of frenzy. He lives again in a new and much more realistic phase of existence, and knows the actual value of mankind's cash-payments! This *you* have yet to learn!"

He advanced a step or two, fixing his eyes more steadily upon me.

"Wealth is like Genius,—bestowed not for personal gratification, but for the benefit of those who lack it. What have *you* done for your fellow-men? The very book you wrote and launched upon the tide of bribery and corruption was published with the intention to secure applause for Yourself, not to give help or comfort to others. Your marriage was prompted by Lust and Ambition, and in the fair Sensuality you wedded, you got your deserts! No love was in the union,—it was sanctified by the blessing of Fashion, but not the blessing of God. You have done without God; so you think! Every act of your existence has been for the pleasure and advancement of Yourself,—and this is why I have chosen you out to hear and see what few mortals ever hear or see till they have passed the dividing-line between this life and the next. I have chosen you because you are a type of the apparently respected and unblamable man;—you are not what the world calls a criminal,—you have murdered no-one,—you have stolen no neighbour's goods—, your unchastities and adulteries are those of every 'fashionable' vice-monger,—and your blasphemies against the Divine are no worse than those of the most approved modern magazine-contributors. You are guilty nevertheless of the chief crime of the age—Sensual Egotism—the blackest sin known to either angels or devils, because hopeless. The murderer may repent, and save a hundred lives to make up for the one he snatched,— the thief may atone with honest labour,—the adulterer may scourge his flesh and do grim penance for late pardon,—the blasphemer may retrieve his blasphemies,—but for the Egoist there is no chance of wholesome penitence, since to himself he is perfect, and counts his Creator as somewhat inferior. This present time of the world breathes Egotism,—the taint of Self, the hideous worship of money, corrodes all life, all thought, all feeling. For vulgar cash, the fairest and noblest scenes of Nature are wantonly destroyed without public protest,[5]—the earth, created in beauty, is made hideous,—parents and children, wives and husbands are ready to slay each other for a little gold,—Heaven is barred out,—God is denied,—and Destruction darkens over this planet, known to all angels as the Sorrowful Star! Be no longer blind, millionaire whose millions have ministered to Self without relieving sorrow!—for when the world is totally corrupt,—when Self is dominant,—when cunning supersedes honesty,—when gold is man's chief ambition,— when purity is condemned,—when poets teach lewdness, and scientists blasphemy,—when love is mocked, and God forgotten,—the End is near! I take My part in that end!—for the souls of mankind are not done with when they leave their fleshly tenements! When this planet is destroyed as a bubble broken in the air, the souls of men and women live on,—as the soul of the woman you loved lives on,—as the soul of the mother who bore her, lives on,—aye!—as all My worshippers live on through a myriad worlds, a myriad phases, till they learn to shape their destinies for Heaven! And I, with them live on, in many shapes,

---

5. Witness the destruction of Foyers, to the historical shame and disgrace of Scotland and Scotsmen.

in many ways!—when they return to God cleansed and perfect, so shall I return!—but not till then!"

He paused again,—and I heard a faint sighing sound everywhere as of wailing voices, and the name "Ahrimanes!" was breathed suddenly upon the silence. I started up listening, every nerve strained— Ahrimanes?—or Rimânez? I gazed fearfully at him, . . . always beautiful, his countenance was now sublime, . . . and his eyes shone with a lustrous flame.

"You thought me friend!" he said—"You should have known me Foe! For everyone who flatters a man for his virtues, or humours him in his vices is that man's worst enemy, whether demon or angel! But you judged me a fitting comrade,—hence I was bound to serve you,—I and my followers with me. You had no perception to realize this,—you, supreme scorner of the Supernatural! Little did you think of the terrifying agencies that worked the wonders of your betrothal feast at Willowsmere! Little did you dream that fiends prepared the costly banquet and poured out the luscious wine!"

At this, a smothered groan of horror escaped me,—I looked wildly round me, longing to find some deep grave of oblivious rest wherein to fall.

"Aye!" he continued—"The festival was fitted to the time of the world to-day!—Society, gorging itself blind and senseless, and attended by a retinue from Hell! My servants looked like men!—for truly there is little difference 'twixt man and devil! 'Twas a brave gathering!—England has never seen so strange a one in all her annals!"

The sighing, wailing cries increased in loudness,—my limbs shook under me, and all power of thought was paralysed in my brain. He bent his piercing looks upon me with a new expression of infinite wonder, pity and disdain.

"What a grotesque creation you men have made of Me!" he said— "As grotesque as your conception of God! With what trifling human attributes you have endowed me! Know you not that the changeless, yet ever-changing Essence of Immortal Life can take a million million shapes and yet remain unalterably the same? Were I as hideous as your Churches figure me,—could the eternal beauty with which all angels are endowed, ever change to such loathsomeness as haunts mankind's distorted imaginations, perchance it would be well,—for none would make of me their comrade, and none would cherish me as friend! As fits each separate human nature, so seems my image,—for thus is my fate and punishment commanded. Yet even in this mask of man I wear, men own me their superior,—think you not that when the Supreme Spirit of God wore that same mask on earth, men did not know Him for their Master? Yea, they did know!—and knowing, murdered Him,—as they ever strive to murder all divine things as soon as their divinity is recognised. Face to face I stood with Him upon the mountain-top, and there fulfilled my vow of temptation. Worlds and kingdoms, supremacies and powers!—what were they to the Ruler of them all! 'Get thee hence, Satan!' said the golden-sounding Voice;—ah!—glorious behest!—happy respite!—for I reached the very gate of Heaven that night, and heard the angels sing!"

His accents sank to an infinitely mournful cadence.

"What have your teachers done with me and my eternal sorrows?" he went on—"Have not they, and the unthinking churches, proclaimed a lie against me, saying that I rejoice in evil? O man to whom, by God's will and because the world's end draws nigh, I unveil a portion of the mystery of my doom, learn now once and for all, that there is no possible joy in evil!—it is the despair and the discord of the Universe,—it is Man's creation,—My torment,—God's sorrow! Every sin of every human being adds weight to my torture, and length to my doom,—yet my oath against the world must be kept! I have sworn to tempt,—to do my uttermost to destroy mankind,—but man has not sworn to yield to my tempting. He is free!—let him resist and I depart;—let him accept me, I remain! Eternal Justice has spoken,—Humanity, through the teaching of God made human, must work out its own redemption,—and Mine!"

Here, suddenly advancing he stretched out his hand,—his figure grew taller, vaster and more majestic.

"Come with me now!" he said in a low penetrating voice that sounded sweet, yet menacing—"Come!—for the veil is down for you to-night! You shall understand with WHOM you have dwelt so long in your shifting cloud-castle of life!—and in What company you have sailed perilous seas!—one, who proud and rebellious, like you, errs less, in that he owns GOD as his Master!"

At these words a thundering crash assailed my ears,—all the windows on either side of the saloon flew open, and showed a strange glitter as of steely spears pointed aloft to the moon,— . . . then, . . . half-fainting, I felt myself grasped and lifted suddenly and forcibly upwards, . . . and in another moment found myself on the deck of 'The Flame,' held fast as a prisoner in the fierce grip of hands invisible. Raising my eyes in deadly despair,—prepared for hellish tortures, and with a horrible sense of conviction in my soul that it was too late to cry out to God for mercy,—I saw around me a frozen world!—a world that seemed as if the sun had never shone upon it. Thick glassy-green walls of ice pressed round the vessel on all sides and shut her in between their inflexible barriers!—fantastic palaces, pinnacles, towers, bridges and arches of ice formed in their architectural outlines and groupings the semblance of a great city,—over all the coldly glistening peaks, the round moon, emerald-pale, looked down,—and standing opposite to me against the mast, I beheld, . . . not Lucio, . . . but an Angel!

XLI

Crowned with a mystic radiance as of trembling stars of fire, that sublime Figure towered between me and the moonlit sky; the face, austerely grand and beautiful, shone forth luminously pale,—the eyes were full of unquenchable pain, unspeakable remorse, unimaginable despair! The features I had known so long and seen day by day in familiar intercourse were the same,—the same, yet transfigured with ethereal splendour, while shadowed by an everlasting sorrow! Bodily sensations I was scarcely conscious of;—only the Soul of me, hitherto dormant, was awake and palpitating with fear. Gradually I became aware that others were around me, and looking, I saw a dense crowd of faces, wild and wonderful,—imploring eyes were turned upon me in piteous or stern agony,—and pallid hands were stretched towards me more in appeal than menace. And I beheld as I gazed, the air darkening, and anon lightening with the shadow and the brightness of wings!—vast pinions of crimson flame began to unfurl and spread upwards all round the ice-bound vessel,—upwards till their glowing tips seemed well-nigh to touch the moon. And He, my Foe, who leaned against the mast, became likewise encircled with these shafted pinions of burning rose, which like finely-webbed clouds coloured by a strong sunset, streamed outward flaringly from his dark Form and sprang aloft in a blaze of scintillant glory. And a Voice infinitely sad, yet infinitely sweet, struck solemn music from the frozen silence.

"Steer onward, Amiel! Onward, to the boundaries of the world!"

With every spiritual sense aroused, I glanced towards the steerman's wheel,—was *that* Amiel whom I had instinctively loathed?—that Being, stern as a figure of deadliest fate, with sable wings and tortured countenance? If so, I knew him now for a fiend in very truth!—if burning horror and endless shame can so transfigure the soul of man! A history of crime was written in his anguished looks, . . . what secret torment racked him no living mortal might dare to guess! With pallid skeleton hands he moved the wheel;—and as it turned, the walls of ice around us began to split with a noise of thunder.

"Onward Amiel!" said the great sad Voice again—"Onward where never man hath trod,—steer on to the world's end!"

The crowd of weird and terrible faces grew denser,—the flaming and darkening of wings became thicker than driving storm-clouds rent by lightning,—wailing cries, groans and dreary sounds of sobbing echoed about me on all sides, . . . again the shattering ice roared like an earthquake under the waters, . . . and, unhindered by her frozen prison-walls, the ship moved on! Dizzily, and as one in a mad dream I saw the great glittering bergs rock and bend forward,—the massive ice-city shook to its foundations, . . . glistening pinnacles dropped and vanished, . . . towers lurched over, broke and plunged into the sea,— huge mountains of ice split up like fine glass, yawning asunder with a green glare in the moonlight as the 'Flame' propelled, so it seemed, by the demon-wings of her terrific crew, cut through the frozen passage with the sharpness of a sword and the swiftness of an arrow! Whither were we bound? I dared not think,—I deemed myself dead. The world I saw was not the world I knew,—I believed I was in some spirit-land beyond the grave, whose secrets I should presently realize perchance too well! On,—on we went,—I keeping my strained sight fixed for the most part on the supreme Shape that always confronted me,—that Angel-Foe whose eyes were wild with an eternity of sorrows! Face to face with such an Immortal Despair, I stood confounded and slain forever in my own regard,—a worthless atom, meriting naught but annihilation. The wailing cries and groans had ceased,—and we sped on in an awful silence,—while countless tragedies,—unnameable histories,—were urged upon me in the dumb eloquence of the dreary faces round me, and the expressive teaching of their terrific eyes!

Soon the barriers of ice were passed,—and the 'Flame' floated out beyond them into a warm inland sea, calm as a lake, and bright as silver in the broad radiance of the moon. On either side were undulating shores, rich with lofty and luxuriant verdure,—I saw the distant hazy outline of dusky purple hills,—I heard the little waves plashing against hidden rocks, and murmuring upon the sand. Delicious odours filled the air;—a gentle breeze blew, . . . was this the lost Paradise?—this semi-tropic zone concealed behind a continent of ice and snow? Suddenly, from the tops of the dark branching trees, came floating the sound of a bird's singing,—and so sweet was the song, so heart-whole was the melody, that my aching eyes filled with tears. Beautiful memories rushed upon me,—the value and graciousness of life,—life on the kindly sunlit earth,—seemed very dear to my soul! Life's opportunities,—its joys, its wonders, its blessings, all showered down upon a thankless race by a loving Creator,—these appeared to me all at once as marvellous! Oh for another chance of such life!—to redeem the past,—to gather up the wasted gems of lost moments,—to live as a man should live, in accordance with the will of God, and in brotherhood with his fellow-men! . . . The unknown bird sang on in a cadence like that of a mavis in spring, only more tunefully,—surely no other woodland songster ever sang half so well! And as its dulcet notes dropped roundly one by one upon the mystic silence, I saw a pale Creature move out from amid the shadowing of black and scarlet wings,—a white woman-shape, clothed in her own long hair. She glided to the vessel's edge, and there she leaned, with anguished face upturned,—it was the face of Sibyl! And even while I looked upon her, she cast herself wildly down upon the deck and wept! My soul was stirred within me, . . . I saw in very truth all that she might have been,—I realized what an angel a little guiding love and patience might have made her, . . . and at last I pitied her! I never pitied her before!

And now many familiar faces shone upon me like white stars in a mist of rain,—all faces of the dead,—all marked with unquenchable remorse and sorrow. One figure passed before me drearily, in fetters glistening with a weight of gold,—I knew him for my college-friend of olden days; another, crouching on the ground in fear, I recognised as him who had staked his last possession at play, even to his immortal soul,—I even saw my father's face, worn and aghast with grief, and trembled lest the sacred beauty of Her who had died to give me birth, should find a place among these direful horrors. But no!—thank God I never saw her!— *her* spirit had not lost its way to Heaven!

Again my eyes reverted to the Mover of this mystic scene,—that Fallen Splendour whose majestic shape now seemed to fill both earth and sky. A fiery glory blazed about him, . . . he raised his hand, . . . the ship stopped,—and the dark Steersman rested motionless on the wheel. Round us the moonlit landscape was spread like a glittering dream of fairyland,—and still the unknown bird of God sang on with such entrancing tenderness as must have soothed hell's tortured souls.

"Lo, here we pause!" said the commanding Voice—"Here, where the distorted shape of Man hath never cast a shadow!—here,—where the arrogant mind of Man hath never conceived a sin!—here, where the godless greed of Man hath never defaced a beauty, or slain a woodland thing!—here, the last spot on earth left untainted by Man's presence! Here is the world's end!—when this land is found, and these shores profaned,—when Mammon plants its foot upon this soil,—then dawns the Judgment-Day! But, until then, . . .

MARIE CORELLI

here, where only God doth work perfection, angels may look down undismayed, and even fiends find rest!"

A solemn sound of music surged upon the air,—and I who had been as one in chains, bound by invisible bonds and unable to stir, was suddenly liberated. Fully conscious of freedom I still faced the dark gigantic figure of my Foe,—for his luminous eyes were now upon me, and his penetrating voice addressed me only.

"Man, deceive not thyself!" he said—"Think not the terrors of this night are the delusion of a dream or the snare of a vision! Thou art awake,—not sleeping,—thou art flesh as well as spirit! This place is neither hell nor heaven nor any space between,—it is a corner of thine own world on which thou livest. Wherefore know from henceforth that the Supernatural Universe in and around the Natural is no lie,—but the chief Reality, inasmuch as God surroundeth all! Fate strikes thine hour,—and in this hour 'tis given thee to choose thy Master. Now, by the will of God, thou seest me as Angel;—but take heed thou forget not that among men I am as Man! In human form I move with all humanity through endless ages,—to kings and counsellors, to priests and scientists, to thinkers and teachers, to old and young, I come in the shape their pride or vice demands, and am as one with all. Self finds in me another Ego;—but from the pure in heart, the high in faith, the perfect in intention, I do retreat with joy, offering naught save reverence, demanding naught save prayer! So am I,—so must I ever be,—till Man of his own will releases and redeems me. Mistake me not, but know me!—and choose thy Future for truth's sake and not out of fear! Choose and change not in any time hereafter,—this hour, this moment is thy last probation,—choose, I say! Wilt thou serve Self and Me? or God only?"

The question seemed thundered on my ears, . . . shuddering, I looked from right to left, and saw a gathering crowd of faces, white, wistful, wondering, threatening and imploring,—they pressed about me close, with glistening eyes and lips that moved dumbly. And as they stared upon me I beheld another spectral thing,—the image of Myself!—a poor frail creature, pitiful, ignorant, and undiscerning,— limited in both capacity and intelligence, yet full of strange egotism and still stranger arrogance; every detail of my life was suddenly presented to me as in a magic mirror, and I read my own chronicle of paltry intellectual pride, vulgar ambition and vulgarer ostentation,—I realised with shame my miserable vices, my puny scorn of God, my effronteries and blasphemies; and in the sudden strong repulsion and repudiation of my own worthless existence, being and character, I found both voice and speech.

"GOD only!" I cried fervently—"Annihilation at His hands, rather than life without Him! GOD only! I have chosen!"

My words vibrated passionately on my own ears, . . . and. . . even as they were spoken, the air grew misty with a snowy opalescent radiance, . . . the sable and crimson wings uplifted in such multitudinous array around me, palpitated with a thousand changeful hues, . . . and over the face of my dark Foe a light celestial fell like the smile of dawn! Awed and afraid I gazed upward, . . . and there I saw a new and yet more wondrous glory, . . . a shining Figure outlined against the sky in such surpassing beauty and vivid brilliancy as made me think the sun itself had risen in vast Angel-shape on rainbow pinions! And from the brightening heaven there rang a silver voice, clear as a clarion-call,—

"Arise, Lucifer, Son of the Morning! One soul rejects thee,—one hour of joy is granted thee! Hence and arise!"

Earth, air, and sea blazed suddenly into fiery gold,—blinded and stunned, I was seized by compelling hands and held firmly down by a force invisible, . . . the yacht was slowly sinking under me! Overwhelmed with unearthly terrors, my lips yet murmured,

"GOD! God only!" The heavens changed from gold to crimson— anon to shining blue, . . . and against this mass of wavering colour that seemed to make a jewelled archway of the sky, I saw the Form of him whom I had known as man, swiftly ascend god-like, with flaming pinions and upturned glorious visage, like a vision of light in darkness! Around him clustered a million winged shapes,—but He, supreme, majestic, wonderful, towered high above them all, a very king of splendour, the glory round his brows resembling meteor-fires in an Arctic midnight,—his eyes, twin stars, ablaze with such great rapture as seemed half agony! Breathless and giddy, I strained my sight to follow him as he fled; . . . and heard the musical calling of strange sweet voices everywhere, from east to west, from north to south.

"Lucifer! . . . Belovëd and unforgotten! Lucifer, Son of the morning! Arise! . . . arise! . . ."

With all my remaining strength I strove to watch the vanishing upward of that sublime Luminance that now filled the visible universe,—the demon-ship was still sinking steadily, . . . invisible hands still held me down, . . . I was falling,—falling,—into unimaginable depths, . . . when another Voice, till then unheard, solemn yet sweet, spoke aloud—

"Bind him hand and foot, and cast him into the outermost darkness of the world! There let him find My Light!"

I heard,—yet felt no fear.

"God only!" I said, as I sank into the vast profound,—and lo! while the words yet trembled on my lips, I saw the sun! The sweet earth's sun!—the kindly orb familiar,—the lamp of God's protection,—its golden rim came glittering upwards in the east,—higher and higher it rose, making a shining background for that mighty Figure, whose darkly luminous wings now seemed like sable storm-clouds stretched wide across the horizon! Once more. . . yet once, . . . the Angel-visage bent its warning looks on me, . . . I saw the anguished smile, . . . the great eyes burning with immortal sorrows! . . . then, I was plunged forcibly downwards and thrust into an abysmal grave of frozen cold.

XLII

The blue sea—the blue sky!—and God's sunshine over all! To this I woke, after a long period of unconsciousness, and found myself afloat on a wide ocean, fast bound to a wooden spar. So strongly knotted were my bonds that I could not stir either hand or foot, . . . and after one or two ineffectual struggles to move I gave up the attempt, and lay submissively resigned to my fate, face upturned and gazing at the infinite azure depths above me, while the heaving breath of the sea rocked me gently to and fro like an infant in its mother's arms. Alone with God and Nature, I, a poor human wreck, drifted,—lost, yet found! Lost on this vast sea which soon should serve my body as a sepulchre, . . . but found, inasmuch as I was fully conscious of the existence and awakening of the Immortal Soul within me,—that divine, actual and imperishable essence, which now I recognised as being all that is valuable in a man in the sight of his Creator. I was to die, soon and surely;—this I thought, as the billows swayed me in their huge cradle, running in foamy ripples across my bound body, and dashing cool spray upon my brows,—what could I do now, doomed and helpless as I was, to retrieve my wasted past? Nothing! save repent,—and could repentance at so late an hour fit the laws of eternal justice? Humbly and sorrowfully I considered, . . . to me had been given a terrific and unprecedented experience of the awful Reality of the Spirit-world around us,—and now I was cast out on the sea as a thing worthless, I felt that the brief time remaining to me of life in this present sphere was indeed my "last probation," as that Supernatural Wonder, the declared Enemy of mankind, whom still in my thoughts I called Lucio, had declared.

"If I dared,—after a life's denial and blasphemy,—turn to Christ!" I said—"Would He,—the Divine Brother and Friend of man,—reject me?"

I whispered the question to the sky and sea, . . . solemn silence seemed to invest the atmosphere, and marvellous calm. No other answer came than this, . . . a deep and charmëd peace, that insensibly stole over my fretting conscience, my remorseful soul, my aching heart, my tired mind. I remembered certain words heard long ago, and lightly forgotten. *"Him who cometh unto Me will I in no wise cast out."* Looking up to the clear heavens and radiant sun, I smiled; and with a complete abandonment of myself and my fears to the Divine Will, I murmured the words that in my stress of mystic agony had so far saved me,—

"God only! Whatsoever He shall choose for me in life, in death, and after death, is best."

And closing my eyes, I resigned my life to the mercy of the soft waves, and with the sunbeams warm upon my face, I slept.

I WOKE AGAIN WITH AN icy shudder and cry,—rough cheery voices sounded in my ears,—strong hands were at work busily unfastening the cords with which I was bound, . . . I was on the deck of a large steamer, surrounded by a group of men,—and all the glory of the sunset fired the seas. Questions were poured upon me, . . . I could not answer them, for my tongue was parched and blistered, . . . lifted upright upon my feet by sturdy arms, I could not stand for sheer exhaustion. Dimly, and in feeble dread I stared around me,—was this great vessel with smoking funnels and grinding engines another devil's craft set sailing round the world! Too weak to find a voice I made dumb signs of terrified inquiry, . . . a broad-shouldered bluff-looking man came forward, whose keen eyes rested on me with kindly compassion.

"This is an English vessel," he said—"We are bound for Southampton. Our helmsman saw you floating ahead,—we stopped and sent a boat for rescue. Where were you wrecked? Any more of the crew afloat?"

I gazed at him, but could not speak. The strangest thoughts crowded into my brain, moving me to wild tears and laughter. England! The word struck clashing music on my mind, and set all my pulses trembling. England! The little spot upon the little world, most loved and honoured of all men, save those who envy its worth! I made some gesture, whether of joy or mad amazement I know not,—had I been able to speak I could have related nothing that those men around me could have comprehended or believed, . . . then I sank back again in a dead swoon.

They were very good to me, all those English sailors. The captain gave me his own cabin,—the ship's doctor attended me with a zeal that was only exceeded by his curiosity to know where I came from, and the nature of the disaster that had befallen me. But I remained dumb, and lay inert and feeble in my berth, grateful for the care bestowed upon me, as well as for the temporary exhaustion that deprived me of speech. For I had enough to do with my own thoughts,—thoughts far too solemn and weighty for utterance. I was saved,—I was given another chance of life in the world,—and *I knew why*! My one absorbing anxiety now was to retrieve my wasted time, and to do active good where hitherto I had done nothing!

The day came at last, when I was sufficiently recovered to be able to sit on deck and watch with eager eyes the approaching coast-line of England. I seemed to have lived a century since I left it,—aye, almost an eternity,—for time is what the Soul makes it, and no more. I was an object of interest and attention among all the passengers on board, for as yet I had not broken silence. The weather was calm and bright, . . . the sun shone gloriously,—and far off the pearly rim of Shakespeare's 'happy isle' glistened jewel-like upon the edge of the sea. The captain came and looked at me,—nodded encouragingly,—and after a moment's hesitation, said—

"Glad to see you out on deck! Almost yourself again, eh?"

I silently assented with a faint smile.

"Perhaps"—he continued, "as we're so near home, you'll let me know your name? It's not often we pick up a man alive and drifting in mid-Atlantic."

In mid-Atlantic! What force had flung me there I dared not think, . . . nor whether it was hellish or divine.

"My name?" I murmured, surprised into speech,—how odd it was I had never thought of myself lately as having a name or any other thing belonging to me!—"Why certainly! Geoffrey Tempest is my name."

The captain's eyes opened widely.

"Geoffrey Tempest! Dear me! . . . *The* Mr. Tempest?—the great millionaire that *was*?"

It was now my turn to stare.

"That *was*?" I repeated—"What do you mean?"

"Have you not heard?" he asked excitedly.

"Heard? I have heard nothing since I left England some months ago—with a friend, on board his yacht. . . we went on a long voyage and. . . a strange one! We were wrecked, . . . you know the rest, and how I owe my life to your rescue. But of news I am ignorant. . ."

"Good heavens!" he interrupted quickly—"Bad news travels fast as a rule they say,—but you have missed it. . . and I confess I don't like to be the bearer of it. . ."

He broke off, and his genial face looked troubled. I smiled,—yet wondered.

"Pray speak out!" I said—"I don't think you can tell me anything that will deeply affect me,—*now*. I know the best and worst of most things in the world, I assure you!"

He eyed me dubiously;—then, going into his smoking-cabin, he brought me out an American newspaper seven days old. He handed it to me pointing to its leading columns without a word. There I saw in large type—"A Millionaire Ruined! Enormous Frauds! Monster Forgeries! Gigantic Swindle! On the track of Bentham and Ellis!"

My brain swam for a minute,—then I read on steadily, and soon grasped the situation. The respectable pair of lawyers whom I had implicitly relied on for the management of all my business affairs in my absence, had succumbed to the temptation of having so much cash in charge for investment,—and had become a pair of practised swindlers. Dealing with the same bank as myself, they had forged my name so cleverly that the genuineness of the signature had never been even suspected,—and, after drawing enormous sums in this way, and investing in various 'bubble' companies with which they personally were concerned, they had finally absconded, leaving me almost as poor as I was when I first heard of my inherited fortune. I put aside the paper, and looked up at the good captain, who stood watching me with sympathetic anxiety.

"Thank you!" I said—"These thieves were my trusted lawyers,—and I can cheerfully say that I am much more sorry for them than I am for myself. A thief is always a thief,—a poor man, if he be honest, is at any rate the thief's superior. The money they have stolen will bring them misery rather than pleasure,—of that I am convinced. If this account be correct, they have already lost large sums in bogus companies,—and the man Bentham, whom I thought the very acme of shrewd caution has sunk an enormous amount of capital in a worn-out gold mine. Their forgeries must have been admirably done!—a sad waste of time and cleverness. It appears too that the investments I have myself made are worthless;—well, well!—it does not matter,—I must begin the world again, that's all!" He looked amazed.

"I don't think you quite realize your own misfortune, Mr. Tempest"— he said—"You take it too quietly by half. You'll think worse of it presently."

"I hope not!" I responded, with a smile—"It never does to think the worst of anything. I assure you I realize perfectly. I am in the world's sight a ruined man,—I quite understand!"

He shrugged his shoulders with quite a desperate air, and left me. I am convinced he thought me mad,—but I knew I had never been so sane. I did indeed entirely comprehend my 'misfortune,' or rather the great chance bestowed on me of winning something far higher than all the coffers of Mammon; I read in my loss of world's cash the working of such a merciful providence and pity as gave me a grander hope than any I had ever known. Clear before me rose the vision of that most divine and beautiful necessity of happiness,—Work!—the grand and too often misprized Angel of Labour, which moulds the mind of man, steadies his hands, controls his brain, purifies his passions, and strengthens his whole mental and physical being. A rush of energy and health filled my veins,—and I thanked God devoutly for the golden opportunities held out afresh for me to accept and use. Gratitude there should be in every human soul for every gift of heaven,—but nothing merits more thankfulness and praise to the Creator than the call to work, and the ability to respond to it.

England at last! I bade farewell to the good ship that had rescued me, and to all on board her, most of whom now knew my name and looked upon me with pity as well as curiosity. The story of my being wrecked on a friend's yacht was readily accepted,—and the subject of that adventure was avoided, as the general impression was that my friend, whoever he was, had been drowned with his crew, and that I was the one survivor. I did not offer any further explanation, and was content to so let the matter rest, though I was careful to send both the captain and the ship's doctor a handsome recompense for their united attention and kindness. I have reason to believe, from the letters they wrote me, that they were more than satisfied with the sums received, and that I really did some actual good with those few last fragments of my vanished wealth.

On reaching London, I interviewed the police concerning the thieves and forgers, Bentham and Ellis, and stopped all proceedings against them.

"Call me mad if you like,"—I said to the utterly confounded chief of the detective force—"I do not mind! But let these rascals keep the trash they have stolen. It will be a curse to them, as it has been to me! It is devil's money! Half of it was already gone, being settled on my late wife,—at her death, it reverted by the same deed of settlement, to any living members of her family, and it now belongs to Lord Elton. I have lived to make a noble Earl rich, who was once bankrupt,— and I doubt if he would lend me a ten-pound-note for the asking! However, I shall not ask him. The rest has gone into the universal waste of corruption and sham—let it stay there! I shall never bother myself to get it back. I prefer to be a free man."

"But the bank,—the principle of the thing!" exclaimed the detective with indignation.

I smiled.

"Exactly! The principle of the thing has been perfectly carried out. A man who has too much money *creates* forgers and thieves about him,—he cannot expect to meet with honesty. Let the bank prosecute if it likes,—I shall not. I am free!—free to work for my living. What I earn I shall enjoy,—what I inherited, I have learnt to loathe!"

With that I left him, puzzled and irate,—and in a day or two the papers were full of strange stories concerning me, and numerous lies as well. I was called 'mad,' 'unprincipled,' 'thwarting the ends of justice,'—and sundry other names, while scurrilous civilities known only to the penny paragraphist were heaped upon me by the score. To complete my entire satisfaction, a man on the staff of one of the leading journals, dug out my book from Mudie's underground cellar, and 'slashed' it with a bitterness and venom only excelled by my own violence when anonymously libelling the work of Mavis Clare! And the result was remarkable,—for in a sudden wind of caprice, the public made a rush for my neglected literary offspring,—they took it up, handled it tenderly, read it lingeringly, found something in it that pleased them, and finally bought it by thousands! . . . whereat the astute Morgeson, as virtuous publisher, wrote to me in wonder and congratulation, enclosing a cheque for a hundred pounds on 'royalties,' and promising more in due course, should the 'run' continue. Ah, the sweetness of that earned hundred pounds! I felt a King of independence!—realms of ambition and attainment opened out before me,—life smiled upon me as it had never smiled before. Talk of poverty! I was rich!—rich with a hundred pounds made out of my own brain-labour,—and I envied no millionaire that ever flaunted his gold beneath the sun! I thought of Mavis Clare, . . . but dared not dwell too long upon her gentle image. In time perhaps, . . . when I had settled down to fresh work, . . . when I had formed my life as I meant to form it, in the habits of faith, firmness and unselfishness, I would write to her and tell her all,—all, even to that dread insight into worlds unseen, beyond the boundaries of an unknown region of everlasting frozen snow! But now,—now I resolved to stand alone,—fighting my battle as a man should fight, seeking for neither help nor sympathy, and trusting not in Self, but God only. Moreover I could not induce myself yet to look again upon Willowsmere. The place was terror-haunted for me; and though Lord Elton with a curious condescension, (seeing that it was to me he owed the free gift of his former property) invited me to stay there, and professed a certain lame regret for the 'heavy financial losses' I had sustained, I saw in the tone of his epistle that he looked upon me somewhat in the light of a madman after my refusal to take up the matter of my absconding solicitors, and that he would rather I stayed away. And I did stay away;—and even when his marriage with Diana Chesney took place with great pomp and splendour, I refused his invitation to be present. In the published list of guests, however which appeared in the principal papers, I was scarcely surprised to read the name of 'Prince Lucio Rimânez.'

I now took a humble room and set to work on a new literary enterprise, avoiding everyone I had hitherto known, for being now almost a poor man, I was aware that 'swagger society' wished to blot me from its visiting-list. I lived with my own sorrowful thoughts,—musing on many things, training myself to humility, obedience, and faith with fortitude,—and day by day I did battle with the monster, Egotism, that presented itself in a thousand disguises at every turn in my own life as well as in the lives of others. I had to re-form my character,—to mould the obstinate nature that rebelled, and make its obstinacy serve for the attainment of higher objects than world's renown,—the task was difficult,—but I gained ground a little with every fresh effort.

I had lived for some months like this in bitter self-abasement, when all the reading world was suddenly electrified by another book of Mavis Clare's. My lately favoured first work was again forgotten and thrust aside,—hers, slated and screamed at as usual by the criticasters, was borne along to fame by a great wave of honest public praise and enthusiasm. And I? I rejoiced!—no longer grudging or envious of her sweet fame, I stood apart in spirit as it were, while the bright car of her triumph went by, decked, not only with laurels, but with roses,—the blossoms of a people's love and honour. With all my soul I reverenced her genius,—with all my heart I honoured her pure womanliness! And in the very midst of her brilliant success, when all the world was talking of her, she wrote to me, a simple little letter, as gracious as her own fair name.

Dear Mr. Tempest,
    I heard by chance the other day that you had returned
to England. I therefore send this note to the care of your

publisher to express my sincere delight in the success your clever book has now attained after its interval of probation. I fancy the public appreciation of your work must go far to console you for the great losses you have had both in life and fortune, of which I will not here speak. When you feel that you can bear to look again upon scenes which I know will be sure to rouse in your mind many sad and poignant memories, will you come and see me?

Your friend
Mavis Clare

A mist came before my eyes,—I almost felt her gentle presence in my room,—I saw the tender look, the radiant smile,—the innocent yet earnest joy in life and love of purity that emanated from the fair personality of the sweetest woman I had ever known. She called herself my friend!— . . . it was a privilege of which I felt myself unworthy! I folded the letter and put it near my heart to serve me as a talisman, . . . she, of all bright creatures in the world surely knew the secret of happiness! . . . Some-day, . . . yes, . . . I would go and see her, . . . my Mavis that sang in her garden of lilies,—some day when I had force and manliness enough to tell her all,—save my love for her! For that, I felt, must never be spoken,—Self must resist Self, and clamour no more at the gate of a forfeited Paradise! Some day I would see her, . . . but not for a long time, . . . not till I had, in part at least, worked out my secret expiation. As I sat musing thus, a strange memory came into my brain, . . . I thought I heard a voice resembling my own, which said—

"*Lift, oh lift the shrouding veil, spirit of the City Beautiful! For I feel I shall read in your eyes the secret of happiness!*"

A cold shudder ran through me,—I sprang up erect, in a kind of horror. Leaning at my open window I looked down into the busy street below,—and my thoughts reverted to the strange things I had seen in the East,—the face of the dead Egyptian dancer, uncovered to the light again after two thousand years,—the face of Sibyl!—then I remembered the vision of the "City Beautiful," in which one face had remained veiled,—the face I most desired to see!—and I trembled more and more as my mind, despite my will, began to weave together links of the past and present, till they seemed growing into one and the same. Was I again to be the prey of evil forces?—did some new danger threaten me?—had I, by some unconscious wicked wish invited new temptation to assail me?

Overcome by my sensations, I left my work and went out into the fresh air, . . . it was late at night,—and the moon was shining. I felt for the letter of Mavis,—it pressed against my heart, a shield against all vileness. The room I occupied was in a house not far from Westminster Abbey, and I instinctively bent my steps towards that grey old shrine of kings and poets dead. The square around it was almost deserted,—I slackened my pace, strolling meditatively along the narrow paved way that forms a short cut across into Old Palace Yard, . . . when suddenly a Shadow crossed my path, and looking up, I came face to face with—Lucio! The same as ever,—the perfect impersonation of perfect manhood! . . . his countenance, pale, proud, sorrowful yet scornful, flashed upon me like a star!—he looked full at me, and a questioning smile rested on his lips!

My heart almost stopped beating, . . . I drew a quick sharp breath, . . . again I felt for the letter of Mavis, and then, . . . meeting his gaze fixedly and straightly in my turn, I moved slowly on in silence. He understood,—his eyes flashed with the jewel-like strange brilliancy I knew so well, and so well remembered,—and drawing back he stood aside and—let me pass! I continued my walk steadily, though dazed and like one in a dream,—till reaching the shadowed side of the street opposite the Houses of Parliament, I stopped for a moment to recover my startled senses. There again I saw him!—the superb man's form,—the Angel's face,—the haunting, splendid sorrowful eyes!—he came with his usual ease and grace of step into the full moonlight and paused,—apparently waiting for some one. For me?—ah no!—I kept the name of God upon my lips,—I gathered all the strength of faith within my soul,—and though I was wholesomely afraid of Myself, I feared no other foe! I lingered therefore—watching;—and presently I saw a few members of Parliament walking singly and in groups towards the House,—one or two greeted the tall dark Figure as a friend and familiar, and others knew him not. Still he waited on, . . . and so did I. At last, just as Big Ben chimed the quarter to eleven, one man whom I instantly recognised as a well-known Cabinet minister, came walking briskly towards the House, . . . then, and then only, He, whom I had known as Lucio, advanced smiling. Greeting the minister cordially, in that musical rich voice I knew of old, he took his arm,—and they both walked on slowly, talking earnestly. I watched them till their figures receded in the moonlight, . . . the one tall, kingly and commanding, . . . the other burly and broad, and self-assertive in demeanour;—I saw them ascend the steps, and finally disappear within the House of England's Imperial Government,—Devil and Man,—together!

A Note About the Author

Marie Corelli (1855–1924), born Mary Mackay, was a British writer from London, England. Educated at a Parisian convent, she later worked as a pianist before embarking on a literary career. Her first novel, *A Romance of Two Worlds* was published in 1886 and surpassed all expectations. Corelli quickly became one of the most popular fiction writers of her time. Her books featured contrasting themes rooted in religion, science and the supernatural. Some of Corelli's other notable works include *Barabbas: A Dream of the World's Tragedy* (1893) and *The Sorrows of Satan* (1895).

A Note from the Publisher

Spanning many genres, from non-fiction essays to literature classics to children's books and lyric poetry, Mint Edition books showcase the master works of our time in a modern new package. The text is freshly typeset, is clean and easy to read, and features a new note about the author in each volume. Many books also include exclusive new introductory material. Every book boasts a striking new cover, which makes it as appropriate for collecting as it is for gift giving. Mint Edition books are only printed when a reader orders them, so natural resources are not wasted. We're proud that our books are never manufactured in excess and exist only in the exact quantity they need to be read and enjoyed.

bookfinity™

Discover more of your favorite classics with Bookfinity™.

- Track your reading with custom book lists.
- Get great book recommendations for your personalized Reader Type.
- Add reviews for your favorite books.
- AND MUCH MORE!

Visit **bookfinity.com** and take the fun Reader Type quiz to get started.

Enjoy our classic and modern companion pairings!

Classic & Modern